ALSO BY EMILY MCINTIRE

Be Still My Heart: A Romantic Suspense

THE SUGARLAKE SERIES
Beneath the Stars
Beneath the Stands
Beneath the Hood
Beneath the Surface

THE NEVER AFTER SERIES
Hooked: A Dark, Contemporary Romance
Scarred: A Dark, Royal Romance
Wretched: A Dark, Contemporary Romance
Twisted: A Dark, Contemporary Romance

CROSSED

A Never After Novel

EMILY MCINTIRE

Bloom books

Published by Bloom Books, an imprint of Sourcebooks
P.O. Box 4410, Naperville, Illinois 60567-4410
(630) 961-3900
sourcebooks.com

Cataloging-in-Publication data is on file with the Library of Congress.

Printed and bound in the United States of America.
VP 12 11 10 9 8

Playlist

"Seven Devils"—Florence + the Machine
"My Mind & Me"—Selena Gomez
"Come as You Are"—Nirvana
"Unholy"—Sam Smith, Kim Petras
"Monster"—Shawn Mendes, Justin Bieber
"God Is a Woman"—Ariana Grande
"Elastic Heart"—Sia
"Lovely"—Billie Eilish, Khalid
"Bleeding Out"—Imagine Dragons
"Figure You Out"—VOILÀ

For anyone who's afraid of making mistakes.
To err is human. Give yourself some grace.

When I had seen you twice, I wanted to see you a thousand times, I wanted to see you always. Then—how stop myself on that slope of hell?—then I no longer belonged to myself.

—Victor Hugo, *The Hunchback of Notre-Dame*

Author's Note

Crossed is a dark, contemporary romance. It is a fractured fairy tale, not fantasy or a literal retelling.

The main character is a villain, If you're looking for a safe read, you will not find it in these pages.

Crossed contains mature and graphic content that is not suitable for all audiences. **Reader discretion is advised.** I highly prefer for you to go in blind, but if you would like a detailed trigger warning list, you can find it on EmilyMcIntire.com

PROLOGUE

Cade

FESTIVALÉ, VERMONT, LOOKS DIFFERENT IN THE dead of night.

It's a dirty town.

Filthy. Teeming with darkness.

My superior sent me to revive the historic area. To bring it back to the path of righteousness where it's been missing for far too long.

When I first arrived earlier today, it sent a shot of nostalgia through me. I sat in the passenger seat of the SUV as it rolled slowly down the roads, the French Colonial architecture reminding me of my childhood—of growing up in the back alleys of Paris, begging for scraps and stealing just to keep myself alive and fed.

This town, much like Paris, drips of sin, although it lacks the finesse.

Instead of holding on to what *should* be a rich history, preserved from when Vermont was part of New France in the 1700s, Festivalé seems like a caricature. A farcical ode to somewhere it doesn't belong. The name of the town itself isn't even real French.

Still, if I were a man of hope, I'd look through the dusty windows and see potential. But there's evil polluting the air, making it thick and muggy, a dark cloud that blankets the valley and creates disease in everything it touches. I can smell it with every inhale. Taste it with every breath. A part of me worries it will infect me too, but I cast the thought aside quickly, feeling my defenses fortify until they're as strong as steel.

I'm not sure what time it is now, just that it's hours after my arrival, and when I left my new home, it was nearing midnight. I hadn't meant to venture outside so soon after arriving, but there was a *need* surging inside me, a familiar one that I try to ignore.

And I'm only human.

When my own sickness comes to fruition, I'm helpless against its pull.

Il est miséricordieux.

He is merciful.

Tonight, the air is cold, and I rush down the cracked sidewalks and back alleys, a hint of frost nipping at my nose and the tips of my ears until a stinging numbness skates across my skin. I dip my head, the collar of my black peacoat chafing against the sides of my neck as I make my way through what I'm guessing is the roughest part of the city.

The full moon casts an eerie glow on the quiet streets, my footsteps echoing through the otherwise still air.

Suddenly, a door to my left opens, yellow light bleeding from the entrance, highlighting the silhouette of a woman. Her voice bounces off the crumbling brick buildings that have rotting boards and broken glass for windows.

I hesitate, frowning from beneath the wide brim of my hat as she saunters off her stoop and moves toward me. I scan the area. There's nobody outside except for us.

She stops directly in front of me, her hazy gaze peering up into mine, pupils dilated, making her eyes as black as coal.

My stomach drops.

Une démone.

A demon.

"You're new," she croons. Her voice is raspy in a practiced sort of way that I'm sure has been honed to make a man's cock twitch and his baser instincts surge forward. But I haven't had a single sexual urge toward a woman in years.

Disgust burns the back of my throat, and a voice whispers in my mind, but I try to ignore the wicked thoughts. I didn't come outside to *act* on my impulses, only to clear them from my psyche.

I stare down my nose at her, towering over her wiry frame, though she isn't short by any means. A burst of icy wind whips across my face, my teeth clamping to keep from chattering.

Goose bumps sprout along the woman's creamy exposed chest, and she shifts, leaves crunching beneath her feet.

Her palm reaches out and ghosts down the lapel of my black coat, and it spurs me into movement, snapping out my gloved hands to grab her fingers tightly. A surprised gasp leaves her sloppy red lips.

"What's your name, démone?" I rasp.

The shock melts from her features, a gleam of curiosity taking its place.

"That's quite the accent." She steps in close. "You can call me whatever you want as long as you can pay, baby. Cash or...or smack if you've got it."

My sickness sings.

And before I can shove it back down, my monster—that *sickness*—explodes, sinking into my bones until they ache.

I drop my hold from the woman's wrist and give her a curt nod.

Her grin stretches until it reaches the corners of her sunken face. "Follow me."

She spins and walks back to her open door, and I scan the area one last time, ensuring no one is around to see.

Still alone.

Her place is small and filthy. Just a single room with a dirty mattress on the floor and a lamp with no shade flickering in the corner. The bed itself is riddled with stains, and I can smell the unholy matings permeating the air, so thick it makes me feel like I can't breathe.

Years ago, I would have been envious of this space. I would have longed for a mattress beneath me at night and a roof over my head.

But that was before.

The woman turns to face me, and I notice the pock marks scattered along her gaunt face, a feral desperation swimming in the depths of her features, reaching out to capture *my* energy with its shadowy black claws.

The man in me wants to step away, but the monster calls her closer.

Her bony hips sway as she saunters over, and something sour teases the edges of my mouth as I watch her malnourished body attempt seduction. Her hands slip up the front of my peacoat, undoing the buttons slowly. I let her, and when the material gapes open, her eyes lock on the distinct collar around my neck, widening as her head snaps up to meet my gaze.

She jerks, but I grab her hard enough to bruise, dragging her flush against me.

"Le diable est à l'intérieur de toi," I hiss.

She shakes her head. "I don't...I don't know what that means."

I lean down until my words whisper against her coarse, tangled hair. "It means the devil is within you."

My hands skim up her arms until I'm wrapping my palms around her fragile throat, the thrum of her heartbeat so loud I can feel it through the leather of my gloves. Excitement bursts like a piñata in the base of my stomach, and now my cock *does* twitch.

I don't care that she's clearly a sex worker. It isn't *what* she does that calls to my monster, it's what's *inside* her. I only wish to free her of her demons.

"Don't worry, my child," I continue. "I've come to help."

And then I press down, applying pressure to her delicate windpipe. The sleeves of my coat rise with the movement, and her fingernails dig into my exposed wrists, gouging the skin, making my muscles tighten.

I enjoy the way she fights. Releasing her right before she loses consciousness, I undo the scarf from my neck and wrap it around her throat, crossing the ends and pulling.

Slowly, her body slackens, and it's only when I see the life leave her doped-up eyes that the violent *need* within me fizzles out until it's nothing but burnt ash, my sickness dissipating like it was never there at all.

I lay her corpse on the ground, breathing deep as I take back my scarf, rebutton my coat, and crouch over her body. My fingertips touch her forehead, then her lower chest, before creeping across each shoulder in the sign of the cross.

"Give thanks to the Lord, for He is good," I murmur.

Already the tendrils of guilt are weaving through my middle, coiling until my breaths become choppy and my vision starts to shake.

But I can't control it.

I've had this *thing* within me since I was born, damned from my very first breath. It's only in servitude that I can attempt to cleanse my soul.

"There's a monster in you, child. And God wants me to beat it out."

I shake off the voice from my past and stand up quickly to make my way outside, ensuring the coast is clear before I head back to the center of town.

To my new home.

It will be a long night. I won't be able to rest until I atone, both for the sinful act of taking the life and for my lack of remorse after doing it.

Guilt squeezes my middle for *not* feeling anything at all.

I'll welcome the pain.

He is merciful.

I grit my teeth against the harsh air while I walk, trying to remember where I packed my discipline: the whip I keep for times like this.

It takes me twenty minutes to get back, the Notre-Dame Cathedral gleaming in the full moon, its two intricately designed bell towers looming over the main square like a promise. The outside architecture is very Gothic and a nearly exact replica of the cathedral with the same name in Paris, although on a much smaller scale.

This entire town is like a time capsule, history that doesn't *truly* belong to these people or this country suffocating the air with its ill-placed potency. It draws tourism and money though, and if the United States excels in anything, it's greed.

I quicken my steps and am just about to head beyond the doors and around to the back courtyard where the rectory is when movement at the base of the cathedral steps catches my eye.

There's a man leaned against the stone, his eyes closed and his hair tangled as he tries to keep warm beneath a holey blanket and fingerless gloves.

My throat tightens. I know how unforgiving the cold nights can be when you're sleeping on concrete streets.

I stride over and rest my hand on his shoulder, squeezing gently when he jerks awake. My eyes flicker over where we touch, a few deep scratches marring my pale wrist, and a vivid memory of my fingers wrapping around that woman's throat just a few moments earlier makes my blood heat and a burst of adrenaline rush through me.

"Come inside before you freeze." I nod to the cathedral doors.

The man's gaze widens, and he hesitates for only a moment before mumbling out a thanks and following me up the stairs. We head past the stone gargoyles that line the front and into the warmth of the narthex, which is the lobby just beyond the vaulted entrance.

"You can sleep here or in the nave if you wish." I jerk my chin toward the pews of the sanctuary before spinning to move down the hall that will take me to the back exit, to the small cottage at the rear of the church property that I now call home.

"Who are you?" the man asks, his voice echoing off the high ceilings and stained glass. "I've never seen you before."

I pause but don't turn to face him.

"I am Monsieur Frédéric. But you may call me Father Cade."

CHAPTER 1

Amaya

"FUCK."

I suck in a breath, pulling my hand away from the gas stove, and rush to the sink, flipping the taps so water cascades over my singed skin. Tears prick behind my eyes from the sharp pain, but I clench my teeth, letting the lukewarm liquid soothe the burn.

I'd like to blame the shoddy appliances for my mishap, but it was just me getting lost in my thoughts. Even now, as I watch the water pour from the rusted nozzle of my kitchen sink, the small waterfall breaking apart as it meets my finger, I start to drift away, lost somewhere in the back of my mind. Somewhere I don't feel the sting. Somewhere I don't feel anything at all.

Shaking my head, I turn off the faucet, sighing as I glance around the one-bedroom apartment, looking for my little brother.

"Quin," I call out when I don't see him.

Noise from out front seeps through the paper-thin walls of the small living room, and my brows furrow. I make my way to the door, the cold air from the bitter Vermont fall bleeding through the cracks, making a shiver race down my spine. I glance up, noticing the lock I keep high on the door is unlatched, and a heavy feeling drops in my gut. I *always* keep it locked.

Quinten elopes, and it's my job to make sure he stays safe when he's self-regulating.

I can't believe I didn't lock it.

There's a shawl I keep hanging on the coatrack, and I reach out quickly, ripping it down and wrapping it around my shoulders as I wrench open the door and step outside onto our front stoop. The icy breeze punches me in the face, but I ignore it, my eyes darting around the crumbling sidewalk and down the street.

As soon as I see the huddle of kids on the corner, my throat tightens and I race toward them, my long legs eating up the distance.

One of the boys laughs, his foot coming back like he's about to kick something in front of him. "Cat got your tongue, you fucking *idiot?*"

My chest spasms.

"Hey," I yell.

The little asshole's leg freezes, and he turns around, along with the other four kids: two boys and two girls who are flanking his sides. My stomach drops when I see who the main one is.

Bradley Gammond. *That little fucker.*

His mother is a defense attorney for the state, and she absolutely hates me, the same way she hated my mom. And the same way that, apparently, Bradley hates Quinten.

When did kids get so mean?

Their eyes widen when they see me, and Bradley's cheeks tinge pink beneath his fair skin. His hand jerks out, grabbing the arm of the boy next to him. They all rush away, their quick footsteps smacking against the pavement.

My brows crease as I move forward, seeing a hunched-over form with short, fluffy black hair rocking back and forth in the middle of the sidewalk.

Quinten.

A lump of guilt swells in the middle of my throat. I can't believe I didn't realize he was out here.

"Fucking bullies!" I scream after the kids, picking up a medium-sized pebble and throwing it at them before crouching down next to my little brother. The chill of the concrete creeps up the insides of my long, flowy purple skirt and latches onto my skin, but I don't mind. I'm no stranger to cold weather in Vermont, and I became a pro years ago at pretending that my thin clothing provides enough warmth.

Quinten is shaking, his hands curled into fists so tightly, his smooth, tawny brown skin is blanching white, and I know without seeing that his nails are cutting into his palms. I send up a quick prayer that he isn't bleeding enough from the self-infliction to need antiseptic.

He hates having things touch his hands. Honestly, he hates being touched in general.

"Quin," I murmur, making sure I don't grip his arm until he acknowledges me.

His head turns toward me, his green eyes identical to mine big and round, but he doesn't make a single sound.

Shit.

He doesn't speak often, and when he does, it's normally phrasing he's picked up from others. It's only in the past year that he's started to manipulate the words into his own sentences, and when emotions run high, he tends to shut down, so his silence right now doesn't surprise me.

It wasn't until his third birthday that he started to form words at all, echoing people around him and scripting things he'd already heard.

Echolalia and gestalt language processing, his therapists call it.

But that doesn't mean he's not smart, despite what those kids were saying. Quinten is the smartest six-year-old kid I've ever known. And the best. Period.

"They're jerks, okay?" I say, not sure who I'm trying to soothe: myself or him.

He drops my gaze.

A sense of failure drips from the knot lodged in my throat and cascades down my insides, making my heart pinch. I tighten my jaw, not wanting to show my struggle in front of Quinten.

It's my job to be strong for him.

And I try, *God* do I try. But sometimes it's so damn hard.

It's a cruel place here on earth, filled with people who don't get it. Who *choose* not to understand that just because someone is different, it doesn't mean they're less than. Quinten deserves the whole world, and I'd do anything to shield him from the harsh reality of one that refuses to offer him even a small piece.

The people in Festivalé make it even worse. Quinten being my little brother makes him guilty by association. I'm the town outcast, and he's *different*. Although they blame that on me of course, along with everything else that goes wrong in this town.

I can't even count how many times I've dreamed of packing us up and disappearing to somewhere else. Somewhere we can start again.

Just like my mom always used to do.

But that's unrealistic. I have bills and Quinten's therapy and a thousand different types of responsibilities here. Besides, I can't just rip him away from the only home he's ever known.

When I was little, long before Quinten was born, my mom used to pack us up right after I'd get comfortable in whatever place we were in and then plop us down somewhere new. I learned quickly that making friends was a useless skill and that having a sense of belonging was a pipe dream I read about in books, not one I got to experience in real life.

The last thing I want is for Quinten to have that same experience with me.

He's my world. The only thing that matters.

I reach out my hand, holding it in front of his curled-up form, waiting until he places his palm in mine. I squeeze, giving a broad smile as I pull him to a stand and lead him back into our home.

Once we're inside, he immediately walks to the small rectangular kitchen table and slips into the worn wooden seat, grabbing his tablet and getting lost in his safety net. Can't say that I blame him; if I could, I'd be running to curl up in my bed or headed to the nearest pole studio, just to blow off steam and get lost in my body instead of my mind. Pole dancing is the only thing that's ever made me feel like *me*.

The unpaid internet bill winks at me from the kitchen counter where I've stowed it away and tried to forget that it exists. But this morning and the way Quinten just ran to his tablet are stark reminders that his apps aren't just a luxury, they're a *necessity*, and if I can't pay the bill, then he can't feel safe in his own home.

Tonight's Monday, which is usually my night off, and it's one I had planned on spending with Quinten vegging out and relaxing, but before I can second-guess myself, I grab my cell phone to send a message to my only friend—and roommate—Dalia as I drop down in one of the chairs.

There's a missed call and I cringe, my stomach twisting when

I read the name Parker on the screen, and I swipe away the notification to type out my text.

> Me: Hey, I'm going into work tonight. Can you watch Quin?

A reply comes through quickly, and I sigh in relief.

> Dalia: You bet. I'll be home at 4.

I run a hand over my forehead and glance across the table at my younger brother. His face is emotionless, like whatever happened didn't even affect him. Like he's forgotten about it already.

But looks are deceiving.

Quinten never forgets a thing.

Besides, even if he appears to bounce back quickly, I don't. The feeling that comes along with knowing some asshole kids were trying to physically harm him will stick with me forever, another notch sliced into the already marked-up surface of my heart.

In the really hard moments, I wonder if those notches will turn to scar tissue, making an impenetrable wall too thick to breach.

Some days, I wish for it.

My phone rings again, and I look down, *Parker* flashing across the screen.

My heart falters, but I silence the call. It's way too early to deal with him.

Parker Errien is the bane of my existence and the reason

Quinten and I live in perpetual debt. He first showed up when he was dating my mother, after we moved here a little over five years ago.

I'm not sure how she got involved with him, but it didn't come as a surprise. My mother was a beautiful woman. Similar to me in almost every way with her long black hair and striking green eyes. Her legs for days that accented her thick thighs and hips. When necessary, she looked the part of money easily even when she had none, and she was a siren to men, calling them over and casting them under her spell with a single look.

She and Parker started dating almost immediately after we arrived, and it was only after she disappeared that I learned he was secretly "renting" her out to his friends in high places. The type of friends who need discretion and are willing to pay a pretty penny to ensure they get it. But in public, Parker Errien and Chantelle Paquette quickly became the talk of the town, and for the first time, I felt a sense of belonging. Even when his stares lingered just a little too long and his hands wandered a little too far.

Only when she disappeared, he didn't. He simply switched his focus from her to me.

He didn't like that she left him high and dry, leaving his "clients" out of a woman to warm their bed and money they'd already paid for the privilege. So now, I'm stuck paying off her debts. Most of the money I make ends up in Parker's dirty hands, and he thrives on making me need him in any way he can.

A shiver sprints up my spine, and I shake my head, turning my attention to Quinten.

"You hungry, Quin?" I ask, my nails tapping on the worn wood of the table. It's a piece of shit, just like everything else in this place. I grabbed it from the dumpster down the street five years ago right after my nineteenth birthday, which was also right after our mom made me the town enemy and then disappeared, leaving a note that said six words.

I'm done. He's your responsibility now.

Funny how having a daughter when she was fifteen was manageable, but an oopsy baby with one of the many "loves of her life" at thirty-three who showed signs of being on the spectrum was too much to bear.

Fuck her.

I dragged the table inside and then spent a few days sanitizing it until my fingers bled, but I didn't care. I was just happy to give Quinten and I somewhere to eat that wasn't the floor, determined to prove that I was better than our trash egg donor who didn't love us enough to even *try*.

"Quin."

Quinten doesn't look up, and dread starts to grip my insides, knowing I don't have his normal scrambled eggs to offer because I just fucking burnt them all on the stove. It's been his comfort food for the past six months, the *only* thing he'll eat for breakfast, and if there's anything I want to do, it's comfort him.

"How about some chocolate chip waffles?" I smile wide, trying to entice him. I think there are some left. They might be a little freezer burned, but they'd do in a pinch.

He shakes his head, making a clicking sound in the back of his throat before saying, "You want eggs?"

It's not a question. The phrasing is just part of his gestalt language processing.

"I want eggs," I reply.

"I want eggs," he echoes, then adds his own thought. "That sounds good."

"You got it, dude." My throat tightens as I bob my head, knowing I'll have to run next door and ask Mr. Brochet for some, and he's a skeevy, grumpy old man who doesn't like to be bothered.

But I do it anyway, because if Quinten wants eggs, that's what I'll make sure he gets.

CHAPTER 2

Cade

PARKER ERRIEN.

I knew the name before I even came to town. My superior, Bishop Lamont, mentioned him frequently enough that I know Parker is the catalyst that inspired me being sent here. But this is the first time I'm meeting him in person.

He's a decently attractive man with porcelain skin, light blond hair that's graying around the edges, and an air of pompous ego that I'm salivating to grind into dirt. He waltzed into my office in the back hallway of the church twenty minutes ago, acting as though he owned the world, which I suppose, at least in this little spot in the universe, he does.

Parker runs Errien Enterprises: a holding company that owns seventy percent of the *other* companies between here and the neighboring towns. Parker's name graces the sides of almost every affluent building in Festivalé. It goes without saying that he's filthy rich, best friends with the mayor, and one of the biggest local donators to the Notre-Dame Cathedral, and he's the quintessential king of Festivalé.

And he has my superior, Bishop Lamont, in his pocket.

But I can feel the evil bleeding from his soul, and I wonder what it is a man like Parker has to do to ensure his throne can never be touched. How many people he pays off, how many sins he's willing to commit.

I find it very difficult to believe I was brought here to truly turn the town around, and my assumption is that in Parker's eyes, I'm just another pawn for him to puppeteer.

After all, my predecessor, Father Clark, was vocal in his last days. I heard him on the phone raging in Bishop Lamont's ear about how Mr. Errien was not his master and he wouldn't bow down to anyone other than God.

Parker will be very disappointed to learn that I'm no different.

"I heard you were old school," Parker says, eyeing me as I sit behind my large walnut desk.

My fingers are steepled beneath my chin, elbows digging into the arms of my cushioned chair.

"Uptight even," he continues.

Still, I don't respond.

He scowls. "Do you speak English, Mr. Frédéric?"

I quirk a brow. "Depends on if there's anyone worth speaking to, Monsieur Errien."

A dark look coasts across Parker's gaze as he settles back into the seat, his legs spreading wide. I'm sure he thinks it's an act of dominance, lazing about in *my* office like he owns it, but all it does is show that he's a man who doesn't know what to do with the dick between his legs.

"Is that some type of Catholic thing?" he snarks. "Priests who think they're beyond reproach?"

The muscle in my jaw twitches. "And to what religion

do *you* prescribe, Monsieur Errien? I had presumed you *were* Catholic."

His brows jump to his hairline. "Of course I am."

Humming, I stand up, moving around the edge of my desk until I'm hovering close enough that he has to crane his neck to meet my eyes.

"I am a man of God, Monsieur Errien, which means I am *more* subject to reproach," I say. "Despite the fact that I forgive many things a lesser person would not, for the sake of our future… *relationship*, I think we should establish boundaries."

"I'd agree."

"Perfect. I'll start." I smile. "It doesn't matter how much money you throw around or how many others drop to their knees and worship you as some sort of false deity because of said money. I will not tolerate disrespect."

Parker's teeth grind together, loud enough for me to hear it. "Neither will I."

I chuckle, leaning forward until my shadow looms over his frame. "Don't come into my office, into *His* place of worship, and flaunt your disregard, implying that my faith is something to mock. Here, in this house, *I* am the power."

"You're only in this position because I wish for it," Parker spits back. "You have *no* idea what I'm capable of."

Straightening, I run my hand down the front of my black button-down and lean against the lip of my desk. "That's true. And the church is forever grateful for your more than generous donations. I know that you and Father Clark didn't see eye to eye on cleaning up the streets of Festivalé, so I suggest you take a moment of reflection and search deeply for the gratitude you should be feeling, knowing I've heard your pleas and support your cause."

He scoffs, but I don't miss the minuscule way his shoulders slump, his arrogance cowering in the way false confidence usually does when hit with a strike of dominance.

"Do we understand each other?" I press.

He doesn't reply other than a sharp nod, and a grin tips up the corners of my mouth. I let the silence thicken the air and puncture his skin until he shifts in obvious discomfort.

"Where did you say you were from again originally?" he finally asks.

"I didn't."

"And how long have you been a priest?"

"Long enough."

The starched collar chafes around my neck at his question, and I clear my throat.

Parker hums, tapping his thick fingers against the wood of his chair, his eyes calculating in a way they hadn't been before.

It was probably a mistake to be so harsh with him, but being here, in this town, has thrown me off-kilter. My temper is short and my fuse is lit.

"I have some ideas for your homily this Sunday," he says, changing the course of our conversation.

My spine bristles.

"I'd expect nothing less," I reply, waving my hand toward the door. "Unfortunately, duty calls and I don't have time to hear it. If you require confession, you may speak to Father Jeremiah, the curate who's taking them today."

Parker shoots to a stand, buttoning his suit jacket before placing his palm in the air between us, ever the businessman. I stare down at it, but I don't take the offering of a handshake. He's insulted me, and I have no intention of letting him find comfort within these walls.

Not today.

"We're not so different, you and I," he muses. "And regardless of the title you may hold here, Mr. Frédéric, I'd suggest *you* remember why you hold it."

"No need for formalities, Parker." I smile. "Please, call me Father."

His jaw tightens but he nods. "Have a good day, Father."

And then he's gone.

I let out a slow breath, moving my head to the side until a sharp crack rings in my ears, the tension morphing into relief. Maneuvering back around my desk, I sit down, picking up a pen and tapping it in a methodical rhythm against the wood, my eyes trained on the door where Parker just left. I shouldn't have goaded him, should have bit my tongue and smiled, allowing him to think he holds the power.

But there's something off about him. A darkness in his eyes that reminds me of my past. Of Sister Agnes when she'd beat me black and blue.

"Cade Frédéric!" Sister Agnes screeches, her voice echoing off the concrete walls in the dining hall.

I cower behind the longest table in the back, trying to conceal myself in the corner, keeping to the shadows and hoping that she can't see. If she finds me, she'll surely take the belt to me again, and I still haven't healed from last week when I stole that new boy's toy. This time, I didn't do anything.

Not really.

Footsteps draw near, and I hunch down farther, sliding from being on my knees to on my belly, trying to keep myself as flat to the floor as I can. My eyes are peeled for a sign of her, and my heart shoots to my throat when I see her plain black shoes stomping into the room. She moves closer, and with every step, my stomach sinks, regret for losing control of myself and smashing those plates in the kitchen hitting me full force.

But I was just so...angry. And I needed to get it out.

Her footsteps halt right in front of the table where I'm hiding, and her knees crack as she crouches down, her habit making her seem even more threatening than if she was in plain clothes.

Her lips pinch. "Come out from under there this instant."

My stomach drops and I crawl out from beneath the table, my head down and my hands clasped behind my back, but I don't say a word. I don't like to speak English with her. I stumble over my words and forget proper phrasing. Every time I mess up, she adds another lashing.

She reaches forward and grips my ear tightly, twisting until it feels like she might rip it off altogether. I hiss but know better than to fight against the pain.

"I see you've made a mess of things again, child. Always getting into trouble. Do you know how much money you've cost us this time? Dozens of dishes, shattered in the kitchen. So much destruction for a five-year-old."

"Je suis désolé," I mumble.

She twists my ear harder. "English, child."

"S-sorry, Sister. I'm sorry," I stutter.

She lets go of my ear, pain radiating down the entire left side of my face as she does.

"What caused you to do it this time?" She looks down her nose at me.

"André's p-parents came back for him."

She crosses her arms. "And that made you angry?"

I nod. It did make me angry. And jealous. "Oui."

Sighing, she says, "It isn't your fault, Cade. You're sick."

Swallowing, I nod again. "I know."

"Come on." She grips my arm and drags me behind her through the dining hall and into the kitchen. Dozens of shattered dishes litter the ground, and she places me in the center of them before walking over to grab a thick wooden spoon.

When she's standing directly in front of me, she leans in close, her gaze meeting mine. It's quick, but I swear I see her pupils dilate and a flash of black coast across her eyes. It makes my shoulders tense and my mouth run dry.

"There's a monster in you, child. And God wants me to beat it out."

Sighing, I come out of the memory and glance down at the calendar that takes up the majority of the empty space on my desk, a reminder that my duties are ingraining myself into the spaces here, getting to know the parish, overseeing the curate—Father Jeremiah, the apprentice of mine whom I've yet to meet. I'm here to lead people back onto the path of Christ. To help Festivalé become a righteous land instead of a sinful pit.

I already know I'll be doing none of those things today.

Instead, I follow Parker, needing to know more about the man who has the ear of the bishop and the stink of corruption.

CHAPTER 3

Amaya

I HOP OFF THE BUS AT THE EDGE OF CARNIVAL Street, heading around the corner to where the Chapel sits, the strip club I've danced at for the past three years. A bright purple cross—shattered in the middle—flickers above gold neon lights, like a homing beacon for the depraved to gather.

The club itself is two towns over in Coddington Heights, about an hour away from Festivalé. Close enough to get to but far enough to maintain anonymity without too much worry.

That's not because I'm ashamed of what I do—quite the opposite, really. I just can't risk Parker finding out where I work. If he knows, he'll ruin it, just to make me depend on him more. And that's not something I want to deal with.

But I love exotic dancing.

I *enjoy* seeing the lust in people's eyes when they watch me onstage, using the hollow steel pole as a blank canvas while I paint my body around it like a brushstroke. And I especially like the way it feels to control my sexuality, bleeding money from the people who come to watch. Counting and wrapping the stacks of bills at the end of the night sends a rush through me, one that feels a hell of a lot like success—no matter how fleeting the feeling is. I've been objectified for as long as I can remember, puberty hitting me early and showcasing just how little people care for a girl's age as long as she's aesthetically pleasing to their baser instincts. It's one of the many reasons my own mother was a piece of shit. She was a bitter woman, one who couldn't handle both an autistic son she never wanted *and* a well-endowed daughter who garnered more attention simply by existing.

If it was random people on the street, she got annoyed. When it was the men she'd bring to our home, she'd get jealous.

When I was young, the subtle jokes and leering glances made me afraid. But once I became a nineteen-year-old left to care for myself and Quinten, I learned that it's *women* with the real power, only most women don't realize it. I did. I mastered how to utilize everything in my arsenal, so now I'm the one in control. At least in all the areas that I can be.

It's the main reason why I don't date. Have zero interest in the opposite sex, actually. I've spent my entire life witnessing what happens when you get close with a man through the lens of my mother, and it's always the same.

Hearts in the eyes, can't eat, can't sleep kind of infatuation. Flowers and gifts and "Oh, *this* time, it's different, baby girl. He's the one."

Then come the sharp words, the bitter fights, the sound of fists hitting faces. The late-night crying and the need to have your daughter take care of *you* instead of the other way around.

And then, finally, the disappearance. Packing up and leaving when you realize the man you fell for isn't the man you thought he was at all.

My mother was a nomad at heart, and it was damn near impossible for her to stay still long enough to dig her heels into the ground. The second she started to sink in too deeply, she'd rip herself away, and I was the unfortunate luggage that got dragged along while she looked for something that always seemed just out of reach.

I wonder if she's still searching now that she's been without us.

Realistically, she's probably dead in a ditch somewhere, suffocated by her vices or one of the men she claimed to love.

When I was little, I'd pretend that I was a lost princess, stolen away from my castle and toted from place to place, hidden away on purpose so my fictional parents, ones who would love me right, wouldn't be able to track me down. It was comforting, thinking there were people out there desperate to find me. As I got older, I stopped seeking out my imagination and started watching my mother instead. Easier to be prepared that way.

Similar to religion, her patterns never changed.

When her smile started to thin and the flowers turned into ice packs, I knew it was time to leave.

Chantelle Paquette could only take so much abuse, only get in *so* deep with the men she thought loved her, before she'd sneak us off in the night like criminals slipping through metal bars. Another city. Another man. Same neglectful parenting.

But experience shapes us whether we'd like it to or not, and the *experiences* she gave me were valuable lessons.

I learned to not plant roots when you wouldn't be around to tend to the soil.

How to care for my brother by remembering all the ways I wished she had cared for me.

Most importantly, I learned not to trust anyone who says

they love you, because in the end, they always love themselves the most.

And despite all that, despite me seeing it happen with her time and time again, I never in all my life thought she would leave *me*.

But things changed once she had Quinten.

I shake the memories away. I'll *never* be like her.

My ratty black high-tops crunch on the gravel in the parking lot of the club, and I head toward the employee entrance that's situated in the back, my leggings, ball cap, and oversize hoodie engulfing me in its fabric.

Benny, one of the bouncers, is standing outside, his bulky frame and curly hair casting a shadow from the yellow streetlamp hovering above the door. There's not much to watch, but there is a back alley that's hidden from the exterior cameras and connects to the main street, so usually someone's out here just to make sure nothing goes awry.

He gives me a nod and moves, unlatching the door handle so I can slip inside.

I smile my thanks before the door latches behind me, and I head down the hallway, the shiny linoleum floors squeaking beneath my sneakers as I head into the back room.

The other dancers are lounging around, each one taking up their own vanity, adjusting themselves as they either rest between their sets or get ready. I know most of them by appearance, but that's it. I'm not sure I'd notice them on the street, and in any case, none of them are chummy with me.

I haven't tried to get to know them. I'm not here to socialize.

Quinten's therapy is expensive, and between the astronomical price of insurance, trying to keep the lights on, and everything else in my life, I need all the money I can get. These women are my competition as much as I'd like them not to be. Most of them are tight-knit with one another, and I ache for that type of camaraderie.

The only person I've found it with is Dalia, and she doesn't work here anymore.

So I keep my head down and focus on what matters.

I drop my bag in one of the small gray lockers that line the back wall and spin the lock I clicked into place, making sure my belongings are safe.

When I turn, Phillip, the owner, is waltzing through, and I give him a tiny wave as he moves past me to talk with one of the other girls.

Out of all the men I've ever known, he has to be the one I hate the least. He gave me a job when no one else would, and when I wanted to stop being a cocktail waitress and learn pole, he hooked me up with the best dancer—Dalia—and had her give me lessons while he footed the bill. He pretended like he was simply being nice, but I'm not naive enough to truly believe that. I know that most likely it was because he saw potential and thought I'd be a worthy investment. Either way, I appreciate what he's done. Pole dancing is my outlet. Besides, he lets me use the empty studio he owns on the other side of town to dance on my days off, and that alone is worth its weight in gold.

He's not necessarily attractive in the classic sense, with his spiked-up blond hair, fair skin, and muddy brown eyes. He has a softer jawline than most, and I stare down at him when I wear stage heels, but he's bulky, and I like a man who makes me feel safe without being overpowering.

Like I said, I don't enjoy losing control.

He moves right past me, not sparing me a single glance, and I ignore the way a slight pinch of jealousy hits me when he stops and grins at another one of the dancers. Not because I want his attention on me but because there's a familial type of energy with everyone in the club, one that I'm excluded from. The same way I'm excluded back in Festivalé.

Gritting my teeth, I internally smack the shit out of myself and move to an open vanity.

It's time to transform from Amaya to *Esmeralda*.

Twenty minutes later, I'm done, my raven-black hair hidden beneath a red wig that cascades down to my hips, secured by tape and bobby pins, purple-colored contacts, and full makeup, my long sparkly lashes brushing against the undersides of my eyes every time I blink. And when I finally waltz out to the main stage, the DJ's voice booming out my introduction, I become someone else entirely.

I feel sensual as I move across the raised platform and around the pole, slowly stripteasing, allowing the eroticism of the moment to blend with the artistry of my craft. I imagine my energy as a pulsing red color, pouring out and covering the entire area, drawing everyone's eyes and, more importantly, dollars to *me*.

Losing myself in the moment, my mind floats away, all my worries and troubles ceasing to exist as the power of holding attention cascades down my limbs and around my nearly naked form, infusing me with confidence and sensuality.

But then something sharp and hot pierces through the hazy numbness, my eyes popping open and swinging across the main floor.

My heart stutters in my chest when my gaze locks on a dark figure in the back corner, behind the plush couches with table service. He's leaning against the wall, his hands in his pockets and his body turned toward me. I can't make out any features—other than the fact that he towers over everyone else—but his face is covered by the brim of an old-school black hat, like he's some type of 1920s mafioso, and the rest of him is enshrouded in the shadows. And somehow, I know like I know *anything* that he's the reason for the heat currently slicing through my calm.

I shake my head and look away, not liking the way it feels, and scan the eager faces near the front of the stage instead. I reach above me and grip the pole, sliding my ass down the metal until I'm squatting with my legs parted in invitation.

A stocky man with slicked-back blond hair and a pinched nose is front and center, and my stomach somersaults violently when I recognize him. I lose my footing, stumbling enough to feel a small tug in my ankle.

Parker Errien.

Fuck. Fuck. Fuck.

Panic jumps along my nerves and my palms grow clammy as I straighten and continue with the rest of my set, my fingers slipping on the pole, making my movements appear sloppy and unsure. I grit my teeth, rushing through the last few moments of my dance, and the second it ends, I jerk forward, grabbing my clothes and the few bills thrown on the stage before hobbling off. I don't stop, don't think, don't *breathe* until my back hits the wall in the employee hall, my limbs shaking.

I don't think he recognized me but Jesus.

What the hell is he doing here?

I peek back around the hallway once my heart calms down and scan the main floor, anxiety tormenting my mind with what-if questions. It's a risk to walk out there and try for private dances because I *really* don't want him to recognize me, but my need for money wins the battle.

Besides, if he does, I'll just explain that *he's* part of the reason I need the cash in the first place. Cringing, I visualize how that outcome would go. Probably the same as last time I tried telling him I wasn't paying off my mother's bullshit debt, and the cat that I had rescued two months earlier, one that Quinten had grown severely attached to, showed up dead with its head severed and placed in our mailbox. I found random pieces throughout the week, slipped into air vents in our home, underneath the cupboard, beneath the slats of my bed.

Bile rises in my throat as I remember the realization that Parker was far more dangerous than I gave him credit for. That the businessman front was just the tip of the iceberg. That he could come into my home anytime, and there was no way I could keep him out.

And then he proved that to be true a month later when he decided to take what he wanted from me without my consent.

My throat grows dry as I think of what he'll do next time I decide to disagree.

Blowing out a deep breath, I stiffen my shoulders, shaking my fake red hair until it tickles the middle of my back, and I make my way onto the floor, making sure to keep to the edges in case I need to hide myself away.

It isn't until a gust of hot air whispers along the back of my neck, goose bumps sprouting along the length of my arms, that I realize just how distracted I am. And then a voice rumbles, so deep and commanding that I swear to God it vibrates through my bones.

"Hello, petite pécheresse."

CHAPTER 4

Cade

I'VE CONVINCED MYSELF THAT FOLLOWING PARKER all day is recon work. He thinks I'll be his puppet, and Bishop Lamont seems to have brought me here under false pretenses of helping, just to tell me I need to acquiesce to Parker's requests. But I bow before no one but God, and it makes me uneasy, knowing my superior is easily swayed by something as simple as greed and money.

Plus, on a more personal level, my monster *aches* to rid Parker of his demons.

And now he's here.

Péchant.

Sinning.

Just like the rest of them.

I'm not surprised. Parker Errien has a lot of money, innumerable amounts, and that's what money does. It turns and tortures and corrupts until there's nothing left but an inflated ego and an empty soul. Again, my mind flies to Bishop Lamont. To the church that I've taken vows for. Dedicated my *life* to. This can't be what God has in mind for His people.

I move through the crowd scattered around the strip club, disgust churning my stomach as I burrow deeper into my coat and hat. The club itself is far enough away from Festivalé that I don't have to worry about being recognized, but I'm always cautious, just in case.

The Chapel is filled with religious artifacts being desecrated, and it makes my skin itch. I find a hidden corner behind long plush purple couches and lean my shoulder against the wall, watching Parker push his slimy body through the crowd toward the front of the stage.

His head bobs and weaves, and my view of him keeps being momentarily blocked by a stripper on the couch in front of me, her barely clad pussy grinding against the lap she's on.

My upper lip curls, irritation and judgment bleeding from my insides. I skim my gaze around the room, cataloging all the lost souls here. I imagine most of them are empty, searching for something to fill the gaping holes inside themselves, aching to feel as though they have purpose. Meaning.

They won't find it here. I'm not sure if they'll find it *anywhere*, not that I'd ever admit that piece out loud.

Parker falls in my line of vision again at the head of the main stage, his attention rapt on the woman who's spinning effortlessly around the pole in the center.

Esmeralda, I think the DJ announced.

Her knee is wrapped around the metal and the rest of her body is floating in the air, her hands running down her front, a large green stone shimmering from a necklace that dangles in the valley between her breasts. Her complexion is flushed a light blushing brown, and it makes her look ethereal, like a sparkling topaz gemstone. The way she uses the stage and flings her body in the air around the pole makes it seem as though she's flying, high above the ground, her muscles tensing and forming around the silver bar. It's art, pure and simple, and it chips a piece of ice away from my chest, heat blasting through my center.

All thoughts of Parker fade away.

She's mesmerizing.

My cock thickens, and I clench my jaw to keep from shifting to ease the discomfort.

If being here is sinful, then this woman is sin, wrapped in a fiery bow.

My stomach dips, a shot of panic washing over me. Watching her makes me feel like *I'm* the one spinning, my focus being thrown off-kilter until my feet are scrambling to find solid ground. A thin layer of sweat breaks across my brow the longer I swim in these unfamiliar emotions, and my tongue sticks to the roof of my mouth.

Look away, I tell myself.

But I don't. I can't.

She flips around, slinking her body back to the ground, her knees spreading apart, flashing the white silk of her underwear, leaving just enough to the imagination. But I know every man here is thinking the same things I am. Picturing what's beneath the fabric, desperate to see if her cunt is pink and flush, begging for a tongue to soothe its ache.

Before I can even attempt to put up a fight, my monster surges up, tearing through its cage like it's trying to burst through my skin and devour her whole, carnal attraction blazing in my veins until all I can see is her.

Her long red hair cascades down her body like a waterfall, caressing her curves similar to a lover, but the way she moves on the stage is what really steals the energy from the room. Something scratches at the back of my brain while I watch her. A small, timid voice, screaming for me to look away. To remember everything I've promised.

But temptation is a devastating mistress.

It's not my fault, I remind myself. I'm only human. And she is…all-consuming.

Like hellfire.

Our eyes meet and an unhinged possessiveness pounds through me. I don't understand it, but I can't control it, and although it doesn't make sense, I have to bat away the voice blaring in my ears, telling me to mutilate every single person who has their beady eyes on her.

They don't deserve to look at her.

The unhinged thoughts, so violent and visceral, make me see red, and somewhere, mild and meek in the back of my mind is my sanity, begging me to remember who I am. Who I *strive* to be.

"You're sick, Cade."

Whip.

Slash.

Pain.

Sister Agnes's voice rears its ugly head just in time, and it does the trick, allowing me to regain a modicum of control. Enough to feel the way my throat has gone dry and my muscles are drawn tight, ready to do…*something bad*.

I lost sight of myself so quickly with her. She's like a drug for my sickness, making it scream in delight. That's the only explanation for the obsession that washes over me like a tidal wave and drowns the spaces in my soul that should be reserved for Him.

She rips her gaze away, severing our connection, and it feels like a piece of my chest is torn when she does. Her eyes widen as they zone in on something close to the stage, and she stumbles. I follow her line of sight, irritated that I don't hold her attention any longer. My vision narrows on Parker, who's drinking her in like ambrosia.

Does she dance for him? Sit on his lap and grind against him until he groans and makes a mess in his thousand-dollar suits?

My jaw ticks.

She rushes off the stage before the last note of the song hums through the speakers, and although I try to fight it, to stuff the urge to follow her down and keep it locked up tight, I can't.

God forgive me, I can't.

I'm after her just as quickly as she left, unable to think past the pulsing need to be closer. I'm a simple man who's been reduced to his base instincts to hunt, capture, keep.

I want to hear her voice.

Smell her skin.

Paint my sickness on her soul.

A single glance in her direction and I'm a ravenous dog, desperate for a crumb. My shoulder sinks into someone as I move by them, and they yell out an insult, but I ignore them.

Let anyone try to stop me.

I find her past a sign that says *Employees Only*.

She's against the wall with her clothing pressed to her heaving chest, eyes squeezed shut and pouty mouth open like an invitation. She's vulnerable right now. It would be so easy to waltz over, drop her to her knees, and slide my thick cock down her tight little throat.

The visual is so strong, it makes my footsteps stutter, the familiar twinge of guilt nipping at my middle, different than it normally is because usually, I don't have these sexual desires. Just violent ones, and those violent ones, I've come to terms with. Made a deal with God, reminding myself that He is merciful in all ways. As long as we repent.

Will he be as forgiving for sins of the flesh?

She redresses quickly and starts moving, and my logical reasoning dissipates.

I follow her back onto the main floor, noting the way she sticks to the edges, as though she's fighting with herself on whether to stay hidden or come into the light. My stomach tangles into a thousand knots as I step close enough to breathe down her neck. Close enough to see the fine hairs on her body rise as goose bumps sprinkle across her skin like raindrops.

"Hello, petite pécheresse," I whisper in her ear.

She stiffens and I move in closer, the back of her head hitting my lower chest. My fingers tense, wanting to grip her hips and pull her flush against me until my cock can slide between the crack of her ass cheeks.

No touching.

Thoughts are easier to repent for than action, and my back is already raw from last night's atonement.

The air shifts as though it's under her command and she spins, craning her neck to smile up at me. It's a practiced grin, and I hate it. Almost as much as I hate the fake purple of her irises and her sparkly lashes.

I long to see her bare, wearing nothing but that sparkling green gem that's wrapped around her neck.

"Hello," she rasps.

She doesn't appear to be as affected by me as I am by her.

Does she do this to all the men she sees?

I glare down at her, the thought lighting a match to my short temper, and she starts to shrink back but stops herself and stands taller instead.

"Do you not speak English?" she tries again, her head tilting.

"I do."

Her thick, dark brows lift, and she nods slowly, her ripe plump bottom lip turning glossy when her tongue swipes across it. My eyes follow the movement, locking on to the wetness.

She reaches out brazenly, her short nails scratching against the lapel of my coat. I watch the movement, disgusted at the knowledge she's probably done this same move with hundreds of others yet too transfixed to stop it.

"Do you want a dance?" she asks.

My spine stiffens. "Absolutely not."

Her smile drops along with her fingers, and I blow out a small sigh of relief when she moves back, a tiny bit of logic filtering in with the miniscule space she's created by stepping away.

She seems disappointed.

"Not used to your witchcraft failing?" I ask.

I'm not sure why the words slip from my lips, but it's the only thing I can think of. Why else would she bewitch me in such a way if it weren't on purpose?

Her brows furrow with concern as though being called a witch is something that hits too close to home, but then her features smooth and a tinkling laugh pours from her mouth.

A rumble vibrates through me in return.

My mind spirals along with the beat of my heart that's stomping like a stampede through my chest because I've never reacted to *anything* the way I am to her.

"You're French," she states.

I step in closer, bending so my lips ghost across the shell of her ear. *No touching*, I remind myself, but I just as quickly ignore it. Maybe to see how much my control can stand, if I can survive being so close to her without ever enjoying her taste. "Oui."

Clearly, I'm a masochist.

Her breath hitches. "If you don't want a dance, then what *do* you want?"

"I'm not sure," I say honestly, straightening back up. The flip-flop of control wavers between my sickness and what I know is right, making my stomach churn and my palms grow clammy and stick to the inside of my gloves.

If we were alone…if we weren't in public, I would allow the darkness to seep from my pores like tentacles and wrap around her delicate throat, squeezing until the sultry tone of her voice ceases to exist.

My fingers twitch, wanting to do it anyway, despite the fact that everyone will see.

Her eyes flick behind my shoulder, scanning our surroundings, and just like it did when she was on stage, losing her attention bothers me. My hand snaps toward her, my fingers gripping her chin and turning her back to look at me.

A small puff of air escapes her, and my stomach cramps in fear because even through the leather of my gloves, touching her this way is what I imagine a shot of heroin would feel like swimming through my veins.

"Eyes on me," I demand.

She nods slowly, and her acquiescence sends a bolt of lust down my spine.

"I won't fuck you, if that's what you're after."

My thumb pinches her chin until her mouth parts with a

slight *pop*, and the tip brushes along her bottom lip, anger cracking against my nerves like lightning.

"I have no interest in *fucking* you," I lie, even as the image of her beneath me while her nails split the scarred skin on my back assaults my brain. A shiver crawls up my spine like spiders, and my monster laps them up like meat.

Something dark passes over her face, but it's fleeting, and then she's ripping herself from my hold, her eyes widening as they move behind me. I cock my head, watching as she spins around, rushing away and back through the employee hallway.

For a split second, I consider chasing her, my heart thumping quickly at the thought, but I shake myself out of it, realizing this must be His grace, giving me reprieve from temptation.

I glance around to see what spooked her, and I'm wholly unsurprised when Parker is standing close by, a drink in his hand and his eyes scanning the room.

So she knows him.

Seeing Parker reminds me of why I came here in the first place, and it surely wasn't to fall prey to a dangerous woman who offers nothing but damnation.

It was to learn more about Parker, because he is surely my nemesis here and not my friend, and in order to keep him in check, I need to know what makes him tick.

But even reminding myself of this, recognizing how she affects me, and knowing I should keep far away, I don't stay to spy on Parker.

Instead, I stalk the shadows, waiting for Esmeralda to leave. I know the moment she does, even though her perfect body is hidden beneath a large hoodie and the long hair spilling from beneath a baseball cap is black instead of red. She glances around as she steps beneath the street lamp, her face flashing in perfect view, and the way it sends fire through me veins has me following her all the way to the bus stop.

And then I hop in my car and continue following her all the way back to Festivalé. I'm not surprised she lives here, not after seeing her visceral reaction to Parker.

It was foolish to speak with her.

I wonder if maybe her sins are too strong and that's why I feel the pull.

Because there's a monster inside her, a *demoné*, and it's my job to snuff it out.

CHAPTER 5

Cade

I AM A HOLY MAN, BUT MY MONSTER IS FROM HELL.

Sister Agnes tried for the first seven years of my life to temper that part of me, and her teachings stuck long after I ran away. But no matter how I try to extinguish the disease inside myself the same way as I do for others, I'm weak to its call.

If I don't feed the beast scraps, it's ravenous by the time it surfaces. So I give in to the cravings. I listen to the whisperings in my head—the quintessential devil on my shoulder—because it allows me to keep a semblance of control.

When people come for confession, I relate to their plight, and over the years, I've come to terms with the fact that my relatability to their failings makes me a better listener. A better priest. I *understand* darkness because it exists within me.

In my darkest of moments, I wonder if the Lord gave me the world's sickness so I'd recognize it in others. Living in its shadow while searching for the light. I don't *hate* the people I kill, quite the opposite in fact. I sympathize with them. I wish to free them in a way that I'll never free myself. And then I hope God understands why I must.

Not many men would be strong enough to weather the storm raging within them, and when the disease blankets my mind like a fog, it's a terrifying place. One where I don't care for morals. For right and wrong. I only care for my next hit. Adrenaline floods my veins like a drug, scorching everything in its wake, leaving behind nothing except potent satisfaction that warms my insides like a shot of whiskey.

In those moments, *I'm* a god.

But the crash back down to earth is a stark reminder that it's only in repentance that I can be temporarily freed. I don't feel remorse for the murders. I feel guilt that God may not approve.

I first went into seminary because it was easy. The church sheltered me when I was in need, offered me respite from an empty belly and a tortured past. Father Moreau took me under his wing and taught me how to seek forgiveness. How to be a better man. How to let go of the petty crimes and the meaning- less sex and find sanctuary in something other than myself.

I wasn't a religious person growing up. I had been an orphan, and the only adult figure in my life was Sister Agnes. Then I lived on the streets once I escaped her prison the day I turned seven years old.

But despite Sister Agnes being my only experience with religion, the church offered me warmth.

Food.

Purpose.

And I work every day to be what I set out to be.

But even the most loyal of soldiers have their weaknesses.

And right now, I am not a worthy man.

Not when I'm neck deep in black waters, wading through this

obsession that's reached out and wrapped itself around my neck like a noose, choking me until I can't suck in air.

Esmeralda.

Although I'm sure that's not her real name.

My slacks are open the second I make it back to my office, my cock in my hand before I can lock the door, and I stroke my length furiously for the first time in years, desperate for relief. It's *painful*, this desire. A throbbing in my body, an ache that has my balls heavy and my mind hazy with lust. I've always prided myself on being a logical and steady man, but this is far from logic. Before I entered seminary, there were several women, and men as well, but those trysts were inconsequential compared to even a single thought of her.

I've never experienced anything like it.

Still, if I don't take care of the desire, then I won't be able to function.

I drag my palm upward, twisting my hand at the top of my cock where I'm already leaking cum. I spread it down the length of me, creating lubrication that has my hips thrusting and a groan falling from my lips.

It's been so long since I've felt sexual pleasure.

I had forgotten the way it softens edges and clouds the pain.

My movements speed as I lean over my desk, my free hand slamming down on the oak as a sharp spike of pleasure splices through my core. My fingers tingle at the memory of Esmeralda's skin, the way her big doe eyes portrayed the perfect mask of innocence. And then I imagine her on her knees, needy and begging at my feet as I grip her chin the way I did at the club, resting my cock on her pouty lips as my cum sprays across the flat of her tongue.

I'd cinch her mouth closed and stroke her throat, feeling the act of her swallowing every drop of me.

The visual makes my sack tighten. More precum drips from my tip and slides down my length, coating the top of my knuckles with arousal.

Another groan escapes my lips and I throw my head back, abs constricting as pleasure, white-hot and blinding, courses through the marrow of my bones and explodes through my pores, my balls pulsating in a steady rhythm as my shaft jerks wildly in my palm.

It's dirty.

Depraved.

Incredible.

My vision goes black, cum spurting out forcefully, landing across the few papers and the large calendar that marks my responsibilities to the church.

It takes minutes, maybe hours until my breathing regulates and I'm able to relax back into my seat, taking stock of what just happened and how I feel now that I've found relief. I had hoped the act would rid me of the temptation, but I can immediately tell that isn't the case. It's only burrowed in further, purring like a cat, creating a hum that vibrates through my chest.

I frown at the feeling, that same sense of panic from when she was near reaching up and gripping me tightly, squeezing until my vision blurs.

She's a problem that I'll need to take care of as quickly as possible.

I tuck my now-flaccid dick back into my slacks, relieved that at least the tight knot of tension has loosened and a bit of clarity has seeped through the muddled edges of my mind, but it isn't long until the guilt settles in, coating my tongue until I'm nauseous from the taste.

And there's only one cure for that.

I jolt forward, ripping the stained calendar from its base and tossing it in the trash before rushing around my desk and making my way out of my office. My hurried footsteps echo through the long hallway and out the back exit that leads to the detached rectory. It's a small cottage, made of dark wood and a small wraparound porch, and I throw open the front door forcefully, desperate to make amends for my transgressions.

I'm loud as I stomp through the living room, unable to take in my surroundings, but it doesn't matter. No one else lives here, my curate Father Jeremiah living in the smaller place a few yards away.

My breaths come sharply when I make it to my bedroom, and I slam my hand against my chest, trying to beat my lungs into submission. My fingers tear at the roots of my hair as I pace in front of the modest full-size bed and empty end table.

Il est miséricordieux. He is merciful.

The phrase doesn't lessen the anxiety because I'm not sure He is when it comes to this type of sin. I've reasoned away the violent acts, knowing there's a purpose behind what I do. But this...this has no reason.

Just a weak man giving in to temptation.

But as long as we repent, He will forgive.

Nodding to myself, I drop my hands and straighten, my vertebrae slotting into place with purpose, the panic ebbing away. I reach down, unbuttoning my dress shirt, the thin layer of sweat coating my body making the fabric stick to my skin. My back stings, the raw and scabbed-over wounds from last night pulling with the motion.

I revel in the pain, using it as a reminder of how weak I truly am.

Once my shirt is off, I lay it down on the mattress, smoothing out the wrinkles before I walk over to the wooden chest that's pushed into the corner of the room. I open it, the brass hinges creaking, and I bend down and grip the discipline in my hand, running the coarse tassels of rope along my palm.

"It shall be a holy convocation unto you; and ye shall afflict your souls," I murmur to myself as the knotted rope scratches against my skin.

With a deep breath, I stand, my body stiff and my muscles locked, my fingers tightening around the thick base of the whip. My nostrils flare as I picture *her* face, a bolt of lust driving through me even now, even when I should be living for only Him.

I bring my arm up high and strike it down over my opposite shoulder, the multiple tassels with knotted ends slicing into the open wounds on my back. I repeat the motion, and my teeth grit against the burn.

For as much then as Christ hath suffered for us in the flesh, arm yourselves likewise with the same mind: for he that hath suffered in the flesh hath ceased from sin.

My movements quicken, my cock shamefully hardening as my mind and body buzz from the pain. I beat myself harder until warm liquid drips down my spine and drops onto the floor in dots of red.

One strike for every impure thought, ten for every sinful stroke.

I continue until I can barely stand, my body wet with blood and my head dizzy from the punishment.

Usually, I feel relief afterward. As though my soul has been cleansed, my purpose brought back into view like a dirty window washed clean. But as I lie in my bed, taking in the sharp stabs of pain radiating through my back and down my limbs, I don't feel as though I've suffered enough. Terror seizes my lungs and steals my breath because I'm unsure if I'll ever feel cleansed again. Because even now, she's already creeping back in.

This stranger.

Ma petite pécheresse.

My little sinner.

CHAPTER 6

Amaya

MY MOTHER WASN'T A GOOD PERSON, SO IT makes sense that she wasn't a particularly good Catholic. Not that it ever stopped her from dragging me out of bed every Sunday morning for Mass.

I'd dress up in the nicest clothes I owned and we'd walk to whatever church was in the area. We moved around a lot, but no matter where we went, religion never seemed to change. Always the same stringent rules and regulations.

Do this. Don't do that. He is forgiving, yet He will smite you down.

It was enough to convince me that we were committing sin just by *being* there. Visions of a lightning bolt splitting apart the clouds and thundering down the center of the sanctuary filled my head. I was sure that seeking forgiveness for something we weren't truly sorry for was blasphemous enough for hell. And I know my mom wasn't remorseful over her actions because she continued to do them over and over again.

Still, every week, we went, and every week, nothing ever happened.

And nobody in the church ever seemed to catch on that my mother was a hypocrite. A fake. Or maybe they did, and they simply stayed quiet. After all, people often ignore traits in others that exist within themselves.

Perhaps we just didn't stick around in a single place long enough for anyone to really care.

But when we showed up in Festivalé, all that changed.

Because somebody *did* care.

Florence Gammond.

We've been in Festivalé for months now, and I think I can count on one hand the number of times my mom has stayed around for an entire day. She chugs coffee, her hair pulled back in a ponytail as she flits around the small kitchen in our apartment, humming to herself while she gets ready to leave.

"What time will you be home?" I ask, tapping my nails on the table. Irritation simmers deep in my gut as I watch her.

"Hmm?" She spins around, her eyes not even able to meet mine. "Oh, late probably. I have some errands to run, and then Parker's taking me up into the Green Mountains for a weekend getaway. Isn't that so romantic?"

Her cheeks flush and my stomach drops.

"But Quin has an appointment today. You promised you'd be here."

She waves me off. "You can get him there, yeah?"

I sigh as a heavy weight drops down in the middle of my chest. "Yeah, Mom. I'll take care of him."

I don't add that I'm always taking care of him. That I'm pretty sure he's supposed to be mimicking by now or smiling and making noise. Bringing up my concerns will just make her angry, and she likes to throw things when she gets mad. Her mood can flip as quick as a switch, and I learned years ago to pick my battles.

Besides, this isn't anything new. Mom disappears most days, leaving me alone to care for Quinten. Ever since she came home from the hospital.

She's never even told me who his father is.

After she leaves, I strap Quinten in a stroller and take to the quaint city streets to pass the time before his checkup. We live on the edge of town, where the French architecture is starting to crumble and the homeless sleep in tents, but it's only about a twenty-minute walk from the main square, and I like to go there whenever I can to take in the dark brick exteriors and steep roofs. There's something so magical about Festivalé, something that makes me want to immerse myself in its history and soak up the culture.

The square itself is teeming with people, most of them likely tourists, coming to the area to experience "Little France" without leaving the country. The main attraction is the Notre-Dame Cathedral, which was erected in the late 1800s and has been preserved beautifully ever since.

We go there on Sundays for Mass, but otherwise, I stay far away.

Religion creeps me out.

The sun beats down on my head as I push Quinten's stroller past the Champlain Patisserie and am about to turn around and head to the doctor's office when a sound rings out from the back alley and draws my attention to the noise.

My jaw drops as I take in the sight of my mother's boyfriend. Parker has a woman pressed up against the brick wall, her pasty white leg wrapped around his hip and her auburn hair stark against his blond.

I stop in my tracks, jerking the stroller so harshly that Quinten begins to cry.

Both Parker and the mystery woman's bodies fly apart, and as they do, she comes fully into view.

Florence, the woman who's always helping with Communion during Mass and is always glaring at my mother. She smooths down the front of her skirt, her giant diamond wedding ring glinting in the afternoon sun, and Parker's eyes narrow when they zone in on me.

I spin around and scurry away before either of them can say a word, my heart pounding as I try to compartmentalize what I just saw and whether I should tell my mother.

If I tell her, I'm sure she'll have us packed up and ready to leave before the sun can fully set. And I love it here. I want to stay.

No matter what.

Three nights later, long after I put Quinten to bed and lay down to fall asleep, Parker crept into my bedroom.

I remember my blood pumping in my ears and my stomach tightening in fear when the mattress dipped behind me, his large frame cocooning mine as his hand reached around my side and up to cover my mouth.

"Don't make a sound," he said.

I didn't.

"Whatever you *think* you saw the other day, your mother doesn't need to know. Nod if you understand."

Slowly, I nodded. My mouth ran dry, but I bit my tongue to keep quiet.

"I can make your life *very* difficult, sweet Amaya. I'd hate for you to find out just how depraved of a man I can be."

His hand ran down the front of my nightgown and slipped between my legs, and my teeth chomped down on my tongue so hard, the taste of copper started flooding my mouth. Tears pricked behind my eyes, my muscles tense and ready to fight, but his next words stopped me in my tracks.

"Say a word and I'll kill her in front of you and then take this little pussy for myself while she bleeds out at your side. Is that what you want, sweet girl? You want your mother's last vision on earth to be the man she loves fucking the younger, *tighter* version of her?"

Bile surged up my throat, and I shook my head, my lungs burning from the need to let out a sob.

"Good."

He pressed a kiss to my cheek and then he was gone, just as quickly as he had arrived.

I never did tell my mom.

But she found out about Florence anyway.

And after she made a scene in front of the entire town, she disappeared, the way she always had before. Only this time, she didn't take us with her. And whether she knew it or not, she handed me over to Parker on a silver platter.

But there's nothing I can do about it now. Not if I want to keep Quinten safe and a roof over our heads, and Parker's weird fixation on me lends itself to a type of protection that I wouldn't get anywhere else. He's the mayor's best friend. He's a dangerous and powerful man. And although people still sneer and whisper about the rumors my mother left in her wake, when he's around, at least they don't say it to my face.

"Amaya," Parker says as he walks into his office.

The lock clicks as he closes the door, and his voice grates over my skin, leaving it raw.

"Parker." I force a tight grin.

I peer at him closely, trying to figure out whether he recognized me at work. He's never been there before, and him popping up out of the blue worries me. The thought of him stripping away the last piece of my freedom makes me sick to my stomach. As it is, he thinks I make my money from doing freelance data entry work from the comfort of my home.

His fingers coast along the back of my neck as he breezes by where I'm sitting, the touch so light it could be considered an accident. But I know better. Parker doesn't *have* accidents. Everything he does is methodical.

He moves to sit behind his desk, his gaze undressing me like I'm a gift sent just for him.

I don't like his staring, and I like staring at *him* even less.

It's not that his face isn't appealing; it is, and most women in this town drool at the sight of him simply because his money makes him the most eligible bachelor in Festivalé. But to me, he's just another filthy creep. A bad man dressed up in thousand-dollar suits.

He continues to watch me, and my hands grow clammy in the silence. If he doesn't speak soon, I might throw up all over his fancy wood floors.

"You look nice," he finally says. "Everything good with Quinten?"

"He's fine." My chest smarts. I don't like him pretending that he cares.

He nods slowly. "School treating him well?"

I grit my teeth because *no*, it isn't, and I'm pretty confident that Parker knows that. Quinten and public schooling don't mesh. There are too many students and not enough support for someone on the spectrum. He doesn't do well with standing in lines or with having to keep still and quiet at a desk, and no matter how many times I fight for accommodations that allow him to feel safe and comfortable, his teachers shut it down. His iPad is part of his self-regulation, and they don't allow that in class. So he acts out, and then I get a phone call where I end up fighting back tears as I beg for them to reevaluate his IEP: his individualized education program. The school is understaffed and underfunded, and they don't care about *why* Quinten might be struggling. They only care that he is.

But I can't afford to put him anywhere else.

"It's the same as always," I reply carefully.

Parker sighs, standing up and moving until he sinks down into the chair next to me, reaching out to grasp my fingers. "I don't know why you insist on resisting this. I could take care of you."

How many times can we have this same conversation?

"I'm not interested in the ways I'd have to pay for that." I pull my hand back.

The muscle in his jaw ticks, and he runs his hand through his slicked-back hair. "Would it really be so bad? To be with me?"

"It's not that it would be *bad*," I say, even though it would be. "It just wouldn't be real."

"I can shelter you," he argues. "Take care of you. Put Quinten in the best private school in the state. You'll never want for anything again."

I would be lying if I said I wasn't tempted, but him using what I care about most to try and control me makes hatred burn through my veins. Parker knows me well enough to know I would do absolutely anything for Quinten, and my biggest fear is one day having no choice but to shackle myself to a man who would use stability and the people I love as a bargaining chip.

He's already taken so much.

"Parker," I plead, wishing he would stop doing this *every* single time. "I can't."

"Fine." His features drop, the softness molding into harsh edges, a coldness entering his gaze. "You got my money?"

A sharp laugh escapes me before I say, "Don't I always?"

"I don't see what's so funny," he spits.

"You." I wave my hand in between us. "*This.* You want me to be with you, to *marry* you, but you're the reason we're struggling so much in the first place."

He scoffs, picking an invisible piece of lint off the arm of his suit jacket. "I'm a businessman, Amaya. Your mother made a deal with me, and she left before fulfilling her end. As her next of kin, it falls to you."

I lift a brow. "You pimped her out to your clients. You didn't sign a million-dollar contract. It would hardly stand up in court."

"Semantics." He shrugs. "It holds up where it matters. Should I remind you of that again?"

I swallow around my suddenly dry throat, because *no*, he doesn't have to remind me. I got the message loud and clear after Mom left and I tried to tell him no.

Huffing, I reach into my worn purse and pull out the wad of bills, almost everything I was able to make this past week, dropping it in the small space between us.

He snatches it up immediately, his thumb flicking through the tops of the rubber-banded bills. "This feels light."

My heart stutters. "Just by a hundred bucks, Parker. I need...I need to keep the internet on."

"That's not my problem."

I swallow.

"You won't *let* it be my problem," he amends.

"Well, paying you isn't supposed to be *my* problem either," I bite back.

Chuckling, he reaches out and cups my cheek. To an outsider, it would look like a tender moment between us, but his grip is tight and his eyes are empty. "As long as your last name is Paquette, it is."

He stands up then, clutching the money in his fist and turning his back, effectively dismissing me. I follow suit, my legs tingling from the blood rushing back into them, and I walk to his office door, flicking the lock open.

"Same time next week, Amaya," I hear from behind me. "And don't be short or you won't like how I'll make you pay."

CHAPTER 7

Cade

FATHER JEREMIAH IS A RECENTLY ORDAINED PRIEST in his early twenties. He's youthful and eager to learn. His eyes still sparkle with mirth, and there's hope and innocence weaved into his gaze, the kind that only exists when you haven't experienced heavy things like grief spawned from trauma. He was the apprentice of my predecessor, Father Clark, so when Clark was pushed out and I was brought in, Jeremiah stayed on to ease the transition.

A twinge of guilt hits me when I think about how it's been days and we're just now meeting. He should have been the first one I sought out, but distractions seem to latch on extra tight here in Festivalé. Jeremiah doesn't seem to mind though. Within the first ten minutes of being together, he's at my heels like a dog eager for a bone, which is just fine by me. He'll be beneficial to have at my back.

We're driving to the monastery today in the thick of the Green Mountains. It's about an hour away from town, and the second Jeremiah mentioned it to me, I decided it was imperative to visit. Apparently, it's a well-kept secret, one that's attached to the local church but kept away from the people of Festivalé and surrounding areas. It's reserved solely for the Carmelite nuns who vow a life of solitude. And I'm always looking for a quiet spot when I need to get away. Sometimes, a silent mind and a place to recover from my nights of self-inflicted wounds are the only things I want.

"Have you lived in Festivalé your entire life?" I ask him.

"Yep, born and raised," he replies.

"And you like it?"

He shrugs. "As much as anyone does. My mom runs the café down on Champagne Street, so this town and its people are all I've ever known."

My fingers tap against the car door as I take him in. "And what made you want to be a priest, Jeremiah?"

He grins, his teeth bright white and sparkly against the deep brown of his skin. "It was either that or become a tour guide."

I laugh. "Not much to tour in Festivalé outside the town square, is there?"

He shakes his head. "I suppose not. But there's history in everything. Most of these buildings have been around since the 1700s, you know? Great Britain won the territory in the Seven Years' War, but our French roots are strong."

"I think you would have made a wonderful tour guide, Jeremiah."

He laughs. "The church is my calling, Father. Same as you, I'm sure."

Doubtful.

I nod instead of voicing my thoughts.

"I've never wanted to do anything else," he continues.

"You're young," I state.

"So are you."

"Thirty-six isn't *that* young." A grin tugs at my lips. "So besides the history of Festivalé, what is it you love about the town?"

"It's just home."

Envy hits me hard, because I can't relate. I've never had a home. Not really anyway.

"Mr. Errien seems to think the people are straying too far from God." I look over at Jeremiah as I say this, gauging his reaction. I don't really need to hear his answer. I've already come to the conclusion that Parker just wanted me here to have another person in his pocket, but I'm curious about what Jeremiah thinks of him.

"Well, he'd probably know," Jeremiah says.

"Would he?"

"People don't come to Mass the way they used to. They don't seek confession. Things are…quiet."

"Hmm." I'm not surprised to hear him say it. "And you trust Parker?"

"Sure." He shrugs. "He's never given me a reason not to. He does a lot for the town. Got his own best friend the mayor gig, I'm sure of it."

"And do you not think that's wrong? To use your money and influence to ensure certain people end up in office?"

Jeremiah purses his lips. "With all due respect, Parker's untouchable in this town. He funds the city programs and preserves the history by buying up the buildings instead of letting others tear them down. If he *sent* for you, it's because over the past few years, we've seen the drug epidemic bleeding onto the streets. Poor people panhandling at car windows.

Father Clark didn't care to help his own parish when they were in need."

I quirk a brow. "So why doesn't Parker handle it himself with his massive wealth and endless reach?"

"Well…" Jeremiah's head tilts. "That's why he called you here, isn't it? To help."

"Hmm, perhaps so." I turn to stare out the window, letting silence envelop the car.

The seasons are on the cusp of changing, the icy blue sky like a painted canvas against the leafless branches and dark green pines. It's different from what I'm used to, and the peace that comes with untouched nature skates over the tree line and paints itself on my soul. I sink into the feeling, knowing it's a temporary respite from the constant battle I'm waging inside.

The tires of our car crunch over loose gravel as we turn off the mountain road and trek up a long, winding driveway, stopping in front of a cabin.

It's an older building with a faded red roof. A-frame peaks jut out, shading the arched windows underneath. I wouldn't say it's an expansive place but large enough to comfortably house a handful of rooms and a small place to worship, and there's a definite woodsy vibe that complements the atmosphere.

I get why the Carmelite nuns stay here. Solitude doesn't sound so bad when this is what you're existing in.

"How many people live here?" I ask, unbuckling my seat belt and opening the door to step out.

Jeremiah's car door slams after mine, and he stretches, his back popping as he flips the car keys on his forefinger. "Sister Genevieve."

I lift a brow. "And?"

"That's it right now."

"She lives here alone?" I twist toward the building, staring up at the second-story windows.

He nods as we make our way up the small pathway to the front steps. "Not many people know of this place. And she prefers solitude."

Despite the barren feel of the upcoming winter, this is a lush land, teeming with life. The smell of pine is strong, and there's a small creek running along the left side of the driveway and disappearing beyond the monastery, the water gleaming with patches of thin ice, teasing the change of seasons.

The double front doors have intricate carvings, large crosses smack-dab in the center, and when we open them and step inside, the heat blasts against my face, making the tips of my ears burn from the change in temperature.

I pull off my gloves slowly as I glance around.

It's a comfortable cabin with deep cream couches in the small, quaint living room, a wood fireplace crackling in the corner and a Bible on the end table next to a reading chair with a plaid throw. There's a small sanctuary off to the left with three rows of old wooden pews and a staircase directly in front of us that I assume leads to the bedrooms.

"Sister Genevieve will be around here somewhere," Jeremiah murmurs as he walks farther into the room.

There's a creak of wood and then a woman appears from around the corner, dressed in a simple black habit.

"Here she is." Jeremiah grins.

She's different than I expected.

Her eyes are striking, a bright green that accents the deep bronze of her skin, spearing wherever she gazes, and she's much younger than I pictured, although the lines around her face carve out a story of a rough life. She's small in stature, but there's an energy that whips around her, one that tells me there's darkness within her just as there is within me.

I imagine she locks away her demons, whereas I let mine out to play.

And those eyes…there's something almost haunting about them. Like déjà vu or a memory that I can't quite grasp.

"You must be Father Frédéric," she says with a small tilt of her lips.

"Father Cade is fine." I incline my head. "Sister Genevieve, I'm guessing?"

"That's right," she replies. "Please, both of you come inside and get warm."

She whisks us away quickly, leading us to the small living area and then disappearing into the kitchen.

The warmth of the wood fire is strong against my side as I settle into the couch and wait. Jeremiah sits across from me, his ankle crossed over the opposite knee while he lounges comfortably as though he's been here a thousand times. Maybe he has.

Before long, Sister Genevieve is back, setting down a tray of small pastries before perching on the reading chair next to the fire. "Sorry I don't have anything better to offer. I didn't know you'd be making the trip."

"We won't keep you," I promise. "Just making the rounds. You know how it goes."

"Hmm," she hums.

"How long have you lived here?"

"A few years," she replies. "I was in a novitiate here with Sister Anna."

I lift my brows. "Novitiate? You're still in training?"

It surprises me because she seems practiced, refined in a way that newer nuns normally aren't. And she's a little older than most of the novitiates I've seen. Usually, they take their vows young.

I can't help but wonder what type of life she must have lived before and what turned her toward Christ.

She shakes her head. "Not anymore. I took my final vows last year shortly after Anna passed."

I nod slowly, cataloging the way her body shifts uncomfortably, tightening with each of my questions. She's on guard, and I want to know why.

Unfortunately, I don't find out. While we do speak for a few more minutes, we're simply filling the air with inane chatter, and I couldn't tell you what was said. I'm too busy watching her body cues. The way her eyes flick behind us to the staircase like she can't wait to be done entertaining our presence and how every so often, her fingers twine together and squeeze, blanching her skin.

Normally, it would draw my attention to the point of me not being able to focus on anything else. But even now, even when I'm here, my mind drifts to a sinful woman who's entirely out-of-bounds and definitely someone I shouldn't be thinking of at all. The same way she's been filtering into my thoughts since the moment I met her. The urge to go to where she lives and perch outside her window just to sate this *need* is strong.

"Are we interrupting something, Sister?" I finally ask, unable to take the tension wringing her body tight.

She shakes her head. "I'm sorry. I'm not used to having people here. I like my solitude. Guests make me nervous."

I nod and stand, gesturing for Jeremiah to do the same. "Then by all means, let us get out of your way."

She smiles tightly, following as we head toward the door.

When we reach it, I look down at Genevieve, fastening my peacoat and donning my gloves while Jeremiah holds open the front door. "Will you be present for the Holy Mass?"

I already know the answer.

She laughs, a light, tinkling sound. "Oh no, Father. I don't leave the monastery."

My eyes flick over the lines of her face. "Pity."

"You know how to reach me." She inclines her head and I smile, enjoying the subtle show of subservience, even when I know I shouldn't. "But just a gentle reminder, this place is a *private* sanctuary away from all the noise. We like to keep quiet about its whereabouts."

"I understand."

Once we're back in the car and I'm not hurling questions at Jeremiah, he's quiet, almost pensive, and I wonder if he's always this subdued or if it's because of me. I can't find the will to care either way, my mind already drifting off to places it shouldn't, wondering if I'll be able to slip away without anyone noticing who I am or that I've gone.

Even if they *did* notice, I hardly doubt it would stop me. And now that I've been to the Green Mountain Monastery, I have a place to hide away and heal if the whip cuts too deep.

Whether Sister Genevieve wants me there or not.

CHAPTER 8

Amaya

"DO YOU EVER MISS IT?" I ASK DALIA, PLOPPING down into the light wood chair of the dining table and wrapping my hands around the mug of hot tea.

We're having a drink before she makes dinner for Quinten and I leave to go to work, which is something we try to do every day. Just a chance to check in and have some private girl time.

Unfortunately, the apartment is small, so sitting at the table in the middle of the square kitchen, surrounded by chipping pale green cabinets and mismatched dish towels, is as private as we get.

It doesn't matter. I love these simple moments. I like to think of it as replacing the bitter memories my mom and Parker infused in this apartment with new ones. *Better* ones.

Dalia blinks at me with her doe-brown eyes from over the rim of her own cup. "Miss what?"

"Dancing."

She shrugs. "Nobody can dance forever, you know?"

I know she's right, even if I don't like to think about it. "Yeah."

Her answer is the same every time I bring it up, but for some reason, I keep asking, like if I push enough, she'll change what she says and admit the emptiness that flits through her gaze is from losing a piece of her when she lost the ability to dance.

Dalia and I met through our boss, Phillip. Well, I guess only my boss now. She was the best damn performer there, and when I first came in to be a cocktail waitress, barely knowing how to balance on bare feet let alone platform shoes, Phillip linked us up. We hit it off right away, and she's been the only person in my life I've truly been able to call a friend. She sparkled in the spotlight, and I admired her, envied her even, because she always seemed to know exactly who she was. Even more than that, she *loved* who she was. A long lean body, russet-brown skin, and a large chest, she was a favorite at the Chapel. And then, one night, a drunk driver sideswiped her while going eighty in a thirty-five, and they had to use the jaws of life to cut her out of the car. She hasn't been the same since, and neither has her right leg, which was shattered on impact.

With no job and no money, she was shit out of options. So I had her move in with Quinten and me. Free room and board if she'd watch him while I brought in the cash for us both. There's not much space, barely enough for Quinten and me, with a small living room and one hallway off the kitchen, but there are three bedrooms, and the one that was my mother's was just sitting unused. I couldn't really force myself to go in there, so having Dalia take it over was cathartic in more ways than one.

Dalia swears up and down that she's fine, that she's happy. But despite what she says, every time I leave to go dance, I have to swallow down the guilt.

"That's why it's good you work so much now," she continues.

"Save up everything you can, Amaya. Make that money and then put it away for when you need it."

Her words drop on my shoulders like slabs of concrete. God, I fucking *wish* I could put away enough money to have some savings, but that's just not my reality. I could have it rain down in the thousands, and Parker would still make sure I don't keep enough to stay afloat.

Not unless I agree to being his.

But I can't tell her that because nobody knows about my shady dealings with Parker. He's my dirty little secret, with grit that burrows into my pores and is impossible to wash clean.

Besides, knowing Dalia, she would never let sleeping dogs lie, and I don't need her trying to solve my problems like they're her own.

"It's annoying that you always ask me that, you know? About dancing, I mean," she snips.

I shake my head, taking a sip of tea. "I'm not trying to be annoying. I'm just…I love you and I want to make sure you're happy."

She scrunches up her face. "Please. We've got the perfect setup. Are you kidding? Quin's my dude."

"I know, but—"

"But nothing, girl. Things are good. *I'm* good, okay?"

"Okay." I nod but we both know I'll probably ask again. I can't help it. The last thing I'd want is for her to realize that what she's got going on here isn't enough and pack up to leave us and find a new purpose.

I shake the thought from my head.

"I have to tell you something," Dalia sighs, her mug clunking on the wood as she chews on her bottom lip. "It's about Candace."

"Oh god, what is it?" I groan.

Candace is Dalia's cousin, and even her name irritates the hell out of me. She's been around since the beginning of my and Dalia's friendship, especially considering she lives here in Festivalé and, until recently, Dalia lived in Coddington Heights. They've never been close, but every once in a while, they chill, and I don't like her around here. Candace is a raging addict, and I don't want to put myself or Quinten in her path any more than necessary. Plus, Candace is a nasty thing, taking every opportunity to dig her words into my sides, making sure they leave a scratch.

I know people aren't themselves while they're in the clutches of addiction, and hating her probably makes me a shitty person, but I can't help it.

I take another sip of tea.

"She's dead."

My chest burns, hot liquid spewing from my mouth as I spit my drink across the room. "*What?*"

Dalia's eyes are solemn, her lips pursing while she nods slowly, clearly trying to keep her emotions at bay, and empathy hits me square in the chest. Sure, I didn't like the woman, but death is so…final.

"Jesus, Dal."

She shrugs, but I see the way her jaw stiffens like the sharp edge of a knife. "We all knew it was coming eventually. I just always figured it would be the dope that took her, not a *person*."

My head tilts. "What do you mean, 'a person'?"

Dalia shakes her head, wiping the back of her hand over her mouth. "She was murdered. Strangled to death. Her slimeball landlord found her when he stopped by to demand her rent for the month."

My stomach twists. "Holy shit."

I've never been good when people show me emotion, and saying I'm sorry doesn't feel like it would be enough, but I'm not sure how to show support when I don't feel sad over the loss.

"Do they—do you know if there are any leads?"

Is that an appropriate thing to ask?

She scoffs. "Probably that old bastard landlord. Or maybe his wife. Everybody knows how Candace was paying rent when she had no money to give."

"Is there an investigation?" I ask.

"Maybe." She shrugs again. "Even if there is, how much effort do you think they'll put into a dead sex worker with a drug problem who was constantly asking the worst of the worst to come into her home? They're probably happy she's gone."

I nod slowly, but my body is coiling tight. Candace's apartment is only a few blocks away from ours.

"So it could have been anyone," I say, glancing down the hall to where Quinten's playing in his room.

My eyes meet Dalia's, my earlier calm ebbing away like the moon when it drags out the tide.

She winces when our gazes clash, her tongue swiping out across her lip. "Candace was into a lot of bad shit with a lot of terrible people, Amaya. I doubt it was random."

"You're probably right," I reply, standing up and moving across the table to her. I lean down and wrap her into a hug. "I'm really sorry about your cousin, Dal."

I feel her head move against my shoulder, the sound of her shaky breaths in my ear. "Yeah…me too."

Releasing her, I walk down the hall until I'm peeking into

Quinten's open door, watching as he kneels at the foot of his bed, inspecting his figurines before placing them in perfect rows.

"Quin?" I call out. "I'll be back later, okay? Be good for Dalia."

He doesn't acknowledge me, but I know he heard.

"Can I have a hug?" I try again.

This gets his attention, and he drops the toys he's lining up and rushes over, leaning his body into me with his hands by his sides. He doesn't lift his arms, and he doesn't wrap them around me, but I don't care. This is more than enough.

I breathe in his scent, my heart feeling heavy. "Love you, kid."

"Love you back," he murmurs.

I make it to the front door, twisting the knob and stepping outside with one foot before I hesitate, Candace's death fresh on my mind. I twist to look at Dalia, who's at the sink rinsing out our cups, her back to me.

"Dalia," I say.

She pauses but doesn't turn around.

"Lock up behind me, yeah?"

And then I'm gone to the Chapel, where I can leave Amaya's problems at the door.

CHAPTER 9

Cade

I'M TAKING CONFESSION TODAY.

I'll admit I wasn't sure what to expect. With the way Bishop Lamont and Parker both talk about Festivalé, I wondered if anyone would come at all, but there has been a steady stream of people here to cleanse their souls before they take Communion tomorrow. I've listened to everything from a housewife crying over sleeping with her stepson to a young teen who steals spare change from the register where she works so she can feed her family. Compassion lights up my heart for the latter, and my monster surges forward wanting to rid the demon from the former. As the morning bleeds into the late afternoon, the people dwindle down until there are long lags in between. I'm about to head back to the rectory when a shuffling noise hits my ears, followed by the light, airy breaths of someone new entering the other side of the confessional booth.

A pleasant smell wafts through the partition, like campfire and vanilla, a heady mix that I've already committed to memory. One I inhaled when *she* was close enough to touch. Every muscle in my body freezes, nerves zapping along my skin like an electrical shock.

Petite pécheresse.

I watched her dance again last night at the Chapel, keeping myself hidden in the shadows and then following her home. I had planned to kill her then, to rid myself of her, but I couldn't, although I'm not sure why.

"I don't…I don't know what I'm doing here," she whispers softly.

Blood floods my groin at the sound of her meek voice, and my hands curl into fists to keep myself in check. I'm unprepared for her to be here, and it makes me feel incredibly vulnerable.

"How long has it been since your last confession?" I rasp, licking my lips as though I'll be able to taste her in the air.

"Years," she murmurs, even softer than before. "I didn't plan to come here. I just…I was walking by, and for some reason…"

My eyes flutter closed, and I count to three, desperation latching on to my bones, *needing* to hear her sins. "What is your name, child?"

I'm not foolish enough to believe it's Esmeralda.

"Amaya."

My heart stutters, and it makes me angry that once again, my body is not under my control when she's here.

"Amaya," I repeat. The syllables form on my tongue and settle in like a permanent aftertaste.

I wonder if she recognizes my voice. We only had a brief interaction at the Chapel, but selfishly, although I know it's not probable, I hope she's here to seek me out, that she's spiraling in the depths of obsession just as surely as I am and somehow tracked me down and found out who I was.

"Am I… Should I say a certain thi—"

"Tell me why you've come," I say, cutting her off. It's not the appropriate way to lead a confession, but I don't care.

Now that she's here, my mind is muddled to everything except for her. *Again.* I'm feral to hear her transgressions pass her lips.

"Oh, I…" She pauses again, and I dig my nails into my palms so I don't leap from my side of the booth and pry the words from her throat myself. "I don't know. I worked late last night and then couldn't sleep so I took a walk today, and I kind of…"

"There's no judgment here," I soothe. "Only forgiveness."

"It's not that," she snaps. "I just…I don't know what to say. Sinning is subjective."

Her naivete makes my cock thicken. Shamefully, I reach down and press my palm against it, willing it back down. It only makes it stiffer.

"Then tell me about you," I force out. "What do you do for a living, Amaya?"

I like the way her name feels rolling off my tongue, like a ripe berry that bursts on my taste buds, the perfect mixture of sugar and bite.

"I dance," she replies, and I can hear the smile in her voice.

"How do you dance?" I press, wanting her to say it plainly.

"Pole. And I strip," she rushes out. "But I don't think that's a sin."

She's wrong. Her dancing will create enough sin to overflow the city streets. I want to lash out, to say that *anyone* seeing her body other than me will only ensure their death. But that would be ridiculous, because the thought itself is ridiculous, so I push back the words.

"So do you believe your sexual immorality will inherit the kingdom of God?"

"I don't know that I *want* his kingdom," she says. "Besides, I enjoy what I do."

"Sin is often steeped in pleasure," I note, the open wounds on my back stinging with the reminder of how true my words are.

"I pay off my mother's debts. And *that* makes me feel dirtier than any type of sex work ever could."

My spine stiffens, my gaze snapping toward her, so laser focused I'm surprised it doesn't singe through the barrier between us. "Pay off debts *how*?"

"Are all priests so pushy?" she questions.

I chuckle, lifting slightly as I adjust my pant legs, trying to give my cock breathing room from where it's being suffocated by the fabric.

There's a rustling noise and then a faint, "I shouldn't have come," before she's out of the confessional, her footsteps echoing through the dome ceiling and stone walls.

Everything inside me wants to chase after her, spin her around and force her to her knees as I drag her secrets from her lips, then taste her death as I steal her last breath, but I don't. Instead, I grip the bench beneath me so tightly my fingernails feel like they might split.

Finally, I leave the booth, staring at the empty space where I foolishly hoped she'd still exist.

"What was *she* doing in here?"

I glance behind me, my mind trying to catch up to the present. Jeremiah's holding an unlit white candle and glaring at the sanctuary's entrance.

"You know her?" My stomach tightens.

His lips twist. "Everyone knows Amaya Paquette."

"How so?" I press.

"Her mother used to date Mr. Errien."

My brows shoot to my hairline.

"I was gone to seminary when she lived here, but apparently they all used to come with him to Mass. One day, there was a fight out front in the main square."

My brows rise. "A fight?"

He nods. "With her and her mother."

"Where's her mother now?"

"Gone." He shakes his head, staring after where Amaya just was. "Her mom called her a witch. Said she *hexed* the town."

"Ridicule."

He nods. "You'd think but…after they moved here, things started to fall apart in Festivalé. Poverty started hitting the streets. People strayed from the path of God."

My stomach sours. "People blame Amaya's mother for the downturn of this town?"

Jeremiah shakes his head. "People blame *Amaya*."

"Non, la sorcière?"

Is it possible she's truly using witchcraft? She ensnares me so easily.

He nods. "Cursed, at the very least. Ever since she's come to town, it's been nothing but trouble. The only reason she hasn't been run out is because Mr. Errien won't allow it. He has a soft spot for her, I think."

I stare at the empty space where she was moments ago. I wonder if I breathe deeply enough whether I'd be able to inhale her scent or if it's faded away as fast as her physical form. "She's all alone then?"

He frowns. "She shouldn't be here."

"All God's children are welcome," I reprimand.

"She's beyond saving, Father."

I clench my jaw, half of me wanting to reprimand him for not accepting my word as law and the other half reveling in the thought of being the one to rid her from the earth. If what he says is true, then she has a demon inside her that needs to be eradicated.

And it's up to me to free her soul.

"No one is beyond saving. That's why I'm here."

CHAPTER 10

Cade

I THROW THE PEN DOWN AND RUN MY HAND through my hair, tugging on the roots. I've been trying to write Sunday's homily for the past two hours, but my mind keeps wandering back to Amaya like a nightmare that lingers in the daytime.

I'm not somebody who believes in love at first sight, and I'm under no illusion that what I feel for her is anything close to the emotion, but clearly lust has dug its talons deep. Just a moment in her presence and she's become the biggest temptation of my life.

Glancing down at my words on the paper, I curl my lip, hating the red lines marked through the passages.

It needs to be perfect, but I can tell with every swipe of my pen that my personal demons are slipping into the teachings.

For the first time, I wonder if *I* need the reminder as much as everyone else. I shake my head to dispel the ridiculous notion. I just need to kill Amaya, that's all. As long as she's around, she'll be a distraction, and I've never needed focus and clarity more than I do right now. Maybe she's a test sent from God.

Clicking my tongue against the back of my teeth, I flick my gaze between the clock on the wall and the papers on my desk, debating what I should do. It's already the evening, and it's painfully obvious that I'm unprepared for the morning's Holy Mass, but the need for preparation dulls like sunshine on an overcast day when my mind clouds with thoughts of Amaya. Where she is. What she's doing.

Before I can stop myself, I'm leaving the church entirely, and when I end up nearing the bus stop at the end of the block—having memorized the schedule that runs to Coddington Heights, the town where Amaya works—I slip off the collar from around my neck, shoving it deep in my jacket's pocket.

Because I've memorized the schedule, I know there's twenty minutes before the next bus, and in that time, I've halfway convinced myself to turn around, but my feet are rooted to the ground like they're covered in cement.

I'm going to kill her tonight.

The thought is quite erotic, actually. There's something so deeply satisfying about hunting my prey. A heady rush of capturing them and holding their life in my hands.

Large round headlights cut through the crisp December evening, blinding me to reason as the bus rolls down the street, brakes whirring and screeching as it pulls to a stop, the accordion door opening, a large plume of smoke emitting from the back. I move onto the steps, glancing over the empty seats before tucking my chin into my neck and sitting at the very front so I can get off quickly if I need.

It's mostly empty.

There's an older man with a pot belly in the middle row, his eyes closed and arms crossed as he leans against the window, and a young woman in the very back, her eyes glued to the screen of her phone. Giant headphones cover the sides of her face like earmuffs. I don't pay any more attention to them, and they completely ignore me, which is just as well. So far at least, anonymity still has its grip on me. But I know that after Holy Mass tomorrow, that won't be the case.

The bus lurches forward, and then we're on our way out of Festivalé. Just like that, there's no turning back, not that I would even if there was. Adrenaline percolates through my veins in a steady drip, nerves dancing beneath my skin like sparks of fire, that dark feeling I keep locked up in the daytime eager to come out and play.

It takes over an hour to get to Coddington Heights, and before I can blink, I'm at the Chapel, paying the twenty-dollar entry fee and hiding in the shadows, the same way I did last time.

It's busy tonight, but it's no matter. I find her almost immediately, her aura like a lighthouse, blinding me with its dangerous glow.

She's chatting with a man at the end of the bar, her head flying back with her tinkling laughter while she weaves her magic like a spiderweb, luring another poor sap into her clutches. He leans in and whispers something in her ear, and she grins before nodding, the fake red hair whispering against the small of her back, making me jealous of synthetic strands.

And then they're off, maneuvering between tables and the plush sofas along the walls before they disappear into a hallway, where I assume the private rooms are.

A wave of possessiveness pours down my spine, thick and hot.

There's a split second where I consider my choices. Where I *try* to be a decent man. But that's all it is: a second.

I stride across the floor with purpose, retracing their steps until I'm hovering in front of a closed-off room, separated by a heavy purple curtain instead of a wooden door. I glance around, looking for staff, for a bouncer or somebody who will see what I'm doing and rip me away, but there's just an empty chair in the far corner of the hall and the thump of the bass that's so loud it rattles my insides. My fingers glide along the velvety material of the curtain, and I slide it open just enough to peer inside, my heart pounding so fast it makes my chest cramp.

My throat dries, a violent current of...*something* rushing through me at the sight that greets me. It's different from what I'm used to, but it rains down on me like a monsoon, the sickness inside me making me ache and throb for pleasure instead of pain.

The two of them are near the far wall of the small room, catty-corner to where I am, just her side profile visible. Amaya's on the man's lap, her heavy breasts kissing the open air, and it's enough to drive me mad, quick flashes of her pebbled nipples torturing me like a storm cloud that never rains as she twists and grinds on someone who isn't me.

He's completely consumed by her.

I can relate.

For the first time since I was a child, I grow angry with God.

How *easy* this would all be if I didn't have morals separating what I crave from what I know is right. *Why would you put her in my path?*

The gold of the man's wedding band shimmers as his hands rise from his sides and he digs meaty fingers into the flesh of her gyrating ass, a deep groan rumbling from him as he thrusts his hips up, simulating sinking himself inside her.

I grit my teeth, my cock aching and hard and my chest burning with envy.

"No touching," Amaya snaps, reaching back and removing his touch. "You know the rules, Andrew."

"Esmeralda," he rumbles, his hands dropping back down onto the couch. "Such a fucking tease."

There's a stack of bills lying next to them on the couch, and he moves to grab a bill from the pile, slipping it into the band of her G-string. I imagine breaking off his fingers one by one, reveling in the screams that would accompany the *snap*.

He smirks and she giggles, light and airy and fake as hell.

My monster rears its head like it smells fresh meat.

I soak in every detail of Amaya's bare back, the indent in her waist that flares out to perfect wide hips, the small glimpses of pebbled dark areolas silhouetted by the curve of her breast.

My cock leaks as arousal makes my balls heavy with want.

"Hey, what the fuck are you doing?" A deep voice cuts through the moment, and I straighten, irritated that I got so lost in the moment that I stopped paying attention to my surroundings.

I don't reply, stepping away from the curtain and letting it drop back in place before twisting to face whoever's caught me red-handed.

"Hey," the bulky man repeats, walking closer. "I asked you a question."

I smile when he gets close, dwarfing the man in the shadow of my height.

His brows furrow, nostrils flaring. "You can't be back here."

"I was just leaving," I reply, walking backward slowly with my hands held up high.

He doesn't do anything, although I'm not sure why. He just

crosses his arms and nods toward the exit, and I take the opportunity, slipping out the door into the alley behind the club.

But I don't leave.

The hours pass and my fingers grow numb and stiff, even while wearing my gloves, and my legs scream in exhaustion as I perch near the employee parking lot, watching and waiting.

I tell myself that it's just to follow her home, to finish what I came here to do in the first place.

Kill her and be done with this sorcery.

But when she makes it back to her apartment, I don't leave then either.

Instead, I stand by the side window off the alley, the poor excuse for shrubbery digging into my side as I stare through the smudged glass, watching her sway her hips as she undresses in what she believes is the privacy of her bedroom.

I should go in and murder her. My body is *humming* at the chance to take her life in my hands, to see the spark dim from her eyes and feel my obsession drain away with it.

But I don't. I leave her in her bed, safe and alone, while I go back to the rectory and whip myself for my weakness.

"Give, Lord, strength to my hands to wipe out all stain so that, without pollution of mind or body, I may dare to serve You."

The water is cool as it runs over my fingers, and I continue with my prayers as I grab my amice, a white cloth that I wrap around my shoulder and neck.

Today, the fabric feels like it's choking me.

After that comes the alb, and I slip it on, the robe dusting the floor. "Wash me clean, Lord, and cleanse me from my sin that I may rejoice and be glad unendingly with them that have washed their robes in the blood of the Lamb."

My back is raw and tender, making me hiss as the vestments scratch against my skin, the guilt and self-loathing running through me like rotting trash, rancid and strong.

Then comes the cincture. The ropelike texture rubs against my palms as I tie it around my waist, and I'm reminded of how I atoned with similar material last night. Every move I make is painful from the lashes.

"Gird me, Lord, with the belt of faith, my loins with the virtue of chastity, and extinguish in them the humor of lust that the strength of all chastity may ever abide in me."

My chest tightens in regret as I speak the words, hating myself for the way Amaya makes me feel, the things she makes me do.

Next, I grip the purple silk of the stole tightly, lying it over my shoulders, letting the material drape down the front of my body. "Restore to me, Lord, I beseech Thee, the stole of immortality, which I lost in the transgression of the first father, and though unworthy I presume to approach Thy sacred mystery with this garment, grant that I may merit to rejoice in it forever."

Breathing in deeply, I exhale my mortality, allowing His word to flow through my veins and into my heart, because it is He who celebrates the Mass. And even while I'm in turmoil, today isn't about *me*.

Then, finally, I reach for the chasuble. The sleeveless, ornate outer vestment slips over my head with ease, dropping over the length of me like a waterfall that pools on the floor.

A bead of sweat trickles down the back of my neck, sneaking its way beneath the layers of clothes and stinging the whippings on my back. I use the pain as fuel, a sense of rightness clicking into place as I prepare to face the people of Festivalé for the first time as Father Cade Frédéric.

But during the homily, my gaze scans the pews, and then I'm spiraling, wondering where *she* is and how *she's* doing. If she would scream louder when she comes or when she dies. How once I do the latter, I'll never get the chance to hear the former.

My chest tightens at the thought.

My mind is still in a fog as I give Communion, and I glance down at the woman kneeling before me and murmur softly, "Corpus Domini nostri Iesu Christi custodiat animam tuam in vitam aeternam, amen." I place the body of Christ on her tongue, the motions monotonous in a way they've never been, because I'm mentally so far away from where I'm meant to be.

The line for Communion continues, one by one, bits of bread and sips from the chalice until everyone is in silent prayer back in their pews.

It's a heavy atmosphere, and my voice booms, echoing off the arches and stained glass. "Go in peace to love and serve the Lord."

I say the words, and I *mean* what I say, but at night, as I make my way back to a run-down apartment, staring in that same bedroom window as before, unable to rid myself of this sick obsession, it's not the Lord I'm serving.

And I feel nothing close to peace.

CHAPTER 11

Amaya

QUINTEN SKIPS DOWN THE AISLE, DRAGGING HIS toes on the ground while I push the grocery cart behind him. It's Monday afternoon, and just like every other week, right after I pick him up from school, we head to the store so we can stock up.

Today, I'd rather be anywhere else. The overhead lights feel like they're hammering behind my eyes, and my attention is torn, making sure Quinten doesn't trip while he hops around on his tiptoes while also trying to grab our groceries.

The credit card burns in my wallet, practically screeching at me to keep it locked away and start actually paying *off* the debt, not adding more. But I don't have a choice. Every transaction is another pile of dirt on my unmarked grave, burying me alive. And the only person who can dig me out is the same man who's got the shovel.

I could scream, but there's no one around who would care.

Reaching out, I grab three giant boxes of the off-brand shells and cheese, tossing them into the cart. It's been what Quinten has requested for dinner without fail every single night for the past three months, and while I know it's coating his insides with synthetic cheese, at least I know he's eating.

"Watch where you're going," a sharp voice hisses.

My head snaps up just as Quinten cowers back, running toward me and gripping onto my pant leg, his lips sucking in to keep from showing emotion.

I narrow my eyes as I zone in on Florence Gammond.

She sneers as she looks me up and down, her pinched face souring like she's sucked on a warhead. Her auburn hair is exquisitely curled and her pantsuit is perfectly pressed, and I lift my chin to keep from feeling two inches tall in her presence.

"Amaya," she says, her muddy brown eyes cutting.

"Florence."

"Keep that kid in line," she snips.

My fingers grip the handle of the grocery cart so tightly my knuckles blanch.

"You can't just let him run off and into people," she keeps going. "If he doesn't have the capacity to pay attention or to apologize like a normal person, then maybe he shouldn't be in public places like this."

Anger floods through me so quickly my body shakes. I glance down at Quinten, but he's already on to the next thing, tracing the faded letters of the store name on the side of the cart. Still, I know he's paying attention, so I try to contain my anger.

"You're the adult, Florence. Maybe *you* should be the one paying attention." My voice comes out surprisingly steady.

It's in moments like this that I thank God for my poker face.

Florence loves to sniff out even the slightest weakness. With me especially, she'll find one and use it to cut me down until I'm nothing but loose thread that's frayed on the floor. She hated my mother for having Parker, and she hates me because I'm all he wants. But I wish she'd get it through her thick head that I don't want *him*.

She scoffs, and I lightly touch Quinten's back to get his

attention before moving to walk past her. In this town, avoidance is *key*. We veer almost all the way to the right-hand side, which is plenty of room to steer clear of the hag, but she moves into *my* path, her shoulder ramming into mine until my feet stumble.

I pause, gritting my teeth to keep from throat punching her.

"You know," she whisper hisses. "You should be more careful, Amaya."

Anger weaves its way through my body, knocking on my calm like a hammer on a nail.

"I'd hate for Quinten to keep having run-ins at school," she continues, glancing down at her nails. "You know I had the superintendent over for brunch just last week. I hear he's on his last strike as it is."

Deep, steady breaths. In and out. Don't show the emotion on your face.

It's difficult because the *emotion* is rolling through me like a banging drum, growing louder with each violent beat of my heart. She knows damn well it's not Quinten causing the issues.

"I don't think we're the ones who need to be careful, Florence."

Her eyes flash with alarm, but she covers it quickly. "Are you threatening me? Is that some sort of spell?"

I smirk. The ridiculous people in this town still think I'm a witch, as if anyone here is important enough for me to expel *any* energy toward. All because my mother called me one when she lost her mind in the middle of the square after finding out I knew Parker was fucking Florence and hadn't thought to tell her.

My mother's mad at me today.

What else is new.

"Sit up straight, Amaya. Your slouching is ugly," she hisses at me.

We're at Mass again, and like usual, I'm bored out of my fucking mind. The only thing that holds me together is paying attention to Quinten, who's just turned one and is currently fussing in Mom's arms. Parker looks down at him and glares.

Mom immediately stiffens before nudging me with her elbow hard in the ribs and then passing Quinten over. "Take him somewhere else. He's causing a scene."

Indignation burns through my chest, but I take him from her and stand up from the pew, eyes falling on me as I interrupt the service to leave.

Quinten cries, his little chubby fingers gripping the front of my dress, and I smooth my hand over the back of his head as I carry him out and into the lobby.

We must be out here for twenty minutes, and I've plied him with those nasty raspberry tarts that are always next to the coffee. Now he's passed out, sleeping peacefully on the cushioned bench in the hallway that leads to the offices.

"You're good with him."

I suck in a breath and spin around, coming face-to-face with Parker.

"You scared me." I press a hand to my chest, looking behind him. "Is it over? Where's Mom?"

He steps in closer, until I'm back against the wall. "No, I just wanted to give you your birthday gift."

My stomach tenses. "Oh."

"Nineteen's a big number, huh?" His eyes strip me raw as they graze down my body, and my arms move in front of me like I can shield myself from his gaze.

Another step closer. I look over to Quinten, then back. "I—"

"What the hell is this?" My mom's voice pierces through the air, and I close my eyes, my heart dropping to my feet.

Parker backs up and smiles over at her. "Calm down, Chantelle. I'm just wishing your daughter a happy birthday."

Her lips pinch as she glares between the two of us. "Service is over."

Parker nods, stepping to her and gripping her by the back of the neck. It's a power move, and I would swear a flash of panic flits through her gaze.

"Get yourself together, and then meet me out front. I don't like to be kept waiting."

The second he's gone, her eyes are on me, sharp as a blade.

"Mom, it wasn't—"

"Quiet. Grab your brother, and let's go."

Swallowing back the words I want to say, even though I know they'll be pointless, I move to where Quinten is and pick him up gingerly, letting his head rest on my shoulder while he continues to sleep.

We walk outside, through the people lingering in the narthex and into the main square. It's a sunny day, and I soak in the rays as we walk down the front and past the gargoyles.

Mom stops short once we hit the bottom steps, and I run into her back. Quinten jolts awake and squirms until I let him down. "It's okay, buddy," I whisper.

He wobbles on his little legs, having just learned to walk a month ago. I keep his hand in mine.

My stomach drops when I follow my mother's gaze and see her zoned in on Florence and Parker, smiling wide at each other in front of the world.

She storms over.

"Get away from him, you fucking slut!" she screeches so loud that I swear every single head turns our way, silence blanketing the square like it's empty.

Florence looks over, her eyes widening. But she listens, and she takes a step away. And then she turns her gaze to me, and her features twist into a scowl. "You told her?"

I suck in a breath, shaking my head. What is she doing saying it out loud? Doesn't she care that anyone can hear?

Mom whips her head toward me, her eyes blazing with betrayal.

"Mom, it isn't—"

"I want you gone," she snaps.

My breathing stutters, because I must have heard her wrong. "I... what?"

"You heard me, you little witch. I won't let you ruin what I have with Parker."

My jaw drops, disbelief washing over me. "I want nothing to do with Parker."

Florence huffs out a laugh. "Please."

"I don't," I snap, not taking my eyes off my mom. "I'm not going anywhere. If I leave, who's gonna take care of Quin, huh?"

Mom scoffs. "He's my son."

"About time you remembered," I hiss back.

She moves forward and smacks me, my face flinging to the side, forcing Quinten's hand to drop from mine.

Audible gasps ring out around us, but no one steps in. No one intervenes.

Mom blows out a breath and straightens, flexing her fingers as she stares at me with nothing but ice in her gaze. "Watch your mouth."

I shake off the pain, holding back the tears that are threatening to spill.

"Chantelle." Parker's voice is stern.

She whips toward him. "You're taking her side? After all I've done for you? All I constantly do?"

His features harden, and he moves away from Florence and closer to her, dropping his voice until it's nothing more than a whisper. "Think carefully before you speak again."

She swallows and shakes her head but looks around. She must realize then what a scene she's made. But it doesn't stop her from turning back on me. "It's you."

My jaw drops, chest cracking open at how she's turning against me so quickly, so publicly.

"You are a disease on everything you touch," she spits, reaching down to pick up Quinten like it's me he needs protection from. "A little witch, seducing men right out from under me."

My eyes widen because I'm seriously becoming concerned about her state of mind. "Mom, be serious. Please."

Voices murmur in the distance, but I don't listen to what they say.

Parker steps in between us then, almost like he's shielding me from her.

"You'll see. You'll all see." She raises her arms like she's talking to everyone in town. "She'll curse this town just like she's been a curse on my life!"

"Chantelle," he says again. "You're embarrassing yourself."

My mother stiffens her spine, nostrils flaring as she looks from him to me.

And from the corner of my eye, I see Florence doing the same. Glaring at me, like somehow Parker's weird fixation is my fault.

That night, my mom disappeared.

And Florence made it her personal mission to make my life a living hell.

I'm not one. A witch, I mean. Although, I *do* believe in a lot of their practices. Nature is all about balance, and I believe energy can absolutely be wielded and manipulated. Maybe if any of these people took time to actually learn about what they're afraid of, what they're *biased* against, they'd realize there's nothing to fear at all.

Still, I lean in to their terror, because if nothing else, they're so afraid of me cursing them or bringing the town to ruin that they take to avoidance rather than full-on hate. Well, most of them. Florence is a rare breed.

I shrug, reaching beside her and grabbing a can of tomato sauce, plopping it into my cart. "I hear karma's a vengeful bitch."

This time when I walk past her, she doesn't move an inch, and I quicken my footsteps, dragging Quinten along as we round the corner, my heart racing so quickly I can feel it thrumming in my neck.

It isn't until we're three aisles over that I let out the breath I was holding.

"You handled that well."

The accented voice floats over me like a warm blanket, and the familiarity makes me pause. I've felt this before. The other night at the Chapel. And then again when I made the last-minute decision to waltz into the church like I belonged and confess my sins because it's cheaper than therapy.

It hits me, so suddenly that I feel like a fool for not noticing it before. Maybe it's because French accents aren't entirely uncommon in Festivalé, or maybe it's because the idea itself of a priest being in a strip club is ludicrous.

But I can't deny it when it's staring me in the face.

My mystery man and the new priest of Notre-Dame are one and the same.

Holy shit.

Slowly, I twist around.

His face is stern, all sharp angles and haunted shadows, and his hands rest in his pockets like he can't be bothered. He's dressed in a simple black button-down, the color matching his hair perfectly, and a long peacoat over the top. I can see the smallest hint of his clerical collar peeking at his neckline.

What the hell was he doing in a strip club?

I lift a brow. "You're a priest?"

It's only after the words slip from my mouth that I realize they may have been a mistake, because why would I be surprised by that unless I had another idea of him in my head? I don't think he recognizes me from the club, but there's a chance he does and that's why he approached me.

I shake off the panic that's mounting in my gut, reminding myself that even if he does, I doubt he'd acknowledge that he was there.

My anxiety eases when recognition doesn't even flicker in his gaze.

"Is it that obvious?" His mouth tilts up as he stares down at himself, like he's surprised with what he's wearing.

He's joking, but all I can do is nod, my throat suddenly too thick to even swallow. My tongue swipes out across my bottom lip, and his grin drops as he tracks the movement.

Clearing my throat, I look down at Quinten as he hovers near the cereal shelf a few steps away, reading the words aloud on the front of every box.

"Cade Frédéric." He reaches out a hand, drawing my attention back like a homing beacon.

I slip my palm into his, but I don't offer my name in return. I expect a handshake, but he brings it up to his mouth, skimming his lips over the back.

My stomach jumps. This hardly seems appropriate.

"Nice to meet you, Father."

Something flashes in his dark brown eyes when I speak, and he drops my hand like it's coated in acid.

"That woman was very rude to you, no?" He jerks his head toward the other aisle.

"You know how it goes," I say, brushing it off. "Maybe she needs Jesus. I bet you could convince her to come and confess her sins."

He chuckles, stepping forward until the tips of his shoes press against mine and leaning in like he's about to tell me a secret. "Ah yes, but there's one problem. I'm not sure I'd want to offer her forgiveness."

My stomach clenches, and I suck in a small, surprised breath that I hope he didn't notice.

God, how embarrassing to react this way to a freaking priest.

He glances down to Quinten, who's crouched on the floor with three giant family-size boxes of cereal laid out in a row. "And who's this?"

"That's Quin, my little brother."

He squats down to be on Quinten's level and smiles wide, dimples creasing the sharp hollows of his cheeks. "Hey, Quin, I'm Cade."

Quinten stares at him before grabbing the Flintstones Fruity Pebbles and shoving it in his face. "Hi. Look, a dinosaur!"

Cade's eyes flick to the box. "You like dinosaurs?"

Quinten starts rocking in place, and my lips break into a wide smile. I've always loved how Quinten shows his happiness, and right now, his excitement is a tangible thing. It vibrates through his body and lights up the space like a thousand rainbow prisms reflecting the sun off a diamond.

"You like dinosaurs? *I* like dinosaurs," Quinten says.

"Me too," Father Cade replies, turning to me and winking. "Don't tell anybody."

Quinten shoots upright, jumping wildly on his toes. "Me too!"

I swear to God my chest feels like it might explode, he's so happy and free.

A lump forms in my throat, and I will back the burn behind my eyes as I watch them together. I'm so fucking angry that this is even a thing I *have* to feel, that someone treating Quinten like a human being is a gift and not the bare minimum.

But the truth is the truth, no matter how ugly it feels. And the *truth* is that I'm not used to someone interacting with Quinten and being so...normal. Not in this town anyway. People do one of two things. They either overcompensate, trying to accommodate Quinten so much that they end up alienating him from everyone else, creating resentment with the other kids, or they avoid him all together, giving quick wide stares and ushering their own children away because he doesn't act like them.

Guilt hits my chest that I can't take those experiences from Quinten and lay them on my shoulders instead.

I'm not sure if Cade realizes what he's doing, but he's done it all the same, and gratitude fills me up so intensely I can hardly breathe.

Cade stands back up, and as he does, I take him in again, that small interaction having shifted my view of him into something else. Something softer.

He's tall, like, *really* tall. And even with mirth dancing in his eyes, he's an imposing figure, his tousled black hair matching the darkness in his eyes and the clerical collar around his neck doing nothing but making him seem even *more* intense. Power bleeds from his pores. He's not even *moving*, and I feel like he's taking up more space with every second.

My hand drops from the grocery cart's handle as I step closer.

"You know, you're kind of intimidating for a priest," I blurt.

"Oh? Have you met a lot of us?"

"I've met enough," I say, lifting my shoulders and walking back to my cart.

"I didn't see you yesterday at Mass, did I?"

Laughing, I grab the Fruity Pebbles from Quinten's hand, toss it in the basket, and then move down the aisle. "Nope."

Father Cade follows. "Why not?"

"Because I didn't go."

He reaches out and touches my forearm lightly, his palm so hot it sears through my long sleeve, up my arm, and burns through my chest. I jerk to a stop, rooting my feet to the ground despite every single nerve in my body blaring like a foghorn to run the other way.

"I'll see you next week then?"

His eyes meet mine, a challenge sparking in his gaze as his demand falls like a lyric from his lips.

I scoff. "Doubtful."

He blinks at me, and his hand, which is *still* on my arm, squeezes the smallest amount. "You'll come."

Then he turns around and disappears, leaving me with irritation simmering like fire beneath a boiling pot.

I let out a huff, going over that bizarre interaction in my head. Does he think I'll do whatever he says just because he was nice to Quinten? Fuck him. I won't let him make demands of me like I'm a child. I'm half tempted to march after him and tell him where he can shove his Holy Mass, but instead, I stuff it down and smile at Quinten. "You ready to roll, dude?"

"Ready to roll?" he parrots. "Let's go home."

Suddenly, I can't wait to leave. We make our way down the aisle and to the front of the store quickly, my insides vibrating with impatience as Betty, the checkout lady, takes her sweet-ass time ringing up every item.

My eyes scan the area for Father Cade while I wait and then again as we walk through the parking lot, bags weighing down my arms as we start our half a block trek to the bus stop.

But he isn't there. And I'm not sure why I feel a twinge of disappointment when he's not.

CHAPTER 12

Cade

ANOTHER WEEK, ANOTHER HOLY MASS IN THE books.

And I still haven't done anything other than the bare minimum for the parish. I've barely met the people.

I've been too distracted by Amaya. Stalking in the shadows and waiting for my moment to pounce. Or maybe waiting for a reason not to. The indecision is tearing me in two, the man warring with the monster. Only this time, it's the *man* who wants to rid her from the earth.

All things come with time, I remind myself.

After this week's Mass, I'm annoyed that once again, she didn't show up. Even though I specifically told her to be here. I want to see how the townspeople interact with her in this setting. When the *witch of Festivalé* comes to pray.

I use the term witch loosely; they treat her as more of a bad omen than anything else, but I'm not convinced. She's able to put *me* under her spell with ease, and I'm a believer in dark magic.

"The Festival of Fools is coming up."

I glance over at Parker as he sits in an ostentatious black chair behind his giant desk, watching me from over the rim of his reading glasses.

"And?"

I had no idea the Festival of Fools was even celebrated here. It's not widespread or well known outside history books, and the church banned the festival in the 1400s. I'm not sure how to feel about it being resurrected, although the few that I *have* seen are nothing more than a common carnival. Street performers doing cartwheels for little kids with cotton-candy fingers and powdered-sugar mouths.

"It'd be good to put a stop to it." Parker says this like a command, and it makes my jaw lock.

Here it is. The first of his "suggestions." I've known since arriving that I wasn't truly called here for what Bishop Lamont said. While the people *do* live in sin and there is poverty and strife in the streets, it isn't to the level I was led to believe.

Parker Errien wants me to be his puppet in a way Father Clark was not. But I take orders from no one but God.

"Surely it's little more than a street festival," I reply. "It can't be like it was in the Middle Ages."

"It's *blasphemous*."

My brows rise and I bite back the retort that wants to escape. Rich of Parker to remember his religion when it suits him.

"Blasphemous is a powerful word." I lean forward in my chair, resting my elbows on my knees and cutting him with a knowing look. "Are you sure this is about disrespect to the church and not about the personal slight?"

Traditionally, the Festival of Fools was a celebration on January 1, where the peasants would be the power for a day, appointing a king of the fools to sit on the bishop's throne and lord over his people. But as with all things, the devil infects where there's a weakness, and the church banned the celebration when the townspeople became belligerent, drunk, and unholy.

Normally, I'd agree with Parker that this must be eradicated. But he doesn't need to know that I'm on his side. Showing people your cards means they can plan a next move without you, and that's the last thing I want Parker to do.

Besides, I've found that I quite like making him squirm.

"It's all in good fun, Parker. Let the people have their joy." I wave him off. "It's all pretend. Take it as a compliment. They want to *be* you."

"It's not a laughing matter, Father." Parker's voice is low and dangerous.

The smile drops from my face, and I lean in, that familiar burning starting to take root in the deepest parts of my body. "And tell me, *Parker*, what is it you expect me to be able to do?"

"You're the *church*." He waves his hand aggressively. "Aren't you supposed to be all-powerful?"

I am.

It seems like our initial chat didn't sink into his pigheaded brain, which isn't surprising. Words won't hit their mark when you're saying them to someone who thinks they know the world and all its secrets.

But my ire grows with every breath he takes. I stand up, taking the time to grab my peacoat and slip my arms slowly into the warmth before grasping my leather gloves and putting them on. I take three large steps then to his desk, pressing my knuckles against the edge and leaning in until he jerks back in a gorgeous show of submission.

"And what makes you think that you command the *church*?"

"I command *everything*," he replies. "You should learn that quickly."

"The festival will go on as planned." I straighten before he can continue and button the front of my coat. I'm done with this conversation. "In fact, I think it may do the church some good to get involved. A show of good faith to the community."

A smile breaks across my face when I see the anger growing on Parker's already ruddy cheeks.

He opens his mouth to respond, but a knock sounds at his door, the handle turning before he can tell them to come back later.

I twist toward the noise, using my opportunity to slip away, and when I've made it to the door, it flies open, leaving me chest to face with the little sinner of my nightmares.

My stomach tightens, blood pounding in my ears, remembering how she stuttered on stage when she saw Parker in the crowd. How he was a man on a mission, like a hunter trying to capture prey.

The expression on Amaya's face changes from shock to confusion so quickly that I'm sure the shift is from the fire flashing through my gaze.

Her eyes lock on mine, and time slows until there's nothing except for us.

A throat clears somewhere in the distance, and it snaps her out of the trance, a beautiful smile stretching across her face. "Father Cade, what a surprise." She glances past me to flick her eyes toward Parker.

My chest pulls at the split in her attention.

"I hope I'm not interrupting," she says.

I don't take my eyes off her, even now, even when I can hear Parker moving closer, his feet shuffling on the floor, can see in my peripheral vision the moment his dirty hand *dares* to touch her shoulder.

You shouldn't care, I tell myself. *She'll be dead soon anyway.*

"Don't be ridiculous, sweet girl. You're never an interruption." He drags her in close, pressing his slimy lips to her temple, and my stomach twists.

She shifts uncomfortably, taking a small step away, and I let the air out of my lungs.

"You've met Father Cade already?" he asks her.

She shrugs. "Hasn't everyone by now?"

"Amaya was *supposed* to be at Mass yesterday morning." I lift a brow as I stare down at her. A challenge sparks in her gaze and my cock twitches.

She tilts her head. "You must have confused me with somebody else."

I smirk at her defiance and can't resist taking a step closer. "Impossible."

Parker clears his throat again, his eyes blazing. He turns toward her, reaching out his hand and tipping up her chin as though she's his. "Get comfortable, sweetheart. Let me walk Father Cade out."

She nods and moves farther into his space like she's always belonged. The thought bothers me more than it should, and for a single solitary moment, I wonder if she *is* his. But then another thought grips me.

I pay off my mother's debts, and that makes me feel dirtier than sex work ever could.

"Amaya," I bark. My voice is loud and gravelly, my eyes

flickering between the two of them. "My door is always open if you need it."

She nods, a small grin tilting the corner of her lips as she makes herself comfortable in Parker's office.

I turn back to Parker. "I can see myself out."

He nods, slamming the door in my face, clearly as desperate to get away from me as I am to leave. Or maybe he's just desperate to get back to her. I relate to his plight.

Has she bewitched him too?

I should go back to the church. Or maybe head around the community and make sure the homeless are ready for the cold front expected to hit in the next few days. Maybe set up a place for them to stay dry and warm.

But deep down, I know that I'll do none of these things. Not today.

And when I see Amaya's angelic face walking out the Errien Enterprise doors, I follow her all the way back to her run-down apartment, a possessive fire burning through my veins.

CHAPTER 13

Cade

"I'M THINKING WE'LL TAKE PART IN THE FESTIVAL of Fools coming up."

"Why?" my superior, Bishop Lamont, grunts on the other end of the line. "Parker says he wants it stopped, and I can't say I disagree."

"Well," I start, tapping my fingers on the edge of my desk. "He has enough power to stop it if he truly wished. He doesn't need us for that. Besides, it's tradition in the town, and what better way to gain the people's trust than to ingratiate ourselves in the fabric of what they love?"

Silence.

"Without the church, it's just them mocking us. It's embarrassing that Father Clark allowed it to go on for so long without trying to intervene, honestly." I pause. "Or maybe Parker hasn't stopped it because he knows it would paint him in a bad light. You don't think he's trying to make the *church* look like the bad guy, do you?"

"Fine," Bishop Lamont replies, his voice rough and choppy.

"But you need to work with Parker. I don't appreciate being called and informed that you're making things difficult. He's very important to the church. He singlehandedly keeps Notre-Dame afloat in Festivalé."

Irritation stabs at my chest. He's only *important* because of the money he provides. Parker is not a godly man. This isn't His way. It's the way of greed and corruption. "Understood."

I hang up the phone and scowl down at it right as Jeremiah walks in.

"What's wrong?" he asks.

Sighing, I run a hand through my hair and lean back, the chair rocking on its hinges. "Bishop Lamont would like us to get the church involved in the Festival of Fools this year."

It's not entirely the truth, but making it seem as though it's my superior's idea may smooth over anyone's reservations.

Jeremiah eyebrows lift. "Really?"

I nod. "Do you have any recommendations on where to start?"

He moves into the room and sits down across from the desk, crossing his legs and rubbing his chin. "You could try Louis Elementary. They always do a big production right out front with all their kids."

My face twists.

"Plus, Principal Lee is a devout Catholic. She'll be over the moon to know the church has decided to take part."

Speaking with Principal Lee is a chore. She's a dowdy woman with black hair so dark it hints at blue and a god complex that goes unchecked from the power she wields over the minds of our future. I've only been here for a few moments, but I can already tell that Louis Elementary in general is a drag, but I'm here for a reason, and I won't leave until that purpose is served.

Jeremiah told me the elementary school usually puts on a play during the festivities and that the principal was one of the few women who would bend over backward for the church. Now that I'm looking at her, I realize I've seen her every Mass. She's never missed. Jeremiah is right. If we want to take an active part in the festival, then she's the place to start.

So first thing this morning, I made a spontaneous trip to the school, assuring Principal Lee that the church would love to support their efforts. To say she's thrilled is an understatement.

"More than anything, we need a place for the kids to rehearse," Principal Lee says. "We have our auditorium, but it's taken up by the *actual* school play rehearsals, and nowhere else in the building can accommodate so many students at once."

"They can use the church for rehearsals and the play," I cut in. "We have plenty of rooms in the basement."

A flash of relief coasts across her eyes, and a peal of distant laughter rings through the open door at my back. I turn to see what it is, looking past the front office and into the hall, noticing a large boy crowding a smaller one, a piece of paper falling from the younger kid's hand when he gets shoved into the wall.

I squint my eyes, realizing that it's Amaya's little brother.

What was his name? Quinten.

I hadn't realized he went to public school. Just like the first time I saw him, an odd sense of familiarity whips through me, warming me to his presence. There's something about him that reminds me of myself when I was his age, and it makes me protective in a way that I'm not used to feeling. I assume it's because of my sick obsession with his sister, and it's manifesting in Quinten as another way to feed my addiction to her.

Or perhaps it's because I remember being that child, huddled in the corner while the other kids in the orphanage pointed and laughed.

Children—once they lose their innocence—are some of the cruelest creatures on earth.

Quinten curls in on himself. The larger boy bends over, picking up the fallen paper and holding it in front of his eyes, a cruel smirk twisting his features. The way his face twists with menace reminds me of Parker's.

In fact, a lot about this child reminds me of him.

Does Parker have children?

I tilt my head, watching as the boy murmurs something, but I'm too far away to hear. He leans in, ripping the paper right down the middle, then drops it before stomping on it with his boot.

"Who is that?" I ask.

Principal Lee sighs, and I glance back to her, annoyed at her pinched expression.

"That's Quinten Paquette," she says with a monotonous voice. "And Bradley Gammond."

I lift my brows. "Gammond? He looks so similar to Mr. Errien, I almost assumed that the boy was his."

Principal Lee laughs tightly, shifting in her chair. "Yes, well… no. His mother is Florence Gammond, a defense attorney for the state. And her husband is *Samuel.*"

"And what does Samuel do?" I press.

"High-ranking military. He's gone a lot." Her eyes flick down the hall and then back.

"And this is common?" I nod toward the commotion.

"What is?"

I motion to the hall. "For you to allow children to behave in such a way?"

"Boys will be boys. You know how it goes." She waves her hand in the air like she's fanning smoke.

"No," I say slowly, leaning in. "How *does* it go?"

"Bradley, get to class!" An adult voice rings through the hallway. I look back, seeing what I assume is a teacher making her way toward the two boys.

"See?" Principal Lee smiles as she stands, moving toward her door and closing it before spinning back around to face me. "Lydia, Quinten's handler, is there. No harm, no foul."

Her lack of care scratches against my nerves like nails on a chalkboard, flashes of Sister Agnes finding me bruised and making them worse instead of helping me heal.

"Does Amaya know her brother is bullied?"

Principal Lee's brows shoot to her hairline. "*Bullied?*"

"What else would you call that?"

She huffs out a disbelieving breath, crossing her arms and moving to sit back in her chair. "With all due respect, Father Cade, I'm not sure you understand what kids are like."

Her words break the dam, and bitter memories of my time in the orphanage burst through like flooding waters. Times when Sister Agnes's cruelty whispered through the halls and gave the other children free rein to take out their own trauma on the skin of my arms or the back of my legs. The way the adults who were in charge would avert their eyes or whisper that *I* was a troublemaker. That I deserved it.

Nobody stood up for me then, the same way nobody is standing up for Quinten now.

My chest smarts, and I press my lips together.

"I take it you've met Miss Paquette then?" Principal Lee continues.

"Only in passing."

She nods slowly, her lips thinning as she stares at me. "May I offer a word of advice, Father?"

I incline my head.

"I'd keep away from her."

I frown. "You know, everyone continues to say that, yet no one ever gives me an actual reason why."

She shrugs. "She's a bad influence. Everyone in Festivalé knows it."

A smirk tips the corner of my mouth. "And you think I can be *influenced*, Principal Lee?"

I say it in a mocking tone, but the truth is that my insides are uneasy from the conversation. I *am* influenced by Amaya, more than I ever have been by anyone else, God included. Both the monster *and* the man.

My stomach twists up in anxiety the second I think of it, so I swallow around the panic and push it back down.

Principal Lee leans forward, her brows furrowing. "This town is steeped in superstition, Father. We've learned long ago not to question when something stinks of evil. We'd rather rip it out at the root. I'd hate to think that our very own priest doesn't support the culture of Festivalé, one that's been passed down through generations."

"Hmm," I hum. This is the first someone has said it so plainly. About Festivalé and the eerie feeling that blankets the air. But I believe what she says, as surely as I believe in Him. "And what part will Quinten be playing in the production?" I pivot the conversation.

Principal Lee laughs, like I've made a joke.

"Oh no. Quinten wouldn't know how to do that."

"Presumption is a sin against hope, Principal Lee." It's more than obvious she doesn't care about the boy's well-being. "Have you ever given him the chance?"

"Well, I—" she sputters.

"Is he not still made in God's image?" I cut her off.

"No, of course he is. I just—"

"Great. It's settled then. Quinten will take part in the production."

Her brows draw down and she shakes her head. "Now, wait a minute, Father. I can't just *guarantee* him a part."

"If you want the support of the church, you will." I stand up, heading toward her door. "I'll be back tomorrow, and I expect to hear good news."

CHAPTER 14

Amaya

THERE'S A SMALL STUDIO CLOSE TO THE CHAPEL that my boss owns. He lets any of the dancers use it as long as there aren't any classes, and Wednesdays are usually pretty sparse, so I always head over while Quinten's in school to make use of the space.

It's nothing fancy, just plain wooden floors with smudged-up mirrors along the back wall and a pole installed right in front of them. I've got my phone blaring music through the Bluetooth speaker that Dalia lets me borrow, and my muscles ache from having been here for the past few hours. It's a feeling I've come to love, and I wonder how I got through so many years without knowing that pole was where my soul feels most at home.

By the time I stop, my body is drenched in a thin layer of sweat, and my mind is calm for the first time since I met Father Cade in the grocery store and he threw my world off its axis.

Seeing him in Parker's office was unexpected, and it sent my stomach flying into my throat, my heart dancing around like a schoolgirl with a crush.

A crush on a fucking priest. Leave it to me to finally have sexual attraction to a man who's so off-limits, he's a one-way ticket to hell.

I roll my eyes and groan as I make my way over to the stool and pick up my phone, glancing down at the screen. I rotate my neck, stretching the tight muscles, a satisfying pop rippling through me as I pull up my missed calls.

Louis Elementary.

Great.

Dread plops in my middle as I press play on the voicemail, Principal Lee's voice coming over the line. It's never a good thing when the school is calling me.

"Ms. Paquette, this is Principal Lee, As I'm sure you know, the Festival of Fools is coming up. We'd love for Quinten to be part of the play we're putting on, but since most of the rehearsals will be taking place off campus, we need you to come in and sign a permission slip. Thank you."

A breath of relief whooshes out of me.

I had braced myself for the worst with this call, knowing everyone at that school is just itching for a chance to throw Quinten out, but maybe I've been projecting or putting the feelings of a few on the shoulders of all, expecting everyone to be the same. Hope flickers in my chest. They've never asked to include him in something like this before.

My stomach drops at the thought of taking part in something I've actively campaigned against for years. Well, not the festival itself per say, just the ridiculous, outdated name.

It's insulting.

But on the other hand, how could I tell Quinten no to being part of something with his peers? To being treated like any other kid?

My chest pulls tight.

I can't. He'll need to learn to navigate this world that won't change for him, and I'd be doing him a disservice by keeping him from spreading his wings just because other people are stuck in their ways.

Grabbing a small towel, I wipe the sweat from my face and pack up my meager belongings before locking up and heading home for a quick shower.

It's less than two hours later, and I'm walking down the halls of Louis Elementary, the unease in my stomach growing even as that tendril of hope has fully taken hold, wrapping around my nerves and making me imagine that maybe we're on the tide of something new.

Still though, I hate coming here. My experience in school wasn't the best time, having moved around so much it was impossible to make friends. And being back in halls that smell like rubber sneakers and arts and crafts shoots the feeling of loneliness to the forefront of my mind. It's so weird that no matter how much time passes, a simple scent can bring emotions you've buried for years roaring back as though they never left in the first place.

There's a gymnasium to the left of the entrance, filled with the high-pitched squeaks of shoes and loud shrieks of children. I walk past it, taking in the wide hallways that are lined in colorful art, displayed like Monet himself created the pieces.

When I round the corner, I stop short in my tracks, seeing Principal Lee shaking hands with Father Cade, her smile wide and teeth gleaming, her neck craned uncomfortably to look him in the eyes.

Why is he suddenly everywhere I am?

His stare immediately finds mine, and like a moth to a flame, I take an involuntary step closer.

He pulls away from the principal and moves toward me, his hands slipping in his pockets as he stops just inches away.

"Amaya, we meet again?" He grins. "God surely has me in His favor."

I lift a brow, a quiet hum filling up my body. "Stalking me, Father?"

He chuckles, his gaze looking up and down the empty hallway of the school before he leans in and lowers his voice. "And what if I am?"

I shrug. "It's probably a waste of your time. I don't live an interesting life."

"Non, ridicule." His voice curls around the French like smoke. "You *are* the interest."

Something about his tone makes my stomach clench tight, and there's a niggling feeling, like if I don't step away now, I never will. But the weight of his energy pressing into mine is so intense, it's physically holding me captive.

"What will it take to see you in my church?"

I snort, shaking my head as a small smile plays on my face. "A miracle."

His eyes scan the length of my body. And I swear to God it feels like he's stripping off my clothes piece by agonizing piece. I swallow, *hating* how out of control he makes me feel.

He's a stranger, Amaya.

"Then I'll pray for a miracle."

A sharp stab of heat strikes between my legs, and I curse myself for having such a visceral reaction to somebody who is so out of reach that he's not even on the map.

After losing my virginity to Parker when he first came back around once my mom left and I dared to say no, my sexual desire has been at an all-time low. Nonexistent.

My body has *never* reacted so viscerally to someone else before.

"What are you doing here anyway?" I ask, finally forcing myself to take a step back.

He follows, keeping himself so close, frissons of electricity dance off my skin.

"I thought you already knew?" He smirks, leaning down until I'm engulfed in his shadow, his lips skimming across the shell of my ear. "I'm stalking you, petite pécheresse."

Goose bumps sprinkle down my spine.

"Miss Paquette," a sharp voice rings from down the hall, followed by a click-clack of heels.

Father Cade backs up immediately, but I would swear on everything that his lips just brushed against the top of my head before he did.

"Au revoir, Miss Paquette."

And then he's gone, his long strides heading away from me and out of the building entirely.

My heart flutters, completely out of my control, and I fucking hate the way it feels.

I flip around and try like hell to clear my expression. "Principal Lee, I was just coming to see you."

Her eyes flick past me to where Father Cade just was and then back again. "You should have called before coming in."

Her coldness doesn't detract from the light in my heart at Quinten being included, so I brush off the biting words and force a sympathetic look. "I'm sorry. I figured I'd drop by on my way to pick up Quin. It's just a couple of permission slips, right?"

"That's right."

"Thanks for including Quin," I say. "I can't explain how much it means to—"

"Every student can participate, Miss Paquette," she cuts me off. "Normally the slips get sent home, but, well...I wasn't sure they'd ever make it to you."

Her subtle jab hits me right beneath the ribs as I follow her into the main office. It smells like reheated lasagna and stuffy air, and I crinkle my nose as we make our way to the front desk.

"Carla, make sure Miss Paquette signs the permission forms for Quinten to take part in the children's play during the festival," Principal Lee directs the school secretary.

I smile at Carla before giving my attention back to Principal Lee, who's staring at me with her hip leaned against the desk and her arms crossed over her chest.

"I didn't know you were still a practicing Catholic," she says.

"I'm sorry?" It's hardly her business what religion I am.

"Father Cade." She nods toward the open door.

"Oh." I tilt my head. "I didn't realize you needed to be Catholic to talk to him. What was he doing here anyway?"

It's not really my concern, but I ask anyway, the curiosity overwhelming my need to be polite.

"Father Cade's been here all afternoon helping us get ready for the festival." Her lips thin. "I figured you knew that already."

"Why would *I* know that?"

Her attitude is tiring, and honestly, I don't have the energy to keep entertaining her snide remarks and less than subtle innuendos about...whatever it is she's trying to insinuate.

She blinks at me in confusion before tapping the papers Carla just placed on the desk and sliding them toward me.

"Because he's the one who suggested Quinten be in the play."

CHAPTER 15

Cade

IT WASN'T MY INTENTION TO RUN INTO AMAYA AT Louis Elementary, but even with the threat of other people around, I find her impossible to resist.

Worse than that is the sense of ownership that sparks through me like kerosene, lighting my veins on fire when I see her. When I so much as *think* of someone other than me touching her. It's bothersome, and quite frankly, it makes me furious having to constantly balance on the tightrope between killing her quickly or keeping her alive so I can watch her every breath.

This obsession makes no sense, and I don't like being so helpless to its pull.

But I refuse to be a victim any longer, which is why tonight, despite every fiber of my being aching to go and peer in her window, I don't. Instead, I sit in my cozy little cottage and let my television drone on while I break apart a chocolate bar that's the size of my forearm, preparing to drop it into the milk I have boiling on the gas stove.

It's a treat, one that I don't often indulge in, but tonight I'm feeling nostalgic, wanting to remind myself of where I come from and how far I still have to go, and hot chocolate brings back the memories of when I first got off the streets for good. When Father Moreau took me in and convinced me to come back by plying me with sugar cookies and warm drinks, not realizing I would have done it for a single night with a roof over my head.

My stomach grumbles, echoing off the large stone outside Notre-Dame de Paris Cathedral. My face heats at the noise, but nobody turned my way, so I can only hope they didn't notice.

Maybe my hunger isn't as loud to everybody else as it is to me.

There are a lot of people here today on the Île de la Cité, traipsing around and taking photographs, but I don't care about anybody other than the group of three American women who I've been tracking since they walked out of their ritzy hotel forty-five minutes ago. They don shawls around their shoulders, whispering about how archaic it is to have to cover their skin if they want to see inside, and their giggles ring off the high arches and intricate Gothic carved structures as though it's appropriate to be so disrespectful in a place so full of beauty.

I move slowly behind them, keeping enough distance that I disappear into the scenery, because the last thing a pickpocket wants is to stand apart from the crowd. And I learned to blend in long before I ran away from the orphanage ten years ago.

Besides, blending in is easy enough to do here. Paris is teeming with tourism, full of people who are too busy looking up to see the hand sliding in their pockets and sneaking out their wallets.

As the group of women head closer to the door, I pick up my pace, cutting across the concrete-lined bushes and the open square to deliberately stand in their way right when they reach the entry to the church.

The short brunette slams into me, and I jerk back, gripping her around the waist to catch her.

Her purse sways at her side.

"Je suis désolé, belle. Est-ce que tu vas bien?"

The girl's eyes widen, and she leans in closer. "What?"

I offer her my most devastating smile. I've been told that when I can keep myself at least moderately bathed and my anger in check, I have a certain type of charm. It usually seems to work in my favor when trying to woo a pretty girl, but I can't be sure if it's my face or my accent that does the trick here.

Tourists are terribly predictable.

My hand holds her side tightly, squeezing in comfort, but my other one has already slipped into the side of her bag and grabbed her wallet, moving it from her purse into my pocket. My heart slams against my rib cage, adrenaline flooding through my system like a drug, and I walk away, smiling and apologizing as I slink backward until I reach the door.

Then I'm spinning around and speeding off, wanting to leave the scene before she realizes what I took.

Hopefully, there's cash in here. Tourists usually carry some around, but cards, while not impossible, are more difficult.

"Hey!" she yells behind me.

Merde.

I break into a sprint, pushing two bystanders out of the way as I cut across the open courtyard, garnering attention from the people standing by. A flock of pigeons is huddled by a lamppost, and I run straight for them, hoping the distraction of them flying and flapping will help me get away.

And I almost do. Get away with it, I mean.

But then a man steps in front of me, gripping my arm tightly and swinging me around, my heart pounding in my ears and my stomach tightening around the emptiness.

Disappointment rattles in my hollow bones as I look up at my captor, realizing Archbishop Moreau has me in his hold.

"Suivez-moi," he says simply, telling me to follow him.

I expect him to take me back to the cathedral itself, but instead he walks to a small patisserie and sits us down at the front corner table, Notre-Dame towering over everything in the distance.

The smell of rich chocolate and freshly ground coffee fills the air, and my stomach cramps.

I've known of Archbishop Moreau—it's almost impossible not to if you live in the area—but I never imagined he would seem so...normal. Although beyond scouting for people to steal from, I've never given much thought to the church in general, if I'm honest. Religion brings back memories of Sister Agnes. Of a time I try to forget.

He waves over one of the baristas and orders two sweet crepes and cups of hot chocolate, choosing to let us both sit in silence until the young man comes back with our order.

My mouth salivates at the buttery pastry in front of me, but I'm too nervous to pick it up.

He sits back in his chair, rubbing his scruffy chin as he watches me. His hair is graying at the temples, and his skin is pallid, a pasty white that makes me wonder if he might be ill. Then he asks my name. "Quel est ton nom, cher enfant?"

"Cade Frédéric," I mutter.

I'm not sure why I don't lie to him. Maybe it's because he gives off a vibe of trustworthiness. Or maybe I'm just hoping if I cooperate, then I won't feel like I owe him something once I take his offerings of food.

He nods and reaches forward, the tips of his fingers pushing the
small, round white plate closer to me.

"I'm sure you're hungry, no?" he says in English. "Eat."

And I did. He didn't ask any questions, just fed me and kept me
warm with hot chocolate.

So when he asked me to come back again the next day, I did.
And the next.

Until my hopelessness was replaced with faith and my anger
replaced with Him.

At least that's what I assumed.

Foolishly, I even had the passing thought that Sister Agnes
would be proud of how far my soul has come, of who I've become.
The most broken part of me wanted her to see me now, to feel
pride that I finally rid myself of sickness.

But monsters love to hide in the shadows, just waiting for
the perfect moment to strike. And mine came rearing back after
being subdued for too long, ravenous as ever.

Snapping out of the memory, I pound the candy bar harder
than necessary, pieces of broken chocolate flying off the sides
of the wood cutting board. Shaking my head, I grab the cocoa
powder from the spice rack and move to the stove, sprinkling
some into the milk, mixing it in with a wooden spoon.

As I stir, I ruminate.

Since the moment I've entered the church, I've never
questioned God. Never questioned His path for me. And I'm still
rigid in my beliefs. He tests His strongest soldiers, and this is no
different. Amaya Paquette is a test to my chastity.

And I'm terrified I'll fail.

She's a wrecking ball, upheaving the clarity I've spent years etching into stone until it's nothing but cracked marble.

This isn't my first bout of balancing the temptation of evil with the path of righteousness, but it's a new one. An untraveled road that I'm heading down blind. I've come to terms with coexisting with my monster and the sin that it begets, but this *lust* is all-consuming in a way that I'm not sure I can balance.

Gritting my teeth, I take the small mallet and smash it down on the dark chocolate, a shot of *need* breaking through the moment as I compare the feel of the cocoa breaking to something else.

Something more fragile.

Something that will scream out until it fades into nothingness.

Bones are harder to fracture than a simple candy bar, but the comparison sends a sick thrill through me anyway. I sink into the moment because at least the violence is familiar.

I'm dropping the smashed-up pieces into the pot of milk when a knock sounds on my door. My brow furrows, and I lower the heat to a simmer before heading to the front and opening it, coming face-to-face with Amaya Paquette.

Everything that I've just told myself, everything I've spent the past day *convincing* myself of—that I won't follow her around, that I'll kill her and be done with it—all of it falls away the moment I see her standing in the doorway to my cottage.

She looks ethereal in the night, surrounded by falling snow. Her hair dances slightly as it's picked up by the icy wind, and her cheeks are as flushed as the tip of her nose from being kissed by the cold.

I lean against the doorframe as I take her in, the sight of her making it hard to breathe.

She smiles, her pouty lips parting as she shakes her head,

white drops of snow melting into the strands of her hair until it looks as black as the sky.

"I wasn't sure if this was where you lived," she says, her eyes glancing behind me into the small living room.

I quirk a brow, sinking my shoulder farther into the door's frame. "You were looking for me, petite pécheresse?"

Her hand raises to wrap around the ends of her hair before she pauses, blowing out a deep breath. "Yes, but I—" She shakes her head. "It's late and I shouldn't have come. I didn't wake you up, did I?"

I smile because it's *always* her keeping me awake, whether she's here or not.

"Non," I reply. "I'm always available for you, no matter the time."

Moving to the side, I gesture for her to come in, although there's something screaming deep in my gut to turn her away. That if I let her inside, there will be no going back. Her scent will be in my home, and the memory of how she fits here will be etched into the walls like scripture on stone.

She moves through the entry, and my stomach twists when she brushes by me.

I turn and close the door, flicking the lock in place and staring at her back as she stands in the center of the living room, looking around.

I could kill her now and be done with it.

My fingers twitch at the possibility, my mouth going dry at imagining her heartbeat growing faint beneath my hands. I move closer, my muscles tensing in anticipation.

She shakes her head again, spinning to face me, and when her eyes meet mine, my footsteps halt.

"I probably shouldn't have come." She smiles. "I just needed to think and kind of ended up here."

The need inside me mutates into curiosity. "And what is it you have to think about that you can't do at home?" I press, taking another step toward her. "Do you need to confess, Amaya?"

She laughs and it makes my chest pull tight.

"According to you? Probably." Now it's her who moves closer. "Truthfully, I've been debating all day whether I should hunt you down and thank you."

She continues toward me until she's mere centimeters away, her neck craned and her green gaze peering at me through her lashes, like an innocent doe presenting herself at the feet of a predator.

My cock pulses, blood rushing to fill it until it presses uncomfortably against my slacks.

As usual, when she's around, there's a battle waging war inside me.

"So thank me then," I demand.

She bites into her lower lip as she blinks at me, and the urge to reach out and replace her teeth with my own is so strong, my stomach flips.

"I know it was you who requested Quin be included in the festival," she states.

"Oui."

She moves in again, the smell of vanilla wrapping around my senses and tugging until my equilibrium feels off-center.

My cock is throbbing now, and I slip my hands into my pockets so I don't grip her arms and haul her into me, just to feel how warm she is against my flesh. My jaw ticks when her mouth parts, her breasts moving in an uneven rhythm from her heavy breaths.

Merde.

"I'd do the same for any child," I force out, although it's far from the truth.

My words do the trick, and her gaze clears, widening slightly as she takes a giant step back.

"Right." she says, running a hand through her wavy hair. "Anyway, I should go home. I just…"

I don't reply, allowing her to move past me and make it all the way back to the front door.

"Amaya," I call out right before she leaves.

Come back here. Let me taste you. Touch you. End you.

"Come to Mass on Sunday."

The corner of her mouth tilts up, her eyes meeting mine for a split second before she's gone.

CHAPTER 16

Amaya

I DON'T KNOW WHY I'M HERE AGAIN.

Last night, coming to Father Cade's home was easy to reason away, because I couldn't get my mind off what Principal Lee told me, about how it was Cade who ensured Quinten would be included. I thought about it for the rest of the night and all the next day. It was on my mind during every single performance at work until my brain felt so frazzled I knew I *had* to see him. I needed to thank him properly, let him know how grateful I am that he's here. So I left the Chapel, and instead of taking the bus all the way home, I got off two stops early until I was standing at the base of the stone steps to Notre-Dame, indecision weighing me down. It was the stony eyes of the gargoyles lining the entrance that spooked me away until I walked around the perimeter and decided to try the first of two small cottages at the back.

Honestly, I hadn't expected him to answer. It was three in the morning, and any normal person would be sleeping. *Any normal person wouldn't be knocking on someone's door.*

Tonight, I don't have an excuse.

But here he is again, answering the door in gray sweats and a black T-shirt, looking nothing like a priest and everything like a statue made by the gods.

My heart races at the sight of him leaning against the doorjamb with his hands in his pockets, and I curse myself for being weak enough to come here. He makes me *feel*, and I know better than to allow myself close to anything that threatens my control.

But it's nice to have someone who doesn't sneer at me when I walk past or think I'm the reason bad things happen.

"Salut, petite pécheresse. Back again so soon?"

My stomach flutters at the nickname. I almost looked it up, curiosity getting the best of me, but stopped myself. Not knowing is better, because what if it's something sweet? Or worse, something that's not.

His eyes scan the open space behind me before coming back to rest on me, and I wonder if he's worried that someone might see us. I also wonder if he's even allowed to have me back here or if it's a rule I'm forcing him to break. Guilt starts to rear its head.

He gestures for me to move inside again, the same as he did before, and I shake the thought away.

I'm living in the moment. I can worry about everything again tomorrow.

We walk through the doorway, and I take in the small space. Last night, I was too shaken, so nervous from being here that while I saw everything, I didn't get to soak it in.

Tonight, I take my time lapping up every detail. There's a log fireplace crackling in the right-hand corner of the living room surrounded by bookshelves and a cozy oversize recliner next to it with an open book turned down on the end table. A large couch with worn plaid fabric takes up the majority of the space, and a small oval coffee table sits in the center, a vase of white flowers perched right in the middle. There's a television fixed to the wall, but it's turned off, reflecting the glow from the fire.

To the left is the kitchen, a small mobile island in the center, painted forest green with an oak cutting board for its top. A tea kettle sits on the gas stove, and a dark green hand towel is draped over the faucet in the sink.

It's so…different from what I expected. So normal. I guess it's never occurred to me to think about how priests live. That they have a life outside their job.

And that's what it is at the end of the day, isn't it? It's a job just like any other.

"Cup of tea?" Cade asks, already moving through the small living room and into the kitchen.

I clear my throat. "Sure."

Maybe I should be following him, but I stay in the living room instead, moving to the bookshelves that surround the fireplace, tilting my head to read the titles.

Frankenstein.

Middlegame.

The Art of Alchemy.

Suddenly, a tingle trickles down my spine, Cade's breath on my neck.

"See something interesting?"

His voice is low and raspy, and it makes the hair on the tops of my arms stand to attention. "Alchemy is an interesting subject for a priest."

He nods, jaw ticking. "I like to be aware of all practices. Helps my faith be well-rounded and secure."

I turn around, allowing a small smile to grace my features as I take the cup of tea from his hand. "I didn't expect your place to look like this, I guess."

A piece of dark hair falls on his forehead as he grins, and when he pushes it back, I'm struck again by how attractive this man is without even trying.

Not for the first time tonight, I question what the hell I think I'm doing and then soothe my unease by reminding myself that there's a boundary here that can't be crossed. Despite how out of control he makes me feel, *nothing* can happen between us. Nothing will.

So it doesn't matter if he makes my stomach tense and my heart pound.. Because he's a priest. He's taken his vows. He's married to the church. And I'm not even sure if I actually *like* him or if he's safe. So out of bounds that my defenses lower, and I'm able to ignore the way he puts me on edge.

He's taken a vow of chastity. And there's a type of safety net in that.

"And what did you expect?" he asks.

"I don't know." I shrug. "When it comes to you, I'm starting to think I shouldn't expect anything."

That stray strand of hair falls in his face again, and I reach out before I can stop myself.

He jerks away almost violently and winces, a slight hiss leaving him as his entire body stiffens.

My hand flies back to my side. "Sorry. Are you okay?"

He chuckles, but the sound feels forced. "It's better if we don't touch."

"Why?"

His eyes darken, and heat splits through my middle, striking between my legs.

"I think you know why."

My mouth goes dry as I nod. Because he's right. I do. A little piece of that safety net disintegrates with his words. I had assumed this was one-sided.

I must zone out or get lost in the moment, because next thing I know, he's turned toward me fully, his other hand reaching out and smoothing away the furrow in my brows. Even though he just said we shouldn't touch.

Even though I agreed.

"You're much too beautiful to look so sad, Amaya."

My chest squeezes tight. "You have to say things like that because you're a priest."

He shakes his head, stepping in closer, his hand coming up to cup my cheek fully now, sending my heart careening off the cliff it's been teetering on.

"Non," he whispers. "I *shouldn't* say that *because* I'm your priest."

My breath hitches as I stare at his face, my eyes dropping to his lips and then back up again.

I want him to kiss me. I know it's impossible and so, so wrong on a thousand different levels, but...

I want him to kiss me.

Clearing his throat, he steps back, taking the still-full cup of tea from my hands and spinning around to set it on the coffee table.

"It's late," he says.

Disappointment sinks inside me like a rock, but it mixes with a heavy dose of relief. "Yeah, I'm...I'm really sorry I bothered you, Father."

I use his title to remind myself of who he is. Of *what* he is.

"Cade," he replies sharply.

"What?"

He sighs, running a hand through his mussed-up hair. "When it's just the two of us, you can call me Cade."

Calling him Cade feels personal, and I don't want us to *be* personal.

But I don't listen to the warning sirens blasting through my mind, and I nod slowly. "Okay, Cade."

"I'm surprised you even *want* Quin involved," Dalia says the next evening, scrunching her nose.

I tilt my head as I drain the pot of macaroni shells, confused by her statement. "What? Why wouldn't I want him included?"

Moving to the side of the sink, I cut open the foil packet of cheese and pour it in the bottom of the heated pot before grabbing the macaroni, dumping it back in, and mixing it.

"Quin!" I yell. "Dinnertime!"

The pitter-patter of footsteps comes down the hallway, Quinten appearing in the kitchen doorway. "Finish this first and then dinner," he says.

"Deal." I nod.

I don't know what "this" is, but he loves to barter, and usually I allow the compromises, wanting him to have a sense of self-agency.

He smiles, and the sight of it makes my chest warm. When he goes to his bedroom to finish whatever task he was on, I put my attention back on Dalia.

"I mean, it's called the Festival of *Fools*, Amaya," she continues. "It's ableist as fuck."

"Well...yeah," I reply slowly. "I'm not a fan of the title, but what can I do about it? You want me to keep Quin from being able to be part of something to make a statement?"

Guilt swims through me, but it's irritating to have Dalia talk to me like I haven't agonized over every aspect of anything involving Quinten.

I shake my head, mixing the shells and cheese to keep it warm. "That won't do anything except keep us in solitude and ostracize us even more."

"You don't know unless you try."

I slam down the wooden spoon, splatters of orange skating across the counter. "I *have* tried, dammit. You really think I sit by and do nothing? The first year after my mom left, I went to the county meeting, begging them to change it." I spin around, crossing my arms over my chest. "And do you know what they said? 'It's tradition. It's not about *you*. It's about history.' And then I went the next year. And the next. And the fucking next."

"Oh," Dalia says.

"Yeah, *oh*. And fuck you, Dal, for assuming."

"Look, I'm sorry, okay? I just…" She sighs, rubbing a hand over her face. "He's my little dude, you know? I can't stand the thought of anything hurting him."

Empathy douses my anger. "Yeah."

Dalia glances down the hall. "I just worry he'll look back one day and think we were complacent, you know?"

I grab a bowl from the cupboard, scooping the shells into it and moving to the table where she is. Sitting down, I reach out and grip her hand in mine. "I get it, okay? *Believe* me. But the truth is that we can only protect him so much, and even when we *do*, we're still going to live through it. It's painful sometimes to realize that other people don't understand or…or don't care. And it fucking sucks." Emotion clogs my throat, tears burning behind my eyes. "It sucks to know you have the best kid in the world and can't protect him from everyone else's ugliness."

She nods.

"But he's got me." I shrug. "And now he's got you too. And he *knows*, Dalia. He knows we'd burn the world just to make him smile. And I have to believe that one day, he'll have others. Not everyone can be as awful as the people in Festivalé, right?"

Dalia sniffles, wiping a stray tear from the side of her cheek. "You're right. I'm just a sensitive bitch."

I laugh, squeezing her hand.

"Do you think he even wants to be in the play?" she asks.

I shrug. "He seemed excited about it when I told him. Quin!" I holler out again, standing up and walking to his room.

He's on his iPad, his finger moving furiously over whatever app he's playing.

"Dinnertime, dude. Just bring it with you."

He grabs it without ever looking up and makes his way into the kitchen, climbing into his chair and picking up the fork to his side, stabbing one piece before slipping it in his mouth and going back to his game.

I watch him as he eats one shell at a time, ensuring none of it makes a mess and that none of it gets on his hands.

My chest feels heavier after my talk with Dalia, but the love I feel when I look at Quinten eclipses any amount of hardship I could ever endure.

"Quin," Dalia says. "You excited about the play?"

"Yes or no?" he says, his legs starting to kick violently. If he was standing, he'd be jumping in place right now.

"Yes or no?" Dalia repeats, asking him.

"Yes!" he squeals.

I look over at Dalia with a beaming grin, as if to say, *See? Told you.*

The alarm on my phone beeps and I jump in place. "I've gotta go."

There's only twenty minutes until the next bus comes by, and I have to work tonight.

Dalia waves me off. "Yeah, yeah. We've got it under control here."

CHAPTER 17

Amaya

ANDREW GLEESON IS MY BEST REGULAR.

He's also the most obnoxious. He comes in four to five times a week, and while he's a big spender, he always gets a little *too* grabby.

I let it slide because whenever I smack his hands and tell him to remember the rules, he listens.

But tonight, before things even get started, I can tell that something's not quite right. There's a glaze to his eyes that isn't normally there, his pupils blown like he's snorted a whole eight ball up his nostrils. I ignore it, because I need the money, and like I said…normally he listens.

So even though he gets pushy during my set onstage and is a little too jittery when I meet him in the private room, I push the feeling aside and remind myself that he's harmless.

The music pumps through the surround sound speakers, a sultry bass vibrating through me as I attempt to slip into the role of Esmeralda, the way I always do, sauntering toward him to put on my show. Only as I sink into his lap and feel his erection pressing against me, I'm still just *me*. My alter ego is nowhere to be found, lost somewhere like a ghost in the wind.

Well, this is problematic.

I try to fake it till I make it, going through the motions even though my mind is on a thousand different things, but Andrew notices almost immediately.

"What's wrong?" he snaps.

I shake my head, smiling at him and throwing my arms around his shoulders as I swivel my hips in a figure eight on his lap. "Not a thing, handsome."

We both know it's a lie.

This isn't the first time I've had trouble sinking into the role of Esmeralda, but it's never been with a man like Andrew, an overbearing slimeball of a regular who should really be at home with his wife and not paying me to grind against his dick until he comes inside his pants.

My dances still satisfied, and I always felt good about the money I was making.

But tonight, Andrew's wandering hands feel like slime coating my sides.

And that has everything to do with him and nothing to do with me.

"No touching," I say, pushing myself off his lap and bending over, trying to get some space while continuing to dance.

"Get back over here," he demands.

I bristle at his tone, gritting my teeth. He's never been so sharp with me, but I listen to him, wanting to keep him calm and just finish this and be done with it. Spinning around, I sit back down on him, looking into his hazy eyes.

He's definitely on something.

His hands come up and grip me tight again on the hips, and then he thrusts himself up between my legs, so hard that it hurts.

"Fuck, Andrew. *Stop*." My voice is firm, and I quit moving entirely.

"Then get it the fuck together, Esmeralda. Jesus. You feel like a damn robot."

I know what I should do, what the smart thing is to do. I should smack him in his disgusting face and call Benny the bouncer in to take out the trash. But then I think of Parker saying what would happen if I was short on money again, and I close my eyes, swallowing down the urge to leave.

Instead, I let my mind wander, and when Father Cade's face flashes in my mind, I suck in a sharp breath at the spark of heat.

I latch on to his image, even though it feels wrong, and suddenly every roll of my hips is on top of *his* lap, and every time I feel a wandering hand, it's *his* fingers skimming across my flesh.

The fabric of my G-string dampens as arousal flushes through my system, my clit swelling as I grind myself down, able to feel how hard he is as I rub myself just the right way along his thick cock.

Fuck.

My eyes squeeze tighter, reveling in the way it feels to give in, to let myself *feel*.

To be the reason he breaks his vows.

Strong hands grip my breasts, ghosting over the fake emerald necklace I wear while I'm Esmeralda, and a moan escapes me, my hips working faster against his erection, the slight thrust of his hips hitting me in just the right spot. Pricks of pleasure skitter through my middle and dance between my legs, and I hear a low groan from in front of me.

"Goddamn, Esmeralda. I knew you wanted it. You're soaking me, baby."

My eyes snap open and I stumble off Andrew, reality crashing back down on top of me until I feel shattered and trapped beneath the rubble.

Andrew's hands fly up and grip my waist tightly, meaty fingers digging into my skin until I wince. "Where are you going?"

"The song's over, Andrew," I say, ripping myself away. "I've gotta go."

Forcing a grin, I lean in and press a swift kiss to his cheek before rushing out the door, not even remembering to get the money I'm owed.

I've never, *ever* gotten that way when I'm at work. It's not about sexual pleasure for me. It's business. A way for me to regain agency with my sexuality after it being stolen from me when I had just turned nineteen.

And it's extremely concerning that with a single *thought* of Father Cade, I lost myself in a fantasy.

Ridiculous.

I'm still beating myself up over it twenty minutes later when I rush out the back entrance, desperate to get home and curl up beneath my covers and pretend tonight never happened.

Usually there's a bouncer at the door, but when I leave, there's no one there, and I put my head down and hustle over the few steps, calculating how long I'll have to wait to grab the next bus home. And maybe that's why I don't hear footsteps coming up behind me until I feel the strong grip on my arm that pulls me into a hard body.

My breath whooshes out of me.

"You forgot your money," Andrew rasps in my ear.

I press my lips together, shaking my head, fear piercing through me like needles. "Oh, did I?"

My heart slams against my ribs, beating out the words "*get away*" like a giant red flag waving in the wind. I listen without a second thought, trying to pry from where he has us stuck together so I can leave, but he just tightens his hold and then drags me back into the alley behind the club, slamming me roughly against the side of the building.

"Don't run, baby," he whispers against my neck, his hips thrusting against my ass as he presses me into the brick. "Finish what you started. You were into it. I *know* you were into it."

"No, Andrew. It's a job." I struggle against him, my stomach heaving with nerves, adrenaline pumping through my veins. Flashes of Parker waltzing into our apartment in the middle of the day and me smacking him in the face as he demanded for the thousandth time to know where my mother went coast through my mind. The way his hands reached out and gripped my throat, slamming me on the couch. His meaty paws ripping away my clothes as he told me he was trying to find her. That until she came back, it was up to *me* to make sure he got paid.

How when I told him no, he made it hurt worse.

"It's *just* a job for me," I cry out. "Stop it."

"Quit *lying*, dammit." He pushes me harder into the wall, my cheek scratching against the rough surface until it stings.

A crack sounds from beside the large dumpster at the end of the alley, and it's loud enough to make us both jump and for Andrew's grip to slacken. I don't waste the opportunity, ramming my elbow into his stomach and slipping beneath his arms, my stomach heaving as I sprint away.

I don't stop and I sure as hell don't look back, only slowing down when I make it to the bus stop where there's a few people already waiting. There's safety in numbers.

Glancing behind me and not seeing Andrew, I relax, hunching over and resting my hands on my knees, my lungs burning from the exertion and my body stinging from the shock. My hands shake and my mouth turns sour, and I close my eyes to keep from throwing up.

It's ten minutes before the bus shows up, and it takes every single one for me to calm down. To convince myself that everything is fine. That I'm overreacting. That if I talk to my boss, Phillip, he'll ban Andrew from ever coming back in the club and everything can go back to the way it was before.

By the time I make it back to the apartment, I've done my best to wipe the experience from my mind, not wanting Dalia to pick up on anything being wrong. Luckily, she's not even awake when I get home, so I slip in as quietly as possible and closing the door once I'm in my room.

And that's where I stay for the rest of the night. In my bed, burrowing in the covers and pretending that I'm choosing to stay awake.

CHAPTER 18

Cade

WHEN I WAS A YOUNG CHILD, I WAS FILLED WITH untenable rage. It crashed through my system like a hurricane, lighting up every single nerve and throwing it into chaos.

I was angry.

Angry at my parents, whomever they were, for giving me up as soon as I was born.

Angry at them for dropping me in a dumpster, like it was just *that* easy to take back the gift of life.

Angry at the people who found me and took me to that terrible orphanage instead of anywhere else.

And angry at the world for not giving me anyone who cared when I ran away from that horrid place at seven years old.

It was only when I found seminary that I was able to compartmentalize properly. To take things apart, analyze them, and then put them back together, fitting them into a new mold and learning that if I put all my faith in Him, He wouldn't lead me astray.

Because *He* cares. And He forgives.

The reason became clear one night during prayer, my insides

aching with scars as I asked *why?* And I heard His voice as surely as my own, whispering the answers.

It was an epiphany realizing that all the pain, all the strife, all the *unfairness* of life was thrust upon me because I was His loyal soldier: here to experience the worst of the worst and come out stronger. To recognize it within myself so I could help heal it in others. I fell into the role effortlessly, and for a brief moment in time, I believed I was cured myself.

But then another voice slithered its way back into my head, one that convinced me healing them wasn't enough. A need, putrid and violent, rose up inside me like it never left, and when I took a nighttime walk to try and cast it away, whatever *it* was took the reins instead.

That was the first night I killed a man.

It felt incredible. I reasoned away the guilt while it was happening, that voice in my head saying it was our *duty*. That he was sick with demons, the same way I was as a boy.

"There's a sickness in you, child, and God wants me to beat it out."

Sister Agnes's voice murmured in my head, telling me I was doing the right thing.

The *righteous* thing.

It was only once the adrenaline left and the thrill of holding another man's life in my hands faded away that I was able to feel the gaping hole of truth.

There's still a sickness in me too.

So I went home, and I beat it out.

The cycle continues to this day, but none of it—not a single moment of that anger—compares to the fury that's coursing through me at the sight of another man touching Amaya in the private rooms at the Chapel and her *liking* it.

They're both lucky that she came to her senses before I could rip open the curtain and tear his eyeballs from his sockets. Even now, as I wait for her in the back alley, I'm shaking with the unsteady feeling.

I pinch the bridge of my nose, and visions of her eyes closed, mouth parted, and chest flushed with her arousal flash through my mind, my chest burning with jealousy.

Footsteps crunch over the gravel, the slush of melted ice audible as someone walks close by. My back straightens from where I'm leaned against the wall, hidden beside the large green dumpster.

It stinks, but I ignore the stench.

And then there that enfoiré is, standing at the edge of the building, watching the employee entrance like a dog waiting for its master.

My teeth grind together.

Is he waiting for her?

He shouldn't be allowed to breathe the same air as her, let alone touch her. And just because I can't have her doesn't mean anyone else can.

I breathe deeply, trying to find my center or a justification for why I should absolutely walk out there and take this man's life, for any reason *other* than touching what I wish I could have. I cannot take a soul for selfish gain.

He's married, I reason with myself. That much is obvious by the gold wedding band on his finger, and adultery *is* a sin.

Righteousness swarms through my veins, and I straighten my spine, flexing my fingers in my gloves as my purpose locks in place.

This man needs his demons freed.

Before I can make another move, Amaya comes rushing out the back door, my hand flying to my chest when I see her. The pinch of my heart turns to indignation when I see the man move forward, gripping her *again* with his filthy fingers and pulling her against him like he deserves her warmth.

He pushes her into the concrete wall and then drags her farther around the corner, hidden from view and away from the security cameras lining the parking lot, and the burning in my chest explodes in a fiery blast.

I don't have any weapons on me. Honestly, I never do. Part of the satisfaction comes from experiencing the bones breaking and cartilage crunching beneath my hands. The act of *feeling* the demons detaching from the soul and scampering back to their place in hell beside the devil is all part of the whole.

But now, I fear, I *am* the devil.

My fist slams against the side of the large green dumpster, the boom echoing down the alley, and then I'm walking toward them before I can stop myself, a red haze clinging to my vision and envy scratching against my skin.

I barely notice when Amaya gets free from his grasp and races away, I'm so laser-focused on my goal.

He moves to follow, but then I'm there, my gloved hand wrapping around the back of his neck and tugging harshly, his short and stocky frame flying through the air until it's *him* that's shoved against the brick.

"What the fuck?" he yelps.

He struggles almost immediately, and the scabbed-over wounds on my back stretch and rip, making me suck in a sharp breath. But the pain fuels me.

He is merciful.

My forearm presses into the man's windpipe as I shush him.

"Shh, mort vivant," I murmur quietly as I increase the pressure on his throat.

My other hand reaches down and grips his disgusting prick, enraged that it got hard for her. That it was *so* close to her sweet and sinful cunt—the one that I'm *dying* to taste.

I twist, trying to rip it off his body, until his face turns red and his mouth opens in a silent scream. I assume it would be louder, but his vocal cords are compressed by the immense pressure of me cutting off his air supply with my forearm.

"Tell me, do you pray?" My voice is low and silky, and I let his groin go, moving my free hand up to pat the side of his cheek instead. "Non, it doesn't matter," I continue. "I want you to know something." Leaning in, I press my lips against the side of his ear, his body flailing against my grasp. "You will die tonight."

As soon as I release the pressure on his throat, he drops to the ground, his hands flying to his groin and cupping while he writhes in pain.

I step forward, my shadow looming over him, nothing but a single flickering yellow streetlamp there to illuminate his fear.

"I–I...*please*," he stutters.

His begging makes me smile, but I need him to stay quiet. Reaching around my neck, I unwrap my long scarf and shove it into his mouth until he's gagging on the fabric.

He groans, although it's muffled, and I crouch down, my knee pressing into his sternum and the bottom of my coat dusting along the wet concrete. I reach out, gripping his hand in mine, bending his wrist at an angle that keeps him immobile in my grasp.

"I'm jealous of your hands," I note, resting the palm of mine against his, trying to steal the memory of her skin from his. "And I don't enjoy being envious. It's a nasty emotion."

I bend his pointer finger back harshly until the snap of his bone reverberates off the brick.

He screams but it's barely audible behind the makeshift gag.

"If you stop fighting, this will go faster," I muse, leaning more of my body weight into him while I straighten his middle finger and repeat the snapping motion. A rush of satisfaction floods through me at the sound of the fracture.

Another muffled scream.

And then a different noise, one in the distance but close enough to cause concern. Muted laughter and voices.

Sighing, I glance back down to my victim, disappointment mixing with the adrenaline when I realize I'll need to end this quicker than I'd like. Normally, I'd have ensured we were in a place more private, but this kill is fueled by passion, and it's made me sloppy.

I release his mangled fingers and drop them to the ground where they fall limp to the side. His eyes are bloodshot, tears slipping down the side of his cheek and hitting the concrete beneath him, and I cluck my tongue.

"A quick death is more than you deserve."

Leaning in, I slip the scarf from his mouth and wrap it around his throat. I crisscross the ends, one in each hand, and pull, soaking in the way his body jerks and flails beneath me as his throat is crushed from the soft fabric. His eyes bulge, and his mouth parts.

The sound of him unable to breathe and the sight of him realizing these are his last moments make my cock harden and my spine tingle with pleasure.

It's erotic taking a life.

And then he falls silent, his body dropping limp until he's prone and still on the cold, wet ground.

It's not enough to temper the jealousy of having Amaya on his lap and in his grasp, but it will have to do.

Standing up, I brush down the front of my pants and rebutton my coat. There's wetness seeping down my back from where a few of my newer lashes split open, but I ignore them. They'll be worse by the end of the night anyway.

I don't bother to clean up the body, instead heaving him into the giant dumpster and leaving him there to rot, just like he deserves.

When I make my way back to Festivalé, I debate on heading straight to Amaya's. To suffocate her the same way I did him. It isn't fair that she gets to live while torturing me this way.

But I'm starting to realize that when it comes to her, I am weak in every way that matters. And I'm wondering if I'll be able to kill her at all.

CHAPTER 19

Amaya

"DID YOU HAVE FUN WITH MISS GABBY?" QUINTEN
says, hopping out of his occupational therapist's room. "*I had
fun.*"

Gabby walks over, her amber-colored eyes sparkling as we
watch him prance down the hall. "He did a great job today. We
worked with spatial awareness, and I got him halfway into the
body tube and rocked him back and forth. He loved it."

My brows rise. "How many times did he want to get out?"

"Only a few." Her grin spreads.

I throw my phone into my purse and dig out Dalia's car keys,
thankful she lent me her ride for the day so we don't have to trudge
through the slush to make it to the bus station. I'm eager to leave
before Abby, the owner of Little Hands and Hearts Therapy—
which is where we are right now—comes into the hallway and
asks me if I've been getting her messages.

"Hey, did Abby talk to you?" Gabby questions.

My stomach drops. "Nope."

Gabby nods. "I think she needed to talk to you about some

insurance stuff. Probably no big deal. I think there was some mix-up with what they'd cover for Quin."

I roll my eyes and sigh, putting on the same front I always do, pretending it's a simple misunderstanding. But Quinten's care is hard for me financially, and I can't always make my part of the payments. Insurance *does* cover most of it, but they fight me harder because I don't have Quinten in ABA therapy.

But ABA therapy doesn't *work* for Quin. Play therapy does.

Besides, insurance is a scam, made specifically to ruin my fucking life, but even I know it still needs to be paid. *I will pay for it*, I console myself. I feel guilty enough I'm only able to bring him in twice a week and barely able to handle the co-pay on that.

Anger buzzes beneath my skin when I think of all I *could* do if it weren't for fucking Parker.

My phone starts to vibrate in my hand at the same time as Quinten runs up to me and pulls on the sleeve of my arm. "Ready to go home?" he asks.

"Let's roll, dude." I smile at Gabby and slip my phone into my pocket. "See you next week."

She tosses a wave and I follow Quinten down the carpeted hallway where he's skipping his way to the exit.

My phone vibrates again, but despite the salted sidewalks, the concrete's still a little slippery, and I don't want Quinten to trip or for me to fall and take him down with me, so I ignore it.

Probably just Dalia checking in anyway, and we're about to see her.

Or maybe it's Parker, who I definitely *don't* want to talk to right now.

I get Quinten buckled in and set up with his headphones and music, and then we're off, nothing but the roads and the silence, leaving plenty of room for me to ruminate in my thoughts. It's been a few days, and I haven't been back to work. I've made excuses with my boss, saying that I'm sick, but Gabby bringing up the insurance issue is a stark reminder that I really can't afford to not be bringing in nightly money.

It's just…every time I think about going back in, I imagine Andrew showing up to finish what he started.

My phone rings again, vibrating in the center console right as we pull into the open space in front of our apartment.

I barely have the key in the lock when it's swinging open, Dalia's wide and frazzled eyes meeting mine. "Where the hell have you been?"

The look on her face makes my stomach drop. "Quin's therapy. Why? What's wrong?"

Quinten hops in place beside me before slipping between Dalia's body and the doorframe to disappear into the living room. She doesn't even spare him a glance, and now I'm really concerned.

"I tried to call you. I've *been* trying to call you, Amaya. Jesus Christ." She reaches out, gripping my forearm tightly.

"Miss Paquette?" A deep voice comes from behind Dalia.

She sighs when I look around her, seeing the two men standing in our kitchen.

I push her to the side and make my way in the house. My eyes immediately find Quinten, who's in the living room, side-eyeing the strangers but keeping his distance.

"Miss Paquette?" the man on the right says again.

"Who's asking?" I don't like random men in our apartment when it's supposed to be our safe place.

"I'm Detective Fuller, and this is Detective Allan," the same man says, his graying brows furrowing as he gestures toward his partner. "We'd just like to talk to you for a minute, if you don't mind."

I cross my arms and look at Quinten then Dalia before jerking my head toward the living room to let her know she should keep him occupied. She nods and sucks on her lips before moving, and I make my way closer to the detectives, a sick feeling creeping into my stomach and up my throat.

Is this about my mother? Ridiculous. It's been years.

"Sure," I finally reply, reaching into the fridge to grab the creamer before I turn to make a pot of coffee. "Either of you thirsty?"

Detective Fuller smiles, his thin lips stretching across his tan face as he shakes his head. "We won't take up too much of your time."

Nodding, I reach up to grab the coffee grounds and start scooping them into the filter. "What can I do for you two?"

Detective Allan pipes in, his blue eyes sharp and his voice clipped as short as his buzzed hair. "Where were you three nights ago around the time of one forty-five?"

I pause with the grounds halfway poured, my brows drawing in.

What the hell?

"Uh…at work, probably."

Detective Fuller frowns in a way that highlights the deep set of wrinkles around his mouth. "At the Chapel."

My heart stutters. This is starting to border heavily on invasive territory. These men aren't from Festivalé—at least I've never seen them—but if they know where I work, that means other people might know too.

The thought makes my stomach cramp.

"That's right," I confirm.

"And what time would you say you left for the night?"

I spin around completely, leaning against the counter and crossing my arms over my chest. "I'm not sure. I think I got home around three? It was kind of a hectic night."

Detective Allan lifts a brow, rubbing the salt-and-pepper scruff that sprinkles his chin. "Was it?"

I shrug, biting my lips.

"Do you have anyone who can corroborate that time frame, Miss Paquette?" Detective Allan questions.

"I'm sorry. I'm just a little confused," I say, pinching the bridge of my nose. "What is all this about?"

My eyes flick past them into the living room where Dalia is coloring with Quinten, her gaze firmly on us. My chest tightens. I don't want her to hear about what happened with Andrew; in fact, I've been actively trying to forget anything happened, but the more questions these guys ask, the more I think this all might be connected to the other night with him.

But how would they even know?

Detective Fuller blows out a breath, his eyes cataloging what seems like every single movement of mine before he looks around at the kitchen. "Small place, huh?"

I cross my arms. "And?"

He lifts a shoulder. "Decent money at the Chapel?"

"What's that have to do with *anything*, Detective?" I snap.

He chuckles, shaking his head. "Do you know an Andrew Gleeson, Miss Paquette?"

"Yeah, yes." I nod, my heartbeat pulsing in the side of my neck. "He comes into the club."

"And you dance for him?"

I swallow, unease swirling through my veins. "Sometimes."

"Your boss, Phillip, said you were his favorite. That when he was there, no one else could ever get anywhere near you."

My muscles tense. I'm not sure what these detectives want or what's going on, but if they're talking to Phillip...

This whole situation is weird.

"Listen, Detectives, not to be rude, but it's been a long day and will be an even longer night, so if it's all the same to you..." I wave my arm between them. "I'd like you to leave."

"Unfortunately, it's not that simple." Detective Fuller steps closer, the heel of his dress shoe clicking on the tile. "You see, Miss Paquette, Andrew Gleeson is dead. And you were the last person he was seen with."

CHAPTER 20

Amaya

I'VE NEVER ACTUALLY BEEN INSIDE A POLICE station before, and for some reason, after Detective Fuller asked if I'd come to the precinct, I expected to stay in Festivalé. Instead, we drove to Coddington Heights.

Makes sense Andrew would go to a local strip club.

He's dead.

I'm not torn up over it. Honestly, I never am with things like this. Sometimes I wonder if there's something wrong with me because when it comes to death, everyone grows sick with grief, but my insides stay a steady numb slate like a hard drive that's been wiped clean.

I feel a similar sensation now, except there's a fog of curiosity looming over the situation. I'm assuming they're calling me in because I was the last person to see him, but other than the information I already gave, I'm not sure how I can be of much help.

Serves the prick right for trying to assault me, quite frankly.

But the farther we move into the station, the heavier my body feels, and when they lead me to a small room with a metal table and chairs, a wrecking ball blows apart the numbness. Because this feels a lot like I'm a suspect.

Breathing deeply as I sit down, I tell myself that I don't even know if there's been foul play, and it doesn't do me any good to jump to conclusions. They probably just want to ask me some questions, which makes sense if I was the last person Andrew was with and now he's dead.

The back of my mouth sours, and my knee hits the bottom of the table every time my foot taps on the ground.

I'm jittery. *Does that make me look guilty?*

"Do you want something to drink?" Detective Allan asks, closing the door behind him.

"I'm fine," I reply. "Am I…I'm not—"

I don't finish the sentence, because I'm afraid of what they'll say, and right now I only have assumptions. I shift in my seat, staring down at my hands, fingers tangling in my lap.

"You seem nervous," Fuller notes, slinking across the table and tapping his fingers on the metal top.

"You guys aren't really forthcoming with information, and this all feels very…aggressive. Wouldn't you be nervous?"

He shrugs. "Not if I was innocent."

"I *am* innocent," I snap back before the weight of his statement sinks in. "Wait, am I a *suspect*? Was Andrew—was he murdered?"

My lungs clamp down tight in panic.

"We're just ruling out everything we can, Amaya." He smiles. "Can I call you Amaya?"

I think I nod, but I can't be sure. My vision narrows into a tiny circle, edged by black. My chest is heaving and I'm certain my heart's beating at a rate that *can't* be sustainable for a long period of time.

Maybe I'll just drop dead of a heart attack right here.

That only makes my chest squeeze tighter because if I'm gone, what will happen to Quinten?

"It's all right, *Amaya*," Detective Fuller says, dragging the chair beside his partner out and sitting down. He leans back, one knee propped on the other like he's relaxed. Like he has all the time in the world, and this is just an average conversation. "Just take a few deep breaths, and tell me about that night."

My head is spinning but I try to think logically. I *know* I'm innocent, but I also know at face value I'm a low-income stripper with almost no family and no friends. It'd be so easy for them to pin this on me, lock me up, and throw away the key. And I don't know *what* the hell to say to convince them otherwise, because my last interaction with Andrew doesn't exactly scream I'd like him alive.

Slowly, I take a deep breath and force my head up until I'm looking Detective Fuller in the eyes.

"I think I'd like a lawyer."

––––––––

I've been sitting in silence for the past two hours.

My ass is numb from this metal chair, and my ears ring from how quiet it's been. There's a long wall of mirrors on the far side of the room, and I cross my arms, staring directly into them. I just *know* somebody is on the other side watching my every move.

Anxiety slowly eats away my insides like maggots on rotten food.

There's been plenty of time for my thoughts to spiral until my cuticles are picked clean and my lips are chewed through.

The door opening jars me from where I've been burning a hole through the two-way mirror, and I twist toward the noise.

Anticipation fills my chest…

And in walks Florence Gammond.

"Amaya Paquette."

She looks as professional as ever, a dark-blue pencil skirt with a crisp white blouse tucked in at the waist. She saunters over, sitting down across from me with a smirk. "Who knew I'd be defending you?"

"No." The word passes my lips without even having to think about it. I look toward the mirror, sitting forward, jabbing my finger in the air. I *know* somebody is watching me. "I want someone else."

Florence shakes her head and sighs, pinching the bridge of her nose like I'm an annoyance. "Who are you talking to, Amaya?"

I look back to her, the panic I've been trying so goddamn hard to keep subdued rearing up and smacking me in the face. "Don't belittle me, Florence. This is a *major* conflict of interest."

A slow grin spreads across her face, and she leans in. "You're right, it is. But I'm your only choice. Take it or leave it. Now… tell me about the other night. When you were working at…" She looks down at her file and then back up. "The *Chapel*."

My stomach sours.

Fuck. Fuck. Fuck.

I press my lips together instead of saying what I want to say because there's no chance in hell that Florence Gammond is going to represent me.

"I'm not telling you anything, Florence. Get out of here. I don't want you."

She cocks her head. "It's either me or no one, honey. You made your bed, and I can't wait to see you lie in it. Does Parker know you've been stripping?"

I grit my teeth. "Don't talk to me about Parker."

"Can't imagine he'd still want you if he knew." She sneers down at me. "Although you'd think everything else about you would have turned him off, so who knows what he wants?"

Her words burn.

"You're right," I say. "Easier to know what he *doesn't*."

I shouldn't goad her, but God, she pisses me off.

Her eyes flick to the mirror and then to me before she smiles tightly and lowers her voice. "Keep pushing me, you piece of trash, and I'll make sure you're locked up and never heard from again."

My heart falters.

"Can't wait to see how Quinten fares in foster care."

I stand up so quickly the chair screeches on the tile floor. "Get fucked, Florence."

"Oh, *sweet girl*," she jibes. "No one's as fucked as you're about to be."

She laughs as I march to the door and throw it open, storming out into the hallway where Detective Fuller and his partner are lounging against the wall, the former stirring a stick in his paper cup of coffee.

"Do I have to stay here?" I ask, marching up to him.

My lungs are cramping, and I feel like I'm on the verge of a breakdown.

Detective Fuller straightens, looking past me to the room and then back. "Miss Pa—"

I throw my hand in the air, cutting him off. "Legally, I mean. Do I *have* to stay here?"

He clears his throat. "No."

"Great."

I shove by him, making my way outside, and I don't stop

moving until I'm a block away. A sob threatens to tear free from my throat, but I shove it back down because I'll be damned if I let Florence fucking Gammond be the reason I can't hold it together.

My fingers are shaky as I pull out my phone and dial Dalia's number, and it isn't until she picks me up that I break down entirely, because I have no clue what the hell I'm going to do.

CHAPTER 21

Cade

"I'M SORRY. I DIDN'T KNOW WHERE ELSE TO GO."

The words are out of Amaya's mouth before I even have the door fully opened.

It's almost ten o'clock at night, and I was just settling in to work on this Sunday's homily when there was a knock on the door. Nobody—besides Amaya—comes to my cottage in the back beyond Jeremiah when he needs guidance, and even then, we usually meet in the office at the church, so seeing Amaya isn't that surprising. I glance around the open space behind her, making sure there aren't any prying eyes, before I move to the side and usher her in, quickly closing the door and locking it for good measure. I wince when I turn to face her, the few day-old wounds on my back and inner thighs screaming from the sudden movement, but I don't want her to pick up on my discomfort, so I bite the inside of my cheek until I taste blood and move slowly in her direction.

"What's wrong?" I ask, stopping when I'm a few steps away. I don't dare get too close.

I've thought of little else since the night I killed for her, because as much as I try to justify it, now that the green haze has lifted from my eyes, what else can it be called but a crime of passion?

I've sought penance ever since, although I don't feel remorse for killing him.

I feel guilt that I *don't*.

Still, I haven't gone to seek Amaya out since. I haven't given in.

And I know that I need to get rid of her permanently before I let my addiction to her overtake my entire life. I need to rip it out from the root, making sure it's dead and gone.

But either way, that pathetic man deserved to die, and I'd do it again.

Amaya's frazzled, her eyes wide and red-rimmed, and her hair is a tangled mess, like she's been running her hand through the locks and tugging.

She's upset.

My chest pulls.

"Amaya," I soothe, taking another large step toward her, because I can't *not*.

My fingers tense, wanting to reach out and cup her cheek. I'd turn her face up to mine and force her to look me in the eyes. Then I'd soak in how warm her skin felt and how her pouty mouth would part in invitation if I tugged the smallest bit on her chin.

My cock twitches, and I slip my hands into my pockets instead.

She shakes her head, her gaze growing glossy. "I don't know what to do or wh-where to go, and I know you're not the person I should be coming to, but I don't *have* anyone else."

Now it's her who takes a step closer, and it's so sudden that I panic, jerking back, pulling the scabs apart on a particularly nasty lash across my side. I can't contain the sharp intake of breath.

Her eyes grow wide. "Are you okay?"

I shake off her concern. "It's nothing."

"That doesn't look like nothing." She points to the grimace on my face.

She takes another step forward and I react without thinking, reaching out and gripping her arm tightly. We both freeze when my touch registers, the air thickening around us until it chokes.

My hand wraps entirely around the bone of her wrist, finger-tips meeting on either side, and I'm reminded of just how delicate and small she really is.

I could snap her in half with a simple flick. It would be easy. As effortless as breathing.

Would she drop to her knees? Fall to the floor and beg for mercy?

I quite like that idea.

Her hand flexes as though she's trying to either escape or move closer. Which one, I'm not sure. If she's smart, she'd choose the former.

"Don't," I say, squeezing her close for a split second and then shoving her away roughly, ridding myself of the temptation to do more. My heart pounds as I imagine wrapping my fingers around her throat, just to see if it feels as vulnerable as the delicate feel of her wrist.

Would it be as easy to snap?

She shrinks back, almost like she can read my thoughts.

"Tell me what you need, or leave."

She scoffs, rubbing her wrist and glaring at me. "I shouldn't have come here in the first place."

"That's right, you shouldn't have."

She blinks. "Why are you being so… You know what? Never mind."

She spins around, but before she can make it far, I'm on her, my front flush to her back as I press her into the wall next to the door. Her body tenses against me, and I bring my arms up, caging her in, aching to touch her with every fiber of my being.

I can't *control* either part of myself: the monster who wants to fuck her or the man who wants her dead.

My breath makes the strands of her hair flutter, and I lean in close, licking my lips, wondering if I'll be able to taste her in the air. "Why am I being so *what*, petite pécheresse?"

"So *mean*," she whispers, her voice cracking. "You've never been so mean before."

I give in, the pull to her so strong it floods my veins and makes me high with need. My hand leaves the wall and sinks into her hair, fisting the waves and tugging until her head falls back against my chest. From this vantage point, I can track the delicate veins of her throat, and my mouth parts, going dry as I watch her swallow.

Her breaths come in sharp pants, her windpipe tempting me to crush it.

My fingers twitch at my side.

It would be so easy.

Do it.

I raise my arm up slowly, my body buzzing from anticipation, but then a small moan escapes her, and I drop it back down, fisting her hair tighter with my other hand instead.

"Tu me rends fou," I rasp.

I splay my palm across her stomach, dragging her into me until her ass moves back and meets the thick, hard length of my cock. I groan, my head falling back.

"Cade…" she whispers.

"Do you see what you've done?" I murmur, bending low until my lips scrape against the shell of her ear, my fingers twisting in her wavy, dark strands. "What you've reduced me to?"

I thrust my hips against her, my eyes rolling as my hand slides up the front of her stomach and then over her chest, resting on top of her heart. Her life force drums out a quickened rhythm beneath my palm.

Do it.

In a millisecond, I'm cupping her throat, my thumb stroking her neck to the beat of her heart.

She could become nothing more than a painted memory on my fingers, one I can wash away like chalk in the rain.

I tighten my grip and my balls draw up, my stomach tightening as she sucks in a sharp breath.

Do it, I hear again.

My fingers dig into her skin.

Just a little more now and I could be free. How blessed would it be to feel my obsession drain away along with the light in her eyes?

Out of all the demons I've ever encountered, she has to be the worst. She tortures me until I'm sure I'd miss the pain if she wasn't near.

"Tell me, petite pécheresse, have you thought of your priest?"

She swallows, her throat moving beneath my hand, and I imagine what it would feel like if my cock was fucking it instead. If I'd feel it bulging from the inside while she drank me down.

I loosen my grip, my priorities changing as my mind flips from hatred to lust.

"Tell me," I demand.

"Yes," she breathes out.

My mind goes blank, a primal need rushing through me.

I *need* to touch her.

I *need* to feel her against me.

I *need* to erase what any other man has made her feel, to ruin her for even God, until the only one she can pray to is me.

But it's not my fault. *It's God's for not making man as strong as the devil.*

My hand glides back down her body, memorizing every single curve until I dip in the waistband of her skirt. Precum leaks from my throbbing cock when I meet warm and wet flesh instead of the fabric I expect.

"Fille sale," I groan. "So wet for me."

She moans when I graze my thumb across her clit, fingers slipping effortlessly between her folds from how soaked she is. I bite down on the inside of my cheek until copper floods my mouth.

It's been *so* long since I've touched a woman sexually.

"*Merde.*"

I slide inside her, her inner walls hugging my fingers like a vise and making me hang on to my control by a simple, flimsy thread. I am…*lost* to her.

My thumb continues to stroke her clit until it swells, both of her hands wrapping around my wrist so tightly that her nails break my skin.

The pain makes a small spurt of cum leak from my tip.

I sink my teeth into her neck, her taste exploding on my tongue like ambrosia, and when she starts moving her hips against me, I thrust back, pushing her into the wall and finger fucking her until she cries out.

My other hand, still tangled in her hair, pulls sharply, making her back bow against me, and I swear I could die right now and burn in hell forever as long as I kept the memory of feeling her come undone beneath my hands.

"Cette chatte est à moi," I whisper before swiping my tongue across the expanse of her neck.

"Oh God," she moans.

I pump my fingers harder, my own muscles tensing, my cock growing so thick it's about to burst through my pants. How incredible it would feel to rip away her skirt and sink deep inside her. To split her apart, feel her legs wrapped around my hips and her cunt squeezing me until I paint her womb with my cum.

"Come for me," I command.

My thumb presses down on her clit and she moans, long and loud, her body vibrating as her walls contract around me.

The sounds pouring from her lips send me over the edge, and I explode, blinding white light bursting behind my eyelids as my dick pulses, sharp contractions that drain what feels like years of pent-up sexual frustration. It's hot and messy and I've never felt so much pleasure or relief.

We both stand still for a few moments after, my grip in her hair so tight I'm unsure if I'll be able to untangle my fingers. I rest my forehead in the crook of her neck, my skin sticky from exertion as I try to regulate my breathing.

As soon as I do, the guilt of my actions hits hard.

I push away from her, my limbs cold and emotions wild.

"Leave," I demand.

"I…what?" she asks, spinning around and running her hands through her hair.

"*You*"—I point my finger at her—"are nothing more than a

temptress, a *witch* sent to lead me astray. Just like your mother said."

"Of course you've heard about my mother." And then she laughs.

As though *any* of this is funny.

I rush forward so fast she stumbles into the wall.

"Do you think this is a joke? That me forsaking my vows is something I take lightly?"

She shakes her head, her eyes growing round and wary.

"I have given my life to Him, and *you* come around, *torturing* me simply by existing. No." I shake my head until my skull rattles. "You're a curse. One that will destroy everything I've worked for."

"Cade," she murmurs, her hand reaching out to grasp my cheek.

I rip myself away before I can feel the warmth of her touch, turning my back on her and gritting my teeth.

"I am not *Cade*. I am Father Cade Frédéric. The priest of Festivalé. And you, Amaya Paquette, are worse than a whore," I spit, refusing to look at her. Refusing to acknowledge the way my heart feels like it's splitting with every word I say. "You are the devil, and I want you out of my sight."

There's a strong pinch in my chest when I hear the door slam, and then my stomach is roiling. I race to the toilet, heaving bile until there's nothing left but the bitter taste of regret.

And although I'm already sore, already beaten, I head to my room, grab my discipline, and strike myself for the sin.

He is merciful.

CHAPTER 22

Amaya

"GET OUT OF BED."

Dalia's voice trickles into my room, and I throw the covers over my head, pretending I don't hear her. I dropped off Quinten at school this morning and headed right back here, diving into my covers and wallowing in despair.

I'm stuck between a rock and a hard place, and I'm cursing God—if he even exists—for placing me in this predicament. I try *so* fucking hard, would do anything for Quinten, and yet here I am, lost and drowning with no way out.

Ideally, there'd be no reason for me to worry about things. I'm *innocent*, and if I had any faith left in humanity, I would believe people could see the overwhelming evidence pointing toward me not being the guilty party and actually try to find the real person.

But I know better than anyone that most people will take the easy way out when given the opportunity, and an exotic dancer with a low income and a lot of enemies is easier to pin things on than admitting you have no leads.

Failing at your job doesn't look good on paper. Unless you're

Florence and your personal vendetta against your client super-sedes your need to win. I'm under no illusion she'd go to bat for me. In fact, I'm pretty sure seeing me locked up and called a murderer would give her more joy than winning a case ever could.

"Maybe she'll surprise us," Dalia said when I told her. I laughed, knowing she was full of shit and trying to be optimis-tic. That optimism disappeared as soon as I filled her in on our conversation.

I knew the minute I saw Florence that it was hopeless, so I latched on to the only thing that's given me any kind of peace, the one person I know I should stay away from but never do. Because like the naive, ridiculous person I am, I trusted him. Trusted the way he showed Quinten decency and was clearly mistaken that him giving me attention meant we'd become almost friends.

And then I fucked that up too.

Or maybe he did.

Honestly, I'm not sure how to rectify the two different halves of Cade Frédéric in my head. The God-loving priest and the filthy Frenchman who had me coming on his fingers. They *seem* the same, but that's impossible.

Either way, the safety net I cast around him disappeared in an instant, like it was ripped away in a storm.

Cade Frédéric isn't *safe*.

He's the danger.

"Amaya, come on, girl. You can't wallow in misery all day," Dalia tries again.

"Bet," I mumble back.

Dalia rips the covers from my head, and I grapple to find them. She gets to me before I can, pulling me into her arms and rocking me back and forth. A pathetic sob tears from my throat, puncturing the air.

"I know you're scared," she whispers. "But I've got you. We'll figure it out."

I pull back, pinching my eyes closed to try and stem the tears. I feel like a crybaby. "I'm not scared for me. I just…"

Dalia knows. Of course she does. Out of anyone in the world, she's the *only* one who gets me fully.

No matter what happens, I'll survive. I'll persevere, the way I always do.

But I worry for Quinten. He's my whole heart, and if I'm not around to be with him, how can I protect him? Nurture him? Make sure he's able to thrive and be the fucking phenomenal human I know he is?

"Can't wait to see how Quinten fares in foster care."

Emotion chokes my throat, and I slide my hands down from Dalia's shoulders until they're gripping her hands, and I squeeze tightly. "If things don't work out… Promise me you'll take care of Quin, Dal," I plead.

She protests, shaking her head, her eyes sorrowful and wide.

"No," I say sharply. "*Promise* me."

"Amaya…" She trails off, looking to the side. "I *can't.*"

I rear back, my eyes growing round as disbelief pours through me.

"I want to," she rushes out. "But how can I promise something I don't know I can do? People like us? We don't have the power here, you know that. And I don't want you to hate me forever if I'm not able to stop things."

Her face crumples, and my chest caves in along with it.

I know she's right. I *hate* that she is, but the odds aren't in our favor. They're with the rich. The prosperous. The lucky.

"I'll already hate myself enough," she adds, her voice breaking. "But I promise you I'll try. I'll fight with everything I am to keep Quin safe and with me."

She says it like a reassurance, but her earlier words have already branded their truths on me like a tattoo.

We don't have the power.

But I know someone who does.

Steely determination locks into place like a vault, one agonizing click at a time until my spine is ramrod straight and my salty tears are drying on my cheeks.

I sniff, nodding as my tongue runs over the front of my teeth. "Everything will be okay, Dalia."

Dalia's head cocks, and she wipes beneath her eyes with the back of her hand. "Wh-what?"

Jumping out of bed, I run my palms down my crumpled clothes, resignation thrumming in my veins.

I know what I have to do.

"You said it yourself. We don't have any power." My jaw sets. "So I'm going to someone who does."

Selling my soul feels different than I thought it would.

I'm not sure what I expected. Maybe despair. For depression to sink its devastating claws in and pin me down. But instead, there's…nothing.

No pain left from Father Cade turning out to be a complete toxic waste.

No fear of what will happen to Quinten if I don't get to stick around.

Just a smooth, clear path for me to walk down. Shiny, fortified, bulletproof glass. My hands aren't even shaking as I sit patiently in the waiting room of Errien Enterprises, Parker's personal assistant sneering at me as she click-clacks on her computer.

"Amaya, what a lovely surprise," Parker says, his voice sounding muffled, like my head is underwater.

I stand up and force a smile so wide it strains the muscles in my cheeks, and when he moves close enough, I lean in, pressing a chaste kiss on his cheek and lingering.

It makes me want to vomit.

His body stiffens, most likely in surprise. I've never been the one to initiate closeness before.

"Can we talk in your office?" I glance at his personal assistant, then peer back at him through my lashes. "Or somewhere private?"

His eyes gleam, curiosity rimming the bright blue irises, and he nods, his hand pressing against the small of my back as he leads me through the doors.

Nausea cramps my stomach, slipping through the numbness, and I swallow around the sour tang in the back of my mouth.

His door is partially open, and it's only once I'm fully inside his office that I stop short, realizing we aren't alone.

Father Cade sits in a chair, his eyes blazing as they lock on to where Parker is touching me.

Of course he's here. He seems to always be everywhere that I am.

His leg is crossed over the opposite knee, his stature completely relaxed. There's a type of dominance he exudes simply by *being*, and I wonder if that's something every priest has or if it's uniquely him.

My heart—the traitorous bitch—flutters when our eyes lock.

I break our stare immediately, the reminder of him spitting harsh insults making me *feel* too much. Right now, I need to be a blank slate. I'm not sure I'll survive what I'm about to do otherwise.

Besides, *fuck* Cade Frédéric. He's a hypocrite. A bad priest and an even worse man.

And now I know better than to let him in.

But the way he's looking at me right now makes it hard. His gaze reeks of concern. Of something dark and deep, like he's tearing through my skin and staring directly into my soul. I wonder if he can tell my world has shifted like tectonic plates, leaving me hanging on a jagged cliff's edge with no way out.

I wonder if he'd care.

"Is everything all right, Amaya?"

Cade's voice skirts around me, tempting with its silky caress. I bat it away, my teeth clenching as I hold on to the flare of anger when I think of the things he said. The way he found out about my mother and then used her words against me, flinging them like a thousand blades into my heart.

"Father, you'll have to forgive me for cutting this short," Parker interrupts. "But when a beautiful woman shows up and wants some time, you always say yes. You know how it is." He laughs. "Actually, maybe you don't."

I hold back a snort, and Cade's brow quirks, like he finds this whole thing *amusing*. He chuckles low and dark, and the hurt morphs to rage, snapping like piranhas.

The audacity of this man. Of this *fake* in a clerical collar, pretending to have a direct line to the deity.

Good with his fingers though.

A sharp shot of desire rips through me, and my nostrils flare.

Cade's face changes as he watches me. And somehow, I just

know that *he* knows what's going through my mind. His stare turns so intense it scorches up my side and melts into my skin.

There's a few moments of silence, just long enough to be awkward, and then he smirks, *the bastard*, and stands up.

His every movement is smooth and controlled, and I ache to see what he's like when he's unrestrained. To see him unravel the way he made me, just so I can callously throw him in the dirt and stomp on his ego when it's done.

"Of course, Parker. You can stop by the church. My doors are always open."

I clench my jaw, not looking over, remembering how he's said those words to me before.

Clearly, that's another lie.

"I can come back," I offer. But I know Parker won't send me away. He never does, even when I would wish for him to.

"Don't be ridiculous, Amaya," Parker snips. "Father Cade was just trying to convince me that I should donate to the Festival of Fools instead of getting it shut down completely."

Cade hums as he moves closer to where I am. I stiffen, his woodsy scent wafting through the air and little snaps of electricity sizzling off my skin.

He towers over me, and I *hate* how tall he is and how, even if I lift my chin, it only puts me further at his mercy.

"And can I expect to see you at Mass this Sunday, Miss Paquette?"

His voice curls around me like rope, and I imagine taking a knife and sawing through the threads.

"As long as Parker's there," I reply, a little too sweetly.

It's petty, and I'm one hundred percent doing it to make him jealous. Or maybe to get the point across that what happened yesterday means *nothing*. Less than.

His eyes flare, but then he smiles and nods. "I'll be looking for you then, petite pécheresse."

My chest pulls when he leaves, wanting to follow him and demand an apology for what he's said, but I spin toward where Parker is instead.

Parker leans against the lip of his desk, his ankles crossed and blond hair slicked back as he stares at me. He doesn't speak, just waits patiently.

So I take a deep breath and exhale it slowly, coming to terms with the fact that from this moment forward, my life will change. It's a risk, what I'm about to do. Dangerous, and maybe I'll look back on this moment as the second I fucked everything up for good.

But he's my best bet at making sure nothing happens to me. If I'm safe, then so is Quinten, and I'd rather die a thousand deaths than let anything bad ever happen to him.

Closing my eyes, I enjoy the last few moments of my freedom before opening my lids and staring Parker directly in the eyes, telling him everything.

Admitting that I've been working at the Chapel.

That a regular got too bold and ended up dead.

And then I say the one thing I never have.

I say yes to marrying him.

CHAPTER 23

Amaya

"YOU HAVE NOTHING TO WORRY ABOUT, SWEET-heart. Jason is the best defense attorney in the state, not that I think you'll actually need him beyond this preliminary stage. You couldn't have possibly had the strength to do the things that happened to that idiot, and you're not a suspect, just a person of interest. He'll make it go away," Parker assures, his hand touching the back of my neck.

He's been doing that since I became "his" yesterday. Always touching me. A hand on the knee, fingers on the back of my neck, an arm wrapped possessively around my waist. His tongue down my throat.

And I accept it all, keeping Quinten's face in the front of my mind. His *future*. One that I'll be a part of and that may even be better than it was before.

At least that's what I'm reassuring myself with. Parker's a dangerous man, but he's never hurt Quinten.

"Okay," I reply, staying docile, even though everything in my nature is begging me to jerk away from his touch and tell him that this whole thing is bullshit. I'm *innocent*, for God's sake.

"And you'll never go back to that club, Amaya." Parker's voice is stern.

Sucking on my lips, I nod again, letting the bittersweet emotions pour over me. I'll miss my outlet for pole, but to be honest, I didn't want to go back there. Not after what happened.

It's tainted now.

Right now, we're in the back of Parker's town car heading to my apartment. He wants me to move in with him immediately, but I've convinced him to give me time. I need to ease Quinten into things, and I also need to tell Dalia.

She's going to be so fucking pissed.

Parker leans back in his seat, his legs spreading wide like he owns the world.

I suppose he does.

"I'm glad that fucker's dead," he states.

"Of course you are."

He shrugs. "You're mine, Amaya. I don't like people touching my things."

"I'm not a piece of property. *Jesus*," I snap.

His smirk drops, a cold, icy glare taking over his face. "You should be a little more grateful instead of such a bitter bitch."

My lungs cramp from his words.

"You're tainted goods now," he continues. "In fact, I'm not even sure *why* I'm still going through with it. The board of Errien Enterprises won't like that you're on my arm. It'll be bad for business when it comes out that a *stripper* who murdered a man is the one wearing my ring."

The way he says *stripper* makes me want to lunge across the seat and rake my nails down his face. He makes it sound dirty, disgusting, when it's anything but.

"Dancing is real work," I reply. "It put food on my table and paid my bills. If it weren't for *you*, it would have allowed us a cushy life. I won't act ashamed of it. I'll *never* be ashamed of it."

"Doesn't matter now, does it?" Parker's eyes skate down my body, and I feel sick. "In any case, I'm sure you can make up for the loss of my reputation. It's been a long time, sweet girl."

I swallow back the retorts I truly want to make and nod.

The car pulls to a stop outside my apartment, and Parker sneers out the window. "This place is as disgusting as ever."

"It's home," I reply softly, my fingers already on the door handle.

I step out into the cold, my stomach twisting with nerves.

"Don't be long. We have things to do," Parker's voice commands at my back.

Is this how it's going to be from now on? A man controlling my every move, telling me how to look and where to stand and how many minutes to take?

With every step closer to my front door, I feel the reality crashing down on top of me. I'm exchanging one pair of shackles for another.

But what's done is done.

Dalia's sitting on the couch reading a book when I walk in.

She glances up at me and must see something on my face because immediately she drops what she's doing and sighs, leaning back against the couch. It's incredible, the way she just knows what I'm going to do before I do it, so much so that I've joked about the town needing to look closer at whether it's *her* who's the witch.

"Tell me then." Her voice is resigned. She's been waiting since

I got home last night, but I put it off, claiming I was too drained to explain.

My stomach tenses into knots that I'm not sure will ever unravel, but I don't *want* them to untangle, not when they feel like the only thing keeping me together.

"I'm marrying Parker Errien." The words feel fake as they roll off my tongue and I brace myself for her reaction.

"Okay."

I lift my brows, taking a few steps closer now that I know she won't be screaming at me.

"Okay," she repeats, nodding.

"That's all you have to say?" I press. "You're not…surprised? Or worried?"

"What would you like me to say, Amaya? That I think it's a terrible mistake? I don't." She shrugs. "That I think you're being trigger-happy and jumping into this too fast? Maybe. But what other choice do you have?"

I open my mouth to reply but she continues.

"It's no secret Parker's always been obsessed with you. And time isn't really our friend right now. I think Parker's a little bitch just in the general sense, but he's a powerful bitch. If you think he's the answer, then I trust you."

Swallowing back the thick knot in my throat, I walk over to the couch, grabbing her in a bone-crushing hug. "You don't think I'm making a mistake?" I choke out.

She sighs, her hand rubbing small circles on my back. "Probably. But mistakes are part of life, and I'll be here for you through every single one of them."

I pull back, my vision blurring from the relief. "You're the best friend I've ever had."

"I'm your *only* friend." She smiles.

"Even more reason to feel honored," I jest.

I ignore the hollow look that flashes through her eyes, focusing instead on the small smile she paints across her face. "Don't forget about me once you're loaded."

"Please," I scoff. "Quin and I would be lost without you. And you're staying here anyway. I won't let you lose your home just because I won't be in it."

She waves me off. "You want me around when you tell Quin?"

I shake my head, dread dropping in my gut.

Quinten loves routine, and I'm terrified about what he's going to do when I rip him from what he's known and toss him into this new reality.

At least we'll be together.

"No, I'll do it myself."

She nods and the air grows quiet.

"I've gotta go. Parker's waiting. I just...I'll let you know what's going on, okay?"

"Love you, Amaya. You're a good mom, you know?"

My eyes burn. "I'm not a mom."

"You are. In every way that counts." She laughs, shaking her head. "Now leave before I ruin my makeup from crying."

Warmth fills my chest as I make my way back to Parker's car, his driver standing outside in the cold and waiting by my door, offering his hand for me to slip back inside.

Dalia is the true definition of ride or die, and I promise myself to be a better friend to her. I never fully let her in because of my trust issues, but she's proven time and time again that she isn't like other people. She won't leave.

She'll always be here.

"What now?" I ask Parker after I buckle my seat belt.

Parker glances up from his phone, his eyes sparking and his jaw line set in determination. "Now…we have a wedding to plan."

CHAPTER 24

Cade

I HAD HOPED THAT AFTER LOSING CONTROL WITH
Amaya and then beating myself for the mistake, things would get
better. Foolishly, I assumed that small taste would be enough or
that the regret over my actions would drown out everything else.

Instead, it's only gotten worse. Now I imagine her smell
invading my senses, her skin molding beneath my touch, her pink
cunt gripping my fingers and how it would split apart around my
cock.

Before, she was only in my head, a figment of my imagination,
one I fantasized about turning into a reality although I knew I
never would. But now, she's tangible, real and raw and so delicious
that even days after touching her, I still feel her in my hands.

Seeing her swoon over Parker in his office made my insides
quake. I had my entire day planned out: meet with Parker about
the Festival of Fools, then head back to the church to offer
confession.

Instead, after being rudely dismissed from his office once
Amaya arrived, I waited outside Errien Enterprises for two hours

until she appeared, slipping into her roommate's car and driving back to her apartment.

I followed her there of course, my duties to the parish completely forgotten, and I spent the evening in her bushes, watching the way her chest rose and fell with every breath. Wondering if I was part of the nightmares that made her toss and turn all night. Coming to terms with the simple truth that I won't be able to kill her. I would have done it by now if I could, and every second spent in her presence, the urge mutates into something else. Something no less visceral but…softer somehow.

Then, in the early hours of the morning, I went back home to my small cottage, slipped out of my clothes, frigid from standing in the cold, and whipped myself until I blacked out, hating how weak she makes me.

It took everything in me to stay away the following night. But thoughts still overwhelmed me, until I couldn't sleep and had to atone for the way my cock leaked with desire from remembering how she felt around my hand and moaned in my ear.

Today, the pain of my back is so sharp, I can barely stand.

Sister Genevieve's green eyes widen when she opens the front door of the monastery and finds me there, leaning against the doorframe. I meet her gaze, and something pulls sharply in my stomach when I do, but I brush the feeling aside.

She has darkness in her just like me. That's why I chose to come here.

I'm not used to having to depend on anyone else. I don't like others knowing about the spiritual practices and *failures* I have to atone for, but ever since arriving in Festivalé, the lashings have become more common. More severe. And the pain in my back is becoming too much to bear. I know that if I don't get some help with caring for the wounds, infection could easily set in. That's what happens when rope rips open scabs that haven't had time to fully form.

But going to a doctor or hospital is out of the question. I'm known in the community now, and loose lips sink ships, or in this case, take away the mystery that shrouds me. I don't want people to know anything beyond what I decide for them to, and having multiple eyes on my self-inflicted lashings would be the opposite of controlling the narrative.

What would they think if they knew their priest was so weak that he needs to beat himself to repent? That I'm nothing more than a man disregarding my vows of chastity and being led blindly into lust? I suppose no worse than what they'd think if they knew the truth about what else I get up to in the dead of night.

But I'm much better at keeping that part of myself tucked away and out of sight.

The point is there would be no respect and far too many questions. And maybe there's a small part of me that doesn't want Amaya to become the center of any more hate. If there's hatred at her doorstep, it will be doled out by *me*, not by anyone else. The very thought of someone disrespecting her sends me flying from calm to anger.

I won't have it. Not until I figure out what to do with her now that I've accepted that I can't go through with killing her.

The one thing I *do* know is that I need to keep my hands to myself. I cannot give in to temptation again. I won't survive the lashings otherwise. But part of me fears I'm too weak to resist. My thoughts have only gotten worse since I've had her cum on my fingers and her heartbeat in my palm.

"Father Cade," Sister Genevieve says, moving to the side of the open door so I have room to walk in.

"I need your discretion." I don't bother with pleasantries. It will only waste both our time.

Moving past her, I step briskly into the small living space. It looks the same as the last time I was here, a small log fireplace crackling in the corner and warm lighting that casts a cozy glow throughout the room.

"You have it." Her eyes are curious as they take me in.

I stand taller and nod before stripping off my gloves and coat, folding it methodically and placing it on the back of the couch before reaching for the hem of my shirt and lifting.

Her eyes widen for a split second before she masks the look, and when I spin around, showing her my back, I hear her sharp intake of breath.

I haven't looked in the mirror because I know what I'll see. There's barely an inch of unmarred flesh left. Some scars from years ago—starting when I was a young child—to the most recent ones that still trickle with blood when my skin pulls too tight.

There are several tense moments of quiet before Genevieve moves to my side, her warm hand gripping my forearm and squeezing in comfort. "Don't sit down. Your bleeding will stain the furniture."

I don't move a muscle until she returns, holding a first aid kit and a small wooden stool that she plops down next to me before looking pointedly, clearly implying the seat is for me.

My back stings as I move to sit, and I wince as she perches behind me and starts to dab something cold and wet on the wounds. It stings, and the pain makes my eyelids flutter, a sick sense of satisfaction rushing through me, the way it always does when I can *feel* the atonement staining my skin.

We don't speak while she works, but there's a comfort in the air, and I know without a doubt that I can trust her. And I know that I'll return. Part of me wishes that she wouldn't stay here in solitude so I could have her at my side in the parish to tend to my secrets whenever I need.

She stitches a few of the deeper cuts closed and then spreads a thick, gooey substance that makes the sharp ache ebb away, and I sigh in relief, feeling better than I have in days. She dresses the wounds and then I'm done, being careful as I redress.

"You'll need to take it easy for the next few weeks," she says, her eyes sharp and sure. "You can stay here with me if you'd like."

I pull my gloves back on and move toward the front door, suddenly desperate to leave. I know she's right, but I'm not sure if I *can* take it easy. And I definitely don't want to stay here with her. "That won't be necessary."

"Father." She stops me with a hand on my arm, and I spin to face her, looking down at the top of her head. "It won't do you any favors to hurt yourself until you can't stand. Whatever it is you're doing...*stop*. At least until your body can heal."

Gritting my teeth until my jaw tenses, I give a sharp nod and then head outside to my car.

It's Saturday, and after a morning of confession, I'm in my office, preparing the homily for tomorrow, when an email pings through on my computer. Sighing when I see the name of my superior, Bishop Lamont, on the screen, I drop the pen and click the mouse to open the message.

Father Cade,

Mr. Errien has kindly reached out to inform us that he has upcoming nuptials and would like them at the Catholic church. I've already briefed him on what that will entail, and he would like extra precautionary measures taken for his new bride, including one-on-one lessons to rehabilitate her image. I've assured him we'll do everything in our power to accommodate his requests, including making sure she's an upstanding woman of faith and honor. He has generously donated to the church in thanks.

Please do your best to accommodate any of his requests.

Bishop Lamont

Rolling my eyes, I pinch the bridge of my nose, irritated that I'm at the mercy of Parker. I'd love to put him in his place, but it would make things far too difficult now with how enmeshed in the church he is. And now he's getting married. I smirk at the thought of the poor woman who's subjected to Parker for the rest of her life.

No doubt it's someone marrying him for his money; I can't imagine his *personality* making women swoon and fall to their knees. But relief fills me knowing that soon he'll be officially off the market. Hopefully that means I won't need to watch Amaya in his orbit for too much longer, and all my questions regarding them will disappear.

I stare at Bishop Lamont's name again.

Someone knocks on the door, and I tell them to enter, assuming it's Jeremiah.

But then Parker walks in.

He fills the frame first, his hand wrapping around the small waist of the woman next to him.

Amaya.

My attention is suddenly rapt on her, narrowing into tunnel vision, the sight of her bright in Technicolor while everything else falls away in muted blobs of gray.

"Miss Paquette, what a surprise," I say, reality crashing back in as I realize what it means to have her here with Parker.

His hand possessively around her waist as he leads her through the open door.

Her eyes meeting mine, hurt and anger swirling through their depths.

She's upset with me. Of course she is.

I breathe slow, deep, even breaths, reminding myself that I hold no claim to her. Not truly. Not when I'm already claimed by God. But words don't matter when it *feels* like my name should be branded on her soul, burned so deep the world can feel the letters.

Parker prods her forward like cattle, a haughty look on his face I'm suddenly desperate to disfigure, and when they sit down across from me, his hand slipping to the thick part of her inner thigh, the edges of my vision blur.

My eyes flick to hers.

Look at me, petite pécheresse.

She does. Immediately, as though she can hear my thoughts, and my heart stutters with the knowledge that our connection isn't one-sided. She feels me just as surely as I feel her.

"Hope we're not interrupting, Father," Parker says, breaking the moment.

"Of course not. I'm never too busy for you." I don't take my gaze from Amaya.

She scoffs and then bites her lip like she didn't mean to let the noise slip out.

I lift a brow, daring her to say something out loud.

"Amaya," Parker chides, looking at her disapprovingly. "Don't be rude."

"Yes, Miss Paquette, is something the matter?"

She glares at me, and it makes dopamine flood my system, happy to have her attention when she's here with someone else.

Parker's hand moves higher up on her thigh, his fingers squeezing her supple flesh, and my blood pumps so violently my ears ring. My fingers grip the edge of my desk to keep me in place, my sickness surging up and salivating to take the reins.

Kill him. Snap his neck and watch the life drain from his pathetic, pompous eyes.

I swallow and force the voice back down. I can't *kill* Parker. It would cause far too many problems for me, even though right now, nothing sounds as satisfying as tying him to his chair, breaking every one of his fingers, and then fucking Amaya in front of him and smearing her thighs with *my* cum just to make sure he knows who she belongs to.

My cock hardens at the visual and I shift in place, the sharp twinge of pain down my back making me bite the inside of my cheek, Sister Genevieve's voice smacking me upside my head.

Let yourself heal.

"What can I do for you two?" I ask, forcing my eyes away from Amaya and skimming them over Parker instead.

He grins and I imagine slicing the lips from his face. "I'm

sure Bishop Lamont's already told you, but we're here to plan a wedding."

My heart stalls even though I had already deduced as much.

"Whose?" I ask, needing to hear it said.

I focus back on Amaya, staring her down, daring her to be the one to tell me. *Do it*, I think. *Look at me and say the words.*

She keeps her eyes on her hands.

Parker's hand squeezes her leg until she winces, and my chest squeezes along with it.

"Ours."

CHAPTER 25

Amaya

"WHAT *WONDERFUL* NEWS." CADE'S VOICE IS LIKE ice, so smooth and cool it stings as it sprinkles across my skin.

My gaze is locked on my hands, afraid if I stare at him for too long, I'll snap and do something crazy like reach across the desk and smack him in the face.

"You're worse than a whore. You're a witch. Just like your mother said."

"When is the church available?" Parker asks.

Cade chuckles. "Non, you cannot have it here so soon."

Now I do look at him, snapping my face up and meeting his gaze head-on.

Parker's hand tightens on my thigh until I flinch.

"Bishop Lamont assured me it wouldn't be an issue," he hisses.

Cade clicks his tongue. "*She* is not ready for a Catholic marriage."

My irritation at him intensifies, even as a tendril of unease winds its way around my middle.

"I'm Catholic," Parker argues. "It wouldn't be right to have it anywhere else. And Bishop Lamont said she could take courses."

"It doesn't matter if you're Catholic. *She* is not." Cade waves his hand toward me dismissively.

"I was raised Catholic," I defend.

Cade ignores me like I haven't even spoken, although his next words are aimed toward me. "You haven't been to a single service since my arrival, and I'm sure if I asked anyone in Festivalé, they'd say you hadn't attended in years. You're a *sinner*, Amaya."

"Sinning is subjective," I hiss through clenched teeth.

"It is *not*," he snaps back.

Asshole.

"Okay…" I draw out. "So I'll start to attend with Parker then."

Cade chuckles, low and dark, and then he finally looks back at me, his stare so intense I feel it deep in my core. "So easy to get you to attend Sunday Mass, is it, Miss Paquette?"

I swallow, my tongue sticking to the roof of my mouth.

"Tell me, Miss Paquette. When was your last confession?"

His head tilts, and I glare at him. He knows damn well when it was.

He doesn't wait for a reply, moving his attention back to Parker. "You'll need baptism certificates."

Parker nods. "Not a problem."

My stomach tangles in knots. I've never been baptized. But I won't say that right now, not to Cade. I'll have Parker take care of it.

Blood presses beneath the surface of my skin, heating my cheeks.

"And as far as…everything else," Parker continues, his thumb rubbing tight circles on my leg.

Cade zones in on the movement, the muscle in his jaw ticking. Slowly, his eyes move from where Parker's touching me, up the length of my torso, blazing over my chest and settling on the hollow of my throat.

My heart bangs against my rib cage.

"I will not approve this marriage until I'm sure you're both ready," Cade says, his eyes locking with mine. "And yes, I'll agree to the additional one-on-one sessions with your *fiancée*."

My brows shoot to my hairline. "The what?"

Amusement flashes in Cade's irises, like he knows he has the upper hand. "For someone who claims to be Catholic, you seem to know nothing about the religion, Miss Paquette. Every couple takes a course so we can determine that you're *ready* for the sanctity of marriage."

"And who decides that?"

He smiles so wide, dimples dent his cheeks. "Me."

My heart catapults into my stomach. "And the one-on-one courses?"

Parker clears his throat, side-eyeing me. "I've asked Father Cade to ensure you're well versed and…appropriate."

"Well versed and appropriate," I repeat slowly.

Parker turns in his chair to face me. "That's right. Don't pretend your image is anything other than *trash*." He pauses. "Even Jason thinks it needs an overhaul."

My jaw drops. I can read between the lines, and that's the only reason I don't put up more of a fight, despite the way my body shakes from the disrespect. His name-dropping my new defense attorney Jason means he wants me to seem a certain way in case I go to trial.

A woman who goes to church and is God-fearing is more endearing than one who's called a witch and strips for cash.

Parker's face hardens. "You need to trust me on this."

His phone rings, and he *finally* removes his grip from my thigh as he pulls it out and looks at the screen before slipping it back in his pocket.

But I see the name on the screen.

Florence.

"Excellent, so it's settled," Parker says, not bothering to look up at Cade or me. "I need to get back to work. You two can start right now."

I suck in a breath.

He's leaving me here?

Before the thought can even form fully, Parker's gone, leaving a tense and silent quiet in his wake.

Neither of us speak, and I'm almost certain Father Cade can hear my heart beating against my chest, my anger resurfacing now that we're alone. Slowly, I spin back around from where I was staring at the door and look at him.

He's stood up at some point, and now he's leaning against his desk, ankles crossed and his hands in his pockets. Watching me.

He's always watching me.

Finally, he breaks the silence. "Alone at last."

His voice is smooth as butter, and it pisses me off.

"Unfortunately for me," I snark.

He smirks. "For us both, actually. But let's not waste time pretending you don't enjoy our alone time, Amaya, when we both remember just how much you do."

I sit forward in my chair, pointing my finger at him. "You don't get to do that. You don't get to stand there and act like what we did was fine. Like what you said—" I cut myself off, not wanting to finish the sentence, because it doesn't matter, and me showing emotions like this make me feel out of control, and I *hate* it.

It doesn't matter.

He tilts his head. "You do realize there is no divorce in the Catholic church, yes?"

My stomach cramps because truthfully, I hadn't thought about it. It's not like it matters anyway.

I lift my chin defiantly. "And?"

"Do you often let other men touch you when you're spoken for?" His words are soft-spoken, but I can feel the tension stringing them tight.

"Do you often touch women when *you* are?" I retort, pointedly looking at the clerical collar that's wrapped around his neck.

He frowns, a tendril of his tousled black hair falling on his forehead. He reaches up to push it back. "A mistake I won't be making again."

I don't know why that statement stings, but it does. It's not like I *want* things to happen again. I cross my arms, and his gaze flicks down to my chest.

"My eyes are up here, *Father.*"

His nostrils flare and he straightens, moving forward until he's leaning over my seat, his hands gripping the arms of my chair. "I know every single inch of you, petite pécheresse, as if you were painted by my hands."

My breathing falters, his words slapping against my heart and making it beat out of rhythm.

I sit forward until our bodies are almost touching, a buzzing sensation heating me from the inside out. Our noses brush, and I feel his exhale on my lips.

"And in your painting..." I murmur. "Am I a whore? Or am I a witch?"

The muscle at the side of his jaw twitches, and I just know

he's about to spit something hurtful in the air. Something that will tarnish my view of him even more and make me *hate* myself for not being able to forget what it felt like when his thick fingers spread me wide.

I press my hand over his mouth, his lips burning my skin.

"Don't," I grit out. "Whatever you're about to say, just...*don't*."

Something coasts across his face, and his fingers wrap around my wrist, his thumb pressing into my pulse point like he's searching for the beat. Slowly, he brings my palm down until it's resting in my lap, his hold never loosening.

"You should go," he rasps. "Before I do something we'll both regret."

He drops my arm like it's on fire, spinning until I'm staring at his back. And I rise up and bolt from the room, my muscles tight and my mind screaming, wondering how the hell we'll survive being alone.

CHAPTER 26

Cade

THEY SAY THE FIRST SEVEN YEARS ARE THE BUILD-ing blocks of a child's life. Science points to the fact that during those formative years, our brain waves are in a different state, almost like hypnosis, letting the ideals settle into concrete foundations for what we'll believe. For who we'll be the rest of our lives.

Well, I was seven years old when I ran away from the orphan-age and took to the streets of Paris, and now, twenty-nine years later, it's still those first few years that haunt me the most.

"Little demons who don't learn their lessons get the whip again."

"Please, Sister," I beg. "I didn't mean to do it."

Her eyes blaze as she stares down at me, the smell of dirty concrete and salty tears masking the rest of my senses.

"And what is it that you've done?" she questions, the leather belt hanging loosely by her side.

I swallow, because I don't know what I've done. I never know.

She leans in close, her breath sickly sweet on the shell of my ear.
"There's a sickness in you, child. And God wants me to beat it out."
Whistle.
Strike.
Pain.

The memory of Sister Agnes's voice wakes me from a nightmare, the punishment for being bad sticking to my skin like a leech.

Every action has a reaction, every choice a consequence.

And I learned early that if you do something wrong, you pay with a pound of flesh.

Sometimes I still wonder what it was about *me* that she seemed so hell-bent on beating out. If maybe she could sense the monster blooming inside me before anyone else knew it was there. Or maybe, as she often said, she was trying to cure me, and in the end, I was just too broken to be fixed.

But the most likely reason is that she didn't like the simple fact that I existed.

After all, if even my parents didn't want me, why would anyone else?

But I was still made in God's image, and He listens when I pray. He's happy when I atone.

My penance is my gift. One I'll continue to give, because my self-control is a distant mirage in the heat of Amaya's presence.

She blinds me to my purpose, hiding me from even Him.

And now we're stuck together so I can prepare her to marry another man.

Disgust bubbles in my gut at my thought.

Maybe if I immerse myself in her long enough, it will numb

me to her spell until she's merely another face in the crowd. And now that I've been instructed to appease Parker's ridiculous demands, she'll be talking to me. Tempting me. Close enough to taste and touch and fuck.

Let Parker have her.

My chest twists.

After I sent her away yesterday, I spent the rest of the night in my office, vacillating between the need to whip myself for my sinful thoughts of her and the urge to stalk her and watch her every breath.

The indecision made me stagnant. And that's how I've stayed for the two nights since.

I haven't followed her, haven't sought her out in the crowds. I've put my head down and focused on the parish. On everything I'm supposed to be doing.

But a monster only grows stronger in the dark, and tonight I'm too unwell at the thoughts of where she is, *who* she might be with.

So even though it's the coldest night so far this year, I'm a man on a mission.

My breaths puff from my mouth, crystalizing the second they hit the icy air, and my nose is numb from the cold. But my veins are full of heat as I maneuver between the bushes in front of her apartment and crouch down, peering into her window as I watch and wait.

Again.

Something clicks into place, like a puzzle piece that's been missing as I settle in, peering around to make sure nobody else is near, that I'm well hidden even if they were to walk by.

It's only one a.m., and usually she'd be working for at least another hour before making the trek from the bus stop back to her place. But here she is, the sight of her so unexpected that it steals my breath and cramps my chest.

She's wearing nothing but a fluffy white towel as she stares at herself in a mirror propped above a chipped dresser. Her dark wavy hair surrounds her face in wet ringlets, dripping water down her body in such a tantalizing way that my mouth dries, wanting to lick the wetness from her skin.

Her left hand squeezes the front of her towel together tightly, and even through the window, I can see she's white-knuckling the fabric. Her hold drops, and blood rushes to my groin as I soak in the sight of her wet, naked body.

Merde.

She's beautiful, a goddess, her skin glistening from the shower and her curves perfect and thick. My eyes soak her up greedily, my fingers flexing from the need to pop the button on my pants and grip my aching cock.

I want to stroke myself to the sight of her so badly it hurts.

Her breasts are heavy and full, areolas dark and puffy, and when she reaches up and rolls one between her fingers, I bite the inside of my cheek so hard the taste of copper floods my mouth.

I palm myself over the fabric of my pants, pressing firmly as my hips thrust involuntarily into my hand.

She releases her breast, dropping her fingers to the top of the dresser, her body hanging like she's disappointed in herself for giving in. The new position arches her back, and I'm sure if I angle my vision, I'll be able to see the perfect lips of her cunt peeking from between her thighs.

I move, the bush's leaves jostling when I do. She snaps her head up, and my heart falters.

Because she looks directly into my eyes.

CHAPTER 27

Amaya

IT DOESN'T MATTER THAT HE'S SHROUDED IN THE shadows and his face is hidden by the brim of his hat. I still see him as clearly as if I conjured him up from my thoughts.

Maybe I did.

Father Cade is standing right outside my window in the freezing cold, looking at me...*watching* me, his eyes burning me from the inside out.

I should be revolted. Disgusted. Freaked out. Screaming from the rooftops and calling the cops.

But I'm not.

Instead, I feel a jolt of power, something I've completely lost my grip on since being dragged into a precinct and questioned about a man's murder. I wonder what he's doing here and how many nights he's stood in the bitter cold and watched me. Instead of the revulsion it should send whipping through me, it has me vibrating with a heady type of power.

I have control over this man. This intimidating man who's supposed to be beyond reproach. And maybe it's because I've just been in the shower trying to wash away my own thoughts of him, or possibly it's because I have no say in any other area of my life, but I *like* that I make him weak. That he'd be so perverse in his want for me, he'd do things like stand outside my window or finger fuck me against his door, despite who he is and what he's vowed.

And right now, I'm too tired from another day of sitting in a lawyer's office and being assured everything's fine and too turned on to pretend I feel about Cade any other way.

I keep my eyes locked on him, my heart slamming against my chest as I straighten from where I'm hunched over my dresser, heat swimming through me as I bring my hand back up and glide it from my hip slowly, moving my fingertips over my skin until it pebbles beneath my touch. I can't see anything except the sharp angle of his jaw and the way his mouth parts, but I can *feel* the way he's staring. My breathing shortens when I remember him being the one who touched me, the spark of *wrong* that heightened my arousal, knowing I had the priest of this shitty town doing very bad things to me because I'm a very bad girl. I continue the exploration of my body, the way I imagine he'd be roaming the dips and curves if he were touching me, until I reach my breasts. I grab one, squeezing the flesh tightly, the skin molding beneath the palm of my hand, and when I tweak a nipple, it sends a sharp shot of desire through me, like there's a string connected from the tip to the nerves in my clit.

If he were in this room with me, I'd ask him to make it hurt. To press his touch deep enough to leave a mark. One that I'd feel every time I took a breath, a secret no one else would know.

But *I'd* know. The priest sent to save Festivalé, sinning just for me.

The *witch* everybody loves to hate.

My other hand trails down until I'm ghosting across my pussy, my fingers gliding effortlessly over my clit. I move farther down, circling my entrance and dipping two of my fingers in to the first knuckle, a moan pouring from my mouth because of how good it feels.

He moves closer to the window. I bring my wet fingers up to my mouth and slip them between my lips, my tongue circling them like I would his cock...if only he'd open the window and come inside.

He licks along his bottom lip, like if he tries hard enough, maybe he could taste me too.

I move the hand manipulating my breast up until it skims across my collarbone, lightly wrapping my neck the same way he did when he pinned me next to his front door and let me ride his fingers while he rubbed his cock against my ass.

Oh God.

His gloved hand presses against the window, and it sears through me. It would be so easy to let him in, to sink to my knees and guide his hands up to my head, coaxing them to thread through my hair while I asked him to fuck my face, but I won't do it.

This is all that it can ever be. I'm with Parker now, and I need to *stay* with him to make sure Quinten and I are safe.

And Cade doesn't belong to me. And after what he's said, I'm not sure I'd want him to.

But I'll take this moment, just for me.

My thighs tense as I slide my hand back down to my clit, starting a slow, torturous circle, enough to ramp me up and keep me just beneath my peak.

His head cranes to the side, and I think maybe he's check-ing his surroundings before his attention is back on me, his arm moving to the front of his pants.

My stomach flips when he unbuckles his belt.

My breathing stutters when he pulls down the zipper.

Wetness leaks from me, making a mess on the insides of my thighs when Cade pulls out his hard cock and glides his gloved hand slowly up the length. The dim, yellow streetlight hits him just enough to let me see his movement without allowing me to take in any details, and I ache to get a better look.

I want to watch the vein on the underside of his shaft thicken and pulse as he works himself up and down. I need to see the moment his balls tighten and draw up inside him, making him grow even harder, signaling he's about to come. I want to take in the way his head tilts back, his Adam's apple bobbing as he swallows around the blinding pleasure.

My fingers dip back inside me with urgency, and I lock my eyes on the speed of his arm, matching his rhythm. It might be my own hand making the motions, but it's *Cade* who's going to make me come. It's *Cade's* name slipping off my lips as I explode into a thousand pieces.

Cade. Cade. Cade.

The filthiness of him creeping outside my window when he should be at the church, of him *touching* himself while he watches me, is too much, and my muscles coil tight, white heat growing like an inferno between my legs and bursting through my limbs. My mouth parts on a silent gasp, and I throw my head back, slamming my eyelids closed as I grind my pulsing clit into my palm harshly, dragging out the orgasm.

When I open my eyes, sated and spent, he's gone.

I lie in bed the next morning for a long time, trying like hell to come to terms with what happened the night before and with what my life will be like going forward. I search for the guilt or the disgust at knowing I had a man peering in my windows, but all I feel is a sense of security that wasn't there the night before. Like I'm in control for the first time. I *know* something about Father Cade, something that he can't barter or steal back.

Everyone already thinks the worst of me, but if people were to find out about him...

My momentary feeling of power is doused quickly when I realize that I *do* actually have something to lose now. If Parker finds out, then he'll no doubt abandon me, leaving me to fight against a potential murder charge on my own and leaving Quinten without someone who can care for him.

Which is why I've decided that ignoring it entirely is best. I'll see Cade again at some point, most likely sooner rather than later, and I'll just have to pretend that nothing is different. That he's nothing and no one. Just bland paper on the wall, blending in with the scenery.

The rest of the week moves by slowly. I put off telling Quinten about my upcoming nuptials, and I meet two more times with my new lawyer, Jason. I watch the news every single day, like I can't wait for Andrew's murder to drop, but it's still silence.

I don't know why I'm surprised. Jason told me the authorities were keeping it quiet, not wanting to cause upheaval in the area.

And then at night, I sit and I wait, my insides tense with anticipation to see if Cade will show.

He always does.

Watching me like it's his God-given right to do so.

And now it's Sunday, and a town car's just picked me up, right after I've set Quinten up with Dalia for the morning and dressed in a muted green long-sleeve dress. It's a little tight around my middle and a little low on the top, but it's the most modest outfit I have that's appropriate enough to be seen in church.

Parker made it very clear he expected me there this morning, and while I thought about bringing Quinten along, I can't imagine he'd do well in a long service where he's expected to conform to what everyone else is doing.

Sliding into the car, I beam at Parker, part of me worried he'll be able to look at me and *see* what's been happening late at night for the past week straight.

"Hello, *fiancé*," I say, trying to lay it on thick.

He leans across the seats and presses a chaste kiss to my cheek before pulling back, his eyes scanning my outfit as he slips the phone that he's always on back in his pocket.

"We'll need to get you a new wardrobe."

I rear back. "I'm sorry, what?"

He waves his hand up and down my form. "This is too risqué. You'll be lucky if they let you step foot in the cathedral, looking like a done-up whore. That was your mother's job, not my wife's."

His words would sting less if he had slapped me with them, and I sit back in my chair, crossing my arms, feeling insecure about my outfit. I had thought it looked okay. "That's not fair," I murmur.

Sighing, he reaches out, rubbing a thumb down my jaw, his gaze softening. "Sweet girl, don't look at me with those puppy-dog eyes. We'll take care of it, okay? Just...try not to do anything that brings you attention while we're there."

"Of course not," I bite back. "Wouldn't want to *embarrass* you."

"Right." He smiles. "That reminds me." He reaches into his pocket, pulling out a small blue box, and then grips my hand, pulling my fingers toward him, his thumb rubbing over the back of my third finger. "We also need to take care of this." He opens the box and pulls out a gigantic rock the size of the fucking state and slips it on, then holds it up between us and grins. "You're improving already."

I bring my hand back once he drops it and stare down at the diamond ring as it sparkles and shines. For some reason, this makes it feel more real. More final.

The weight of reality drops in my gut like lead.

I close my eyes, willing away the tension suddenly pulling between my eyes, and don't open them again until we pull up to the side parking lot at Notre-Dame. My stomach flips, knowing Cade is inside, and my mouth goes dry and my heart stutters.

Is Cade having trouble focusing too? Or maybe this is par for the course for him. Being under the guise of a priest and then creeping on unsuspecting women.

Jealousy stabs my chest at the thought of him sharing what we have with someone else, and for the first time since all this started, I finally feel disgust.

But I'm disgusted with *myself* for wanting to feel special. For wanting to be the only one. For lusting after a man who is the actual definition of forbidden and no better than anyone else in town who calls me names.

The car door opens, and a hand appears, helping me out. And then Parker's fingers grip my waist and I follow him inside, wondering just like when I was a little girl if God will smite me down.

CHAPTER 28

Cade

AMAYA'S AT MASS TODAY. I SAW HER THE SECOND I walked up to the altar, before I uttered a single word of the homily.

I *feel* her as surely as I feel Him.

It makes me angry she's here with Parker and not here for me. That I've asked her to show up for the past month, and all it took was another man for her to appear.

A sinner faking as a saint.

Just like me.

She's sitting in a pew next to her fiancé, and I glance around, looking for Quinten but not seeing him.

When I read from the Old Testament, she slips her hand into Parker's and I stumble over my words and rip my eyes away. I can't afford the distraction. Not here. Not right now.

But *not* looking is like forcing two magnets apart.

I'm fairly successful at avoidance until it's time to take Communion, and then my eyes flow back to her—always back to her—as she stands in the pew and repeats the words off my tongue.

Our Father, who art in heaven,
Hallowed be Thy name.
Thy kingdom come
Thy will be done on earth as it is in heaven.
Give us this day our daily bread,
and forgive us our trespasses
as we forgive those who trespass against us,
and lead us not into temptation, but deliver us from evil.

Her mouth caresses the vowels like silk, reminding me of how they parted in the perfect O, mouthing my name over and over again the past few nights while I watched her through her window.

My ire grows.

When it's time for Communion, she moves with the rest to stand in line, Parker's hand squeezing hers as he drags her along.

My envy blooms like a weed.

"This is the Lamb of God who takes away the sins of the world. Happy are those who are called to His supper." The words echo off the high arched walls of the cathedral.

"Lord, I am not worthy to receive you, but only say the word, and I shall be healed."

She doesn't repeat the phrase with everyone else.

By the time she and Parker reach me, my head throbs and my mind is in a daze, furious that she's infected even the most sacred of ceremonies with her presence. Maybe her not showing up before now was a gift, keeping me from this endless cycle of torture.

Parker bows his head as he stands in front of me, but suddenly, it's not enough.

"Kneel, child," my voice booms.

He snaps his gaze up, glancing around when the silence lingers just long enough to be uncomfortable. I lift a brow, and slowly, he kneels.

Amaya fidgets behind him.

I lift the Host. "The body of Christ."

"Amen," he replies, opening his mouth.

My lips twitch at seeing him so submissive at my feet, and he finishes his Communion before jumping to his feet quickly, cutting me a vicious glare before returning to his pew.

And then it's Amaya's turn.

I hear the whispers, people obviously on edge from her being here, but I ignore them, focused only on her, wondering what she'll do.

Our eyes lock, and my cock twitches, my chest twisting when she slowly lowers to her knees. My mouth dries, and my body physically trembles from the strength it takes not to reach out and touch her.

I repeat the same motion as before, holding up the Host. "The body of Christ."

Amaya's tongue swipes across her bottom lip, something dark and delicious flaring in her gaze, and my stomach flips with arousal.

"Amen," she whispers. Her lips part until I can see the pink, wet surface of her tongue, and she cranes her neck, offering her mouth, like an invitation.

My fingers tremble as I reach out, laying the bread on her tongue, and I take just a second too long, allowing her lips to brush against my skin as she closes them. I breathe deeply through the want, anger mixing with lust, furious she'd dare tempt me this way in front of the parish. Furious she's taking my attention away from Him. Turned on that she'd have the gall. The sickest part of me doesn't care for the others here. I bet if I demanded it, she'd suck me down in front of everyone, lapping up my sins while I coat them on her tongue.

And then she's gone, and I'm left behind, repeating the motion with a hundred other people while wishing I could focus on just one.

A terrifying thought, because it forces me to face the truth.

If she were to go up against God, she may come out the victor. My faith keeps me warm, but she burns like molten lead.

She will be my downfall, because I am just a man, and for her, I am weak.

I'm waiting in my office for Amaya the next morning.

She's ten minutes late, and every second that ticks by is another notch of irritation racking up inside me. I didn't go to her window last night, too afraid that if I did, she'd be waiting, that I wouldn't stay outside after the torture of Mass.

And if I'm completely honest, I was in too much pain.

The wounds on my back are worse than ever, and the second I'm done here, I'll be heading into the Green Mountains to see Sister Genevieve. She's the only one who knows and the only one who can help.

There's a knock on the office door, the knob twisting as Amaya walks in.

My anger doesn't cease though.

Immediately, I slip my hands in my pockets, the way I always do around her. At first it was to keep from strangling her in front of others, but now it's to keep from touching her. From claiming her as mine when she's not mine to claim.

She looks different. The most beautiful thing I've ever seen, but *different*. Her raven hair is pulled back in a slick bun, not a strand out of place, The black pencil skirt stops just below her knees but frames her curves in a way that has my body pulsing with want. Red-bottomed heels on her perfect feet and pearls around her delicate neck, with a green gem that reflects the color of her eyes. It reminds me of the large one she wore when she was Esmeralda, and I wonder if that's on purpose.

She's all fine lines and tailored edges. The priest in me approves. It's a perfectly respectable outfit to grace the halls of this church.

It infuriates me.

I want my wild and free Amaya.

"I see Parker wasted no time in dressing up his new doll," I sneer.

She glares at me, closing the door and shaking her head. "You must be the worst priest in the history of the Catholic church."

I move forward until I'm centimeters away, and she falls back, pressing her hands against the wall. I stop myself just before I touch her, lifting my arms on either side of her head, caging her in. Dipping down, my nose runs along the expanse of her neck, breathing in the warmth of her skin. "Oh, petite pécheresse. Who ever said I was good?"

She gasps, and I back up quickly, sharp pain bleeding down my back from the sudden movement.

"I think we need to set some boundaries," she finally says. "You can start by apologizing."

Chuckling, I run a hand down my face. "For? I've done nothing except be weak for *you*."

Her mouth drops open. "So this is *my* fault?"

I lift my arms to the sides. "It's surely not mine."

She nods slowly. "Okay."

Her body goes still, and she mutters something under her breath.

My heart slams against my chest, and I straighten. "What are you doing?"

She peeks out of her left eye before closing it again. "Shh. I'm working."

The hairs raise on my arms, and the rumors of the town whisper in the back of my mind.

She's a witch.

Hexing everyone she meets.

Panic makes my throat swell.

"Stop it," I demand.

She opens her eyes and walks close, inspecting me from head to toe. "Did it work?"

"Did *what* work, you infuriating woman?"

"Do you feel any different?" she presses.

I'm lurching forward and gripping her arms tightly before I can stop myself. "You cast a spell on me?"

She laughs, throwing her head back, molding her body to me from her chest to her hips.

"Jesus *Christ*," she says. "You're just as bad as the rest of the town. Word of advice, *Father*. Don't let superstition rule your life. It might end up killing you."

Scowling, I release her, stepping back and running a hand through my already disheveled hair. "Do *not* curse in my presence."

"I'll do what I want," she bites back.

I pinch the bridge of my nose, closing my eyes, the temper

I've dealt with my entire life bleating against my insides like a battering ram. When I open them again, I see hurt flash across Amaya's face.

And seeing the pain there, even as fleeting as it is, drains away the anger until it's barely there, whispering in the background.

My chest pulls and twists, my heart feeling as though it's splitting right down the middle, and it throbs so intensely my hand reaches up to rub at the ache.

I don't like hurting her.

My brows furrow as I come to terms with this new sensation. With this…power she has over me, stronger than what I had even known she possessed.

Running a hand through my hair, I blow out a breath, my eyes flicking between hers, searching for…*something*.

I reach out and grip the nape of her neck, pulling her even closer against me, her head tilting up and her mouth opening on a gasp. Fire burns from where we touch, my insides being incinerated by whatever this is between us.

"I'm sorry," I say.

Her gaze widens, and I rest my forehead against hers, my jaw clenching as I try—and fail—to keep my emotions in check.

"Do you hear me, Amaya Paquette? I am *sorry* for what I said. For hurting you."

"Did you mean it?" she whispers, her eyes pinching shut.

"In the moment? I lashed out to cause you pain, to keep you away. To try and make sense of whatever this is that you make me feel." I swallow heavily, my mouth going dry. "Because *this*? This is impossible. *We* are impossible."

Her cheeks flush, and she looks down, breaking away from my hold and pulling at the hem of her skirt.

I want to grab her again, to feel her under my hands, to tell her that watching her with Parker makes me *sick*, but instead, I find resolution within myself.

I've hurt her enough. The buck stops here. I cannot kill her, I'm more sure of that now than ever, but I can ease our suffering. *I could leave Festivalé.*

"If you'd like to bring normal clothes to change into once you're here, I won't tell," I say, walking away until there's ample space between us.

Her head snaps up, surprise clear on her face. "Thank you. I'd like that."

I grit my teeth and nod.

"So what do we do now?" she asks, looking around.

"Well, I'm supposed to be *teaching* you, petite pécheresse. But I find that doesn't interest me much. I'd rather learn about you instead. Tell me about your mother."

CHAPTER 29

Amaya

CADE FRÉDÉRIC GIVES ME WHIPLASH. ONE second, he's dominant and dangerous, masking his dark and tortured soul with his devotion to the church, and the next, he's lighthearted and almost…normal.

Like Jekyll and Hyde, flipping personalities with the switch of a light.

He's nice to Quinten, then mean to me.

He finger fucks me in his house, then calls me a whore and treats me like dirt on his shoe.

And even though his "I'm sorry" doesn't make up for the way he made me feel, it's more than I expected him to give. And I know it's genuine.

But his question about my mother feels too close. Too personal. And after everything we've been going through, after him just saying we're impossible, which I *know* we are, I can't go there with him. So I lash out instead. "How many other unsuspecting women do you pretend to be a man of God with and then take advantage of?"

As soon as I say the words, the air shifts and changes, and I close my eyes, rubbing my lips together and wishing with everything in me that I could suck the words back in. I forget just how dangerous he can feel, how it's a tangible thing in the air, so heavy I can reach out and touch it.

Cade straightens like a board, his body stiff like a jack-in-the-box waiting to pop.

Nerves dance through my stomach. "I didn't mean—"

He moves so quickly, wind whips through my hair, and I'm forced back until I'm practically flat against the couch, my neck bent over the arm. Wisps of his energy tangle with mine, lashing across my skin like waves crashing along the shore.

"You didn't mean *what*, petite pécheresse? Didn't mean to throw baseless accusations at a man you know nothing about?"

The hairs rise on the back of my neck.

"They're not baseless," I murmur, because…who the *fuck* knows why? Clearly, I have a knack for self-sabotage. I'm egging him on, but I can't stop myself, wanting to see how far I can push him. At least if he's angry again, he won't want to know about my mom.

His arms come up on either side of my head, the veins in his forearms flexing, and because of the way my hair is fanned out behind me, when he presses down with his palms, it tugs on the strands. I bite back a moan at the sharp stab of pain, and I realize with a sickening realization that even when he scares me, he turns me on.

His breath hits my neck. An inch closer and we'd be flush together.

"How can anyone blame me?" he rasps. "I *am* a man of God, mon trésor, but I am still just a man."

My heart pounds in my chest, my lungs squeezing until my breathing comes in sharp, short pants.

And I wait. Wait for him to touch me. Kiss me. Hurt me. *Something.*

Only it never comes.

Instead, he moves back and sits on the opposite end of the couch, brushing his hand down the front of his shirt like he wasn't just seconds away from ruining my life.

"So we're back to it being my fault then?" I push myself up to sit. "I didn't force you to come to my window at night, Cade. In fact, I should be running for the hills because you do."

"We've both made mistakes." He shakes his head. "And we've both done things we shouldn't have."

"What a cop-out answer," I scoff.

He shoots me a disapproving glare. "I think we need a fresh start, no? Perhaps…friends."

My immediate reaction is to argue, because he has me on edge, and because *no*, I don't want to be his friend. I'm not sure I can be. But the longer I let it ruminate, the more it makes sense.

It's like he said…we're impossible. Whatever *this* is will bring nothing but pain.

Friends.

"Okay," I agree. "Friends."

He smiles, his body relaxing into the couch cushion. "So, *friend*, tell me about your mother."

Sighing, I lean back. I'm too tired to keep fighting and, if I'm honest, too afraid that if I stoke my anger, it will turn into something else. Something that makes me feel and blurs the line from this brand-new boundary we're setting.

"You first," I reply.

There's nothing I want to do less than talk about my mom, but I *do* want to know about him. If I could, I'd dig inside his brain and carve myself out a little hole where I could live while I flip through all his memories.

He runs his hand through his inky black hair, his masculine hands flexing with the movement.

I bite the inside of my lip to keep from reacting the way I want to.

Friends.

"I never met my mom."

I frown. "And your dad?"

"The closest I've ever had to family is a nun named Sister Agnes who would rather have had me die from one of her beatings than take up space in her orphanage."

He says it so nonchalantly, like he's telling me about the weather, but I recognize the hurt in his voice the same way I feel it in my own. And because of that, empathy hits me square in the chest. I know what it's like to feel unwanted. Like you're a plague to the person who's supposed to care.

"I'll be honest, I wasn't expecting you to say that," I jest, trying to get a smile.

His lips tip in the corner, so boyish and innocent it almost feels out of place.

I decide I like the way it looks on him, and I want to see it again. "So you were raised in an orphanage, no friends, no family?"

"That's right." He nods.

"What made you become a priest?"

He tsks, shaking his head. "I've answered your question. Now you answer mine."

I cringe. "Do I have to?"

"Oui. This is just a tête-à-tête."

Swallowing around my suddenly parched throat, I give in. "My mom was...troubled."

"Troubled how?" he questions.

"She had me young." I shrug. "And I think sometimes when that happens, you don't get a chance to grow up yourself before you're expected to raise someone else. I think I fucked her up in a lot of ways. Made her bitter and angry."

Cade's face darkens. "Did she hurt you?"

I smile at him, emotion clogging my throat. "Depends on your definition of hurt."

"Where is she now?"

I laugh, running a hand through my hair, wincing when it gets tangled in a knot. I take the end and start twisting it between my fingers instead. "Your guess is as good as mine. As far as I'm concerned, she's dead."

"Where's Quin's father?"

Sucking on my teeth, I lift a shoulder. "I'm not sure she even knew who it was. At least she never told me, but she never told me about *my* father either."

"Tell me something else about her," he pushes.

My heart pinches. "She had bad taste in men."

"Something that seems to run in the family, no?"

Scoffing, I reach out and smack him in the chest without a second thought, a wide grin splitting across my face. "You talking about you or Parker?"

He chuckles, grabbing my hand and holding it against him. I can feel the warmth of his skin through his clothes. Can almost make out the defined pecs, hard as a rock beneath my fingers.

"Unfortunately, mon trésor, I'm speaking of both. Parker is..."

I wave him off, jerking my hand back and ignoring the way my stomach drops when I do. "You don't have to tell me what Parker is. I already know."

He nods, his fingers brushing along his jaw.

"This is nice," I admit. "This whole friends thing. Is every one-on-one session gonna be like this? Not really the tutoring I expected, I'll be honest."

"Why are you marrying him?" he asks suddenly.

My mouth pops open. Out of everything he could ask, I hadn't prepared for that one. Silly, really. The answer should be primed and ready to glide off my tongue like an oil slick. I haven't told him about the investigation, that I'm a person of interest, and I'm terrified of it turning into something more. And the authorities have done an amazing job of keeping it out of the news, although I suspect Parker has a hand in that as well.

I meet Cade's eyes. "Because I can."

Someone knocks on the door.

My stomach sinks at the interruption, and it drops all the way to the floor when Cade says to come in and Parker waltzes into the room.

"Mr. Errien," Cade greets, crossing his leg over the opposite knee while he leans back.

"Father," Parker replies stiffly. He turns toward me. "Ready to go, sweet girl? Your session ended ten minutes ago."

"I didn't realize you were picking me up," I say, standing and adjusting my clothes. They're uncomfortable, but I woke up to them being hand-delivered to my door, and I knew that meant I was to wear them without question.

Parker walks over, gripping my chin and pulling me in for a kiss. My chest compresses and I freeze in place, not wanting Cade to see Parker claim me so blatantly. His slimy lips against mine feel like poison, and flashes of the first time he forced his way into my mouth make nausea roll around in my gut.

"I'm taking you to my home today. Then we'll talk about you moving in." He beams.

Cade clears his throat from beside us and stands. "You two shouldn't live together until after you're wed. It's not proper."

I bite back the snort at him pretending to be the morality police of what's *proper*.

Parker's face turns to stone, and he spins toward Cade. "I wasn't asking. I'm *telling* you that she's moving in with me. Immediately. I'm putting up with all this other bullshit, but I won't have my woman sleeping anywhere other than my bed."

Cade looks bored as he blinks at Parker.

"And don't think I've forgotten about your little stunt yesterday during Communion," Parker continues. "Making me kneel like some *bitch*."

My eyes widen, head snapping back and forth between them.

Cade smirks, leaning his shoulder against the wall. "I have no idea what you're talking about."

Parker reaches out and grips my hand, jerking me forward in his anger and twisting my elbow. I wince, and Cade straightens, the amusement dropping from his face as he locks on to where Parker's tugging me behind him.

I shake my head slightly, silently begging him to just stay the hell away. He'll only make things worse.

And when Parker drags me from the room and down the hall, I have to force myself not to look back.

CHAPTER 30

Amaya

WE'RE DRIVING FOR THE NEXT TWENTY MINUTES, to the outskirts of the town where the city streets meet the country roads. The largest of Parker's buildings is there, *Errien Hotel* pasted across the front of beautiful French architecture, turning it into an eyesore.

I haven't been anywhere near this hotel since my mom disappeared, determined to stay as far away as possible, because up until recently, any excuse to *not* run into Parker was one that I'd have taken. We pull right up to the front, the town car slowing to a stop and the door being opened by a valet in a black suit with red trim. His white-gloved hand reaches down to help me exit, and I take it, smiling gently as I step out of the car and twist to look up at the giant building.

Parker grips my waist as he follows and he pushes gently forward, leading me right through the front doors. He ignores the staff around him, and they do their best to stay out of his way.

It's a beautiful hotel on the inside, and a bit of unease trickles through me knowing Parker lives like this when so many others go without. Technically, I guess I'll be just as guilty. I've already started to get used to the town cars on demand. How long will it be until I'm also ignoring staff and turning up my nose at other people?

There's a chandelier as large as my living room gleaming in the center of the foyer, gold-lined furniture sprinkled throughout, accented by large vases overflowing with white roses. The floors twinkle from the light's reflection, and my heels click-clack on the marble as we make our way across the space. The reception is to the left of us, and a small line of people are waiting, but we bypass them all, heading to a hallway on the right that opens to a fleet of elevators.

We step inside, and Parker presses a key card to the pad, waiting until it beeps.

"Penthouse, I'm assuming?" I say.

"Smart girl." He lifts the key card. "I'll get you a copy so you can come and go as you please."

My stomach twists, wondering how Quinten will do in a hotel. There's a lot of people and there can be a ton of interaction, both of which are beyond what he's used to.

We'll adapt. At least we'll be together.

The elevator dings and the doors open directly into a large marble entryway that leads into a spacious living room. I step inside, following Parker and taking in the surroundings, trying to imagine my life here.

It's nice, but it's all clean lines and monochromatic furniture, and I can't see myself anywhere in this place no matter how hard I try.

"You can tell you were a bachelor." I smile, because I don't know what else to say.

He ignores me, his attention on the cell in his hand, the same way it always is. I wonder if its work or Florence stealing his attention.

"I have a stylist coming to measure you and replace your wardrobe," he notes without glancing up.

"Okay."

He makes a face at his screen and then slips it back in his pocket, the heels of his polished black dress shoes tapping on the wood floor as he walks toward me. He tips up my chin and I wait to feel *something*. A spark or a flash or something that gives me hope that maybe this marriage won't be as bad as it seems.

But there's nothing. Nothing except for self-loathing at marrying the man who took my virginity by force and fear for what I know he can do. No matter how grateful I'm trying to be that he's here now and helping me out of a shitty situation.

"You're mine now, sweet girl. You need to look the part."

I bite my tongue instead of replying the way I want to.

He moves past me. "I have a meeting, so make yourself comfortable here and then use the town car the rest of the day."

I agree because honestly, I enjoy the town car. It's nice not having to take the bus and even better to have dependable transportation to get Quinten from school and then to therapy and back.

"Hey, Parker?"

He pauses and looks at me.

"Are there any updates? You know…about the case?" I really don't want to ask. It's been kind of nice pretending that it doesn't exist, but avoidance only works for so long until the intrusive thoughts eat away at the middle of my chest. *Not* knowing what's going on is liable to drive me insane.

His lips thin. "Jason's handling things like I already told you. If you haven't heard, then you're still in the clear."

My chest loosens a tiny bit, and I blow out a relieved breath.

His eyes soften and he moves back toward me, leaning down and pressing his chapped lips to mine. "Sweet girl, I've got you. No one's going to do anything as long as you have me."

My stomach rolls but I push back the disgust.

"You're just a person of interest. They probably dragged in a dozen other people along with you." He brushes the hair from my face, and I nod, choosing to believe him.

Three hours later and I've picked Quinten up from school and have him to his therapy, his peals of laughter floating through the door while I sit in the waiting room, my thumb spinning the diamond ring around my finger.

It hasn't been that long since my world went topsy-turvy, but when I think of where I was a few weeks ago, it seems like a different life.

"Amaya, hi."

I twist in my seat, coming face-to-face with Abby, the director of Quinten's therapy.

"Hey, Abby." I smile.

"Have you had a chance to call and talk to your insurance?"

Her words make my stomach dip, out of habit mostly. There shouldn't be any issue now, but I feel like a piece of shit for not even thinking about taking care of it until right this second when I'm reminded.

Parker will handle it if I ask. *I think.* It's habit to throw myself into a tailspin whenever things like this come up, and it will take some time to get used to it being any other way.

"I haven't," I say.

Abby frowns.

"But," I rush out. "Anything the insurance won't cover, I'll just pay out of pocket."

I'm not sure if that's actually the case, but it will get her off my back until I can get Parker in here to help smooth things out. Either he'll pay, or maybe when we're married, I'll get put on his insurance, which would allow a whole new world to open up for Quinten therapy-wise.

I spin the ring on my finger again. "I'm going through some life changes."

Abby glances down to the diamond, her eyes widening before she smiles up at me. "Wow! Congratulations."

Her obvious approval makes me feel sick. I want to reach out and shake her, screaming that it isn't something to celebrate. But when Quinten opens the door and bounces out of the room, all of it falls away, and I beam, remembering *why* I'm doing what I am.

Quinten deserves the best, and I want to be here to share it with him.

"I don't mean to be a pain," Abby continues, drawing my attention away. "They're just breathing down my neck, and whenever I try to solve things with them, I don't get *anywhere*." Her eyes flick to Quinten, who's wrapping his arms around Gabby's legs. "I'd hate to have to interrupt his sessions."

I nod, even though it feels like she's chastising me. Like it's somehow *my* fault that insurance is a fucking scam and I can't afford to pay for things he needs.

"I'll take care of it."

Pulling out my phone, I bring up Parker's name.

Me: Hey, can I talk to you later about Quin's therapy? There's a problem with his insurance and I could use your help.

I stare at the screen, my thumb hovering over Send, nausea rising through my esophagus and burning the back of my throat.

How quickly I went from wanting nothing to do with Parker to leaning on him for almost everything. Just the way he's always wanted.

But desperate times call for desperate measures.

I've been holding on to the tiny sliver of power I felt when I was with Cade, but now it slips away entirely, my life at the mercy of the in-between, straddling two worlds. What life *was* and what it's *about to be*.

My phone vibrates in my hand, and I look down, hope rising in my chest that it's Parker calling to take care of the insurance issue immediately. I'm disappointed when I see my old boss's name, *Phillip*, flashing across the screen.

I cringe, knowing I should answer. Technically, I still haven't quit the Chapel, and while I can go in whenever I want, since there was never a set schedule, I know I should still tell him that I'm done working there entirely.

Only, I don't *want* to. One, I like dancing there, and I guess holding on to the possibility gives me a sense of control, like maybe there'll be some way for me to keep the connection as long as possible. Just in case. And two, the second I tell Phillip, he'll revoke access to his studio. And now more than ever, my body craves the mental and physical release of pole.

If I lose that, what else do I have that's just for me?

Quinten hops over to me, snapping me out of my thoughts, and he's followed by his therapist, Gabby.

"Did you have fun with Miss Gabby?" Quinten says to me, bouncing on his toes.

"I had fun with Miss Gabby. Did you?" I nod.

"Did you?" he parrots. "I had fun."

I glance around for Abby to reassure her one more time, but she's gone. She must have slipped away when I was staring at my phone, lost in thought.

As Gabby tells me what she and Quinten worked on, Quinten walks away, going to stand in front of a young boy who's sitting in the chairs against the wall, his legs pulled up underneath him and his gaze wide and wary as it tracks Quinten's every move.

I hop up, saying bye to Gabby and grabbing Quinten's hat, hoodie, and headphones before making my way over to where he is.

"You ready to go, dude?" I ask, coming to stand next to him. I look over to the boy and his mother. "Hi."

"Hi," Quinten repeats to them, then looks to me.

"Do you want to say hi, baby?" the mother prods.

Her son blinks, curling in on himself more. I put my hand in front of Quinten's face so he sees it coming and then grab his arm, gently pulling him back.

"He's shy," the mother is quick to explain.

I gulp down the sudden emotion clogging my throat. It's always the little things like this that catch me off guard. Things that before Quinten, I never would have thought twice about, but now…my heart aches over what that mom must be feeling, phantom wounds from all the times *I've* felt it pinging against my chest.

The mismatched emotions tearing her in two over feeling the need to explain her son's behavior and feeling guilt over thinking she *has* to explain it in the first place.

I've been there a thousand times with Quinten.

It's a shitty feeling, and it's only been in the past couple of years I've recognized that it literally doesn't matter what anyone else thinks, as long as Quinten is happy and healthy.

Fuck them.

"He's perfect," I reply, smiling. "Quin here took years before he'd come within five feet of anybody. Your boy must have great vibes."

The mother's shoulders visibly relax and she smiles. "This is Stefan's first session here."

I bob my head in understanding. "He's in good hands, Mama."

"Good hands, Mama." Quinten jumps, his little fingers reaching out and gripping my palm. I grin down at him and pull him toward the door, stopping before we leave and doing the same routine we do every time we go outside. Hoodie first, then coat. Beanie on his head and finally covering his ears with light-up, noise-canceling headphones.

We walk out to the town car where Parker's driver, who I'm pretty sure has been put under strict instruction to not even *look* at me, waits with an open door and a stern chin.

Quinten slides in, side-eyeing the man, and then looks at me with a grin. My stomach twists, knowing I need to explain to him that we're moving. I thought I had time, but now that Parker wants us to move in before the wedding, I don't. A few days at the most.

Soon, I decide, watching him scroll through his app, his headphones lighting up the interior of the car with a burst of rainbows.

I'll tell him soon.

CHAPTER 31

Amaya

"TO THE CHURCH, PLEASE," I SAY TO THE DRIVER,
pulling Quinten in behind me and shoving half a breakfast bagel
into my mouth.

It's the first day of rehearsal for the Festival of Fools play, and
we're rushing to make it on time.

"Are you excited for the play, Quin?"

He bounces in his seat, looking out the window, and I smile,
relieved I'm doing something right. If not for myself, at least for
him.

The car rolls down the streets and I peer out through the
tinted glass, watching as people try to stare inside. I feel guilty
we're in here and they're out there, and there's nothing I can do.

If I keep things good with Parker, then maybe one day there
will be. It's what I've decided to tell myself to make my decision
more bearable. If I'm married to the "king of Festivalé," then I'll
have more power to do something.

We pull up to the front of Notre-Dame, and my nerves ramp
up as the car slows to a stop. There's a good chance I'm about to

see Cade. After our talk in his office two days ago, I've been semi-successful in not thinking about him. At least not when it's light outside. At night, I still watch and wait, disappointment sitting like a rock in my gut when he never shows.

The main square is decorated for the holidays, green wreaths and red bows everywhere like Christmas threw up on the town. Quinten's practically vibrating next to me, his little fingers gripping mine as we get closer to the cathedral's steps, the gargoyles judging me with their stony gaze.

They've always creeped me out, but Quinten runs straight to them, crouching down slightly and jumping into the air.

"Hi, gargoyles!" he greets, then turns to me. "Did you say hi to the gargoyles?"

I walk closer, smiling. "Hey, gargoyles."

"Gargoyles are spiritual protectors," he says. "They ward off demons and evil spirits. A gargoyle is carved with a spout designed to convey water from a roof and away from the side of a building."

I bob my head, wondering what he watched that taught him this script. It's a superpower, really, the way he can hear something once and recite it word for word after. His brain is a wealth of knowledge, random facts and tidbits just waiting to come out. His mind is a vault, storing away every single fact and line and keeping them there for a rainy day.

He's beaming right now, the tip of his nose as rosy as his cheeks, and I want to grab him in my arms and bottle up his emotion so I can feel it myself.

"Amaya." Lydia, Quinten's aide at school, smiles as she walks closer.

"Hey, Lydia." I grin back. She wasn't originally going to be at these, but I insisted, knowing she's the only one who really *gets* Quinten and knows him in this setting even better than I do. "Thank you so much for doing this."

She waves me off, walking straight up to Quinten and grabbing his hand. "Please, it's my pleasure." Her smile crinkles the corners of her eyes as she looks down at him. "Let's go inside and see what it's all about. What do you say, Quin?"

He nods and they skip away together.

I frown when I realize they left me just standing here like the stone statues I'm next to. I had hoped that I'd get to be in there with him, but I guess it's probably better that I'm not. Quinten has a tendency to get distracted by me and stick close instead of exploring. I just… I don't know what to do while I wait.

My eyes flicker to the path in the back of the church leading to the cottage where Cade lives, but I quickly talk myself out of that idea.

Ridiculous, Amaya. It's daytime. He's most likely not even there.

To be honest, I have no clue what a priest does beyond Sunday services and confession throughout the week.

A burst of wind whips across my face and I shiver, moving up the steps and into the narthex, the heat wrapping around me like a blanket when I get inside. Immediately I start to wander, memories of when I used to come here every week playing like a movie in my head. I walk down the hallways where the offices sit, my heart skipping as I pretend I'm *not* looking in the windows to seek out a man I know better than to find.

The beige walls and muted carpet of the back halls are so different from the replicated Gothic architecture out front, making it feel like when I'm here, I'm straddling two different worlds, one that transports me into beautiful French history and the other that's plain and an American construct, built quickly just to have it done.

When I hit the stairs leading to the basement, I continue my exploration, assuming it's okay to do since there are no signs saying otherwise.

The basement hallway is stuffy, the air a little moist and the smell a little stale. It's lined with doors, some open and some not, filled with miniature tables and chairs and removable signs on the walls that specify what age range which room is for. I glance into the one closest to me, but there's no one there.

"Peeping in windows, Miss Paquette?"

My heart jumps into my throat and I spin around, pressing my back to the door as I come face-to-face with Cade.

Shit.

I narrow my eyes. "Nah, that's your job."

My pussy clenches at the memory and my cheeks flush.

Friends, Amaya.

He smiles, those annoying dimples showing themselves, and he looks up and down the hallway before stepping in close. And now he's here. *Right fucking here* in my space, making my stomach rise and drop like a roller coaster.

"Thinking of me?"

I swallow, my hands pressing tightly against the wall behind me.

He has me in this position a lot.

"No," I whisper.

His lips are so close to mine that if I breathe too heavy, they'll meet. "Prove it."

There's tension growing between us, slipping into the middle of my chest and latching on, tugging until it hurts. Knowing someone could walk around the corner and see us should make me wary, but instead, it makes fissions of electricity dance up my spine.

My body leans into his. "What if I was?"

His eyes flare, but he doesn't let us touch.

"Tempting me again, mon trésor?"

I shake my head, biting the corner of my lip because being surrounded by him is overwhelming. "We said we'd be friends."

"We are," he groans. "Best friends, even."

And now his lips do ghost across mine, so slight I could have imagined the touch, but it sets my entire body on fire anyway.

I'm two seconds from giving in, because I feel like I might die if I don't, when a door at the end of the hall swings open and slams closed, light footsteps following the jarring noise.

We jump apart like we've been electrocuted, and I run my fingers through my hair, hoping like hell that I don't look too out of sorts.

My panic grows when Florence Gammond walks around the corner, her eyes filled with suspicion as she sees the two of us together.

CHAPTER 32

Cade

I AM A DEPRAVED MAN, AND I FEAR THERE IS NO cure.

And Amaya Paquette is a woman who has far more wickedness in her than the average person. She tempts and torments and teases, and then she smiles and makes me forget why I'm supposed to stay away.

Now here she is in my church, taunting me with more. Granted, I came looking for her, knowing the school is rehearsing in the youth center down the hall.

But when we *barely* miss being caught by someone, reality crashes back in.

I take another giant step back, anxiety stringing up my nerves like Christmas lights, wrapping around me so tight my stomach hurts.

This *obsession* will end, and we can both move on one way or another. I've already known for quite some time that my monster can't kill her—he's as obsessed as I am. But the other idea I had takes root fully.

I'll request that Bishop Lamont transfer me somewhere else. And if he argues, then maybe I'll figure out somewhere else to go, something else to do. They never needed me here anyway. Not really.

Corruption is rife in the church. Parker's moneymaking choices pour from Bishop Lamont's mouth, and I want no part of it.

Besides, if a simple woman can bewitch me so easily, maybe I need more internal reflection than I realized. As if stalking the streets and murdering a man out of jealousy wasn't reason enough.

The acts may sate the monster, but they leave the man inside bloody and torn.

I don't regret it though. Would do it a thousand times over again if given the chance. Although I am surprised they haven't found his body yet, and I wonder if he's still rotting away in the dumpster behind her work.

The work that she wasn't at last night when I went to watch her.

After realizing I wouldn't find her, I forced myself to head back home instead of her house, because I was terrified she'd be there inviting me in. I had set a boundary of us becoming *friends*, and I knew our secret meetings in the window would blast it apart to bits.

Clearly, being around her at all does the same.

Florence walks closer and she glances between us, her eyes softening when she sees me.

"Father Cade." She reaches out to grip my arm.

I paste a smile on my face and nod my hello.

"Amaya." Her smile drops. "Sad to hear I was taken off your defense."

My spine straightens.

Defense?

Amaya laughs. "I'm sure you're devastated."

Florence's gaze drops down to Amaya's hands, and mine follows, my breath whooshing from my chest when I see the giant diamond glinting from her finger.

A claim.

From someone who isn't me.

I knew it was happening, but this makes it feel more real.

Florence smirks. "I see you've grown resourceful. Who's the unfortunate guy?"

Amaya's chin lifts, a bit of haughtiness coming into her features, like she's happy to be able to rub this in Florence's face. Like she's proud to be Parker's.

Something burns in my middle as I see the change.

I hate that it's another man giving her that confidence. It makes me insane with the need to hunt down Parker and beat him to death.

"Oh, didn't you know?" Amaya says sweetly, a sugary sweet grin taking over her face. "I'm marrying Parker."

Florence's mouth pops open, her eyes widening in alarm. "*My* Parker?"

I cock my head. *Interesting.*

Amaya's eyes sparkle. "The one and only. I know you had a *thing* for him once upon a time, so no hard feelings, I hope."

If I have to listen to either of them swoon over Parker for another minute, I'll lose my mind.

"And why are you here, Mrs. Gammond?" I ask.

"Helping with rehearsal." She steps closer. "It's so nice of you to let the kids practice here, Father. You're breathing life back into this parish, and it's amazing to see."

I hum my approval, her words petting me with their praise. It's all bullshit though. I haven't done a thing other than stalk Amaya and beat myself for the sin.

She side-eyes Amaya. "Although I wish we'd be more...*selective* about who we let in the front doors."

Amaya blinks at her, then turns and walks away without another word.

Everything in me wants to follow, but something Florence said keeps me in place.

Taken off Amaya's defense.

Smiling, I place my hand on the small of Florence's back, ushering her into the empty room. "Mrs. Gammond, if I can have a word?"

She follows me effortlessly. "Of course, Father."

The moment we're in the room, I close the door and spin around to face her. "What did you mean about defense?"

Florence bites her lip and looks uncomfortable, shifting the weight on her feet. "I really can't say."

I chuckle, shaking my head slightly and changing my tactic. "Forgive me, I just...if there's something going on in Festivalé, something I need to be aware of with regard to who I let in our church...around our children, I'd like to know."

"If anyone knows I told you, I could lose my job."

"Consider this a confession." I lean in close, frowning. "Your secret's safe with me."

She nods slowly. "Amaya's been instructed not to leave the state."

My brows shoot up, surprise hitting me square in the chest. "Why?"

"Because she murdered Andrew Gleeson."

The statement shocks me, and I physically stumble back. "What?"

She nods. "Well, *allegedly*. She's not really a suspect, but it's only a matter of time. I was the defense put on her case, but she clearly didn't like that much."

Florence chuckles and I cannot, for the life of me, figure out how *anything* about this is humorous.

Memories of the past few days flash like a highlight reel. The way I was consumed with rage and killed Andrew with my bare hands, then tossed him in that dumpster where he belongs.

How a few nights later, Amaya showed up on my doorstep in the middle of the night, eyes red-rimmed and teary, and how instead of letting her speak, I gave in to my weakness and pinned her to the wall.

How the next day, she was engaged.

Regret swims through my veins like poison.

She came to me first.

And I turned her away.

CHAPTER 33

Amaya

I'M SITTING AT A LONG CONFERENCE TABLE IN Parker's office, staring at a TV at the head of the room.

Parker sits to my right, his hand on the back of my chair. My lawyer Jason is across from us on the other side of the table, and for some reason, Cade is here, having been with Parker when I arrived.

I hadn't wanted Cade to know about the whole murder thing, but c'est la vie, I guess. Cat's out of the bag now anyway.

It's been two and a half weeks since Andrew died, and his murder hit the news today.

There's a beautiful woman on the screen, two small children with her. One is a boy with bouncy blond hair and the other a tiny baby, can't be more than a few months old. A microphone is shoved in the woman's face, and someone off to the side hands her a tissue to dab the tears from her eyes.

My stomach is in my throat.

Andrew wasn't an important man, just a midlevel banker from downtown Coddington Heights, but it doesn't matter. Drama is drama, and they're spinning this as something even more grotesque than what I ever imagined.

"The similarities between Andrew Gleeson's death and that of Candace Walker, a woman from Festivalé, are striking. But is there a connection? Or just coincidence? For now, the lead detective on the case says they're not sure."

God, the way my panic is making me spiral.

A serial killer.

They can't *possibly* think it's me.

But it wasn't exactly a secret that Candace and I didn't get along, and I have connections to both of the victims.

The TV switches back from the voice-over to Andrew's wife. "We just want to know what happened. Whoever did this…" She swipes beneath her eyes with the handkerchief and looks directly in the camera. "I hope you rot in hell."

Her voice cracks and it sends guilt cascading through me, almost like I *did* do something wrong, even though I'm innocent.

"Turn it off." Cade's voice is ice.

I don't look over at him because I'm not sure why he's even here. But I wish he wasn't.

Jason and Parker both ignore him, and Jason's eyes meet mine. "Look, it doesn't matter what they're saying—"

"They're saying a lot," I cut in, my voice shaking.

"Doesn't matter," he repeats. "The evidence isn't there."

My leg bounces beneath the table, and my eyes go back to the TV screen.

"I said turn. It. Off," Cade demands.

The temperature in the room drops, the cold slicing through the air like a knife, dragging across my skin.

Jason clears his throat uncomfortably and leans forward, grabbing the remote and shutting it down.

"The way both of you sit here and are willfully ignorant to

how badly she wishes to be *anywhere* else," Cade hisses, throwing a hand toward me.

I suck in a breath, my eyes widening as I stare at him. *What is he doing?*

"She can hardly sit still, and you both speak above her as though she can't hear. Like it isn't *her* life on the line. It's despicable."

Parker stiffens, his arm growing rigid behind me. "Jason's the best. There's nothing to worry about."

My eyes flick up to meet Cade's, and my heart feels like it might beat out of my chest. His face is hard as stone, his hands steepled and jaw tensing over and over.

"Do you think my name will get leaked?" I ask, forcing myself to look away.

"Again, you're not a suspect," Jason says. "Just a person of interest." Jason must see my unease because he shakes his head, his brown hair ruffling from the movement. "They don't have anything tangible. And even if they did…"

Parker's hand moves from behind my chair, dropping on my shoulder and rubbing possessive circles over my skin. I can *feel* Cade staring.

"You have me," Parker finishes.

Jason nods. "Your husband is a powerful man, Amaya. You have nothing to worry about."

"Fiancé," Cade corrects.

All of us whip our heads in his direction, and my stomach tightens, wondering again what the hell he's doing. *Doesn't he know how bad him defending me looks? How much Parker already hates him?*

I glance at Parker nervously.

"That's right." Parker looks over to him with a cold, blank expression. "I'm not her husband *yet*. But by this weekend, she'll be in my bed, where she belongs. And you, Father Cade, will be at the church. Because that's where *you* belong."

Cade doesn't reply, just continues that torturous repetitive ticking of his jaw while he rocks back in the chair.

"I want your word that this won't go to trial," Parker says to Jason.

My stomach tenses as I look between them.

Jason hesitates, then nods. "This won't go to trial."

Parker reaches over to grab my hand, intertwining our fingers and bringing them up to rest on top of the conference table. My palms are clammy, but he doesn't seem to mind, his thumb playing with the gigantic rock on my finger.

"Gentlemen, I need a moment alone with my *fiancée*," he booms.

Jason jumps up immediately, gathering the papers he has spread across the table and packing them away before he leaves the room like his ass is on fire.

But Cade takes his time.

He stretches out his legs, rubs the scruff on his jaw, and stares at us for long moments before slowly rising to a stand and brushing directly behind our chairs, not bothering to close the door on his way out.

Parker sighs, standing up and walking over to shut it and flick the lock.

"Why was he here?" I ask.

"Who, Father Cade?" Parker lifts a brow as he walks back over.

I nod.

"He heard about you being in trouble and wanted to offer support from the church."

My stomach drops. "How did he find out?"

Parker shrugs. "Does it matter?"

I already know.

Fucking Florence.

He grabs my hand. "I was serious about what I said, you know? I want you in my home by the end of the week."

My lungs cramp but I school my reaction quickly, not wanting him to see.

"Father Cade said—"

His fingers tighten on mine. "I don't give a *fuck* what Cade said. I'm only putting up with his ridiculous rules because it will look good publicly, but if you think I'll let you live *away* from me...that I'll allow you to escape me now that I have you in my arms, you're mistaken."

"That's not it," I try to soothe. "I just thought—"

He drops my hand with a scoff, chin raised as he glares down at me. "Do you not wish to marry me, Amaya? Is that it? You want to make me a laughingstock? Use me for my money and resources and not have to hold up your end? Do you think I'm a man who takes kindly to being used and tossed away?"

Panic wraps around my throat like a noose and squeezes. "No. *No,*" I say firmly. "I do want to marry you." Desperation clings to me, and I move forward until I'm between his legs. My hands tremble, but I ignore the way they shake as I reach out, stroking the side of his jaw. "I'm sorry."

I lean in and press a kiss to his stale lips. He doesn't kiss me back, and deep down I'm thankful for it, but in the moment, I need him to give in. I kiss his lips again.

Slowly, he relaxes, the back of his pointer finger brushing down the side of my face. It's a soft motion, but it feels like a razor blade.

"You're lucky I'm such a forgiving man," he croons. "I don't want to hurt you, sweet girl. I've *never* wanted to hurt you. But sometimes you leave me no choice." His finger taps the edge of my chin before he pushes me back so he can stand. "By the way... how's your friend?" He buttons his suit jacket. "What was her name again? Dalia?"

I pry my tongue from the roof of my mouth. "She's fine."

He nods, glancing down the length of me. "You love her, yeah?"

My chest seizes, heart stuttering until I can barely take in a breath. *Is he threatening her?*

"I only wanted to give Quin some time to get used to the idea, Parker." My voice trembles. "That's all I meant."

Parker's face softens. "I'll take care of you and Quinten, Amaya. I've promised you that. Trust me."

I swallow back the nausea and smile.

CHAPTER 34

Cade

I'M HERE AGAIN.

The same place I've been longing for but not allowing myself to go.

I'm planted between prickly bushes in a back alley, watching the object of my desire, the slivers of moonlight slipping through the window I'm currently peering through and caressing a path along her body I wish my hands could trace.

There are a few empty boxes with open lids scattered throughout the area and some taped up and pushed against the wall. I've wasted precious moments where I could have been surrounding myself with her.

And now she's moving in with *him*. About to be completely inaccessible to me in this way.

I've already deduced she no longer works at the Chapel. I went there two nights in a row trying to catch sight of her, and when I couldn't, I convinced myself it was an act of God, trying to keep me from temptation. Somehow, I resisted coming back here to our window.

But as always when it comes to Amaya, I am weak.

After finding out she's in trouble and I'm the reason, I can't seem to stay away, almost as if being here and watching over her will appease the guilt sticking to my insides.

I could come forward, admit it was *me* who did the killings, and maybe if I were a decent man, I would.

But I'm no hero.

Not when it matters anyway.

Almighty Father, what should I do?

I bow my head and close my eyes, straining to hear a resolution. An answer. Some guidance. But instead of His voice, I'm left in the bitter cold with nothing but silence.

Maybe my passion for Amaya has pushed me too far from God. After all, I had *wanted* Andrew's death to be messy. Seeing him with his hands on her body sent fury racing through me, wanting to humiliate him in front of the world, wanting his name plastered across the news and on the front of papers, shamed and disgraced.

But I had never imagined it would come back on *her*.

A foolish mistake.

She'd hate me if she knew the truth.

How I wish I could hate *her* instead. But my feelings for her grow stronger every day. Toxic, twisted, and *greedy*.

She came to me first.

My chest pinches, the way it does every time I realize what she was going through the night I fucked her with my fingers, then used her mother to cut her down.

What could I, a priest bound to his faith, do for her other than offer her prayer anyway?

Parker has money, he has power, and as much as I hate to admit it to myself, he's the better choice.

They have history. But the thought of him kissing her lips, of him feeling her perfect cunt squeezing the life out of his dick, makes me violently ill.

Has she moaned his name the way I ache for her to scream mine?

My jealousy rears up at the thought. The same way it did when I watched them together this morning in his conference room, when his possessive touches and condescending looks made me want to flip the table and gouge out his eyes with the bones I would rip from his fingers.

I shouldn't have been there in the first place, but I couldn't stay away. I needed to find out as much information as I could, and selfishly, I wanted to watch them together, to soothe my green heart by recognizing she's only marrying Parker because she's in trouble.

Amaya's taping up a box and wiping beneath her tear-stained eyes, and I press myself closer to the window, wanting to break inside and gather her in my arms. To apologize for being the reason she's crying.

To try and take away her pain.

My heart fractures as more tears slide down her cheeks.

You did this to her.

It's sick what I'm doing here, what I've *been* doing, watching her most vulnerable moments.

But I know she likes it. And I'm desperate for more of what she'll give, even if it's just despair.

She turns around, standing up and pulling her long, wavy dark hair off her face and securing it with a fluffy purple band. Her shoulders drop, but then, as though she can feel me, her gaze snaps up and locks on mine.

My stomach somersaults, wishing I was next to her.

Would her breathing stutter and her pouty lips part? Would the heat of her skin tempt me with its warmth, making me ache to sink inside her until I've ruined her for everyone else?

She walks up to the window, and now *my* breath hitches, my cock throbbing against the zipper of my pants. I lick my lips as she slips her delicate fingers beneath the spaghetti straps of her purple nightgown. It glides down her body like a waterfall, and she steps out of it, tossing it to the side with her foot. She's standing so close, her nipples graze across the glass, the cold turning them into stiff peaks, begging me to wrap my tongue around them and tug on them with my teeth.

I want her in my mouth.

On my cock.

In my bed.

She doesn't touch herself, not like she has all the nights before, and I don't relieve myself either. But I soak her in slowly, wishing my eyes could feel the same way as my hand.

She presses her fingers to the window, and I mimic her motion, my palm engulfing hers. My stomach flips even though there's a thick pane of glass between us. She exhales slowly, her breasts rising and falling like she's being lulled by the ocean, and then she smiles before turning her back and walking away.

My chest cracks right down the middle, and my hand curls into a fist as I press my knuckles to the glass.

This fucking hurts.

She moves to the bed, pulls back the covers, slips beneath them, and hides herself from my view.

I stay long after her breathing evens out, a black hole festering in my solar plexus, spinning and spitting until an idea forms in my mind. Something that can clear her name.

She came to me first.

I back away from her room, glancing around before heading to the crumbling sidewalk and picking up the largest broken slab I can find. The flickering yellow light of the streetlamp casts just enough light, and I move around the corner to *another* window, one I assume is her roommate's.

There's a chance it's Quinten's, but that's a risk I'm willing to take.

I glance around one more time, just to make sure I'm alone, and then throw the concrete as hard as I can at the glass. It shatters immediately and is quickly followed by a loud scream. I rush away, hiding around the corner, but I don't leave completely until I hear Amaya's roommate yelling for her to call the cops.

Relief pours through me, and I hustle down the street and around the block, knowing I only have a few precious moments to get away.

Maybe I can't come forward to clear Amaya's name...but I can do this.

When I make it to the main square of Festivalé, the one that's centered around Notre-Dame Cathedral, I make a sharp left turn, and I keep going until I'm out of Festivalé and on the back of a bus, headed to Coddington Heights to search out the depraved and the damned.

I'll find a soul trapped by demons, and I'll kill them the same way I killed Andrew Gleeson.

Because I just gave Amaya an alibi.

CHAPTER 35

Amaya

QUINTEN SITS AT THE KITCHEN TABLE, DALIA across from us, both of them staring at me while I slurp off-brand Cinnamon Toast Crunch from my spoon.

I'm too busy zoning out to be of any use to anybody. None of us got much sleep; the person who threw a rock crashing into Dalia's window at three in the morning ensured that today would put us in a zombie-like state.

Dalia has been freaked out ever since, even though I've tried to calm her down, and so did the cops who showed up shortly after to take a statement.

"There's been a lot of burglaries in the neighborhood."

"Probably just some kids."

"We can file a report, but it won't do much."

None of that is why I can't focus. Instead, it's because I keep thinking about how Cade was finally at my window again last night and how instead of being grossed out, I was...comforted.

Like my world stopped spinning because his attention held me steady.

And how I think it may have been *him* who broke the window, but I didn't tell the cops.

I'm demented.

What kind of person is half in love with their stalker?

The same type of person who lets a priest pin her against a wall and fuck her with his fingers, I guess.

Snap out of it, Amaya.

Dalia clears her throat and narrows her eyes at me. She insisted I tell Quinten we're moving this morning. He was freaked out after what happened last night, and it's a good chance for me to spin it in our favor.

He's acting aloof, but I know better than anyone how Quinten likes to internalize. *Must be a family trait.* Still, there's nothing I want to do less than tell Quinten about Parker and me.

I sigh, tapping my nails on top of the table. "Hey, Quin?"

He doesn't look up.

"Quin," I repeat.

Finally he snaps his head up, locking his innocent gaze on me.

"You know how when you were little, I used to read books about princesses moving into castles and knights turned into kings?"

He blinks at me.

My stomach squeezes.

"I found us a better place. Like a castle, with way more space and lots of room for you and all your toys."

"Lots of space," he repeats.

I nod. "That's right. You'll get a brand-new bedroom too. Would you like that?"

"Dalia gets a new bedroom too?" he asks, flicking his eyes to hers then back to me.

Sadness hits me right in the solar plexus.

Dalia cuts in. "Quin, I'm staying here so you can come hang out with me."

His brows furrow and then he nods like he's come to a conclusion. "I'll stay here."

I give him a watery smile. "No, baby boy. I want you to come with me. You remember Parker?"

I'm sure he does. They've only ever met a few times, when I couldn't keep Parker at bay, but Quinten never forgets a thing.

He swings his gaze back to me.

"This will make me happy, and it will be fun! A new adventure." I grin, trying to infuse as much optimism into my voice as possible. "How about next week?"

He's silent for a few long, tense moments, and then I can see when the light bulb clicks on in his brain.

"Want to go to the new house next week with the new bed and line up your toys?" he says, kicking his legs against the legs of the chair.

Relief floods through me and I blow out a shaky breath. "That's right, dude."

And just like that, he goes back to his meal and his learning app, and I look at Dalia with a relieved grin.

"See?" she says, smiling. "Was that so hard?"

"Yes." I cross my arms.

I can tell she's relieved too. That went much better than expected.

Sighing, she chews on the corner of her lip, her eyes skittering around the room.

"Hey," I say, leaning forward and covering her hand with mine. "You sure you're okay to stay here? I mean…I can probably talk to Parker, get you set up in the hotel."

"Parker's already paying for me to stay *here*, Amaya. I'll be fine." She scoffs, rolling her eyes, but I see the wetness lining her lower lids. "What are you doing today?"

I shrug. "Taking Quin to school and then heading to Phillip's studio, probably."

"Have you told him you're officially off the Chapel's roster?"

"I don't *have* to tell him. It's not like I was his property," I snap, defensive because the guilt makes me on edge. "It's been weeks. I'm sure he gets the idea."

She shakes her head. "Well, yeah, but it's common decency, my dude. Let him know you're done."

Sighing, I pinch the bridge of my nose, squeezing my eyes tight. "I don't want him to take the studio away from me."

"Maybe he won't." She shrugs. "You could always pay him for it instead."

I bite back the retort, knowing that Parker wouldn't ever let that fly. I doubt he wants me there in the first place as it is, and I'm constantly worried he's going to find out and strip the last little thing I have left that's just for me.

"Maybe," I mutter. "What about you? You got plans?"

She taps her leg. "Physical therapy."

"Need a ride? I've got this fancy town car now." I wiggle my brows.

She waves me off. "Nah, I can drive myself."

"Suit yourself." I plunk my spoon back into my bowl and stand, placing it in the sink and spinning back around, my hands in my back pockets. "Come on, Quin. Time for school, dude."

Quinten jumps up from the table, and I help him the same way I always do, slipping on his hoodie, then his coat, his beanie, and finally his headphones.

He's used to the town car now, so he follows me outside and slides right in, and I can't help but notice how at ease he is with everything. There's a type of comfort that comes along with having the same driver and the same car every single day, and until this moment, I've never recognized how that would affect Quinten positively. Routine is everything to him.

Satisfaction rushes through me, happy I can give him this.

After I drop him off, I have Barney, the driver, take me to the dance studio in Coddington Heights. I'm not sure if anyone is using it right now, and I'm even less sure about allowing one of Parker's guys to take me there, but the need to carve out a little time to get out of my head and back in my body washes away the reservations.

Instead of focusing on that, I pick up my phone from my lap and dial my old boss Phillip's number, relieved when his voicemail clicks on.

I hate confrontation; this is much easier.

"Hey Phil, it's Esmeralda, er—Amaya. I'm just calling because, well…I'm making some life changes and so I won't be able to dance at the Chapel anymore. I want you to know I truly appreciate everything you've done for me, and maybe I'm a little bitch for telling you this over voicemail, but I really, *really* appreciate you, and I don't want you to try and talk me into staying. But… um…I hope you're cool with letting me still use the dance studio, because I'm on my way there now actually, and I, well, yeah. I don't know. Let me know if it's a problem." I pause, cringing over my word vomit. "I'll see you around, I guess? Okay. Thanks."

I hang up the phone, dragging my hand down my face when I go over everything I just said, realizing that I sound like a disaster. But that's what I am, I guess.

A wreck.

Two hours later and I'm sweaty and spent, feeling more like myself than I have in the past month.

Sweat drips from my brow and my muscles groan with every step, my chest heaving with sharp breaths.

I knew it before, but now I *really* know that I can't give this up. I can't lose myself, not completely.

And maybe that's why Cade affects me the way he does, because he's the only person in the world who puts all his attention on *me* just because I'm me. He's the only other place besides the pole where I feel like myself.

I think back to the first night we met at the club, wondering if he knew who I was already then, if maybe he had followed me there. *What if he had asked for a dance?* If he hadn't been a priest and I hadn't been on edge from seeing Parker, what would have happened? Would he have let me dance for him?

Would I have liked it?

Or is this toxic, weird connection between us only made more intense because things played out exactly as they have?

Doesn't matter now, I guess.

My phone rings and I pick it up, Dalia's name flashing across the screen.

"What up, hoe?"

"Where are you?" Her voice is high-pitched. "Get home. *Now.* And call Parker. They found another body."

CHAPTER 36

Cade

THIS TIME, THE DEAD BODY HITS THE NEWS ALMOST immediately.

The Green Mountain Strangler is what the media has dubbed me, and their lack of creativity is almost insulting. I'm not even killing them *in* the mountains.

And I did far more than just *strangle* them.

In fact, it was almost cathartic in a way that atonement never is to reenact every single step of how I murdered Andrew. I got to replace the random man's face with his, reveling in the satisfaction of broken bones while I snapped every finger for touching what should have been mine.

For thinking he could have her. Hurt her. *Touch* her.

I ache to go to Parker and demand to know whether Amaya's name has been cleared, but I resist. There's honestly no good reason I could give for being *that* invested, and I've been far too messy with my kills to give anybody any ammunition.

Especially someone like Parker.

Other than the murmured whisperings of a killer on the

loose, the rest of the week passes without much fanfare, one day bleeding into the next until it's time for another Holy Mass. And there she is, appearing out of thin air in one of the front pews with Parker on her arm and her chin tilted high.

It takes everything inside me to not rush to her side. To treat her as though she's just another random face in the crowd, when she's anything but. Visions of me dropping to my knees in front of her, spreading my arms wide and begging, "Do you see what I've done for you? What I *will* do for you?" hit me with force, and it's the hardest thing I've done to keep myself away.

I force my mind to jump from her to Him, where it *should* be while I quote the Bible passages to the people.

But the power behind my prayers is weak when she is near.

She's consumed me wholly.

My sickness grows strong in her presence, until I never wish to feel well again.

When I walk into my back office on Monday morning, Amaya's already there, waiting for me.

My stomach flips but quickly falls to the floor when I see Jeremiah sitting behind my desk, his arms crossed and his brown eyes narrowed into slits.

I put him in charge of setting up the Festival of Fools accommodations. It will be cold, and people will want an inside area to keep warm, and I told him we could meet for an update at some point today. I just didn't specify *when*.

"Jeremiah." My voice cuts through the air.

I don't like the way he's looking at her.

His gaze swings over to me and softens before he flicks it

back to her one more time. "Sorry, Father. I wasn't aware you were expecting *visitors*."

Amaya smiles, but her fingers curl into fists. She reins herself in well, the way I've seen her do countless other times with the people in this town. She seems to have an extraordinary amount of control with everyone she encounters...except for me.

"That's right," I say, moving farther into the room. "Miss Paquette is here on the request of her fiancé, Mr. Errien, for tutelage."

Jeremiah's brows lift. "Oh, I didn't know."

"Because it's not your concern," I snap.

A brief look of shock flashes on his face before he schools it, and I sigh while I try to figure out what to do. It isn't his fault I didn't tell him ahead of time, but Amaya's anxious energy is skittering along the walls, like she can't wait for an excuse to escape me.

I run a hand through my hair and shake my head. "We won't be long. You can just wait here and work on the homily for Sunday."

A grin takes over his face, and I know I've made the right decision. It will be the first time I've given him the lead on something like this. In all honesty, I've barely spent any time with him, little more than I've spent focused on Festivalé in general, so letting him spread his wings is the least I can do.

Especially since I've decided to leave Festivalé for good as soon as I know Amaya's name is cleared.

Amaya stares between us, but she keeps quiet.

"Miss Paquette." I turn toward her and my lungs cramp. There's so much I want to say, so much I want to do. So many things I wish I could tell her and even more I know I never will.

"Father Cade." A smile plays on her lips, and a spark of heat whips up my legs and through my middle.

She's so beautiful.

For so long, I hated her because I feared her. And now I fear her because I *crave* her.

But in the end, Parker gets her. The thought of her being with him is an ice pick to the chest, but it's for the best.

There's nothing I can offer her. It's ridiculous to pretend otherwise.

"Fancy a walk, Miss Paquette?" I place my hand in the space between us, knowing I shouldn't allow the touch but not being able to stop myself from offering it.

She nods, her eyes flicking back and forth between me and Jeremiah before she slips her delicate hand in mine.

My stomach flies into my throat, my heart slamming against my sternum.

I pull her to a stand, a little too forcefully, making her legs stumble as she rises. Her hand flies into the flat of my chest. We both suck in a breath, and my palm settles on the small of her back to balance her.

Heat spreads through my arm and settles in my chest.

My fingers tighten in the fabric of her shirt and tug, the smallest amount, and her body skims along the front of mine.

It's just a second. A moment that will surely get lost in infinite space and time. But it shakes me like an earthquake anyway.

We separate quickly, and I open the door, nodding to Jeremiah one more time as I lead her into the hall.

I keep us moving until we're outside and heading down the small path connecting the cathedral to the cottage. Far enough away for the illusion of privacy and close enough to explain it away.

Nobody really comes back to this area anyway.

She looks at me when we near the front door, her body growing tight. "What are we doing here?"

I shrug, because the truth is, I'm not sure. I don't ever know what I'm doing when it comes to her. "Something we shouldn't, probably."

A small smile graces her face, and when I open the front door, she walks inside, stripping off her coat and laying it on the back of the couch. Immediately, I know bringing her here was a mistake.

All I can do is picture the last time she was in my home, how wet and hot and perfect she was.

If I was a smart man, I'd be telling Parker I have no interest in these ridiculous one-on-one sessions.

There's nothing honorable about my intentions with Amaya Paquette, and I should try to hold on to the small shreds of decorum I try so hard to possess. But I cannot help myself.

"Makes sense," she says, spinning to face me. "We're friends now after all. Right?"

No.

"I just thought you'd want to be somewhere familiar," I reply.

"I want to be anywhere that you are." Her eyes grow wide, and my chest lights up like fireworks. "Oh, I didn't mean—well, you know what I meant."

"Non, petite pécheresse." I take a step closer. "I don't think that I do."

She retreats until she hits the back of the couch, and I chuckle, moving past her and into the kitchen, assuming she'll follow.

She does.

When you spend so many moments watching somebody live their life, you learn all the idiosyncrasies that make them *them*.

And I may not know what Amaya's first words were or how old she was when she realized she wanted to dance, but I know she licks her lips when she's nervous and that she mouths silent songs when she's all alone.

I know she loves control and hates being told what to do, and she'll stuff down emotion until she's vibrating from holding it in.

I know her favorite color is emerald green, she hates dressing up, and she's so beautiful even an angel can't compare.

So I knew she'd follow me into the kitchen, because I *know* Amaya Paquette, maybe better than she knows herself.

CHAPTER 37

Amaya

"JASON THINKS I'M FREE AND CLEAR." I RUSH OUT the words, trying to shift the air into something less...whatever this is.

I'm standing in Cade's kitchen and he's staring at me with a look. *That* look, the one he gives when he's about to do something bad. Something forbidden.

His brows lift and he leans against the countertop, crossing his arms. "Oh?"

I nod. I haven't actually talked to Jason, despite me asking Parker if we could once the newest murder hit the news. He said there was no reason to, that the police were in my home because of the broken window when the murder took place, and there's no way I could have been in both places at once.

I have an alibi. *I have an alibi.*

Although they could still try to pin the other murders on me, I suppose, but Jason seems to think they'll be harder to prove since all three victims had the same strangulation marks on their necks, and the last two specifically seem to have been mutilated in the exact same way.

I'm relieved, but after the relief came the questions. I've spent days connecting the dots, and they all lead to one thing.

Cade.

"There was another murder," I say, watching him carefully. "Did you know?"

He nods. "I did."

"Did you care?"

It's a far stretch to think he had anything to do with this, but my intuition is strong and it's never steered me wrong.

I'm still debating on whether the idea horrifies me or fascinates me.

Is it too crazy to think Cade could be the reason behind all this?

He has a tendency to follow me, and there've been numerous times around him when I felt my hair stand on end and the red flags wave, warning me I was in danger. *Was he also at the Chapel that night with Andrew?*

But then I think of Candace also having the strangulation marks, and it just doesn't add up.

It couldn't be him.

Unless Candace was a fluke.

Maybe I'm connecting dots where there's nothing to connect because in some sick, twisted way, the thought of Cade being the one to murder the man who assaulted me and then killing another to clear my name…it's exhilarating.

Nobody has ever protected me that way. No one has ever cared.

"Amaya." His voice brings me out of my thoughts. "Where did you just go?"

Smiling, I shake my head. "Just thinking, I guess."

"Well," he continues, turning to put the tea kettle on the stove. "I *do* care. Of course I care."

"Okay." I chew on my lip, fingering the pearl and emerald necklace around my neck.

He spins back around to face me. "Will you marry him then?"

"I...what?"

"Parker." He takes a step toward me. "Don't tell me you *love* him."

My fingers twist together. "It's complicated."

Cade scoffs.

"He won't let me go," I defend.

Cade's eyes darken and he takes another step.

And another. I put my hand out to stop him when he moves in again, and my palm hits his torso, halting him. I swallow thickly, my chest pulling tight. "You *know* he won't let me go."

I feel his breath on my hair, and I look up, seeing the muscle in his sharp jaw tick. "You don't belong to him, mon trésor."

Our eyes lock, and my fingers curl into the fabric of his shirt. "Then who do I belong to?"

A sharp whistle cuts into the moment and we jump apart.

"Tea?" Cade rasps, running a hand through his hair and turning to take the kettle off the stove.

"Sure, yeah." I twist my fingers together again to stop the tremble.

He pulls down the mugs and prepares the tea, and I step farther into the kitchen, sitting down in one of the chairs.

When he comes to join me at the table, I ask, "Do you think someone saw us come in here?"

He tilts his head. "Does it matter?"

I grab the mug, the heat singeing my skin. I use the slight

discomfort to ground me in the moment instead of letting my mind wander away the way it really wants to.

"You tell me." I lift a shoulder. "You're the one with the reputation on the line."

He sits down, bringing the cup to his mouth and blowing on the hot liquid before taking a sip. I watch the way his lips mold around the cup and then the way his throat works with his swallow, heat spreading down my spine and pooling between my legs.

"We aren't doing anything I wouldn't do with anyone else in the parish," he comments.

That hurts in a way I didn't expect.

"Oh, okay." I nod, bringing the tea to my lips so I don't say something I'll regret. I watch him from over the lip of the cup, that deep-seated curiosity rising up again. "What do you do at night?"

He quirks a brow, taking another sip. "I think you know."

My cheeks flush and my clit throbs, and I'm so. Fucking. Ridiculous. I slam down my mug, hot tea sloshing over the sides. "Are we ever going to talk about things?"

"I'd rather not."

Nodding slowly, I tap my fingers on the table, trying to rein in the sudden rush of anger. "Fine. Well, I meant *after* that thing we're definitely not talking about. Actually, after that last specific time we're not talking about…where were you?"

"Here, obviously." He tilts his head. "Where else would I be?"

I shrug, trying to read between the lines of a man who's impossible to read. "I don't know what you do with your time. Out of the two of us, *I'm* not the one with a habit of stalking."

He blinks, and then a slow grin spreads across his face, and he stands up, chuckling and shaking his head. Like *I'm* the unbeliev-able one.

I pick up my mug again and huff, but before I can take another drink, he's right here in front of me, his fingers brushing mine as he pulls the cup from my hand.

My stomach flips.

"Come on," he says, placing it back down. "We need to head back."

We don't, actually. But I understand his need the same way he must understand mine. It doesn't need to be spoken. He's trying to be good, to not let us stay alone for too long, because we both know what could happen if we do.

Or maybe he doesn't like me questioning his whereabouts.

That intuitive feeling rears its head again, but I don't push him for more. Instead, I nod and agree, already standing up and heading back to the living room to grab my coat and gloves, because I don't trust myself either.

"You know." I look at him from my peripheral vision as we walk down the path back to the cathedral. "You kind of suck at these one-on-one sessions."

He chuckles, his breath blowing into the icy sky like a cloud. "The sessions are only because my superior demands it. Because *your* fiancé has deep pockets and uses them to sway the church."

I bite my lip. "Doesn't that bother you?"

"Oui." He shrugs. "But politics and bribery are the way of man."

I stop walking, glancing over at him, needing him to know.

"Cade," I murmur, my hand reaching out to grasp his forearm.

He stops, looking down at me.

"I'm moving in with him tomorrow."

CHAPTER 38

Cade

DESPERATION SWIMS THROUGH ME BEFORE nightfall even hits. It's existed this entire time, since the moment I laid eyes on Amaya, but it has been simmering just beneath the surface. Her words when she left me this morning lit the fuse and sent it exploding through my veins, blackening my blood with ash and soot.

I *have* to see her one more time.

And then I'll put in my request to leave Festivalé.

The back alley behind her apartment is so familiar to me now, I could maneuver around it with my eyes closed. My chest aches when I get to the bushes, knowing this is my last visit here. These moments, as wrong as they may be, have become something special. Something important. And soon they'll fade into nothing more than a memory.

Yes. It's best if I leave.

I can't stand the thought of sticking around and watching her with Parker.

Longing for her touch.

Wishing she would choose me even though I've never given her the choice.

Non. Impossible.

I peer into her window, my breath stuttering when I see her. She is a vision, sitting in her empty room, nothing but a mattress on the floor.

My knuckles tap against the glass, and she meets my gaze immediately.

Like she was watching and waiting.

Like she knew I would come.

We stare at each other for long, torturous moments, and she walks over slowly, the same way she always does, my heart slamming against my chest even though it's achy and bruised.

Nothing good can come from this, but I'm so far beyond the point of holding myself back.

And if this is our last moment together, I'm going down in flames.

He is merciful.

She reaches the window, and her hands slip beneath the frame, gripping the edge and slowly lifting until there's an opening large enough for me to climb through.

My muscles tense with nerves, but I fold my body through the small gap, holding my breath as she closes the window behind me and lowers the blinds.

She spins to face me.

Neither of us speak, but there's longing, thick and heavy, bleeding through the air. She should have run for the hills. If I were smart, I would do the same.

But neither of us are willing to leave now. Even though we both know what this is.

This is goodbye.

And that's why when she steps into me, her breasts grazing my body, I shake my head and move out of reach.

I cannot touch her.

If I do, I'll never recover. I won't be able to leave her *or* this town.

"Laisse moi te voir, mon trésor," I rasp. *Let me see you.*

I have never known greater torture than staying rooted in my place, knowing I could have her if only I reached out and decided to take.

My gloved finger slips beneath the strap of her tank top and my stomach cramps from wanting to feel her skin so badly. The thin fabric falls off her shoulder, and I follow it with my finger, tracing down her arm, soaking in the way goose bumps sprout in the wake of my touch.

"Tu es magnifique," I murmur, ripping my hand away.

Her mouth parts, and she stands as still as a statue, waiting to see what I'll do next.

I grit my teeth and back away. "Strip for me, petite pécheresse."

Her eyes flare and she lifts her hand, removing the strap from her other shoulder until her top falls down, clinging to the tops of her breasts, teasing me from the way it molds to her cleavage, beckoning me to just give in.

I could cup them in my hands. Slip between them and feel the heat of her skin as I fuck her cleavage and spray cum across her tits. My abs tighten.

"I need you to promise me something," I say.

Her hand moves over the fabric of her shirt, slipping beneath it and flicking it away until her breasts are revealed, one painstaking inch of skin at a time.

Blood rushes to my groin, my cock throbbing.

"Whatever you want," she replies.

"Do *not* let me fuck you tonight."

"Cad—"

I shake my head, cutting her off. "I *can't*, Amaya. I won't survive you if I do."

"Then why did you come?" she asks, her voice sounding pained.

"I wanted to see you one more time." I step forward, testing her, and like the perfect girl she is, she moves, keeping the space between us. "Touch you." I step closer again, and again she backs away. "See if I could reconcile the perfect image of you in my head with the reality of what we must be." One more time, until the backs of her legs hit the bed and she falls onto the mattress. "Show me how you wish to be touched," I plead. "Show me what I'm giving up."

She frowns but crawls farther up the bed until she's in the center.

Her hands glide up the insides of her thighs until she's parting her long legs, allowing me a full view of her glistening, perfect pink cunt.

My mouth waters.

This woman has bewitched me. *Hexed* me. Stolen my voice from God and made it sing just for her.

I move closer, my knee sinking into the mattress as I lean forward, needing to see her closer, imprint her image on my brain so when I'm feeling lost, I can remind myself that once upon a time, at least I had this.

It would be so easy to grip her thighs tightly and drag her until she's at the end of the bed. To hold her legs apart while my tongue drinks her in and I baptize myself in her cum. My body vibrates with the *need* to do it, and I move my hand toward her. But she jerks her leg back so I hit the air instead.

My nostrils flare as I let out a frustrated breath. "Good girl."

With as much restraint as I can muster, I stay in place, watching as she touches herself, moving her fingers from her collarbone over the smooth skin of her stomach and around the wide expanse of her hips.

She glides over the top of her pussy, a moan escaping her lips as she pushes her cunt into her hand.

Precum leaks from the tip of me, and I'm desperate for relief, insane with the need to split her apart and show her how perfectly we'd fit.

I'm barely hanging on by a thread.

I grip the scarf from around my neck and unwind it, wrapping it around my fist and moving forward again until she's forced to lie back even more than she was. She sucks in a breath, arousal playing across her face as I hover over her, holding myself up so we don't touch.

"Slip your fingers in your cunt and fuck yourself the way I would, petite pécheresse."

She follows direction beautifully, a gasp escaping her perfect lips when she dips inside her pussy.

Her eyes flutter and roll back.

"Eyes on me, mon trésor." I demand.

She snaps her gaze back, her pupils blown and her lips a dusky red. I take the scarf that's wrapped around my hand and hold it above her body, letting the end skim across her skin.

Her back arches and her fingers slip deeper, her palm rubbing circles on her clit. I drag the edges of the fabric along her side, in awe at the way her flesh tightens and pebbles under my ministrations.

My stomach flips when I bring the end to her breasts, slowly circling it over one nipple and then the other, my balls drawing up when she moans out my name.

"Cade, I'm…"

She's close. I can tell.

I move my body back until I'm settled in between her spread legs, so close yet so *fucking* far, and skim the fabric across her stomach and then lower over her hip bones while she grinds into her hand, chasing her orgasm.

She moves her palm, allowing me to brush the fabric over the swell of her clit.

Once.

Twice.

And then she comes.

My lips are close enough to suck in her moans, my eyes rolling back from tasting her voice on my tongue.

"Tu es la mienne, au cours de toutes nos vies," I whisper in her ear.

I push myself away from her, forcing the distance I'd do anything to erase.

Then I'm gone, knowing that was goodbye.

CHAPTER 39

Amaya

I KNEW CADE WOULD COME LAST NIGHT.

The same way I know I need to stay away from him entirely. After last night…it's too risky. I don't trust myself, and the last thing I want to do is have Parker find out.

I *have* to stay away.

This strange connection that's threaded us together since the very beginning is gaining strength like a torpedo, and the only way to survive it is to sever it completely.

He can only be the priest of Notre-Dame.

That's all he'll ever be.

Dalia's arms are heavy as they wrap around my middle, squeezing tight like she's afraid to let me go. I'm at the apartment, having just loaded the last box into the back of her car to haul over to my new *penthouse*.

She's nervous to stay here alone after that rock crashed through our window, but she's so stubborn she'll never admit it. I try to convince her not to stay anyway, even though I'm more convinced than ever it was Cade.

"You sure you'll be okay?" I push one last time.

She scoffs, waving me off, but I know she's putting on a front. You live with someone long enough and you learn to read between the lines.

"You can come stay at the hotel if you want," I try, like I have a thousand times before.

She pulls back and makes a funny face, scrunching her nose. "Amaya, *stop*."

"Parker said he'd take care of my family, and you *are* my family." I move my hands down her arms and squeeze her fingers.

"And miss the chance to have this place all to myself on your new hubby's dime?" She scrunches her nose. "Pass."

"Fine." I sigh, slipping my hands away from hers and into my back pockets.

I look around one more time to make sure I'm not forgetting anything of mine or Quinten's, although between the two of us, we don't have much. He's at school right now, and I want to get it all moved before he comes home tonight so he doesn't have to see the process and can just settle into his new space.

"Ready to roll?" she asks.

I give her a sad smile and nod, and we make our way out to her car. Immediately, the music starts blaring out of her speakers, and normally I'd give her shit for it, but now I soak in the noise, hoping it keeps us from having to say our goodbyes. I know she'll be right across town and a phone call away but still. It will be different.

When we pass by where Candace used to live, Dalia sucks on her lips and turns down the volume.

"Any update from Parker or your lawyer yet? About... anything?" she asks.

"Nope," I reply, popping the *p*. "Not since he told me that a man being murdered was 'great news.'"

She laughs. "Well, it kind of is."

"Yeah, I guess." I bite back the smile. "Is it bad I don't feel guilty he's dead?"

"Amaya!" she chastises through her giggles. "You're not supposed to say shit like that out loud."

I grin. "I know but…BFF privilege. You get to hear all the unfiltered thoughts I don't tell anyone else."

She nods. "Well, if that's the case, then as your best friend, I demand you tell me why you're still moving in with Parker if you think your name is cleared."

I tilt my head, chewing on my lip. It's amazing how easily I forget that not everybody knows the same Parker Errien as me. I knew what I was getting into when I agreed to be his, and I'm not naive enough to believe he'd let me go. Now that he has me, he'll never allow me to leave.

Besides, he wasted no time embroiling himself in everything that had to do with my life, making me dependent on him in a way I once swore I would never be. Extra care for Quinten. Paying for therapy. Giving me transportation. Putting Quinten in for an interview with that private school in Coddington Heights.

"Selfishness is an ugly trait, Amaya." My mother's voice rings in my ears.

I nod, sucking on my lips. "He's… He gives Quin a life that I can't give him, you know?"

Dalia's brows furrow as she looks at me from her peripheral vision. "I think you give Quin the best life because *you're* in it. There's no one that kid loves more than you."

"Yeah, well, we're all our own worst critics, I guess." I lean forward and turn the volume back up. I don't feel like talking anymore.

Twenty minutes later and we're pulling in front of Errien Hotel.

The doorman brings out a large gold dolly, and before I can even blink, all my and Quinten's belongings are loaded up and disappearing inside.

"Well then," Dalia says. "That was easy."

"Guess so," I reply, staring up at the deep red brick. There's a sense of dread sinking in my gut the longer I look, but I push it back down.

Dalia whistles. "You're big balling now, sister. Don't forget about us little people."

I snort. "Please. It's insulting you'd even say that."

She leans in, nudging my shoulder with hers. "Come on. I'll help you unpack."

I'm not sure what I expected when we walk into the hotel, maybe for people to look at me funny or for there to be judgment in the air over the fact that Parker chose me for his wife despite who I am and what this town thinks of me, but instead, it's the opposite. I get smiles from every employee, and as Dalia and I make our way through the entrance and over to the elevator, I reach in my back pocket and pull out the key that Parker told me to swipe to grant access to our floor.

It works flawlessly and then the doors are opening straight to the penthouse.

Dalia makes a face. "It just opens up straight into your place like this?"

I shrug. "I guess so." We walk in, my steps echoing on the marble floor, and I spin around with my arms out to my sides. "Here she is in all her beauty."

Dalia nods, looking around. "Kind of boring."

"And big."

"Definitely that," she agrees. "Does he know what color schemes are or you think he went with muted gray tones on purpose to match his personality?"

I laugh, seeing that the doormen put the boxes against the side of the wall here in the living room, and I walk over to them, running my finger over the lettering that spells out Quinten's name.

My heart squeezes.

Dalia walks up next to me. "He'll do fine, girl. He always does."

I swallow around the emotion, nodding. I know he'll be okay, but I still worry. I still wonder if I'm doing the right thing. "Yeah."

"He's got you. And I speak from experience when I say that's really all any of us need."

Chuckling, I roll my eyes and twist toward her. "You're only buttering me up because I'm rich now."

"Ha! You bet your sweet ass I am. Now order us some takeout, and let's get you moved in."

CHAPTER 40

Cade

I HISS AS SISTER GENEVIEVE APPLIES SALVE TO MY back.

"Careful," I snap.

"Apologies, Father."

There isn't anywhere in the world I want to be *less* than in the mountains again. The roads are slick and icy, the weather making the trek terrible to drive, and quite honestly, being here when the conditions could turn too rough to get back to town makes me itch.

There's nothing here except secrets and solitude, both of which I don't want to have. Being alone gives me time to think. About Amaya. About my wavering loyalty to Him. And those secrets are better left buried where even I can't find them.

My heart pangs, and I grind my teeth to drown it out. This *ridiculous* feeling in my chest is why I went so hard with the discipline last night, hoping the physical pain would numb the one ripping through my chest.

I told myself that I wasn't going to think of her anymore.

That I would do what needed to be done. We said our goodbyes, so it's time for my world to stop revolving around her like she's my sun. *I have to leave Festivalé*, I tell myself again.

"What could you possibly have done that requires this level of beating?" Sister Genevieve asks as she bandages the wounds.

"I'm not here for idle chatter, Sister."

She hums, her knees cracking as she stands and starts packing up the first aid kit. "I'm not as innocent as you may think."

I tilt my head, watching her. "No? Yet you're here as a nun."

Her lips thin, her green eyes narrowing. "God forgives."

I nod. "That He does."

"Would you like a cup of tea?" she asks, already making her way into the kitchen.

I sigh, leaning back and staring out the small windows that frame either side of the small fireplace. I shouldn't stay. The snow is coming in thicker flurries, and the roads are surely only going to get worse, but if I go back, I'll have to put on a show.

And here, at least, Sister Genevieve doesn't make me hide.

Besides, my mind needs the distraction so I don't do something wild like think about where Amaya is right now, *who* she's with. What she's doing.

It's not my problem.

Not anymore.

Sister Genevieve walks back in with two cups of tea and hands me one before sitting down on the couch.

"Have you ever been in love, Sister?" I ask, slipping back on my shirt.

She laughs. "Several times, unfortunately."

"Oh?" My brows rise, surprised by her answer.

She smirks at me. "I wasn't always a nun the same way you

weren't always a priest. It took many years of my life to figure out this was where I'm meant to be."

"Did any of them ever love you back?"

She takes a sip of her tea. "Are you in love, Father?"

I scoff. "It's a theoretical question."

"Hmm," she hums, taking another drink. "Well, if you were, *theoretically*, I'd say it isn't worth it. Matters of the heart rarely are."

I'm not sure why her answer sends a spark of something dark through my chest, especially when she's right.

Besides, what I feel for Amaya is beyond love. It's incomparable. And it's clear that whatever Sister Genevieve has felt in her lifetime hasn't come close to anything near that, because if it had, I doubt she'd be here with me.

I leave not long after, and while the wounds on my back feel better, the ache in my heart feels worse.

A week passes, and Amaya is like a ghost. If I didn't have my memories and this obnoxious longing gnawing at my nerves like an addict without their fix, it would be as though she never existed.

But where I had hoped to regain focus, instead, everything seems to have lost its color.

I'm living somewhere between simply existing while I wait to hear back from Bishop Lamont, who I've requested a transfer with, and seeking her out in every face that passes by. And that's the reason I give myself for why I'm constantly strolling into the rehearsal space for Louis Elementary's play, always looking to see her show up, but only seeing Quinten's aide instead.

I know she's avoiding me.

So it's with an anxious type of energy that I get ready for Christmas Mass. Parker will undoubtedly be in attendance, and I can't imagine she *wouldn't* be here with him. I don my garb, repeating the prayers I have so many times before, only this time it feels numb. Where before I'd always feel purpose, now I just feel a hollow silence. It's off-putting and makes me question everything I've ever believed in.

I don't see her right away during service, but like a fallen angel, there she is, wearing a gorgeous red long-sleeve dress, her dark hair swept off her neck and a brand-new emerald necklace dangling from around her neck.

My stomach twists every time the jewel sparkles, and I want to rip it off her throat and shove it down Parker's greasy mouth instead.

My addiction comes roaring back into focus, scratching at my skin with nails as sharp as talons.

I try my best to ignore it because today is a holy day.

Somehow, I make it through the entire service, even though my eyes keep straying toward her hand tangled with Parker's, and as soon as it's over, I bolt, everything in me *begging* to turn around just to be near her. To steal her away and scrub her clean of him.

Instead, I go into my cottage, drop to my knees, and pray.

Two days later, I can't help but stroll by Louis Elementary's play rehearsal again. They're in the sanctuary today, because that's where they'll be putting on the actual play, and my eyes scan for Quinten, hoping that if I get a glimpse of him, maybe it will be enough to sate the urge of wanting to see his sister.

I find him over by the votive candles, taking the unlit ones from their storage and lining them up in a row. There's no one else near him, and I glance around, wondering why he's over here by himself and whether it's by choice or because they placed him here.

The woman I've seen by Quinten before is across the room talking with the art director, Mr. Anderson, and in the aisle between the pews stand Florence Gammond and Principal Lee, looking like two peas in a pod with their heads bent close together.

There's a small group of children on the dais, holding papers and reciting lines, and another small huddle off in the corner laughing quietly, occasionally looking over to Quinten. But no one makes a move to actually include him in anything that's going on.

My feet are moving before I consciously make the decision, taking me toward him. I make sure he can see me before I sit down on the floor, pushing over the storage box that holds the unlit candles. I draw my legs up, resting my elbows on my knees as I lean back against the wall and stare at him.

He keeps inspecting each candle, one by one, before lining them up, and when I look closer, I realize he's also gotten small figurines from the nativity scene we had on display in the front.

I sit with him in silence, watching him work, just keeping him company until he tells me to leave. For the first time in weeks, I feel at peace.

Eventually, he glances up at me, a slow smile spreading across his face. His eyes are the same shade as Amaya's, bright green with splashes of yellow, and a weird feeling of déjà vu fogs up my brain.

"You like dinos," Quinten states.

A small grin breaks out on my face, a little flattered that he remembers me, even though running into them at the grocery store and talking about dinosaurs feels like a lifetime ago.

"That's right." I point to myself. "Cade, remember?"

"Cade," he repeats, rocking his body back and forth and placing another candle down at the end of his line. "Hi, Cade."

"Hello, mon petit." I glance to the dais and back, briefly noting that Florence has her gaze locked on the two of us. *What is she even doing here?* "How come you're over here by yourself?"

Quinten blinks and gets a concentrated look on his face, like he's taking apart my words and reforming them to fit in his brain. He turns to look at everyone on the other side of the room. "I'll stay out of the way, over here."

"Over here?" I point to where we are.

"Stay right here." He repeats my pointing.

"Do you *like* being over here?"

He watches me carefully again, his teeth sinking into his bottom lip. "No."

It's only one word, but it's the most direct answer he's given me so far, and it's pretty clear what's happening.

This boy has no one here who is in his corner. No one here who gives a damn.

Amaya trusts these people to take care of her brother when she's not around, and this is what they do?

Anger races through me as I remember my talk with Principal Lee back when I saw Quinten being shoved around in the halls, and I should have seen this coming. I should have done more to ensure he wasn't going to be treated this way after making her include him. But back then, I was still convinced the extreme emotion I felt for Amaya was nothing more than my monster wanting to see her dead.

"Hey, you want to come hang out in my office for a bit?" I ask him. "We can do whatever you want."

He cocks his head before nodding. "Okay."

I smile. "Okay. Let's go."

CHAPTER 41

Amaya

A HAND SLOWLY CARESSES MY SIDE AND MY
eyelids flutter. Smiling, I stretch my arms above my head and lean
back against the warm body.

Cade.

I'm about to murmur his name when a different voice speaks
in my ear.

"Sweet girl."

My eyes shoot open, and I jerk to a sitting position, whipping
my gaze to meet Parker's.

He's fully dressed and looks like he's about to head out the
door to the office. I bring my hand to my chest, trying to catch
my breath, panic pricking my muscles when I realize I almost
moaned out Cade's name in front of him.

Parker chuckles. "Good morning, wife-to-be. Get some coffee
and get dressed. Jason wants to meet."

This gets my attention and I sit up straighter, running a hand
through my hair as I try to stifle a yawn with my other one. "Oh,
okay. Good news, I hope?"

He grins. "You're free and clear, baby."

My hand drops to my side, and I stare at him, not sure whether to believe it or not. "What? Are you serious?"

He leans in, pressing a kiss to my lips, and I stiffen involuntarily before relaxing into his touch. "I told you I'd take care of you, Amaya."

Relief floods me and I throw my arms around his neck without thinking, holding back the emotion at knowing I'm finally done having this shit hanging over my head. "Thank you, Parker. Thank you, thank you, thank you."

His hands leave my back and slide down to the tops of my thighs, working their way up underneath the bottom of my sleep shorts. "I know another way you can thank me."

Bile rises in my throat, and I force a laugh, smacking his hands off my thighs. I've been lucky that up until now, he's been busy at night with work. "You just said Jason needed to meet, and you look like you're on your way out. Rain check?"

He groans, squeezing me tight enough to bruise before releasing me and standing up to straighten his suit. "Fine, but don't think I'll wait forever. You agreed to be mine, and I've held up my end of the bargain. It's time you start showing some fucking gratitude for everything I'm giving you."

My name has officially been cleared, and I can't wait to grab Quin from his rehearsal at the church and swing by home—I mean Dalia's—and celebrate.

I've been having her pick up and drop him off because I didn't want to chance seeing Cade when I've done so well with avoiding him, but today I told her the good news and decided to say fuck it and head there myself.

Part of me, the most depraved part, hopes to run into Cade anyway so I can let him know too.

"Where's Quin?" I ask Lydia, looking around at all the other students being wrapped up in their coats and herded into the streets.

She scratches at her neck and looks down at the ground, guilt weaving its way onto her face. "Father Cade took him away sometime during the middle of the rehearsal."

My entire body freezes. "*What*?"

Her eyes are apologetic as she looks up at me. "He was doing just fine, so I went over to talk to Mr. Anderson, and when I got back, he was gone. I spent half a damn hour searching high and low before Florence told me she saw them go off together. I figured it was fine since it was Father Cade."

Unbelievable.

"What was Florence doing there?" I spit, then hold up my hand. "You know what? Never mind."

Logic leaves me entirely. *Is this his way of getting me to talk to him?*

I thought we had a deal, albeit a silent one, but I figured we both understood what needed to happen. And I've held up my end of the bargain; I've stayed away. I don't want to ruin his life any more than I want him to ruin mine, and him kidnapping my brother from where he's supposed to be is *not* holding up his end.

"Come on then," I say to Lydia, not waiting for her to follow me. "I'll focus on why you didn't know what happened to Quinten for *thirty minutes* later, and instead, you can come wait with him while I have a chat with Father Cade."

Lydia sucks on her lips and nods, the guilt oozing from her pores.

I look over at her as we walk. "It should go without saying that while you're watching him, you shouldn't let him out of your sight."

A rush of satisfaction pours through me when I put her in her place. *Wow.* Who knew standing up for yourself could feel so good? I'm not the no-power nobody I used to be. And it's about time I learn to use it, especially if I'm going to be married to Parker.

I'm fuming by the time we make it to Cade's office, visions of Quinten finally interacting with his peers, then being stripped of the opportunity and put with a *stranger* racing through my brain.

Is this the first time it's happened? Has he been secretly meeting with Quinten this entire time?

We reach his office, and I give Lydia a look to let her know she needs to stay where she is before twisting the handle and throwing the door open with force, the doorknob slamming on the wall like a thunderclap.

But my ire doesn't last, because what I walk in on shocks me into silence.

Cade and Quinten are sitting in the middle of the floor, and they're...*finger painting*.

My eyebrows shoot to my hairline, and my gaze flicks from where Cade sits staring at me, his white short-sleeved shirt cling- ing to his muscular arms and dotted with rainbows of colored paint, over to Quinten, who has a giant smile on his face and his palms covered in green and blue.

I've *never* seen Quinten with that much mess on his hands before, not even in his therapy sessions, and a swell of elation cuts off my air, making my throat swell. My eyes lock on Cade's.

Quinten smiles, holding up his little fingers and spreading them wide. "Finger paints!"

I break away from Cade's intense gaze and focus on Quinten. "I see that."

Taking a step closer, my anger melts away like snow in the sun, and I glance down at the massive white sheet that's taped to the floor, large and small handprints covering 90 percent of the surface. "That looks awesome."

"Maybe next time, we can paint one just for you," Cade's voice cuts in.

My heart skips. "Yeah, maybe." I crouch down next to Quinten. "Hey, can Miss Lydia take you to the bathroom and clean you up so we can go home?"

He nods slowly, looking between Cade and me. "Can we paint tomorrow?"

"Sure, mon petit," Cade says. "As long as your sister's okay with it."

"He has therapy."

Cade shrugs. "After then."

Lydia knocks on the open door and pops her head in, glancing around before smiling at Quinten. "Let's go get you washed up, buddy."

"Tomorrow?" he asks again.

"We'll see," I reply, my stomach sinking at the thought of Quinten getting more attached than he clearly already is.

Lydia comes forward and grips his hand, and then they're gone, the door clicking shut behind them.

Silence fills the air.

Cade stands up, looking hot as fuck in his white shirt and black slacks, splotches of paint decorating his arms. And just like when we first met at the grocery store, I'm filled with gratitude for the way he is with Quinten.

What-ifs fill my head.

What if he wasn't a priest?

What if I could have him?

What if? What if? What if?

My eyes flicker from his face over his arms and then down farther, and when I raise them again, Cade's irises look like molten fire.

It pisses me off, and suddenly my earlier anger comes surging back in.

Because this is unfair. It's *unfair* that I can't have him. And it sure as hell is unfair that I'm engaged to someone else and Cade is who he is when nobody has ever, *ever* made me feel the way he does.

And fuck him for acting like he has the right to take in Quinten and be so goddamn caring when he isn't available to stay in our lives.

"You really have some fucking nerve," I spit, moving toward him and shoving him in the chest.

He stumbles back slightly. "Excuse me?"

I step forward again, jamming my finger in his chest. "How fucking dare you. What was this, some master plan to soften me up and get me back in your life?"

Cade's eyes grow sad. "Amaya."

"No." I jab him again. "This isn't *fair*, Cade. I can't have you, you know? We aren't good for each other. And here you are, sitting in your office looking like...*that*"—I gesture up and down his body—"and being the way you are with Quin, and I'm supposed to what, forget about everything else?"

He shakes his head. "I don't know what you want me to say."

"The truth!" I yell. "How about you try the truth for once?

Tell me why Quin was in here with you, and then tell me who you really are, because you're sure as hell not a holy man."

He chuckles, and when he brushes a hand down the front of his shirt, his muscles bulge, swirls of rainbow creeping up his arms, splotches of paint dotting his neck and the sharp angles of his jaw.

I *hate* how good he looks right now. How normal. Not when I'm desperate for the reminder of why he's not.

"Here's the truth, mon trésor. You're delusional." He steps into me. Clearly, he's angry. The veins in his neck throb and his nostrils flare like he's hanging on to his control by a thread. "Ungrateful."

I cross my arms and huff. "Don't you tell me I'm ungrateful, you…you *fake*!"

He frowns, then lifts his head until it's facing the ceiling, and he lets out a disbelieving laugh.

The air thins, vibrating like it's soaking up our fury. The moment feels frozen, and I wait with bated breath to see what he'll do. If he'll control himself like he should or if he'll break.

The truth is that I *want* a fight. I want something to shatter this feeling and let me free of this prison.

Cade runs his paint-covered hands through his tousled black hair and tugs on the roots. "You are *infuriating*."

I open my mouth to reply, but then his arms reach out, fast as lightning, gripping me around the waist and pulling me in until I'm flush against his body. I gasp, heat spreading through me like a wildfire. His fingers tense around me like he's warring with himself on either pushing me away or dragging me in closer. I close my eyes, praying to his God that he keeps me close.

This is the most contact we've had in weeks, and like the pathetic woman I am, I melt into the feeling.

"You think I'm *faking*, petite pécheresse?" he rasps.

Shivers scrape down my spine like sandpaper, rough and grating against my frayed nerves.

"You think this isn't real?" He grips my hand and pulls it down until it's covering his hard cock. I bite the inside of my cheek to keep from moaning at the feel, my pussy spasming from want.

"*Fuck. You.*" I rip my hand away, squirming in his hold. I can't think with his arms around me.

The more I struggle, the more his grip tightens. "I thought you wanted the truth, Amaya. How about some more?" He leans in, his teeth nipping at my jaw.

Goose bumps sprinkle across my neck and shoulders, rippling down my spine.

"You pretend to hate me because it makes it easy. You come in here with anger as your shield, striking out before you get struck yourself."

"No." I shake my head, his words spearing through my chest.

"But nothing about us is *easy*. And the only one in this room who's faking anything is you."

A sob breaks free from my throat because I know he's right. I *am* angry, but not at him. I'm angry at the way things are. At how I can't have the one person who finally makes me *feel* so fucking much.

"I just want it to stop," I beg, my fingers gripping the fabric of his shirt and pulling him closer. "I want to be able to exist without you plaguing every single one of my thoughts. I feel sick, and—and obsessed. *Please*, Cade."

He laughs but the sound is hollow. "And what do you know of obsession? You've been tormenting my mind since the very first moment I saw you."

A tear rolls down my cheek and I turn my face away.

He releases my left hip, bringing his hand up to grip my jaw tightly, forcing me to look him in the eye. "Si seulement tu savais quel est mon amour pour toi. You consume me, Amaya. Break apart my faith with the fire of a thousand suns and dominate every nightmare until all I dream is you."

Another tear escapes and then he's leaning in, his tongue swiping out and *licking* up my cheek, his groan reverberating in my ears.

His twisted sentiment smashes through my wall of defense, and I sink into his embrace.

"You think you're *obsessed*, petite pécheresse? You don't know the meaning of the word."

And then he's on me.

Both his palms cup my face as his tongue delves between my lips. His taste floods my mouth, and he inhales my moan, not letting me breathe for even a second as he kisses me in a way no one else has. It's violent, our teeth clashing and nipping, and my fingers fly into his hair, pulling harshly as I climb up his body, trying to get closer, afraid that if I let him go, I'll never get to feel him again.

Something clatters to the floor as he spins me around and presses me into his desk, his body shoving into mine, one of his hands moving from my jaw into the roots of my hair and tugging me back. Our lips break away as he pulls, my back bowing. He smatters kisses along my neck, sharp pricks of pain stinging my skin from the way he sucks and bites as he blazes a path down my throat with his lips.

"Cade," I plead, although I'm not sure for what.

Laughter floats in from outside the door, and it shocks us both back into the present, and we fly apart.

Immediately, he straightens, his eyes dark and his mouth red and swollen. I jerk up from his desk, clearing my throat as I try to calm my racing heart. Reaching down, I straighten my clothes and stand up, blowing out a deep breath.

Jesus.

I shake my head. "That was—"

"An inevitability," he finishes.

He towers over me, his hand tilting up my face until I'm craning my neck to meet his eyes.

"That was an inevitability," he repeats.

"Maybe so," I admit, shaking my head. "But it can't happen again."

"Because you're Parker's?" he sneers.

"Because you're God's," I reply, my hand going to his jaw as I rise on my tiptoes and dust a kiss on the corner of his mouth.

And then I hold my head high and walk out the door to take Quinten home.

My name has been cleared, but suddenly, I don't feel like celebrating.

CHAPTER 42

Cade

MY HEAD IS BOWED AND MY HANDS ARE CLASPED as I kneel in front of my bed.

I pray for absolution. For resolution. For something—*anything*—that will give me some clarity on what I should do. At face value, I know what's right, at least what I've always *thought* to be right. I've walked through my years with one agenda on my mind: being God's loyal soldier, one who condemned the damned while being condemned myself.

But what I've always *known* to be right doesn't feel like it fits anymore. It's shaved down with jagged edges, and I keep trying to shove it into the same round hole.

Now, the only thing that feels right is her.

I still have my faith, still believe in what I preach and in His word. But for the life of me, I can't reconcile the pain I feel inside at not being able to have her as long as I serve Him. It doesn't seem fair.

And I don't like being angry with God.

This is my one last attempt at clinging to my righteousness, to what I've always believed to be so. I pray, and I beg for guidance. But just like before, there's only silence in return.

Amaya's name slaps against my chest with every beat of my heart. Her moans echo in my mind, and the taste of her is imprinted on my tongue.

I snapped. She poked and prodded, and my already frayed nerves broke into a thousand strings pooling at her feet. The endless hours of torment over wanting her, *dreaming* of her, stalking her, culminated in an explosion, and the only way to douse the flames was to drown myself in *her*. So I gave in. I gripped her tight, delving into the delicious, sinful taste of her mouth.

And she's part of me now, integral in a type of way that the sharpest lashing wouldn't drown out.

One blink, one glance in her direction, and my life was irrevocably changed. Twisted and molded into something completely unrecognizable.

Maybe I've become the sinner I've always sought to kill. Or maybe I've always been.

Either way, I'm finding it hard to care.

Amaya is *made* for me. And now that I've accepted what that means, I won't have her any other way except by my side.

Rising from my space beside the bed, I walk to my dresser and pull out my clothes, rushing to get dressed. I slip on my coat and gloves before heading out of the cottage and into the city streets.

It's wildly cold today, and setup is beginning for the Festival of Fools, dozens of workers placing the outdoor heaters and small tents every few meters along the square.

I should stay here and make sure they don't need my help with anything, but that's what they have Jeremiah for. And I can't

CROSSED | 301

be bothered with my duties to the church right now, not when I can't even breathe without seeing Amaya one more time.

Why would God put her in my path if not for her to become mine?

If she is a succubus, then *seduce* me.

If she is my devil, then I will gladly burn.

A few men are salting the concrete steps in front of Notre-Dame as I make my way past, but I pay them no mind. I'm beyond caring who sees that I'm leaving. Let them all know. I'll flee this town and steal Amaya and Quinten away too, making a new life somewhere else.

It's early, just past seven in the morning, and I know that if I hurry, she'll be dropping Quinten off at school. I make it to Louis Elementary just in time; Parker's town car can't be missed for anything in the world.

I tap my fingers on the steering wheel as I pull up to the curb, staying out of the line of cars, and watch Quinten jump out of the back, his aide there to greet him and take him inside. And when the town car pulls away, I put my car in drive and follow.

The same way I've been following her since the beginning.

I'm not sure where I expect her to end up, only that I'll be wherever she is, but when the car continues to drive away from Festivalé and into Coddington Heights, I'm surprised.

She isn't going to the Chapel, surely?

But we don't head that way. Instead, we drive past it, through the city limits until we hit the edge of the town and come to a stop by a small building on the corner of a street. Small businesses line either side, and I tilt my head, trying to look for signage on the front to tell me where we are and what she's doing here.

It's a nondescript building though, and a spike of jealousy

plants in the base of my stomach, imagining her meeting some other man here and giving him everything that should be mine. I scoff, batting the ridiculous thought away. She wouldn't use *Parker's* car to meet with someone else.

I wait with bated breath to see her appear, the memory of her plump lips against mine heating my blood and making my cock fill and harden. She exits the back of the car, saying something to the driver before heading inside, and when the town car drives away, my curiosity is about to eat me alive. I debate for the next ten minutes on whether to stay out here and wait or head inside and let her know I'm here. That she can't escape me again.

That I won't let her run.

Out of the car it is.

I hurry into the building and stop when I make it inside, wondering which one of the several rooms she'd be in. It's a basic beige interior with short, industrial-style carpet and five doors lining each side, each one with a nameplate on the front describing a different business.

Slowly, I make my way down the hall, peeking in the thin window on each of the doors to see if I can spot Amaya.

What is she doing here?

When I make it halfway down the hall, my ears fill with a thumping bass, muted and dulled as it beats through the walls.

Dancing. Of course.

I walk faster, something tugging in the middle of my chest like I'm attached to where she is by a rope, and when I get to the door the music is pouring from, I see her.

And I'm immediately transfixed, the same way I was the first time I saw her. I'm moving before I can stop myself, my hand twisting the doorknob and slipping into the room, expecting her to sense my presence immediately and stop what she's doing to either get angry again or be happy that I'm here. I'm not sure which. With her, it's always a toss-up.

But she's so into whatever she's doing that she doesn't miss a beat. Her eyes are closed and her body is flying around the pole, a single chair perched not too far away.

Desire chokes me like red smoke.

It's a small studio. The back is lined with mirrors, and a little wooden stool is off to the side with a Bluetooth speaker, a bottle of water, and Amaya's phone.

I lean my shoulder against the wall, and I watch her.

She must be dancing for another two minutes before her eyes finally open, and she sees me in the reflection, her body jerking to a sudden stop. Slowly, she slips down the pole, her feet touching the ground.

Her chest is moving up and down with her heavy breaths, her mouth slightly parted and skin glistening with a thin layer of perspiration, and when our eyes lock in the mirror, I smirk.

CHAPTER 43

Amaya

I FELT HIM BEFORE I KNEW HE WAS HERE. THAT sounds silly, but it's the truth. There was a shift in the energy during my dance, and I gave in to the feeling, a heaviness taking over and making my movements more sensual, less rushed. I just didn't know it was *him* until I opened my eyes.

When I'm dancing, I'm in an altered state; my mind turns off and my body takes over, and I find blissful relief from the chaos that's constantly going on in the world. I'm just...*me*. And today, I needed the escape.

It doesn't surprise me that Cade's here. That he followed me.

That's what he does, and I've gone far beyond the scope of pretending that I don't enjoy his attention. We're toxic for each other; therapists would tell me to scream as loud as I can and run in the opposite direction. But I've never been one for doing what I'm told.

The only thing I've ever truly been lacking in is courage. Courage to stand up against the bullies of the town. To not let other people control my life. To dive headfirst into something that could be the greatest thing I've ever known, even though it's fucking terrifying to think of losing it once it's mine.

I've spent *years* working tirelessly to keep everything structured and rigid. Unbendable and routine. Both for Quinten's sake and also for mine. When you don't have deviations from your day, you never meet the unexpected. Every interaction I had was controlled, kept at arm's length. I thought that keeping my heart locked up tight and Quinten and I in a tiny little bubble would protect anyone else from doing what our mother did.

You can't get hurt if you don't let anyone in.

I thought that's what made me strong.

But somehow, Cade worked his way through the shield, and maybe that's what true strength really is. Allowing yourself the chance to be hurt and finding your faith through the fear.

So when I open my eyes and see Cade leaning up against the wall like he's exactly where he's meant to be, I give in.

Fully. Freely. Without restraint.

I'm *tired* of resisting. Tired of worrying about what everyone else thinks and whether Quinten and I will ever fit into the mold.

Tired of caring at all, if I'm completely honest.

The music fades away, one song ending and leaving a few beats of strained silence as we're both locked in each other's gazes, and then a new one starts. Slower. Softer. Sultrier.

The bass pulses through me like a living thing and propels me forward toward Cade.

He's staring at me, because he's *always* staring at me, and I hold his gaze, knowing he likes it when I do.

My hips sway from side to side as I move to him, and when I'm a few steps away, his hand reaches out and flicks the lock on the door, turning to face me straight on.

I stop when I'm in front of him, looking up into his eyes. A slow smile creeps on my face. "Hi."

He straightens off the wall, and my stomach flips in anticipation when he starts to remove his gloves, one finger at a time.

His gaze eats me up, trailing from my exposed collarbone down the length of my sports bra and over my exposed stomach to my shorts and naked legs, then back up again. "Hello, petite pécheresse."

He slips his gloves into his coat pocket and then moves to unbutton it, taking it off entirely and laying it next to him, not caring that it's on the dirty wood floor.

I wait, not wanting to utter another word. Terrified if I do, the spell will be broken. We both might come to our senses and remember we're not supposed to meet like this. We're not supposed to *be*.

The thought propels me into action, because if this is our moment, I'm going to grab on to it with both hands. My palms reach out and rest on his torso, his abs tensing beneath my hands. I glide my fingers up the length of him, spreading them over his chest as I take a step closer until our bodies are centimeters from touching.

Cade stands silent and still as he looks down at me, his eyes dark and fierce. This free rein over his body is intoxicating, and I'm drunk on the feel. I wonder what changed, what made him finally give in to whatever this is between us so fully, but truthfully, I'm finding it hard to care for the *why* as long as it *is*.

The music continues pulsing, and I explore him more, slipping my fingers beneath the collar of his shirt, rubbing back and forth, wishing I was feeling the heat of his skin and not the fabric of his button-down.

I rise on my tiptoes, pressing a soft kiss to the underside of his jaw, and his hands snake out and grip me around the waist, dragging my body flush to his. I suck in a breath at his erection pressing into me, and my fingers dig into his shoulders when his press deeply into my back.

"Do not tease me, Amaya," he growls.

"Nobody's teasing," I assure, pressing another kiss to his chin and pushing myself further against him. "I *need* you, Cade."

He lets out a deep sigh before pushing me back slightly, letting go of my waist and grabbing my hand instead.

I look down at our tangled fingers, my brows drawing in at the simple touch and the way it makes me feel like fireworks are exploding inside my chest. He moves us across the room until we're back by the pole, and he lets me go, sitting down in the chair and gripping my hips, maneuvering my body until I'm standing in between his open legs.

"Dance for me," he commands.

"Did you ever come to see me at the club?" I ask. "Beyond that first time we met, I mean."

He watches me but takes his time answering. His hands move from my hips down the outsides of my thighs, his fingers teasing the bottom of my shorts and slipping beneath the fabric, tickling my skin with his feathery touches. And then he moves them around until he's palming the meat of my ass and pulling me down onto his lap, my legs situating themselves on either side of his hips. My pussy throbs when it feels how hard he is against me, and I have to keep from grinding down on his thick cock.

"Do you want me to say yes, petite pécheresse?" He leans in, licking along the shell of my ear. "It wouldn't be a lie. I've been everywhere you are. Watching you. Aching for you. *Killing* for you."

I moan when he thrusts up into me, his length dragging along the seam of my shorts, and a thrill zips through me like electricity, lighting me up from the inside out.

I'm desperate for more of his words.

More of his obsession.

More of his truth.

"Are you scared yet, mon trésor?" He presses a kiss to my neck before biting down on the flesh and sucking, marking my skin with his mouth.

"No," I say on an exhale.

And it's the most honest thing I've ever said. I know what he's just admitted to me, have known deep down for a while, if I'm honest. And maybe I should be running away, disgusted by who he is and what he represents.

But I don't. And I'm not.

Cade makes me feel free. Makes me feel *seen*.

He makes me feel loved.

And I don't care about anything else.

His right hand moves from my hip and skates up my side until he's threading it into the hair on the back of my head— his favorite spot—and tugging until my back arches. His tongue glides from the side of my neck, and he presses kisses against my throat, and I sink into my weight, pushing my clit against him.

"Good," he whispers against my skin. "I would never hurt you. I'm sorry I ever did." Another sharp sting pierces me when he nips my skin, and then he leans back, his fingers flexing in my hair. "Dance for me, mon trésor."

So I do.

I rotate my hips, my eyelids fluttering when his erection glides along my sensitive nerves in just the right way, and I repeat the motion, wanting to skip the foreplay and take out his cock so it can slide deep inside me. I know he'll make it hurt *so* good.

My body rolls, my chest ghosting across his lips with every forward thrust, and I move to lift my sports bra, fingering the hem before ripping it off altogether and tossing it somewhere to the side.

His pupils dilate and then his mouth is on my breast, his tongue flicking against the nipple before he sucks, *hard*.

"Jesus, Cade," I moan, my hand flying to the back of his head as I grind against his dick.

"Watch your mouth." He groans against me, then moves to pay attention to my other side, and I'm so wet I'm sure I'm leaving a stain on his pants. But I don't care. I need him to fuck me or I think I might die.

"Cade," I mumble, my clit aching more with every pass over his lap. "*Please.*"

He releases my nipple with a pop, his hand leaving my hair and moving to his zipper. I rise up slightly and he undoes his pants, and then his cock is in his hand, precum leaking from the tip. My mouth waters. I rip myself away from where I'm sitting and drop to my knees, swallowing him down my throat before he can tell me no.

"*Fuck*," he moans, his hand going back to fist my hair.

He never curses, and it sends a shot of desire rippling through me, the salty taste of *him* coating my tongue as I move up and down his length.

"That's it, petite pécheresse. Take it down your throat until you choke." He punctuates his words with a sharp thrust, and the tip of him gags me, my eyes watering as he buries himself to the hilt and holds himself there.

I breathe through my nose, desire cramping my stomach.

My head is ripped back, and his dick slides out, angry and throbbing, a thin line of saliva attaching from the head to my lips. I move forward again, my tongue swirling around the tip, desperate for more.

He tsks, jerking the strands of my hair until I wince. The sharp shot of pain makes me see stars, and my pussy is on fire from how badly I need to come. Leaning down, he nips my bottom lip, his tongue swiping along the seam of my mouth and dipping inside like he's trying to taste himself on me.

I need him like I need air.

"Tell me I can have you," he murmurs against me. "Tell me that you're mine."

"*Yours.* Yes. *Please*," I beg. My body trembles as he pulls me up to a standing position, his hands slipping beneath the waistband of my shorts and dragging them down my legs, torturously slow. My heart slams against my ribs as I let him set the pace.

As I give up control and surrender to anything he's willing to give me.

My shorts are tossed to the side, and then his large palm is on the front of my cotton panties and he pulls, the fabric burning my skin deliciously as it tears.

He grips me firmly by the hips and pulls me back onto his lap, and when my pussy touches his naked cock, we both let out a moan.

I have *dreamed* of this moment.

Thought about it every time I slipped my own fingers inside my cunt and longed for it to be him.

"Fuck me till it hurts, Cade. *Please.*"

"I'm not going to fuck you, Amaya." He pulls my hips forward, my pussy drenching his cock from how wet I am.

I whine, squeezing my eyes closed.

One of his hands leaves my hip and cups my cheek. I lean into the touch.

"I'm going to love you. Because loving you hurts so much more."

My heart explodes and he slams me down on his cock, our hips slapping together as he fills me with every thick inch.

He lifts me up slightly with his other hand and then brings me down again, starting a punishing rhythm immediately, and my mind is collapsing and expanding like a galaxy is being born into the stars.

We're a mess of limbs and sloppy kisses and fingers that tug and pull. It's dirty, filthy, *angry*, and it feels like we're on borrowed time.

"God, Cade, you feel—" My voice chokes out as he fucks up into me and steals my breath.

I slip my hand down the front of my stomach, my fingers barely touching my clit before he rips my touch away. "Non," he says. "When you're with me, you're with *me*."

He covers my palm with his and moves us both back to my pussy, his thrusts slowing down as he maneuvers our fingers into a V shape so we surround his length, my hands growing slippery from my wetness on his skin. I lift up slightly so I can feel more of him under my fingers and then lower back down, tension coiling tightly in my abdomen when I touch where he disappears inside me.

I suck in a shaky breath.

"Feel yourself on me, mon trésor? How you drench my cock and how well I fill you up?" He thrusts again, his other hand moving to cup the back of my neck, dragging me forward until our foreheads touch. "Eyes on me, Amaya."

Our gazes lock.

I breathe out. He breathes in.

Everything about us feels connected, and it's intoxicating, making my head spin and my body buzz.

"No other man can make you feel like this," he grits out.

"Cade," I whisper.

"Say it, Amaya."

"Only you," I moan, heat winding into a tight ball at the base of my spine and exploding.

And then I come, my body shaking and my pussy clenching painfully around him, until it feels like my soul is leaving my body and flying into heaven.

He groans, long and low against me, and his cock pulses as he paints my insides with his cum.

I collapse against him, trying to catch my breath.

My body aches and my soul is sated, and I close my eyes and press my ear against his chest, letting myself relax to the sound of his beating heart.

He's right.

Our love hurts so much more.

CHAPTER 44

Amaya

CADE FUCKED ME AGAIN BEFORE LEAVING, AND now I'm back at my new "home," trying to act normal around Parker. I have concealer on my neck, and my clothes are covering every possible inch of my body because Cade's fingerprints are tattooed on my skin in light purple marks.

I feel him every time I move, and I love it.

Parker's home for dinner for the first time since we've moved in, and even if I wasn't feeling awkward and sore, I'd be on edge because this is the first real interaction between him and Quinten. My mind wars between how much I long to make something work with Cade, even though he's never told me he'd give me more than what we've had, and knowing I don't really have a choice.

I've already made a deal with the devil.

Parker's eyes scan me from across the table, and I force myself to stay still even though I want to fidget in my seat.

"How was your day, sweetheart?" he asks.

I shrug.

Incredible.

Life changing.

I can't marry you.

Would he hurt Quin?

I should never have come to him.

More than anything, I ache to speak to Dalia, to confess my darkest secrets and let her give me another perspective, but then I think of Cade. And until I find out more about where he stands, I can't put him at risk of people finding out about us. Even though I trust Dalia with everything in me, the loyalty I feel for protecting Cade and his position reigns supreme.

"Amaya." Parker's sharp voice drowns out my wandering thoughts and I jump in place, holding back the wince from how sore I am between my legs.

Quinten's head snaps up from his iPad at Parker's sharp tone, his eyes narrowing.

The air in the room pulls taut, and I suck in a breath, anxiety making my palms clammy and my throat close up.

"Sorry, my brain's a little foggy today." I grin at him, trying to smooth things over.

He doesn't smile back, and my gut sinks like a concrete boulder.

"Did you do anything exciting?" he continues, taking a bite of his steak and leaning back in his chair, chewing slowly.

My heart jumps into my throat. "Not much. Took Quinten around to school, ran some errands, and then went with Quin to therapy." I stab the lettuce from my salad. "This is delicious, by the way. Thanks for ordering in tonight."

He nods and picks up his tumbler of whiskey, the veins in his neck popping as he swallows and sets it back down, still silent.

Still watching.

Alarm bells ring in my head.

Does he know?

I'm under no illusion he doesn't get reports back from my driver Barney over where I'm going and what I'm doing. But I wasn't thinking of that when I was so lost in everything Cade. Besides, even if I had told Barney some made-up story of why I was going where I was going, it wouldn't have mattered. The man never speaks a word to me.

"How about you?" I ask.

He nods. "It was…illuminating."

"Oh, that's good." I swallow, my mouth suddenly dry. "Is everything okay?"

The second the words leave my lips, I wish I could suck them back in. But I'm trying to appear nonchalant, and I don't know… normal?

"Perfect, sweet girl." Parker's responding smile is a thin line that doesn't show his teeth. "Actually," he continues, looking between Quinten and me, "I've decided we shouldn't wait any longer. I'm tired of playing by the church's rules."

My stomach drops. "What do you mean? I thought the church was important."

"Remind me again what you've learned in your one-on-one lessons?" he asks, tilting his head. "I can't remember."

My heart thumps so loudly, I worry he can hear it from across the table.

"I don't—"

"Right." He nods, rubbing his hand along the bottom of his jaw. "We'll get married next weekend."

My fork drops, the clack of the metal against white china loud in my ears. Parker's staring at me, and I clear my expression.

He places his silverware down gently, grabbing the linen napkin and dotting the sides of his mouth before setting that down as well. "I thought you'd be happy."

I slide my gaze to Quinten, who keeps flicking his eyes to Parker and then to me.

"Can we talk about this later?" I ask, nodding toward Quinten.

Parker sighs, picking up his whiskey and bringing it to his lips, draining the last of the drink. Standing up, he buttons his suit jacket and walks over, pressing a firm kiss to the top of my head, his hand possessively cupping the back of my neck until every hair on my body stands on end.

His fingers press on Cade's marks, and I bite my cheek from the pain it causes when he puts pressure against the bruises.

"No," he says. "What's done is done. My decision's been made."

And then he's gone, back to wherever it is he goes, and I'm left with a wide-eyed Quinten and me trying to smile through the panic so he doesn't know that anything is wrong.

CHAPTER 45

Cade

I'VE HIT AN IMPASSE. A ROCK AND A HARD PLACE. I had thought once I made a firm decision, that would be it. No more looking back, no more questions.

When I'm with Amaya, the urge to beat myself clean fades away.

Turns out once I'm alone, old habits die hard.

As I sit in my room, the smell of Amaya still on my skin, I'm fighting a different type of battle. One that's vacillating between what I've known to do my entire life and what I ache to do now.

Repent. Atone. Regret.

But I've already decided Amaya isn't something to feel bad about, even if it means I lose favor with God.

I stand up, pacing to the corner of the room, staring down into the open chest. Indecision knots up my insides, and I blow out a breath, moving away before stalking back over again. I surge down and grab the discipline in my hand, the rope gripping onto my skin like gritty paper.

Moving back to my bed, I sit and stare at it.

"God wants me to beat it out." Sister Agnes's voice knocks against my brain, the way it has since I was a child, and I know the only way to make her leave is to give in.

But atonement for Amaya makes her feel dirty. Sinful.

She's *everything* to me. Still, the urge crawls beneath my skin like bugs until I want to rip my flesh from bone just to snuff it out.

I shoot to a stand, ripping my shirt over my head and tossing it on the bed, my teeth clenched so hard, it feels like my molars will crack.

"Little demons who don't learn their lessons get the whip again."

My eyes close, my heart fractures, and I raise my hand up slowly, my fingers shaking from how tightly I grip the rope.

Then I bring it down and strike.

One.

I'm taking confession today. It's the last chance for it before the Festival of Fools on the first. I haven't seen or spoken with Amaya in days, both because I've been recovering from the beating I gave myself after I finally had her and because part of me wants her to come to *me*.

It's disappointing that I'm still waiting, although I'm not sure what else I could have really expected. I've decided to give her until the festival, and if she won't give herself to me, I'll accept Bishop Lamont's offer to transfer me back to Paris.

I fear living in her absence will be a torture worse than death. But I would do it, for her.

If she chooses me, I'll turn in my collar.

It doesn't hold the same appeal as it did before, even though my love for God stays strong and sure.

It's late when I leave the confessional booth, my mind as tired as my body is sore. Instead of leaving the sanctuary, I move to the front of the dais, falling to my knees and bowing in prayer, searching for respite from the constant seesaw of questions going back and forth in my brain.

"Please," I whisper, staring up at the crucifix looming over me like a promise. "Tell me what to do."

A door bangs open, echoing off the high-arched walls, light footsteps making their way down the aisle behind me. I rise from my vulnerable position, twisting around to see who it could be, and my lungs collapse, my heart stuttering in its cage.

Of course it's her.

Amaya.

And this is my sign from God.

I'm rushing toward her before she can utter a single word and taking her in my arms, my hands gripping her face tightly as I bring my lips to hers. She moans as she kisses me back, her feelings pouring into my mouth as fiercely as I'm bleeding mine into hers.

Wetness drips over my knuckles and I break away, seeing tears slide down her face. My thumbs brush beneath her eyes. "What is it, mon trésor?"

She shakes her head. "I shouldn't be here."

My stomach twists. "You should always be with me."

Her eyes scan mine like she's trying to peer into my soul. "Was it you?"

My heart stutters. "Was what me?"

"You know what I mean. You—you said it was you. You *admitted* it."

Clarity fills me, remembering my slip of the tongue from the last time we were together, when I told her I had killed for her.

I move my right hand, gripping the back of her neck, my thumb brushing over the faded mark I left on her skin.

Possessiveness flares in my chest, a sick satisfaction flooding my veins like a drug.

"*Please*," she whispers, her hands reaching up to grip my shirt. "I need to know."

I exhale slowly, my muscles pulling tight. "You might hate me once you do."

She shakes her head, pressing herself closer. "*Never.*"

I tilt her head to the side and lean down, brushing my lips against her ear. "I would kill a thousand men if it made sure you were mine."

My hand that was resting against her face drops down to ghost over her collarbone and then along her side until it slips beneath the waistband of her skirt and underneath her panties, dipping into her wet cunt.

She gasps.

"I saw you with him and lost my mind," I say, curling my finger inside her. "I killed him for touching you." A moan escapes her lips, and she falls into my chest. I drag her in until we're flush, pumping into her with a slow and steady rhythm. "And I killed the second man to keep you free."

I push my thumb against her clit, and her pussy clamps around me.

"And Candace?" she asks.

"A tortured soul."

She hesitates. "Was it because she's a sex worker?"

"No," I scoff but then think about what she's asking, my fingers stalling in their ministrations. "I suppose, in a roundabout way. It wasn't about her profession as much as her having demons inside her the same as any other sinner." I pull her by the back of her neck until she's on her tiptoes and her lips are brushing against mine. "Do you hate me now, petite pécheresse? Will you run the other way?"

Her body trembles and my lungs cramp as I wait for what she says, terrified that she'll leave and condemn me to a life without her. Or ask me to repent, replacing His expectations with hers.

I'd do it for her. I'd do anything for her.

"I don't hate you, Cade," she murmurs, her eyes locking with mine. "I'm in love with you."

Her words crash into me like a wrecking ball, and I'm slipping out of her cunt and picking her up in my arms, moving her to the nearest pew and tossing her down. Her skirt flies up, and I push her panties to the side and then my mouth is on her, latched around her swollen clit and sucking like I'll die if I don't taste her.

She screams out and my hand flies up, muffling the noise, and the second I slip my other hand back inside her cunt, she's coming, arching her hips as she grinds into my face, her arousal coating my lips.

I sit back and wipe my mouth with the back of my hand, but she surges up and grabs my head, sucking herself off my tongue. I groan, my cock throbbing. Without looking, I clumsily undo my pants and free myself, lining my tip up at her entrance and pushing her back down onto the wooden pew. I break my lips away from hers and brush her tangled hair off her cheek before cupping it possessively in my hand.

She's so damn beautiful.

"You love me, mon trésor?"

She nods, turning her head slightly to suck my thumb into her mouth.

"I *live* for you." I thrust inside her then, until my hips slap against the insides of her thighs, her hands flying to my back, scratching my barely healed wounds through the fabric of my shirt. The pain makes my balls draw up tight and I groan, my eyes rolling in the back of my head.

This won't last long, but it's just as intense as the first time I sank inside her, and I create a harsh pace, drawing my cock all the way out before plunging back inside. My fingers move to pinch her clit, my free hand still pressing down over her mouth to quiet her moans, and then she's coming again, the slick walls of her pussy hugging my cock as it pulsates.

"Merde," I mumble, tingles of pleasure racing through my limbs. My sack tightens and my vision dims, and I push myself in as far as I can go, pouring my cum into her as she spasms around my dick.

I collapse on top of her, trying to catch my breath as we both come back down from the high. And when we do, reason starts to filter back in. I sit back, running a hand through my hair and glancing around the sanctuary, making sure nobody came in.

Making sure nobody saw.

She makes me lose my mind.

I wait for the flush of guilt to creep over my skin, but it never comes. I feel more sure than ever that she is my future, even if it means walking away from everything else.

"Where's Quinten?" I ask, slipping out of her and rezipping my pants. I move back toward her, helping her straighten her long skirt, and can't resist pressing a kiss to the sliver of skin still visible on her stomach.

The idea of her leaving him with Parker, even though they live in the same place, makes me feel on edge. I find that I care for the boy, and anything happening to him sends a spark of unease down my spine.

"At our old place with Dalia for a 'sleepover.'"

Relieved, I reach up, tangling my fingers in her hair. "Come back to my home for the night."

She frowns, sadness whipping through her gaze, and my chest pulls, disappointment settling in even before she says her answer. She shakes her head. "I can't stay."

I nod. "Just for a moment then."

She hesitates but agrees, and I pull her up, helping her zip her coat back up and straightening her clothes before leading her out the door.

CHAPTER 46

Amaya

I KNEW BETTER THAN TO COME HERE, BUT I couldn't stay away. Cade's words about killing for me were on a constant loop in my head, try as I might to erase them, so when Dalia offered to do a sleepover with Quinten, I took the chance.

It's risky, coming out here, but Parker already said he wouldn't be home until late, and I didn't use Barney to drive me, just in case.

Still, I can feel the pressure of time closing in from every angle, even as I lie in Cade's bed after he convinced me to come back to his cottage.

"I really have to go," I say, hating that I'm breaking up the moment.

Cade lies next to me on his back, half-naked, having lost his shirt somewhere between the time we got home and when he had me laid out on his bed and his face planted between my legs. He sighs and rolls over, standing up and shaking his head.

My eyes follow him, wanting to drag him back. To tell him I didn't mean it, even though we both know I did. The words die on the tip of my tongue as I stare at his back.

I can't help the gasp that escapes, and I shoot up onto my knees, scrambling to the edge of the bed just as he turns around, his hand halfway through his hair.

My face must show my shock because confusion crosses his for just a moment before it drops into realization.

"Cade," I start, my hand coming up to my mouth and my other one reaching out to touch him.

He jerks away, and I try to ignore the way it makes my heart crack.

"It's nothing," he snaps.

Slowly, I shake my head, willing the burn behind my eyes to disappear. "That's not nothing, baby."

I try again, reaching out and grabbing his forearm, and he doesn't move away this time. His body is rigid and his jaw is tense, but he stands still and doesn't fight when I prod him to turn back around.

Heaviness fills up my chest as I take in the marred skin on his back. This is...*years* of markings. Raised and uneven flesh that plays out like a script on his skin. I shake my head slightly, wondering what in the world happened and why so many of them look so fresh. I open my mouth to speak, but nothing comes, so instead I lean in, and I press my lips to one of the scars.

He stiffens.

I don't let it stop me, moving from one to the next, avoiding the ones that are freshly scabbed over. He doesn't encourage the act, but he doesn't move away either, and I take that as a win. After I'm done, I let the sheet drop from my waist and stand up from the bed, moving around until I'm staring up into his eyes.

"How?"

His nostrils flare, his eyes dark with a heavy emotion. "It's the only way I know. I'm a bad man, Amaya. A sinner. This is my atonement."

Breathing out slowly, I nod, trying to school my expression. Somehow, I had a feeling that was what he'd say, and it makes me so incredibly sad to think that he hurts himself to try and feel worthy of God.

I step into him and pull him into a hug, resting my head against his chest and closing my eyes, listening to every beat of his heart, letting it calm me. His arms close around my waist, gripping tightly.

"You said you'd never hurt me," I murmur into his skin.

"*Never* again."

"Every time you hurt yourself, you hurt *me* too," I whisper. "Please stop hurting me."

He doesn't speak, but I feel him nod against the top of my head, and a single tear escapes as I press a kiss to his pec, hating that I'll have to love him and leave.

But I don't know how to be any other way.

The next morning, Parker calls me into his home office. I'm already awake and ready for the day because Dalia's supposed to swing by with Quinten in the next couple of hours, and I want to try and convince her to stick around and hang for a bit since Parker said we weren't going to Mass.

"What's this?" I ask when I walk into the room and see him push a piece of paper across the desk.

"This"—he taps it with his finger—"is our marriage license. I'd like you to sign it, please."

I shift on my feet, nausea tossing my stomach. "Oh, can't we wait until right before the ceremony?"

Parker chuckles and walks around the desk, his stature aggressive and dominating. I take a step back, but he's there before I can get away, gripping me by the front of my throat and squeezing until he cuts off my airway.

My hands fly up to his wrists, trying to dig into his skin to pry him off because I can't *fucking breathe*, but he only grips tighter.

Panic makes my ears ring and my heart falter as I go from trying to scratch at his skin to holding on to his wrists, hoping he decides to let me live.

He drags me in close, his nose bumping against mine, and my head is dizzy, my lungs burning with the need for air. "You must think I'm as stupid as your little brother," he spits.

My stomach drops to the ground, and I try to shake my head and stomp on his feet, *something* to get him off me, but he's too strong and I'm already growing too faint from the lack of oxygen to do any lasting damage.

Genuine fear starts to creep into my system, worried he's going to kill me.

"Do you really believe I haven't known every step you've made since you and your whore mother stepped foot into my town?" he continues, a sick smile spreading across his face. "I am the *god* of this city, and you should be fucking honored I decided to let you be mine. Yet you mock me. Sneak around like a filthy little *slut*, and you think I wouldn't know? I have eyes and ears everywhere, sweet girl. Even in Coddington Heights."

My eyelids flutter as I try to stay conscious, my stomach surging into my chest and then back down, every organ in my body going haywire as it struggles to find breath.

I knew having Barney drive me to that studio was a mistake.

His hand drops and I fall to my knees, my fingers grasping at my sore throat as tears pour from my eyes and I suck in painful heaps of air.

"You'll sign it, Amaya," Parker says as he stands over me. "Because I don't like to lose. Because you belong to *me*." He crouches down next to me, brushing the hair from my face.

My body trembles from his touch, and I wish to God that I had the strength to do anything other than cower in the corner while he slings his hateful words.

"If you don't, I'll go to the church, and I'll find that blasphemous priest and string him up in front of you while I cut off his cock and make him choke on it."

My neck throbs so intensely I know bruises are already forming, but I nod, desperate to agree, to do *anything* so he'll leave me alone. He straightens but doesn't back away.

"Stand up," he demands, kicking me in the thigh.

I wince but push myself to a standing position, wiping the wetness that I can't stop from trailing down my cheeks. I *hate* that I'm crying, because it makes me feel weak.

Powerless.

Which I guess is what I am.

It's what he's always made me.

Parker shoves me between the shoulders until I stumble forward, the front of my legs slamming into his desk, and he moves behind me, grabbing the pen and forcing it into my fingers, his disgusting, meaty hand wrapping around mine as he pushes the pen down to touch the certificate.

"You are not to see him again, *wife*. Understand?"

I hesitate and he slips his other hand up the back of my skirt and rips my underwear roughly from my body.

The burn on my skin doesn't feel good this time.

"Parker, *please*," I beg, a sob tearing out of my throat before I can hold it back. "Don't do this again."

"Sign it."

I close my eyes tightly, praying for a miracle as I hear the clank of his buckle and the pressure of his hand as he presses my front onto the desk.

And when he thrusts inside me, I sign my name, my tears marring the ink.

CHAPTER 47

Amaya

IT HURTS TO WALK.

It hurts to move.

It hurts to breathe.

But I still have Quinten and I still have *me*, even though I'm beat down and quiet.

I'm a survivor.

And I know I'll get through this the same way I have everything before it.

Today is the Festival of Fools, so despite the fact that I'd rather be anywhere other than here, in front of Notre-Dame where I know Cade will be, I paste a smile on my face and fake it for Quinten's sake. He's been in such a great mood since Christmas with me and Dalia.

Parker's arm sits on my shoulders, and the feel of it makes me sick, bile rising in my throat and burning my esophagus until I ache to reach up and rip off my skin entirely.

It's January 1, and the weather shows it, frigid air whipping across my cheeks and freezing the tips of my fingers, even though they're covered with gloves. The entire square is filled with small white tents of vendors and space heaters laid out to keep people warm. Street performers line the walkway, clad in tight spandex clothes while they juggle bowling pins and balance on unicycles, which is only more impressive since there's ice and slush on the ground. Still, there's a general sense of merriment in the air, of people coming together to laugh and celebrate. It's the one day of the year when Festivalé isn't so grim, callous, and *cold*.

The warmth is almost *more* ominous, and I shake off the uneasy feeling that's wrangling my neck like a noose.

The cathedral doors are open today, serving hot chocolate and pastries out of the front entrance, and people mingle just inside, chatting and laughing while they catch up with friends. And in the sanctuary itself, there's a makeshift stage, set up along the dais, where the children of Louis Elementary are about to put on their play.

My stomach rocks back and forth like a ship in a storm as I scan the area looking for Quinten. I haven't seen him since we first got here and I passed him off to Lydia.

Parker and I move down the rows of pews and sit in the very front, waiting for the play to begin. I stay silent and still, trying not to wince every time I move on the uncomfortable wood. I've been bleeding a bit this morning, and if I move too much, it will draw attention.

The only attention I long for today is for Quinten. For *finally* being part of something in town after so many years of being the brunt of everyone's ire.

The thought sends nausea curling through my gut, the same way being in Notre-Dame with the entire town always has, flashbacks of the last time I saw our mother playing behind my eyes on a constant loop.

No. Things are different now. Things are changing, I remind myself. That's why we're here, with Quinten taking part in the community.

I want to glance around and see if Dalia is on her way, but I'm too afraid to look up and see Cade. I can feel that he's here, but I won't seek him out. Parker made it very clear what's expected, and I'm under no illusion he won't make good on his threat.

Besides, I have no doubt that if Cade takes one look at my face, he'll know something is wrong, and I'm still coming to terms with what happened myself. I don't want him to know, because he'll find a way to get to me, and I crave his comfort too badly to stay away.

He could kill Parker for you, a thought whispers.

More voices filter in from behind us, people filling up the pews and chattering while they wait, and my shoulders tense, my body on edge even though there's no logical reason for it. My foot taps against the floor, and Parker's hand moves from my shoulder down to my thigh, squeezing tight enough to make me wince.

I stop the movement, letting the anxiety build inside me instead.

Someone knocks into my shoulder and my heart jolts. I snap out of my daze, looking over into the smiling face of Dalia.

"Hey, girl." She leans forward. "Hey, Parker."

He nods to her, his arm tightening around my shoulders.

I hadn't realized that just seeing a friendly face would make me want to scream, but here we are, with me wanting to do exactly that. "Hey," I force out.

Dalia's smile drops and her brows furrow as she looks at me. I smile at her, trying like hell to be convincing because she can't know anything's wrong.

I don't *want* her to know.

I just want to forget that it ever happened.

"Can you believe Quin's about to be in a play?" I ask, taking the risk and glancing toward the stage.

The concern drops from her face, and she laughs, settling into the pew. "I know. He's gonna be such a little badass. Is he excited?"

I shrug because honestly, this morning he acted like he couldn't care less. "He seemed kind of meh about the whole thing. I don't even know how big of a part he has."

"Doesn't matter." She waves her hand in the air. "He'll be the show stealer either way, obviously."

"You're right," I sigh, shifting and trying not to visibly wince. I glance around again, hoping to see Quinten getting ready, but none of the kids are in sight. I *do* see Florence freaking Gammond though, her beady eyes locked on Parker and me.

I don't have the energy to deal with her, so I pull my gaze away, and then they fall on Cade.

He's standing off to the side of the stage, his shoulder leaned against the wall and his hands in his pockets, clerical collar around his neck, and like usual, he's watching me.

Longing spreads through my chest, sticky and slow like molasses, and I wish *so badly* to stand up and run into his arms. To have him soothe away the pain that's sitting heavy on my soul.

I inhale deeply, and the pain in my side from where Parker kicked me pinches tight, making me wince, my hand flying to the spot.

Cade straightens, his eyes narrowing.

Parker leans in, his lips against my hair. "You better stop looking at him, or I'll be forced to make a scene."

My spine stiffens and I rip my gaze away, faking a smile over at Parker instead.

There's this weird ball of energy swirling in my solar plexus, tightening and tensing like barbed wire about to snap.

People continue to fill in the pews, and then Florence takes center stage, announcing the children and saying what an honor it was for her to work with them. I hadn't even realized she was part of the production, and I chew on my bottom lip, wondering what else I don't know.

I should have paid more attention.

The kids file out onstage, and I scan the area for Quinten, but I don't find him. So I wait. Minutes pass and I zone out, going to the safe corner in my mind where I don't have to feel the things hurtling through my body or my heart.

Dalia leans in when the play is coming to a close. "Where is he?"

I shrug, wondering the same thing, but I don't voice my concern because that ball of energy in my middle is winding up too much to speak. Parker's hand has moved from my shoulder to my thigh, and he squeezes, right on top of a bruise.

I bite my cheek until it bleeds and that odd feeling coils tighter.

The play ends and all the kids take their bows, and I'm fuming that Quinten wasn't there. *Where the hell is he?*

Florence shows up onstage again, her eyes flicking toward me, and I just know like I know anything that something bad is about to happen.

"This year, we're doing things a *little* bit differently." She pinches her fingers together and chuckles. "We thought since the church has been so kind to take part in the festival this year that we'd bring it back to its roots to honor where the festival originated from."

I sit a little straighter.

"And originally, the Festival of *Fools* always crowned a king."

Her eyes meet mine, and dread fills up my stomach.

No.

I try to stand but Parker's hand jerks me back down, and I hit the pew with an audible smack. Tears spring into my eyes from the pain that bleeds from between my legs and spreads up my back.

From the corner of my eye, I can see Cade move off the wall entirely, and I risk a side-eyed glance, shaking my head, hoping he gets the message.

"What the hell is going on?" Dalia asks, nodding toward Florence. "Why is that bitch looking at you like that?"

A couple of kids, her asshole son included, bring out a little makeshift throne, made from a small child-sized chair with streamers down the side and a giant sign on the back that reads "King Fool."

My stomach burns, and my fingernails cut into the palms of my hands.

I look at Dalia. "When you find Quin, you take him from here."

She frowns. "What?"

"Promise me, Dalia. Take him far away."

Slowly, she nods. "I promise."

I turn my head to my husband.

"Parker," I say through clenched teeth. "Let me up."

He looks at me, scowling.

"Parker, I swear to God, if you don't let me up, I will *scream* at the top of my lungs."

His jaw tenses, and for a moment, I think he'll test me, but

I'm banking on the fact that he doesn't like to be embarrassed. It isn't good for his image if his wife seems like she's losing her mind.

He releases my thigh and I shoot up to a stand, shoving my way through the pew and to the side of the stage. Parker's eyes are on mine, and they narrow into slits when they glide just beyond my shoulder, and I know without looking that Cade is right behind me.

I stiffen my jaw and don't say a word.

"Please welcome our King Fool, Quinten Paquette!" Florence cheers.

Laughter and cheers ring out around the sanctuary as Quinten is brought out by a small group of kids.

My heart cracks in half and my eyes blur from rage, because while he may not understand what's going on, I sure as hell do.

She's *mocking* him. In front of everyone.

That tight ball inside me unravels and snaps, and I'm lost to everything except my fury.

Florence moves off the stage, walking right toward me, a smarmy smile on her face that I can't wait to rip off her face.

Because I'm done. I'm sick and fucking *tired* of everyone thinking they can do shit like this and get away with it. She moves by me and into the back hallway, and as soon as I see Dalia snatch Quinten off the stage, I'm after Florence.

I think I hear Parker call my name, but I ignore him, my vision tunneled into a singular focus. He might be following me, but I don't care.

She heads into the bathrooms at the end of the hall, and I'm right behind her, anger snapping and hissing at my back.

"You *fucking* bitch." My voice echoes off the tile, and she halts from where she was leaning over the sink to look in the mirror, slowly spinning toward me and quirking a brow.

"Oh, please. Get over yourself." She rolls her eyes.

My body shakes. "That was cruel. And he may not know it, but I do, and years from now, he'll look back and he'll remember."

She huffs out a laugh. "Don't be so dramatic, Amaya. It's just a little bit of fun."

I step forward slowly, a sense of anticipation thrumming in my veins, and I whip my hand out and smack her across the face, so hard she stumbles into the counter, her head flung to the side.

She sucks in a breath, her palm covering her reddened cheek, and she looks back at me, straightening with a sneer on her face. "You are such trash, Amaya Paquette. *You're* trash, your brother is trash, and your little slut of a friend Dalia is trash."

I point at her, my finger shaking. "Shut your fucking mouth."

"I'm not saying anything that isn't true. Even your own mother knew it." She smirks. "Why do you think she's not around?"

I lose all sense, reaching out and swiping the metal tissue dispenser that's sitting on the sink. I don't even register the weight as I grab it and slam it down on her head.

A door opens behind me, but I don't give a shit who sees, and I slam the metal on her face again. She crumples to the floor, and I follow, hovering over her while I bash her skull in and watch as her blood spills out onto the floor.

Arms surround me and pull me back, and then I'm lifted into sturdy arms and swept away from the room all together, my fingers caked in blood and stuck to the tissue dispenser that's still in my hand.

The familiar smell of pine fills my senses, and I breathe out fully for the first time since yesterday, slumping against Cade's chest while he whisks me away and down the hall.

CHAPTER 48

Cade

"CALM DOWN, PETITE PÉCHERESSE," I WHISPER IN her ear.

I don't even think she's aware that she's trembling in my arms.

My own heart is pounding, and although it's certainly not the appropriate time for it, I'm hard as a rock. She was a vision in her violence, a fallen angel seeking vengeance for being wronged.

She is a masterpiece, and she is mine.

"Cade," she murmurs, her eyes wide and unseeing. She's covered in blood, and the only reason I haven't peeled her fingers off the metal dispenser in her hands is because I don't want her to leave any evidence. I was lucky to beat Parker into the bathrooms in the first place.

"Amaya," I say, rushing us out the back entrance and into the parking lot.

She lets out a sob and curls farther into my arms, and while I want to sit down and rock her, soothe whatever is sitting so heavy on her soul, there isn't time for that now.

There's a *very* good chance she just murdered Florence

Gammond, and I need to get her away so she doesn't end up in jail.

"Amaya," I repeat. "Tell me where Quin is."

"Quin?" She shakes her head, sniffling. "He's fine. He-he's safe. With Dalia."

"You're sure?"

She hesitates but then nods. "Yes, I saw her with him."

I nod because that's all I need to know. Once I get her somewhere safe, I can come back for him.

We reach my car and I fling open the passenger door, shoving her inside and grabbing the seat belt before clicking it into place. I brush the hair from her face and cup her jaw. She stares down at the blood covering her hands, that piece of metal still gripped tight.

"Listen to me. I'm taking you away from here, do you understand? Do you trust me?"

She snaps her gaze up, her eyes red-rimmed and puffy. She nods, leaning forward and pressing her lips against mine.

I close my eyes and force myself to break away because as much as I want to sink into her kiss, there isn't time.

Immediately I know where I plan to take her, and as soon as I make sure she's safe and secure, I'm around to the driver's side and peeling out of the parking lot to the one place I know she'll be hidden.

Where she can be safe until I figure out what the hell is going on.

An hour later and we're high in the Green Mountains. Amaya hasn't said a single word on the drive up; she just sits and stares blankly at the empty trees, occasionally staring down at her hands and then sighing before looking back out the window.

I wish I could say I relate to what she's feeling, but I'm not sure I can. The truth is I felt no remorse the first time I took a life. My guilt has always centered around the *lack* of what I should be feeling, and while I don't know what's going through her head, I can only assume she's at least somewhat affected by what she's done.

Then again, she is my other half, and I had never imagined her capable of smashing someone's head in the way I just watched her do.

We pull up to the monastery and I throw the car in park, getting out and opening her door, cupping her cheek again to make sure she's still with me.

She looks up, giving me a small smile. "I'm not sorry for hurting her," she whispers, her voice shaky. "It felt good."

"Then you are made for me in more ways than one, petite pécheresse." I press a kiss to her forehead. "Let's go clean up."

She lets me unbuckle her from the seat and pull her from the car, and she takes in a deep breath once she's standing, glancing around. "This is beautiful. Where are we?"

"Somewhere no one knows." I grab her hand in mine and lead her to the front door, my stomach tangling in knots at the thought of leaving her here with Sister Genevieve, but I know that until I can grab Quinten and figure out a plan, this is where she'll be the safest.

I don't knock on the front door, choosing to walk right in, and when I don't see Sister Genevieve in the front sanctuary or living room, I lead Amaya up the stairs and into one of the empty bedrooms on the left.

She looks around at the space but doesn't say a word, just follows me into the bathroom suite. The blood has started to dry on her hands, but bits have flaked off onto mine from where we were touching, and I turn on the sink, then prop my hip on the corner and reach out to grasp the metal dispenser that's still tucked away in her left hand. Slowly, I pry her fingers off one by one until it drops, clunking loudly when it hits the ground.

I lean forward, grabbing her hips and lifting her onto the edge of the counter, then I step between her legs, grabbing a washcloth that's hanging from the wall and letting it dampen beneath the sink. Then I lean in and start washing away her sins.

Slowly. Methodically.

One finger clean and I bend down and press a kiss to the knuckle, then repeat it with every one after. Once her hands are done, I move up her arms, wiping away any remnants of red, marveling at the way she sits still and silent, letting me take care of her. The way I'll *always* take care of her.

The water runs red, but her skin is soaked clean, and when I'm done, I grip her chin in my hand and drag her mouth to mine for a kiss. Her body relaxes and she wraps her arms around my neck, pulling me farther into her. My cock hardens and I press myself to her center, grinding against her core.

Her body jerks, but not in pleasure, and she sucks in a sharp breath through her teeth.

I pull back, frowning.

She averts her eyes, twisting her head away.

I grab her cheek and bring her vision back. "Look at me."

She lifts her gaze back to mine, and I see the world in her eyes. Her longing, her love, her suffering.

Her shame.

My chest burns, my monster snapping in its cage, desperate to be released. I exhale sharply through my nose, trying to control my reaction, knowing she needs me to be calm and controlled.

"Are you in pain, mon trésor?" I ask carefully.

"A little." She sucks on her lips and looks away again. "It doesn't matter."

I slam my hand on the wall next to us and press against her, my hand gripping her face until her eyes are wide and open, staring directly into mine. "You are the *only* thing that matters, do you understand me?"

Her breathing stutters, like she's trying to keep from crying out, and then she breaks, a sob ripping from her mouth as she collapses into my hold. "I didn't want to do it, Cade. I—"

I palm the back of her head and hug her against my chest, letting her tears stain my shirt. "Shh, it's okay," I soothe. "Everything will be okay."

We stay like that for a long while, until her sobs quiet into whimpers and her stuttered explanations turn into long, grief-filled confessions. My rage pounds in my ears, but I get the gist of what she's saying.

Parker. Virginity. *Rape.* Forced marriage. *Rape.*

I hold her until she falls asleep in my arms, and then I move her to the bed, tucking her in and pressing a kiss to her lips, whispering my assurances that I'll be back.

Then I close the door behind me and head downstairs into the kitchen where Sister Genevieve is sitting at the table and sipping a cup of tea.

"I saw your car, figured you'd be down here eventually to explain." She grins. "Is it weird I've missed you?"

The first aid kit is out and next to her, clearly having assumed I was here to be sutured up again.

I shake my head, uncomfortable with what she's just said. "I have a friend here. She needs a safe space to stay. Can I trust you to take care of her?"

Sister Genevieve bobs her head, sipping from her cup. "Of course."

"I'll be back as soon as possible," I say. Unease tightens my stomach, not wanting to leave Amaya here at all. But I need to find Quinten.

And now I need to find Parker as well.

"Sister..." I add, right before I walk out of the door. "If something happens to her while I'm gone, I will make the devil look like a saint."

CHAPTER 49

Amaya

A LITTLE BIT OF DROOL IS DRIED TO THE SIDE OF my cheek, and my hair is stuck to it. I blink slowly, gathering my bearings as I reach up and rip away the strands and then sit up entirely, the scratchy blue quilt falling to my waist.

Where am I?

I stretch, lifting my arms above my head and reveling in the way a pop crackles down my spine. Slipping out of the bed, I look around the small room. It's very bland, just a full-size bed with plain sheets and a dark blue quilt and a small desk in the corner with a lamp on the right-hand side. Across the way, there's a door leading to a bathroom, and suddenly the day's events flood through me, reminding me that I'm up high in the mountains, hiding out like a criminal.

Technically, I guess I am one.

I wonder if she's still alive.

My body drops back down on the edge of the bed, and my fingers twist in my lap. I look down at my nails, noticing there's still bits of dried red flakes caked beneath them, and flashes of just how much Florence can bleed assault my memory. I search deep inside me for feelings of remorse, but I come up empty.

The only thing I feel is satisfaction that the bitch finally got what she deserved and a little bit of power flowing back into my soul that I had lost when Parker shoved his filthy cock inside me.

How dare she try to put Quinten on a stage like that. The only thing I regret is doing something that could truly take me away from Quinten now, when I've worked so hard and sacrificed so much to be able to keep myself in his life.

Quinten.

His name is a shot of anxiety straight into my heart, and my stomach rises and drops like a roller coaster. I shove the blankets off me, the fabric suddenly feeling stifling, and I jump up from the bed, pacing back and forth, my fingers tugging at the roots of my hair. *How could I have left him like this?*

I consider looking for my phone but stop myself, assuming Cade took it with him so I couldn't be tracked here. And I get that, I do, but until Quinten is here with me, I won't be able to breathe. Even though I saw Dalia take him away with my own two eyes, and even though I know being here is what's for the best…I still feel like a piece of shit for not being with him right now, when he's the one thing that I need.

Him and Cade.

Cade's going to get him. Everything will be fine.

It fucking terrifies me to trust someone else so fully, but I don't really have another choice. And I can't go back to Parker. Not now. I'm sure he's already trying to hunt me down, either to kill me or to break me, depending on his mood.

Oh God. What if he gets to Dalia?

Bile burns my throat and I race to the bathroom, dropping

to my knees so hard they crack against the tile. I fling up the seat and wait for something to happen, but instead of dry heaves, I just feel *sick*.

Cade will get to them, I tell myself again.

My fingers grip the side of the toilet tighter.

Sharp shots of panic flit around my chest because he knows where Dalia lives.

Cade will bring Quinten to me, and we'll figure out what to do from there.

But I hope he brings Dalia too. She isn't safe in town as long as Parker is there.

I must lie on the cold bathroom floor for thirty minutes until I've worked through the panic, reassuring myself that everything will be okay because it just *has* to be.

Slowly, I rise to my feet, glancing at myself in the mirror and seeing, once again, that I'm filthy from the day. My mind flip-flops, debating on whether I should take a shower or go venture downstairs and see if I'm all alone.

I should introduce myself to whoever's staying here. I glance down at my fingers again, cringing, and decide a shower is absolutely necessary.

The heat of the water eases my sore muscles and relaxes the tension that's been clinging onto my skin for the past whoever knows how long. I still feel sick and torn apart, worried about Quinten, disgusted by Parker, and nervous about what I did to Florence, but something about knowing Cade is in my corner has me breathing a little easier.

He'll take care of everything.

The mirror is fogged after my shower and I stand in front of it, reaching out and swiping a line to look at myself in the reflection. I'm not sure what I expect to find, but I'm surprised when the person staring back at me is still just…*me*.

Nothing extraordinary, no harshness to my gaze that wasn't there before, just plain old Amaya Paquette.

Sighing, I walk back out to the bedroom, scrunching up my nose at the dirty clothes I have to get back into. But it's not like I have any other option. I get redressed, scanning the fabric for bloodstains and feeling lucky that I chose something dark to wear so they don't stand out, and then I leave the room, taking in my surroundings fully for the first time since I got here.

I wasn't exactly in my right mind. Honestly, I'm still not sure that I am.

The stairs creak as I make my way down them, and my hand grips the banister, the wood cool and smelling like Pine-Sol. The entire atmosphere is a little eerie, and goose bumps sprout over my entire body.

There's a fire crackling in the corner of the living room and a small open frame without a door that leads to a narrow kitchen on the left.

Maybe I should grab a drink. Chamomile tea, or *something* to help calm my nerves while I sit here and wait.

I walk into the dimly lit kitchen, past the small white refrigerator that's humming into the air, and open the cupboard next to it, looking for a cup.

The floor creaks behind me right as I grab a glass, and I spin around, my heart jumping into my throat. The glass in my hand drops to the ground and shatters, slicing up my ankles and pooling at my feet. But I don't feel the sting.

The woman's eyes grow wide and she stumbles back, a hand

flying to her chest. "Amaya," she whispers, blood draining from her face.

My mouth drops open and I blink in disbelief.

Because standing right in front of me is my mother.

CHAPTER 50

Cade

I'VE ALWAYS BEEN A RATHER VIOLENT MAN. IT'S something that has existed inside me since I was a small child.

It was the reason Sister Agnes took to beating me with the belt.

Back then, of course, I didn't know how to utilize the feeling. I hadn't yet learned to funnel it into a useful resource. Instead, it would build and build and build inside me until it exploded like fire from a dragon's mouth.

At first, I would tear up stuffed animals or break a dish just to feel it shatter. Sister Agnes didn't like that much, but it wasn't something I could control.

It was only through time, age, and patience that I was able to separate who I was as a man—and then eventually as a priest—from the monster.

Right now, as I swing my car into an empty space outside what used to be Amaya's apartment, the snow crunching beneath the tires, I feel like that little boy again, the fury in me unable to find a source or direction, so instead, it's just marinating in my veins.

Building.

And building.

And building.

It's been snowing since I left the monastery, a thin layer of white making everything glow a little brighter now that the sun has set. I burrow deeper into my peacoat, rushing up onto the small, cracked front porch, a sense of nostalgia hitting me when I glance over and see the edge of what used to be Amaya's bedroom window peeking at me from the corner of the alley.

I maneuver up the icy steps and knock on the front door, my stomach tense from both the need to make sure Quinten is safe and the need to hunt Parker down and get back to Amaya quickly.

Nobody answers, so I knock again, something heavy pressing on my shoulders, pushing down until the weight makes it hard to stand.

Come on, Dalia. Answer the door.

I knock one more time, then hop off the stoop and peer into the front window through the open blinds, but there's nobody inside. At least not from what I can see. I move back to the door again, my breathing growing choppy as I reach out and twist the knob, part of me hoping it's locked, because at least then, I can fool myself into thinking that most likely, they're just not home. That Dalia was smart enough to recognize danger before it happened.

The door unlatches easily, as though it was just barely resting in place to begin with. A lead weight drops in my gut.

It's eerily quiet when I move inside, and a heavy sense of foreboding washes over my skin.

"Quinten!" I call out. "Dalia?"

Nobody answers, and the silence has never screamed so loud.

Moving down the small hallway off the kitchen, I peer in the first room on the right, but it's empty. Nothing but a few shelves and a made-up bed with Buzz Lightyear on the quilt. Then I head back more to where I know Dalia's bedroom sits, the door already ajar. Light filters into the dark hallway, and I push the door fully open with my toe, the creak of the wood sounding like a cannon in my ears.

My hand flies up to cover my nose.

The smell is…*strong*.

Merde.

Dalia is here, but I wish with everything in me, for Amaya's sake, that she wasn't. Her stomach is sliced open from beneath her chest to just under her navel, the bottom half of her body naked and severely abused.

I am a violent man. But even this makes bile rise in the back of my throat until I'm forced to swallow down the vomit.

My heart stalls as I move farther into the room, knowing this is going to break Amaya apart and already trying to come up with ways to make sure she survives the pain. The guilt that I know she'll feel, blaming herself for something that was out of her control.

Breathing through my mouth, I walk over to where Dalia's dead body lies broken and bruised, reaching out and covering her eyes with my gloved hand until they close. "I commend you, my dear sister, to Almighty God and entrust you to your Creator. May you return to Him who formed you from the dust of the earth." I place my fingertips on her forehead and say, "In the name of the Father," then on her chest right above where her body splits and the smell of death emanates from her flayed skin, "the Son," and then both shoulders, "and of the Holy Spirit, amen."

The words feel empty as they roll off my tongue. Simple words that before held so much truth, so much blind faith in every syllable, but now they fall from my mouth and drop onto Dalia's corpse, disintegrating into ash. Meaningless.

I stand rigid at Dalia's side, my hands in fists and my jaw clenching so tightly, pain radiates up my jaw. I spoke His words as though they were my own, the same way I have for years, but instead of finding peace in Him, I can only feel the rage for her. For Amaya. Because I know this will break her heart.

And I've realized that having my faith means nothing if she isn't at the center of it all.

The fury inside me grows, rolling from a small ball into a blazing inferno, the need to make Parker hurt as much as he's hurt Amaya pounding through my veins until I feel it prick against my fingertips.

Spinning around, I take in the scene, debating on whether leaving her here or calling it in is the best course of action.

But then something catches my eye, in the corner of the room next to an overturned table and a smashed-up lamp.

Clearly, she put up a fight.

I walk over to the glimmering object, seeing a small gold cuff link with the initials PE across the front.

Messy, messy, Parker.

My mind buzzes as I come up with a plan.

I need to find Quinten as quickly as possible, but it would be silly of me to not make sure there are no other stops needed after I do. I'm not sure what's coming, but I know when I leave Festivalé, hopefully with Quinten in tow, Parker Errien will be dead and gone. And if things go badly, I need us to be able to escape quickly. So I stop by my cottage first because if I need to flee, I can without worry of what I won't have.

The urge to drop everything and hunt Parker down like a madman is burning through my veins, but I pause when I reach the threshold and see the door is already ajar.

My stomach flips, hackles raising as I push it open, glancing from side to side.

It's dark, not a single light on in the place, but the air is heavy and tense.

There's someone here.

The door closes behind me, but it doesn't latch, and I finger the knob, noticing it's slightly off its center, as though someone broke in and tried to cover it up.

My monster stretches his arms, rumbling in my chest.

"You made it."

The corner of my mouth tilts as I raise my head slowly, flipping around and coming face-to-face with the man I'm on a mission to find.

"Hello, Parker."

He's sitting in the darkened kitchen, his leg crossed over his knee as he leans back in a chair at the dining room table, a gun perched in front of him, next to the white china settings like he's just waiting to shoot me.

I shake my head slightly at his confidence.

"Dinos!"

My body swings to the side, relief filling up my chest like helium balloons when I see Quinten unharmed and at least moderately unfazed, sitting in the corner on the floor, his rainbow light-up headphones flashing blue to green to red on his head.

Apparently Parker has a soft spot for children that he lacks for women. Or he's holding him as bait and knows if he's damaged goods, he won't be as valuable. Either way, I'm thankful.

"Bonjour, mon petit," I coo, flashing Quinten a smile, my eyes scanning his body to ensure he's in one piece. "Parker." I keep my eyes on Quinten. "Let me take the boy away."

Parker chuckles. "I think it will build his character."

I smile. "Undoubtedly." I take a step toward him, my fingers flexing against the leather of my gloves. "But he'll also have nightmares from what he sees you do."

Parker's eyes darken, and I side-eye Quinten, noting the way his eyes are down on his iPad, ignoring us completely again. I've never been more thankful for his propensity for learning apps and headphones as I am at this moment.

"Have you come to kill me, Parker?" I ask, nodding to the gun in front of him.

He shrugs, leaning back in the chair, relaxed, as though he thinks he's already won.

"That depends on what you've done with my *wife*."

I grin. "Which time?"

He jerks forward, his palm slamming against the table until the dishes shake. "You *motherfucker*," he spits. "I want you *gone*. You will tell Bishop Lamont you're leaving, or I swear to that mythical figure you pray to that I'll blow your brains out all over this kitchen floor."

Nodding, I place my hands out in front of me, trying to appear as though he's frightened me. "Calm down, Parker." I glance toward the gun. "You're the one with power here. Just let me take the boy away, and I'll do whatever you wish." I look back to Quinten. "At least to the bedroom."

Parker's jaw tenses as he glances back and forth between us.

"You've already won," I state, sighing and hanging my head in shame. "What more could I possibly do?"

He hesitates for just a moment, and then he jerks to a stand, reaching for his gun.

But I am much larger and leaner than him, my arms eating up the space before he can, grabbing the weapon out from under him with one hand and gripping his throat with the other, hauling his body across the table and slamming him down in the middle until the wood cracks and the china shakes.

He starts flailing like a dog on his back, and my eyes flit to Quinten again, who is staring at us with wide eyes and a slightly parted mouth.

I tighten my grip on Parker's throat.

"It's all right, mon petit. I promise."

Slowly, Quinten nods, looking back and forth between us, his body slightly rocking in place like he can't control the motion and needs to let his energy escape.

Parker's palm flies up and slams into the skin of my wrist, and with my free hand, I take my fingers and dig the tips down into the hollow of his throat, just above his collarbone, until he stops moving entirely, screaming out in pain instead.

"Oui, I know it hurts."

I look back to Quinten, keeping Parker incapacitated by my fingers on his pressure point. He tries to fight, but my body is much larger than his, and he's unsuccessful. Besides, I enjoy it when they squirm.

"Mon petit, I know you're scared," I say to Quinten. "But I'm going to take you to your sister. Would you like that?"

His eyes flash between us again, and now he's fully rocking, his body swaying violently until I'm worried he'll make himself fly into the wall. He bobs his head.

"Good. Can you do me a favor then?"

Parker jerks his hand, swiping out and punching into my gut, making me lose my breath. I grit my teeth and tighten my grip around his throat until his airway is completely cut off, lifting my knee and digging it into his torso to pin him better in place.

"I need you to walk down the hall, and at the end of it is my bedroom. I have a nice set of nativity scene figurines in the top drawer. Can you go find them and line them up for me?"

Quinten's eyes grow larger, but he doesn't make a move.

"Come on, mon petit," I urge with a grin. "After we're done, I'll take you to the store and buy you a new dinosaur. Maybe we can finger paint again."

This gets his attention, his eyes lighting up at my bribe, and he nods, walking slowly, his hands splayed on the wall behind him like he's creeping up on someone until he hits the hallway, and then he darts off, his little footsteps rushing away. I don't make a move until I hear the latch of my bedroom door.

Relief floods my chest, and I look back down at Parker with a smile. "Now, where were we?" I release the pressure point, reaching out to grab a butter knife from the place mat at my side, the weight of us both on the table making it creak. He flails again, his eyes bulging and lips turning blue from how long he's been without oxygen, and I flip the knife around in my hand, adrenaline pumping through my system like kerosene. "I cannot tell you how long I've dreamed of this moment."

I slam the butter knife right into his inner thigh. His mouth opens on a silent gasp, but no sound comes out because the pressure of my hand around his throat restricts his vocal cords as much as it restricts his air. I twist the knife so it rotates ninety degrees in his leg.

"Sorry about that," I wince. "I know it must be *incredibly* painful. I'm certain I've nicked a major artery."

His body shakes, his eyes fluttering like he's about to lose consciousness.

I release his throat and bring my hand up, smacking him across the face. "Oh no, no. You're not allowed to disappear. Stay a while. I want you to really *experience* what I have planned."

His eyes are hazy as he stares up at me and wheezes out. "Fuck. You."

My knee presses farther into his sternum, my hand rotating the dull knife more. "You know, if you play nice, I can take this out, and you'll bleed to death in minutes." I lean down, making sure his eyes lock on mine so I can see the demons that plague his soul and make sure they hear me. "But since you can't find *respect*, I think I'll make it hurt."

I release the handle of the knife and reach out to grab his gun. His movements are still jerky but have much less strength behind them, the blood seeping out from around his open leg wound surely making him light-headed on top of him having been choked within an inch of his life.

Taking my knee from his stomach, I stand up straight, gripping him by the neck again and dragging him up until I toss him on the floor.

He falls like a limp rag doll, rolling onto his hands and knees, that knife still poking from his thigh.

"Surely, you knew it would come to this." I hover over him and kick him in the side, the same way Amaya told me he did to her. He falls and I move, stepping onto his hand, pressing the entirety of my weight against him until I feel the crunch of his bones as they shatter beneath my feet. "After all, you hurt the woman I love. The woman I would do *anything* for."

"She is *my*...my wife, you piece of shit," he yells out, pain and rage infecting every syllable. "She signed the papers, and they're filed with the state. She was mine to do with as I pleased."

Chuckling, I twist my heel and revel in the high-pitched cry that escapes his mouth. I release his hand from under my foot and use the toe of my shoe to flip him over until he's prone on his back, a small puddle of blood forming beneath him from what's bleeding out around the knife.

"And did you also have her sign a prenup?" I ask, staring down at him, clicking off the gun's safety and crouching down beside him, resting the cool metal against his neck. His eyes widen, and I tsk, shaking my head. "Of course you didn't. You're Catholic. Marriage is for life." I lean in, hovering over his broken and bleeding body as realization blazes through his eyes. "Now, what was it you told her?" I move the gun down his frame, resting it on top of his groin. "That you would cut off my cock and make me choke on it?"

He swallows thickly, his Adam's apple bobbing and his body frozen in place, most likely from fear.

This is always my favorite part of the kill: when they realize their life is in my hands and there's no way out.

"She may be your wife, but she is my *soul*," I whisper against his ear. "And I will cut you up piece by piece and burn your empire until it's soot, just so I can watch her be queen of the ashes."

I pull the knife from his leg and jam it down right next to where the gun is pressed, hearing the fabric rip and the satisfying slice of soft flesh being split apart, muscle tearing and a tortured scream releasing from his throat.

I chuckle, the monster and the man inside me finally merging into one, having a singular goal in mind.

Vengeance for Amaya.

"Don't scream yet," I tsk, dragging the knife down until blood seeps through the fabric of his pants.

Parker's eyes roll back, his face growing pallid and strength leaching from his bones like the angel of death is here to suck out his soul.

I jerk the knife back from his groin, smiling wide as I bring it up to my face and see the red blood coating the metal, and then I take my hands and grip his body, flipping him over until he's prone on his stomach.

He groans, and I hurry my movements, knowing there's quite likely only moments left until he loses consciousness entirely. I lean over his back, placing the knife in between his legs, gliding it from where he's bleeding and broken and then up farther until it's resting in another delicate place.

Hovering over him, I grip the back of his neck tightly, shoving his face into the floor.

He whimpers. "Stop, *please*."

"Did she ask you to stop?" I ask. "When you *raped* her…did she ask you to stop?"

My fingers tighten and I pull up his face only to smash it down on the floor again. He whimpers, but it's muffled by how hard I have him pushed into the ground.

"Come again?" I ask.

"Please, *God*," he cries.

Chuckling, I lean down. "I won't tell you to seek absolution from my *mythical figure* tonight, Monsieur Errien. You see, I worship Her now…so it's to Amaya that you should pray. May She have mercy on your soul."

CHAPTER 51

Amaya

I'M SITTING ACROSS FROM THIS ABSOLUTE stranger.

She has my mother's face, but she isn't the woman I know. This isn't Chantelle Paquette.

This is *Sister Genevieve*. A woman of faith. Of renewed hope. One who's been granted forgiveness, though not from me.

The truth in that statement lights my insides on fire until there's nothing but rage left in its place. That same ball of tension from earlier in the church percolates in the center of my gut, coiling tighter and tighter until it pinches my chest and makes my lungs fill with smoke.

She's a fake. A phony. A narcissist wearing a habit and preaching words she's never lived.

"Do you have any—" My voice catches on the knot in my throat, and I try again. "*Any* idea what you've done? The mess you left behind?"

She shakes her head, taking a sip of her tea. "I won't talk about this with you. I've paid my penance. I've lived through my guilt."

"Same old Mom, brand-new packaging, huh?" I eye her outfit with disgust. "Oh my God, do you know Cade?"

Her mouth drops open, something sinister entering her gaze. "Of course. We're…close."

"Really?" I say dryly, although her words make jealousy spear through my middle and wrap around my throat.

"That's right," she continues, a haughty gaze slipping into her eyes. "He *trusts* me. More than anyone else, I'd imagine."

My blood heats with a possessive rage and I lean forward, something dark and wicked spinning through my mind like a spiderweb. "You're not special, Mother. Not like me."

Her face drops.

I smirk because I know how to press her buttons so easily. I spent nineteen years of my life at her mercy. Listening to her tell me I wasn't good enough. That my breasts were too big, my hips were too wide, and I was a distraction to all the men in her life.

And I know envy runs deep. Deep enough to leave your responsibilities at the door. Deep enough to forget about the people you're supposed to love.

I shrug. "Truth hurts, doesn't it, *Mom*?"

She places her mug down on the table and leans back in her chair. It's a comfortable move, one that shows just how settled she is here. *Here*, less than an hour away from where she abandoned Quinten and me, leaving us to clean up her mess.

That knot in my gut cinches tighter. "If I asked him to kill you, he would without blinking."

She scoffs. "He's a priest, child. Please."

"No." I shake my head. "He's *mine*."

"Still the same delusional little Amaya. With bigger dreams than you have tits."

I laugh. "There she is, good ol' Chantelle Paquette. A decent fake but a terrible mother."

"People can change, Amaya."

"Bullshit," I hiss through clenched teeth, smacking my hand on the table. "You fucked up, over and over and over, and then you left, painting me as some witch and leaving me to pick up the pieces. I don't give a fuck if you've changed. I do *not* forgive you."

"Well," she sniffs. "God forgives, and He's all that matters."

A little bit tighter now.

I huff out a breath, sadness filling up my chest, that lost young girl who still aches for a mother rearing her pathetic little head. Maybe she's here because she wanted to be close. Just in case. "Did you ever miss me at all?"

"Oh, Amaya." Her voice is soft, and my naive heart pounds in my chest. "No."

The last tiny strands of hope from that kid inside me break away, leaving behind a lightness that I've been searching for since the day she disappeared.

"How's Qui—"

Boom.

I surge up from the table and am across it before she can blink, wrapping my hands around her throat and squeezing as we both topple to the floor.

She yelps, and I'm fairly certain my rib is cracked from the way we fell, but the fury pounding in my blood silences everything else. I climb on top of her, straddling her lap until she's pinned to the ground, and then the rage pumps into my arm and I swing before I can think, backhanding her across the face, droplets of blood spraying from her mouth.

"Don't you dare say his name!" I yell, my hands going back

to her throat. She fights, and she fights well, nails gouging into the skin of my arm and ripping out chunks of my hair, but I don't care.

She can't hurt me more than she already has.

I tighten my grip, and eventually her flailing turns to jerks and then stops altogether, quiet taking over the room.

My breathing is heavy and uneven, and a clock ticks on the wall. I glance up at it, a delicious buzz racing through my system. And I feel *free*.

The door bangs open from down the hall, and I scramble to my feet, spinning around and racing out of the kitchen toward the front.

Cade stands there like a dark angel, tall and imposing with snowflakes dusting his black hair and Quinten's hand in his.

I let out a sob, rushing to Quinten and grabbing him in my arms, hugging him so tightly he squirms. "All done! All done!" he squeals.

Releasing him, I sit back on my heels, the knot in my chest untangling as I catalog his every feature. Tears flood my eyes again, and I would give anything to stop crying. I've done enough of it in the past few days to fill up a fucking river.

"Everything all right?" I ask, my eyes flicking up to Cade's.

He smiles down at me, but I can sense the worry in his gaze. "Everything is taken care of, mon trésor."

Quinten starts to move past me, looking around this new place he's never been to, and I suddenly remember our mother's dead body in the kitchen.

Panic must show itself on my face because Cade stiffens, his eyes glancing around the room before coming back to me.

"Quin," I call out, my muscles stiff and sore. Now that the adrenaline is wearing off, it hurts to breathe. "Stay close by, dude."

I spin around, watching as he moves into the small sanctuary to the left instead of closer to the kitchen.

Definitely cracked a rib.

Cade moves in front of me, his gloves icy from the winter air as he cups my face, his eyes searching my face. "Are you all right?"

My eyes flutter closed as I sink into his hold. "I did something bad. And I'll need your help to clean it up."

Thirty minutes later and I've finagled Quinten into a bedroom upstairs while Cade is in the kitchen, seeing the damage I've created. I haven't told him who Sister Genevieve really is yet, but I know that to him, it won't matter. I lie down next to Quinten in the small bed, listening to his breathing even out and thanking God—if He exists—for keeping him safe, and eventually I stand up, tiptoeing out of the room and making my way downstairs.

Cade's there waiting with a fresh cup of tea, my mother's body gone and the broken chair cleaned up like it was never there to begin with.

He sets down the mug, stepping into me and pulling me flush against him, one hand cupping the side of my head and his other gripping my jaw.

"I'm sorry if she was your friend. I just—"

"Shh," he soothes, stroking my hair. "I don't care."

And now the emotions that were missing well up in the center of my chest, leaving me tired and ragged and worn. I rest my head against his chest and listen to his steady heartbeat, letting it calm me the way it always does.

"She was my mother."

His body tenses.

"She came up here to, I don't know, stay close but far away? I don't really care why. I just…I didn't mean to kill her."

He leans back, tipping my chin up with his fingers and pressing a soft kiss to my lips. "If she hurt you, she deserved to die."

I sigh, nodding at his words. "Is there something wrong with me?"

Cade smiles, bringing me back into his chest and wrapping his arms around me, cradling me like I'm his to hold. Like I'm the only thing that matters.

It makes my body warm and my fractured heart swell.

"There's darkness in us all, petite pécheresse. We just have to learn to control it." He presses a kiss to the top of my head. "I can help you with that."

The next morning, I wake up feeling tired and sore but ready to face the day. Cade fucked me deep into the night last night, kissing away my tears and breathing life back into my bones. He was gentle, and it still hurt, but it was also cathartic. I *needed* him to wash away the memory of Parker and replace it with himself. Because I *choose* him.

He's sitting on the edge of the bed when I get out of the shower, staring at his hands, that muscle ticking away in his jaw.

My stomach dips. "What's wrong?"

He blows out a breath, running a hand through his hair as he turns to look at me, smiling and reaching out his hand.

I take it, letting him drag me into his body until I'm standing between his legs. My hand squeezes the towel around my body tight, dread over what I can just *feel* is bad news creeping up along my spine.

"I have to tell you something, and it's...I'm not sure how to make it okay."

I back away from him, but he reaches out, gripping my hips and holding me steady. "What's going on?"

He licks his lips and stares up at the ceiling before meeting my gaze. "Dalia, she—Parker got to her and took Quinten before I could…"

My heart drops into my stomach, vomit rising in my throat, and I push away from him, running to the trash can, dropping to my knees, the towel unraveling around my hips as I throw up into the bin, the taste of bile and grief burning the back of my tongue.

Cade moves behind me and holds back my hair as I dry heave.

I look up at him, shaking my head, my vision blurring. "She's dead?"

He nods, empathy swimming in his gaze. "I'm so sorry, mon trésor."

My nostrils flare as I nod, sitting upright, my stomach tossing and turning like a ship in a storm. My heart aches, and there's this pit in my solar plexus, gaping wide and feeling like it might swallow up everything I am.

Sadness grips me by the throat, and I close my eyes, tears squeezing from beneath my lashes and dripping off my chin.

Another notch in my already scarred heart. So many more now than there were a few short months ago. Only now, I'm stronger. I've been through more, and I have someone by my side and in my corner.

I look up at him, my teeth clenching so hard it makes my jaw ache. "Did you make it hurt?"

His hand runs down the length of my hair, something dark flashing through his gaze. "Yes."

Closing my eyes again, I try to control my breathing, the heaviness of this new reality pressing down on the center of my chest.

"Good."

CHAPTER 52

Cade

"I HAVE A CONFESSION TO MAKE," I SAY, STARING down at the hole I've spent the last three hours digging deep in the forest. Sister Genevieve's body is lying next to the suitcase I ~~stuffed Parker~~ stuffed into, and I'm taking these final moments with them both to have a heart-to-heart. "I have a sickness inside me." I rest my hand on top of the shovel. "To which there is no cure. But Amaya…she feeds both the monster and the man. My perfect match in every way. I'm sorry it took both of you to die for us to be together, but He is merciful, and He will forgive."

Pausing, I think about what I've said. While I still have my faith and I still believe in God, things have changed. *I* have changed. I've seen corruption run rife through the church and the "good" men end up being bad. I've seen years of my life that I've struggled to atone for my sickness be wiped clean by simple kisses on my scars.

When I'm with Amaya, the memory of Sister Agnes doesn't scream so loud.

I find my peace in her. She is my sanctuary. My home. My soul.

"But even if He doesn't," I continue, "I'll survive."

It takes me two hours to bury them beneath the trees, and then I drive back to Festivalé to tie up the last of our loose ends. Amaya is grief-stricken from losing her friend, and whether she admits it or not, there's some level of guilt that will follow her like a second skin, as it does with every person who plays God and holds someone's life in their hands.

I head to my cottage to clean up first and then straight to the hospital. It's evening now, past visiting hours, but they won't turn down a priest who's there to comfort a victim.

This will be the last thing I do as a priest.

Fitting, I think.

Walking into the room, I close the door behind me, holding my rosary and Bible as I spin around and stare at the woman resting on the bed in the middle of the room.

Florence Gammond.

Alive and well.

She's hooked up to an IV bag and a heart monitor, and she turns her swollen face toward me as I drag over a chair and sit down next to her.

Her face is mangled, almost unrecognizable, and they had to shave her head to place several stitches along the side of her scalp. But she'll be fine.

And if she wants to stay that way, she'll do exactly as I say.

"Bonjour, Florence."

"Father," she rasps, her voice scratchy and dry. "Did my husband send you?"

"Parker," I state.

Her heart rate monitor beeps faster, and my eyes flick to it before landing back on her. I took a random guess, based on the way she singled out Amaya and always sought him out in every crowd.

I pick a piece of lint off my arm. "Do you remember anything at all about what happened?"

She blinks, as much as she *can* blink with swollen, purple eyelids, and she parts her mouth as if she's thinking. "Am—"

"Non," I cut her off, leaning forward until my face hovers above hers. "I think you're about to be *confused*. Let me help you."

She tries to speak again.

"Shh." I press a finger against her mouth, and she winces when I press down. "Don't speak, my child. Just listen. Did you know Parker liked to make tapes?"

Again, the heart rate monitor increases, and my gaze wanders to it before focusing back. I'll need to hurry. Much more stress and a nurse will show up.

None of what I'm saying is true, but she doesn't know that, and Parker's not around to dispute the claim. "He had a lot to confess over the past few months, *Mrs.* Gammond. His poor, unfortunate soul was more than happy to hand the tapes to the church, to ease his conscience and allow God to grant mercy on his soul." I lift a brow. "Do you think there were any of you?"

She tries to sit, and I move closer, pressing lightly against her chest and keeping her pinned to her bed.

I lean down close and whisper in her ear, "If you don't do exactly as I say, I will release them all. You'll be the laughingstock of Vermont, blacklisted from every *single* career path you wish to take. I'll put it on display so your mother sees it. Your father. Your husband. Your *son*. Do you understand?"

"My husband can't know. He can't—"

"Does he know Bradley isn't his?"

That shuts her up quick. *I had a feeling.*

I whisper her instructions and leave as quickly as I came, heading back up into the mountains to be with Amaya and Quinten.

And then I pray like I've never prayed before, hoping my empty threats will work.

They do.

Three days later, a press conference is held with Detective Fuller announcing that with Florence Gammond's help, they were able to connect the Green Mountain Strangler to Parker Errien.

According to her, he was *obsessed* with his wife, Amaya, long before she agreed to be his. He stalked her to her work, killing Andrew out of a jealous rage. It was a fortuitous coincidence that he also frequented the woman I murdered on my first night.

Florence said she was tired of the games, threatening to tell Amaya about their affair, and he followed her in a rage, beating her to a pulp in the bathroom. When they found Dalia murdered with his cuff link at her side, it was an open-and-shut case.

Both Festivalé and Coddington Heights would rather people stay calm and think they've caught the killer, even if the story doesn't *quite* line up.

I'm just grateful Amaya wasn't the one who ended up stuck in the crosshairs.

Since Parker's not around to dispute the charges, they assume he fled the scene, and a national manhunt is underway.

They won't find him. Not unless I decide they should.

His wife, on the other hand, is free and clear, and after the dust settles and we wind up wherever it is she wants to be, we'll handle the assets that Parker's lawyer insists are now in Amaya's control. He has no living relatives, no working will—the conceited prick—and no prenup signed to prevent her from accessing the funds.

Technically, he's still alive in the eyes of the law, so if a body eventually needs to show up in order for everything to remain hers, I'll make that happen.

I would do *anything* for her.

"Are you all right?" I ask.

I'm in the monastery's living room, looking out at the snow-covered pine trees with Amaya tucked into my side.

She nods, biting on her lower lip. "I'm sad. But if I let my grief consume me, then Parker wins. And Dalia would hate me for it."

I press a kiss to her head, my monster quiet and sated, purring deep in my chest. I'm no longer a priest, not officially anyway. I resigned and left the priesthood yesterday with Bishop Lamont, and he's allowing us to stay here in the monastery until we decide where we'd like to go.

"So now what?" I muse.

She smiles, glancing over at Quinten, who's lining up his new set of dinosaurs that I bought him on my way back from town. She leans into my chest, resting her hand over my heart.

"Now, we live."

I reach down and tip up her chin, leaning down and nipping her mouth with my teeth until the skin breaks and I can lap up the blood. "And, petite pécheresse," I whisper against her lips. "Tell me…who do you belong to?"

"To myself."

My hand tightens on her face.

She grins. "And to you, Cade Frédéric. My heart belongs to you. In all our lifetimes."

EPILOGUE

Cade

I STAND BACK IN THE SHADOWS AND WATCH HER.

Ma petite pécheresse. Mon trésor.

My wife.

She's covered in blood.

It turns me on.

Five years have gone by since I first saw her dancing in the club, and although she was transfixing as Esmeralda—still is, when she chooses to put on private performances for me—she's absolutely stunning like this.

Deadly. Disastrous. Devilish.

There was a lot of inner trauma that Amaya kept bottled up for years, not ever allowing it to rise to the surface, stuffed so deep down that nobody knew it was there. Not even her.

But as monsters tend to do, it grew strong in the dark, feasting on untapped pain and inhaling it like vitamins.

I'm no stranger to the feeling, so I've taught her how to let it free.

And she's taught me how to separate my true faith, my *true* ideals from what I was brainwashed into thinking as a child.

Together, we're balanced. Impenetrable. Unshakeable.

Still, as she stares at me, a bright gleam coming from her smile, splitting apart the splotchy blood-soaked cheeks on her face, there's a hint of *something* that flashes through her eyes.

As though she's waiting for me to tell her what a disappointment she is. Or how she should do things differently. How she should *feel* knowing that what she did is something a former priest of the Catholic church would look down on and condemn.

I smile at her, swooping across the floor of our private cabin, hidden away in the Auvergne Mountains, and I grip her face in my hands, tipping up her chin so our eyes meet.

"Mon trésor, you are a vision."

She grins back, relief coasting across her gaze.

As though I would ever shun her.

There's nothing she can do that I would turn away from.

As a former priest. But even more so now that I'm just a man.

I still have my faith. Still believe in the unshakeable force that is God. It just all pales in comparison to her.

She is my Bible. My scripture. My religion.

She is everything, and I am nothing without her.

There is nothing I wouldn't do for her.

No suffering I wouldn't endure just to make sure she lives a pain-free life.

Which is why, after traveling for the first year after the news broke of Parker being the Green Mountain Strangler, I brought her here to the region of Auvergne-Rhône-Alpes, France. To settle.

Quinten took surprisingly well to the change in routine and blossomed in a way that he never could while he was stuffed into corners in Festivalé, and although he didn't have as much formal therapy at first, once we settled, Amaya found him the best play therapists to work with. He's homeschooled now, with a small group of other neurodivergent children, and I would be lying if I said my heart didn't warm to see him flourish the way he is.

Tonight, actually, he's spending the night with one of his closest friends. So Amaya and I both thought it was the perfect time to let loose and let our monsters *fly*.

Besides, we were just married in a small outdoor ceremony. Not Catholic, of course, but over the years, my beliefs have turned from strict religion into a spiritual faith. God loves me for who I am, *just* as I am. And I don't need to embroil myself in the politics and corruption that is the church.

I press soft kisses down the expanse of her throat, my hands firm in their grip as I turn her this way and that, manipulating her body precisely the way I want it.

"Cade," she moans. "Let me clean up first."

"Hmm," I hum against her skin. "I think I prefer you this way, mon trésor. Dirty and depraved."

She scoffs, pressing against my shoulders, but instead of pushing me away, her fingers dig into the fabric of my shirt and grip me close.

"*Filthy*, even," I continue.

"I…have…"

Her feeble protests break off when I bite down on the juncture of her neck and shoulder and take one of my hands, slip it down the front of her body, and dip into the top of her flowy skirt, beneath her flimsy panties, finding her soaking wet and ready for me.

The way she always is.

"Should I take you here, petite pécheresse?" I ask. "Fuck you with my fingers before I stretch you with my cock?"

"God, yes," she breathes.

I smack her pussy sharply. "Do *not* take His name in vain."

Her eyes flash and my dick pulses.

She knows I still have my faith, and while she'll never be religious, I find that I don't care. In fact, I think she considers it foreplay to piss me off. She thinks I'll make it hurt more when I take her.

Normally, she's correct.

She rises up on her tiptoes and crushes her mouth to mine, her tongue slipping between the seam of my lips and tangling around my own, the taste of her invading every single one of my senses. I groan against her, my sack tightening as I walk her back and slam her into the wall, grinding my throbbing length against her.

Part of me assumed that after a while, my obsession would dull from familiarity, but I've found the opposite to be the case.

Her depravity dives down to meet my monster, and her spirit flies high to give me faith. There is *nothing* beyond Amaya for me.

I drop to my knees, ripping her clothes as quickly as I can, buttons flying from her blouse and torn fabric floating to the side as I expose her wet cunt to the open air.

My forearm keeps her tightly contained against the wall.

"You and your walls," she muses, her fingers running through the messy black strands of my hair.

I smirk as I lean in and blow across her swollen clit.

"Oui. I like you where I can keep you, mon trésor."

And then I lean in and I worship her. The way I was born to do.

She is my salvation.

My hope.

My temptation.

My blood.

My everything.

"Cade," she moans, her fingers ripping the roots of my hair. It makes my cock throb with a drop of cum, aching to feel more of the pain only she can provide.

My tongue laps at her, from the top of her pussy down until I'm circling her entrance, the musky taste of her arousal making me drunk with need.

She pushes her hips farther into me, grinding her clit against my face, and I move back up, sucking it into my mouth and rubbing my tongue flat against the bundle of nerves.

Her legs start to shake, and I move from where I'm holding her down and grip the undersides of her thighs, lifting her up until her knees are over my shoulders and her ass is resting in my hands, making her cunt open up even more for me.

I feast on her. I could suffocate myself in her and it would never be enough.

And then she's coming, *hard* around my tongue, and I'm moving before she can think another word, dropping my pants to the ground and lining my thick shaft up to her hole, her legs wrapping around my waist, before I spear her apart with one single thrust.

Our hips collide, a sharp smack ringing out into the air around us, and my eyes roll back from how absolutely perfect she feels gripping me like a vice. She's still coming, her cunt squeezing and releasing in a torturous rhythm, making my sack draw up before I can think twice.

"You feel so perfect, mon trésor, coming around my dick like my filthy little sinner."

Her head falls back, perspiration lining her face, the blood splotches from the man she killed earlier making her seem like a fallen angel sent to earth just for me.

Groaning, I fuck up into her, over and over until she's screaming out my name again, her nails digging into the scars on my back, even through the fabric, until I feel them bleed.

That shot of pain is all it takes and I'm undone.

Blinding, blistering, all-consuming.

White light dances in front of my eyes as pleasure rushes through me, and I swear that I've never felt closer to God than I do when I'm inside my wife.

Our hearts dance together, our chests pressing against one another as we come down from the high and catch our breath.

This is us at its core.

Wild.

Untamed.

Invincible and brutal in every single way.

I fuck her two more times before we clean ourselves thoroughly in the shower and then head to the living room of the cabin where I make us homemade hot chocolate.

It's tradition.

I heat up the milk, the gas stove ticking as it catches fire, and smile when Amaya walks up behind me with the hammer, her green eyes sparkling like she doesn't have a care in the world.

We work together without speaking, just enjoying each other's company in the silence, and it isn't until we're curled up on the couch in front of the crackling fireplace that she hums as she takes her first sip.

"So what now, husband of mine?"

My heart clenches in my chest and I set down my mug,

moving toward her and pressing my lips against hers softly. "I do love it when you call me that."

She smirks. "You just love that I'm yours in every way now."

My fingers ghost along her cheek, moving back until I'm fisting her curls in my hand. "You've *always* been mine."

"You know, Monsieur Frédéric, I think you're right about that."

Slowly, I move her own cup of chocolate from her hands, placing it on the coffee table.

And then I show her just how much she *truly* belongs to me. The same way I belong to her.

Slow, soft, and tender on the rug in the living room, warm from the fire.

And I love her.

In every lifetime.

Amaya

If someone had told me twelve years ago that I would be a world traveler, I would have laughed in their face. Probably would have thought they were mocking me.

Because twelve years ago, on this day, July 5, I had just turned nineteen years old and my mother had abandoned me with my one-year-old brother.

And now, here I am. Living in the mountains of France, seven years after meeting the other half of my soul, marrying him, and loving without bounds.

It's early morning, and I'm sitting on the balcony of our cottage in the Auvergne Mountains. It's secluded, private. Beautiful.

Ivy traces up the white brick and wraps around the banisters, and there's a cobblestone patio in the backyard overlooking a gorgeous garden of flowers. It's a large space, one that we use to entertain when the mood strikes us. We are, after all, known as affluential people here.

That's what happens when you're a widow to a billionaire mogul who didn't leave a will.

There were, of course, several people who contested it. After all, Parker wasn't *officially* dead, and we were only married on paper for mere days.

But my husband saw to it that we were taken care of.

I don't ask him what he had to do in order to get the others to withdraw their complaints, but I have an idea.

And when the state demanded a body, Parker's suddenly appeared.

And everything he owned was officially transferred into my name.

I used a large portion to inject it back into the community of Festivalé in a way that Parker never did. We got people off the streets, cleaned up the broken sidewalks, and fostered trade schools and small businesses that would allow the community to thrive beyond a money grab of tourism and pretending to be a mini France.

And then I opened up a pole studio and named it Dalia's Dancers. There's now ten of them across the United States and another one opening here in France just next week.

It's the least I can do to honor my best friend's memory.

But the guilt still hits hard whenever I think of her.

And sometimes, I *dream* of her. She comes to me and holds me tight while I cry out my apologies and she soothes me and says there's nothing to forgive. I'll never believe it, but I know she wouldn't want me to wallow in the loss.

So I live for her instead.

Tinkling laughter hits my ears and I smile, draining the last of my coffee before walking into my bedroom and then down the stairs until I hit the French doors that open to the back patio.

I breathe in deep, the air clinging to my skin, a crisp, light breeze blowing through the strands of my hair as I look out over the mountains, and then focus on where Cade and Quinten are huddled together on the ground, right before the stone turns to grass. I smile as I walk closer, my heart expanding when I see that they're painting.

Again.

They've taken to doing it most mornings, and Quinten is an amazing artist.

My heart explodes when Cade turns toward me, smiling wide enough to crease his cheeks with dimples, his eyes sparkling in a way they never did back in Festivalé.

This is what peace looks like.

Although we both still have our moments.

Sometimes, the darkness flashes through his gaze, and I know he's hearing Sister Agnes. Whenever that happens, I crawl up into his lap and hug him tightly, my limbs wrapping around him like a vice as I whisper how worthy he is to just *be*.

That if he hurts himself, he hurts me.

That we're allowed to make mistakes without repenting.

He usually nods against me and whispers prayers to his god while I hold his pieces together until he can stitch them back up on his own.

Then I let our love hurt so good that he forgets the rest of his pain.

"You two look messy," I say, smiling as I walk over.

Quinten laughs as he looks over at me, bouncing on his knees, but then like always, he looks down at his hands and realizes just how colorful they are from paint, and he stiffens before shooting up and running over to the basin of clean water they have placed at the edge of the stone.

He's far more adaptable than even I gave him credit for, and that's yet another thing that makes guilt try to reach up and dig in its claws. And that's when it's *Cade's* turn to remind me that making mistakes is human, and life's about learning. About growing.

And I'll never stop growing with Quinten.

The moment I get close, Cade reaches out, wrapping his arms around me and tugging me into his lap. I squeal, the wet paint on his hands creating purple and gold prints on my skin, physical reminders that I'm his just as much as he's mine.

"Salut, petite pécheresse. You look beautiful today."

He leans in, pressing a soft kiss to my lips and rubbing his nose against mine. I grin, sinking into his touch.

"You got home late last night," I murmur, flicking my eyes toward Quinten, who's scrubbing the paint off his arm and bouncing on his tiptoes.

"I did." He hums.

He doesn't elaborate, and I don't ask him to. Some things about Cade will never change, and I love him wholly, *because* of who he is, not in spite of it.

Even if I do try to let him know that he doesn't have a *monster*, just a damaged little boy who never got the chance to heal.

But his scars tell his story, and his coping mechanisms are his to have, the same way mine are my own.

Like I've always said, our experience shapes us whether we want it to or not.

His large hands glide their way up the back of my spine, sending shivers through my body.

God, I wish we were alone.

Years later and I still can't get enough of him.

"Quin," I yell out, noticing that he's now far down the backyard and smelling every flower. I move to get off Cade's lap, intending to go ask Quinten if he wants to go on a hike today, but before I can, Cade grips me tightly and pulls me back down.

"When we're alone," he murmurs, "I'm going to fuck you right here on this chair and remind you who you belong to."

I scoff. "We'll probably break it."

His eyes glint. "One can only hope."

If he would have said things so blatantly when we first met, I'm sure I would have shied away from his extreme possession. But now...now there's really nothing I crave more. I enjoy being his. *Feeling* like I'm his. Being reminded of it.

I love having a man that even *God* couldn't rule, and I know I could ask him to do anything and he'd give it to me.

The truth is that we both got lost in the world, and the world didn't care to find us, so we found each other instead.

Nobody has ever loved me that way.

Then again, I'm not sure that our love is something common.

It hurts too good.

EXTENDED EPILOGUE

Amaya

TEN YEARS WE'VE BEEN TOGETHER, AND CADE'S bouts of self-flagellation are now far and few between, but they still exist. Trauma doesn't just disappear, regardless of how much distance we gain.

Tonight, for example, he's been out doing...something. I don't ask many questions the same way he doesn't for me, but when I walk into the bedroom, he's home, sitting on the floor, cross-legged with a haunted look in his eyes.

"Oh, baby," I say, dropping the book in my hand and rushing over to him.

He'll call it his "monster" again, but I don't believe in monsters. Not the kind *he* thinks exist anyway. Still, I let him have his beliefs the same way he allows me mine, and I think that when it comes down to it, that's why we work so well together.

We keep each other from falling off the cliff's edge when there's nothing else holding us back.

Sometimes, I still have nightmares of Parker coming back and continuing his years of assault. When I wake up, it's to Cade shushing me and petting my hair, and he loves me soft and sweet, knowing that's what I need in the moment.

And other times, it's like it is right now, with that terrible woman from his past, Sister Agnes, whispering lies in his head. So I do what I've always done. I climb into his lap, and I wrap my arms and legs around him, squeezing until it's hard for him to even breathe.

My muscles ache the longer I hold on tight, but I don't let go. I just grip him close, and his hands paw at me like I'm the breath of air he's been begging for.

Like now that I'm here, he can lose himself in me instead of the memories.

"I love you," I whisper into his ear as he rocks us back and forth.

His fingers slip beneath the waist of my shorts and grip handfuls of my ass, pulling me farther into him.

It's not sexual, not really.

It's comfort.

Because that's what we are to each other.

We're each other's home.

I wait until his heartbeat calms and his breathing evens out, and then I do what I always do in these moments. I start kissing all his scars.

"When you hurt yourself, you hurt me."

"I know," he rasps, his muscles twitching while I slide off his lap and move to face his back, working my lips down his body. "I'm sorry."

"Shh. Don't apologize. Just let me take care of you. Let me take away the pain."

Our lovemaking on nights like tonight is rough and raw. Painful. Violent. Extreme.

It's what Cade craves, so I give it to him, because I'll always give him whatever it is he needs.

I stand up, gliding my fingers down his arm until his hand links with mine and I pull him up too, walking us to the bed and laying him down. Slowly, I strip off his sleep pants, his thick cock bouncing in the air when it's freed. I love to see how turned on I make him, but again, nights like this aren't about sex.

They're about the escape.

I know what he needs, the same way he knows me. After ten years together, he breathes in, and I exhale. It's intrinsic.

There's no time to waste, no foreplay that we need. Not when he's vulnerable and fighting his own demons. I straddle his hips and sink down onto his thick shaft, gasping when he fills me up from the inside out. It's overwhelming, how perfectly we fit together.

His hands fly to my waist, gripping me so tightly I'm sure they'll leave a belt of purple fingerprints.

Marking me. Just the way I like.

I start a fast rhythm, slamming myself down on top of his cock, my nails digging into his chest until they cut crescent-shaped slices into his skin.

"If you need to hurt," I breathe out, "you come to me."

I grip his neck, wrapping my fingers around his throat and putting the weight of my body into it, making sure to use the method he taught me, avoiding his windpipe but giving him the rush of the sting, while I ride him until his dick starts to grow harder inside me.

His hips buck.

And when I lean down and bite into the side of his neck until I taste his blood flooding into my mouth, he comes, hard, filling me up and whispering his devotion in French.

Devotion to *me*.

Not to anyone else.

———————

Cade brought me and Quinten to the new patisserie that just opened down the street from Dalia's Dancers, and now we're all sitting here—the three of us—eating chocolate pastries and giggling like children.

They're simple, these moments, but they're ones I don't take for granted.

I used to think I was destined to live life picking up the pieces that my mother left and somehow figuring out how to stitch them back together. Honestly, I thought I'd be drowning.

But now I'm here.

Funny how life can change in the blink of an eye.

I smile across the table at Quinten, who's slurping down his cold milk and staring at the chocolate chip cookie in front of him like it might bite him if he grabs it. Slowly, he reaches out and takes a bite, his green eyes sparkling while he chews.

"Good, mon petit?" Cade asks him.

Quinten rolls his eyes but nods. He constantly tells Cade he's too old to be called "little one" now, but I think Cade continues to do it just to get on his nerves.

Cade smirks, throwing his arm along the back of my chair, the corners of his lips lifting. There's a softness to his gaze that makes my heart warm, one that only exists when he's staring at me or Quinten.

I take a forkful of the white chocolate croissant that's in front of me and place it in my mouth, the delectable sugar melting on my tongue and making me moan in appreciation.

"Careful, mon trésor, or I'll do things that aren't appropriate for public," Cade whispers in my ear.

I reach out and smack him in the chest, but he just grins and winks, leaning back in his chair.

The little bell hanging over the front of the patisserie door rings, and a group of kids walk in, and Quinten freezes, his eyes flicking from where they are down to the table and then back.

"What's the problem, Quin?" I ask.

He shakes his head, grabbing the noise-canceling headphones from around his neck and putting them over his ears instead, his gaze constantly flickering to the door and then back.

My eyes follow where he looks, my hackles rising the way they always have with him. It's been years since we've dealt with bullies, but last year, Quin decided he wanted to finish out high school in a regular setting. At first, I was against the idea, but Cade talked me down, reminding me that it's Quinten's life and I can't always be there to protect him. He has to let experience shape him the same way it does for all of us.

So he went, and he loves it. I haven't heard a single thing about him being bullied, but it doesn't stop the terror that it's happening from keeping me up at night.

"Who's that?" Cade asks him, his hand slipping onto my thigh and squeezing tightly.

Like usual, he knows exactly what's going through my head, and he gives me the support I need.

"No one," Quinten murmurs. "Just some kids from school."

I'm two seconds away from having us leave, but then one of

the girls lifts her head, her amber eyes catching Quinten's, and then she's on her way over before we can blink. Her intense red hair—obviously dyed—bounces against her smooth and golden sandy complexion, her face brightening as she smiles.

Every step she takes makes my heart pick up speed as I look between them.

Cade leans in and presses a kiss to my cheek. "Calm down, Amaya. Our boy has a crush. Clearly."

I blow out a disbelieving breath, but as I flick my gaze back and forth, I realize he might be right.

"Hey, Quin," the girl says, stopping in front of our table.

I smile wide, blowing out a relieved breath. She seems nice.

"Hi," he murmurs.

She grins and slips her hands in her back pockets, looking over to us. "Hey, you must be Quin's parents? I'm Mina."

I glance back to Quin and then her again. I was expecting French, but she speaks with an American accent.

"Close. Sister and brother-in-law. I'm Amaya and this is Cade."

Cade nods a hello but doesn't talk, and I glance over at Quinten, who's gazing up at her like she lights up the night sky.

Oh my god. He *does* have a crush.

Mina looks back at him, and she rocks on her heels, her teeth sinking into her lower lip. "Some of us were about to grab some snacks here and then head down to the lake for a bonfire. Do you…I mean, would you want to come?" Her eyes bounce back to me and Cade. "If that's okay, I mean."

Quinten looks over to me, delight as clear on his face as the nerves are, and I nod. "Whatever you want to do, dude. Just be back home by ten."

A smile breaks across his face and he bobs his head, standing up and walking away with Mina. She laughs and he grins, and I swear my heart is about to explode.

Sighing, I lean over, resting my head against Cade's shoulder. "I love it here."

"I'm glad." He presses a kiss to the top of my head.

"I love you, Cade," I murmur, turning my head and peering up at him.

He dips his face down, pressing his lips to mine in a possessive kiss. "And I live for you, petite pécheresse. In all our lives."

Character Profiles

Cade Frédéric

Name: Cade Frédéric

Age: 36

Place of birth: Paris, France

Current location: Festivalé, Vermont

Education: Streets and seminary

Occupation: Priest

Income: Modest

Eye color: Dark brown, almost black

Hair style: Black hair

Body build: Extremely tall and lean muscles, 6'7"

Preferred style of outfit: When not wearing religious garb, his wide brim hat, leather gloves, trench coat, button-down shirt, and black slacks

Glasses?: No

Any accessories they always have?: Clerical collar and scarf

Level of grooming: Well groomed

Health: Healthy physically, mentally unwell

Handwriting style: Small and rushed, cursive

How do they walk?: With dominance

How do they speak?: Charming and powerful

Style of speech: Proper

Accent: French

Posture: Perfect

Do they gesture?: Only when making a point

Eye contact: Always

Preferred curse word: Merde

Catchphrase: "He is merciful."

Speech impediments: No

What's laugh like?: Deep and raspy

What do they find funny?: When people underestimate him

Describe smile: Wide with dimples

Type of childhood: Orphan. He ran away from his orphanage when he was seven and lived on the streets until he was around seventeen and was brought into the church for seminary.

Involved in school?: No

Jobs: Petty thief, priest

Dream job as a child: Didn't believe in having dreams

Role models growing up: Nobody

Greatest regret: Letting Parker live long enough to hurt Amaya again

Hobbies growing up: Hurting things

Favorite place as a child: Didn't have one

Earliest memory: Tries not to think about his childhood

Saddest memory: The first time Sister Agnes beat him and told him he was sick

Happiest memory: Sinking into Amaya

Any skeletons in the closet?: Yes, he's a priest who kills people because he craves the violence.

If they could change one thing from their past, what would it be?: Letting Parker live for as long as he did

Describe major turning points in their childhood: Meeting Father Moreau

Three adjectives to describe personality: Cunning, righteous, charming

What advice would they give to their younger self?: You are not your mistakes

Criminal record?: Not officially

Father: Unknown

Mother: Unknown

Any siblings?: Unknown

Closest friends: None

Enemies: Parker Errien and anyone who has demons within them

How are they perceived by strangers?: Charming and trustworthy, but with a dangerous, powerful air

Any social media?: No

Role in group dynamic: Leader

Who do they depend on:

    Practical advice: God

    Mentoring: Father Moreau

    Wingman: Nobody

    Emotional support: Nobody

    Moral support: Nobody

What do they do on rainy days?: Make hot chocolate from scratch

Book-smart or street-smart?: Both

Optimist, pessimist, realist: Realist

Introvert or extrovert: Extrovert when necessary but truly introverted

Favorite sound: Someone taking their last breaths beneath his hands

What do they want most?: To rid the world of sin, but when he meets Amaya, he only wants her

Biggest flaw: His self-flagellation and righteous attitude not allowing anyone to be human and make mistakes, including himself

Biggest strength: His loyalty

Biggest accomplishment: Getting off the streets

What's their idea of perfect happiness?: Being with Amaya

Do they want to be remembered?: No

How do they approach:

   Power: Owns it

   Ambition: Aggressively ambitious

   Love: Doesn't believe in it other than to God, but when he meets Amaya, it is an all-consuming obsession

   Change: Resists it

Possession they would rescue from burning home: His discipline

What makes them angry?: Sin

How is their moral compass, and what would it take to break it?: He pretends it's strict, but under the guise of "the greater good," he'll break it easily and without thought.

Pet peeves: Sinning and disrespect

What would they have written on their tombstone?: He lived for Her.

Their story goal: Cade is a broken man who lives in the trauma and demons of his past. His story arc is that he will be faced with his greatest temptation in a way he hasn't compartmentalized and reasoned is okay. (Amaya, obviously.) He will learn the difference between a righteous, unfailing blind faith and a true faith where he believes in his God but also allows himself the grace to make mistakes. I wouldn't say he'll become "well" because he is shifting his blind loyalty to Amaya and that doesn't change, it only grows, but when it comes to his own healing and trauma, he moves past the self-flagellation and the strict belief that there is something "wrong" with him and moves into a space of accepting himself because the woman he loves accepts him. He will come to terms with the balance of sin and righteousness and will lose himself in Amaya in a way that allows him to let go of everything that has tortured him for years, because she is his other half and they balance each other out.

Amaya Paquette

Name: Amaya Paquette (stage name: Esmeralda)
Age: 24
Place of birth: Unknown
Current location: Festivalé, Vermont
Education: Regular schooling, no college
Occupation: Exotic dancer
Income: High five figures, although most of it goes to Parker

Eye color: Green

Hair style: Black and curly

Body build: Wide hips, long legs, large breasts. Definitely a curvy figure and tall, 5'9"

Distinguishing features: Her eyes and her hair

Preferred style of outfit: Flowy skirts/dresses

Glasses?: No

Any accessories they always have?: An emerald necklace when she's dancing as Esmeralda

Level of grooming: High

Health: Healthy

Handwriting style: Loopy cursive

How do they walk?: Shoulders back and chin high (defensive posture), sauntering when she's Esmeralda

How do they speak?: Normal

Style of speech: Normal/slang

Accent: American, no distinguishable accent really

Posture: Decent

Do they gesture?: Yes

Eye contact: Sometimes

Preferred curse word: Fuck

Catchphrase: Doesn't have one

Speech impediments: No

What's laugh like?: Loud and rich

What do they find funny?: Dry humor

Describe smile: Slightly crooked, wide and perfectly balanced

How emotive?: Very emotive although she tries to control it

Type of childhood: Moved around a lot, single narcissistic mother who was very jealous of her and had a lot of issues with men

Involved in school?: Not really

Jobs: Didn't work as a kid, took care of her little brother when he was born, exotic dancer as an adult

Dream job as a child: Didn't dream of having a job, just dreamed of having a home and a family

Role models growing up: None

Greatest regret: Seems like she has a new one every day but mainly letting her mother walk away without getting answers or closure on their relationship

Hobbies growing up: Daydreaming that she was a princess who was going to be whisked away and find parents who loved her

Favorite place as a child: Anywhere outside her house

Earliest memory: Her mother bringing home a man who sat her on his lap and made her feel yucky when she was three

Saddest memory: When she realized her mother didn't love her the right way

Happiest memory: Seeing Quinten thrive

Any skeletons in the closet?: No

If they could change one thing from their past, what would it be?: Nothing. Past experiences shaped who she is

Describe major turning points in their childhood: Her brother being born, her mother leaving, and all the men her mother would parade in their lives

Three adjectives to describe personality: Smart, seductive, loyal

What advice would they give to their younger self?: Don't be so afraid of love

Criminal record?: No

Father: Unknown

Mother:

Age: 39

Occupation: Unknown

What's their relationship with character like: Nonexistent as an adult, very toxic and unhealthy as a child

Any siblings?: Younger brother, Quinten

Closest friends: Dalia

Enemies: Parker, Florence

How are they perceived by strangers?: Beautiful, mysterious, dangerous

Any social media?: No

Role in group dynamic: Leader

Who do they depend on:

Practical advice: Dalia

Mentoring: Nobody

Wingman: Dalia

Emotional support: Dalia

Moral support: Dalia

What do they do on rainy days?: Dance

Book-smart or street-smart?: Street-smart

Optimist, pessimist, realist: Pessimist

Introvert or extrovert: Introvert

Favorite sound: Quinten's voice

What do they want most?: For Quinten to be happy and for her to find unconditional love and be chosen

Biggest flaw: Avoiding meaningful relationships with most people

Biggest strength: Her loyalty

Biggest accomplishment: Raising Quinten

What's their idea of perfect happiness?: A happy family

Do they want to be remembered?: No

How do they approach:

> **Power:** Scared of it
>
> **Ambition:** Neutral
>
> **Love:** Scared of it
>
> **Change:** Doesn't like it

Possession they would rescue from burning home: Her brother...not a possession but it's all she cares about

What makes them angry?: Bullies

How is their moral compass, and what would it take to break it?: Very bendable, wouldn't take much because things have been building inside her for years and the world isn't a great place for her

Pet peeves: Bullying

What would they have written on their tombstone?: She loved and was loved.

Their story goal: Amaya starts off as a woman who puts up a wall with everyone around her and protects/lives for her little brother solely. She's afraid of forming meaningful relationships because she knows that people let you down and disappear. She has been dealing with years of trauma and abuse but has compartmentalized it and thinks of herself as a survivor who doesn't have time to feel. Her entire purpose is to live for her little brother, Quinten, to raise him and be a better parental figure to him than their mother was to her. Through the story, she will grow from someone who doesn't like power or being controlled to someone who finds escape in it, allowing herself to truly be chosen and loved for the first time in her life. She will let down her walls and start to appreciate that it's worth the risk. She will also have a "reverse good guy" arc that turns her from morally upstanding to morally gray, playing on the "experience shapes us whether we want it to or not" mentality that she has.

JOIN THE MCINCULT!

EmilyMcIntire.com

The McIncult (Facebook Group): facebook.com/groups/ mcincult. Where you can chat all things Emily. First looks, exclusive giveaways, and the best place to connect with me!

TikTok: tiktok.com/@authoremilymcintire

Instagram: instagram.com/itsemilymcintire/

Facebook: facebook.com/authoremilymcintire

Pinterest: pinterest.com/itsemilymcintire/

Goodreads: goodreads.com/author/show/20245445.Emily_McIntire

BookBub: bookbub.com/profile/emily-mcintire

Want text alerts? Text MCINCULT to 833-942-4409 to stay up to date on new releases!

Acknowledgments

First, I'd like to thank my sensitivity readers from Tessera Editorial for reading this and making sure I write everything with authenticity and care.

I'd like to thank my family, my amazing husband, Mike, who stands by me and supports me every single day. Mike: You are a phenomenal father and partner and I'm so happy to have you in my life and at my back.

To my best friend, Sav, thank you for reading all the versions of this, talking through my plots, and reassuring me that everything isn't something to spiral over. Here's to the Smokies.

To my readers, you are the best part of my career. Thank you for showing me that no dream is too big to reach. I love my McIncult.

To my team: My editors, my incredible PR team, my agents, and my PAs who keep my life running smooth… Thank you for making my life and career run smooth. The author version of me wouldn't be half of what I am without you at my back.

To my daughter, Melody, you are now and always will be the reason for everything.

About the Author

Emily McIntire is an international and Amazon top-fifteen bestselling author known for her Never After series, where she gives our favorite villains their happily ever afters. With books that range from small town to dark romance, she doesn't like to box herself into one type of story, but at the core of all her novels is soul-deep love. When she's not writing, you can find her waiting on her long-lost Hogwarts letter, enjoying her family, or lost between the pages of a good book.